Sheila Gilluly was born in Rhode Island and attended school and college in Arizona, graduating from the University of Arizona with a BA in English in 1973. Since then she has earned an MA in Religious Studies from Maryknoll School of Theology, lived in Taiwan briefly, taught for a couple of years in Guam and now teaches English and Creative Writing at a rural district high school in Maine. She has written the Greenbriar Queen trilogy (*Greenbriar Queen*, *The Crystal Keep*, *Ritnym's Daughter*) and *The Boy from the Burren*, *The First Book of the Painter*, which are all available from Headline.

GW00419720

Also by Sheila Gilluly

Greenbriar Queen
The Crystal Keep
Ritnym's Daughter
The Boy from the Burren

The Giant of Inishkerry

The Second Book of the Painter

Sheila Gilluly

First published in 1992
by HEADLINE BOOK PUBLISHING PLC

First published in paperback in 1992
by HEADLINE BOOK PUBLISHING PLC

A HEADLINE FEATURE paperback

10 9 8 7 6 5 4 3 2 1

ISBN 0 7472 3868 5

Printed and bound in Great Britain by
HarperCollins Manufacturing, Glasgow

HEADLINE BOOK PUBLISHING PLC
Headline House
79 Great Titchfield Street
London W1P 7FN

The Giant of Inishkerry

PART ONE

THE HAUNT
OF THE MOOR

CHAPTER ONE

'Ye missed a bit,' a low voice I recognized as Arni's said in the darkness of the granary.

'Where's that?' Pers wanted to know.

'Off in the corner, there. See it?'

'How the bloody hell can I see it?' Pers retorted in a hot whisper. 'Skipper, give us a little more light here, would ye?'

Stationed at the door, I heard the soft thump of Timbertoe's pegleg well-wrapped in a muffling cloth, cross the floor of the huge barn. The place was so quiet you would never have known nearly forty dwarfen pirates were bent to their night's task. The only sounds were the airy whooshing of smiths' bellows and the cautious scrape of wooden shovels, punctuated by a couple of stifled coughs as the grain dust rose in unseen clouds. Even through the concealing black hood of my disguise, the stuff was prickling my eyes and nose. I pitched my voice to carry across to Timbertoe. 'Almost done?'

'Hold your water, Giant,' he growled back. 'Takes even the Haunt of the Moor a while to get every speck. Suppose ye wouldn't settle for—'

'No,' I told him shortly, 'it can't be a sketchy job. The cleaner it is, the more convincing it will be that the Haunt has struck.'

From somewhere near in the darkness, Harrald's voice chimed in, 'Aye, well, us mere mortals what have cold hands can't pick up every mucking kernel, y'know.'

He had one of those whining voices that is like an insect plaguing your sleep: 'If your hands are that cold, Harrald,' I told him, 'go ahead up to the hall and ask them for a pint, why don't ye?' The sounds of riotous merriment rising from the reeve's hall a scant hundred yards up the hill had been rising in volume all night while we'd toiled to empty the warehouse of its treasure of stored oats. The marriage feast for his daughter sounded fairly

3

wild. The skirl of pipes and thumping of dancing feet could be heard plainly even over the hard rattle of sleet against the tiled roof of the granary. So much for the gentry. It must have been brutally cold in the courtyard outside the hall, where the folk of the manor and village were bid to wait attendance, though maybe the Wolfhound overlord had some germ of compassion because we could see leaping log fires up there. To many of the people, the chance of a bit of meat from the feast would have been worth a night in the cold. Powers knew they had had little enough of it this long winter, and the grain that might have held off hunger was locked right there, under seal of the King's reeve. Bloody bastard, I thought, I hope he likes the wedding gift the Haunt will give his daughter tonight.

My attention, which must have wandered a bit because of the cold, was suddenly jerked back to the job at hand when Neddy, our cabin boy, a Burrener refugee like myself, whistled our three-note warning from his position at the overhead hay door. From there, he could see everything between the stout stone warehouse and the reeve's hall. Immediately, all sound inside the barn ceased, and I very carefully leaned a hayfork against the door and stepped away from it. At least if anyone entered, we'd be alerted by the sound.

Timbertoe had shuttered the candle lantern, so it was as dark as the inside of a shark's belly. We waited tensely, straining to hear something above the sleet, the piping and the dancing.

Two voices, thick with drink, coming closer. '—telling you, 's true! Every witch, the order says, ev'ry one.'

'Don't be daft! 'Sides, how the hell could you do it wi' them all riding 'way on their broomstiss?' There was a peal of raucous laughter, and the same voice followed this brilliant sally with, 'Like a great, big flock o' bloody ravens, all on their brooms—' His voice dissolved in drunken laughter, and we heard their staggering steps go by toward the stable. If they were the change of watch, we were in good shape.

A few minutes later, Neddy whistled the two descending notes for the all-clear. Timbertoe unshuttered the lantern, and we took a last good look round. The lads had done a miraculous job, I had to admit. The granary was picked so clean it looked new-built. 'Well done!' I breathed. 'Ye've earned your booty this night, sure!'

4

'Speaking of which,' Pers began.

'Later tonight, my honor as a pirate,' I promised. 'I'll make this worth your while, mates. Come on, Pers, you know the Haunt is good for it!'

Our helmsman's face was as pale as a ghost's in the lantern's light, his dark beard powdered with oat dust, some of which caked off when he grinned. 'Ain't the Haunt I don't trust, pilot, it's you.'

I made him the rude gesture he expected, and the skipper briskly ordered everyone out. Each of the men hefted one of the last remaining sacks of oats and slipped carefully out of the door. Neddy came down the knotted rope, untied it, and he left with them. Timbertoe eyed me over the lantern. 'All set?'

'Aye. Just have Neddy standing by with the curragh to pick me up.' I took the lump of charcoal from my pack and stooped quickly to sketch the sugan Vanu, or Hag's Plait, on the freshly swept floor of the granary. By that mark the Haunt of the Moor had come to be known in the past three years the length and breadth of the Burren. In ordinary usage, it is the straw braid one sees above every hearth and byre in the country to ward off the evil eye, but in the apothecary's notation in which I had been trained as a boy, it is also the symbol for a poison.

'The lad will be there, never fear,' the pirate skipper rasped. 'It's you I'm thinking of. Ye've seemed a bit off all day. Are ye all right, Giant?'

Actually I had a headache that bid fair to split all the badly knit bones of my head, but I answered him lightly. 'Never better, Filthydwarf.' I finished the sugan and dusted my hands before drawing on the black gauntlets and rising. 'This will be all of the vermin, except Cathir, the traitor, and I've saved him till last.'

'Well, just be careful. If this fellow's heard that every other man jack of the troop that first attacked your skellig has been found dead these past years, he may be—'

'Scared witless,' I finished, stuffing the charcoal back in the pack and strapping it. 'I hope so. Three hours, Skipper, no more. Tell Neddy to clear out if I'm not at the cove by then.'

'Don't worry, Giant. We'll desert ye quick enough if it comes to that.' He clapped my shoulder heavily, blew out the lantern, and followed me to the door. Cautiously we slipped out into the ice storm. 'It's doing a nice job of filling in the tracks, eh?' he whispered as he gave me a final salute and stumped quickly away, a hunched figure that disappeared into the wind-driven storm within a few yards.

It was, at that. Already the smooth ground of the threshing floor outside the granary was nearly carpeted with a crunching rug of gray. I pushed home the iron bolts, cursing inwardly at the cold that made them stick, and tickled the works of the lock until it clicked into place once more. Not many locks could withstand dwarfen pirates, and Pers was an accomplished lock-picker. Earlier this evening he had won a bet with Harrald that he couldn't get the thing open by the time Harrald counted a hundred. Pers had it open in under forty. His tab at the alehouse in our home port of Inishkerry was now Harrald's responsibility.

I drew a deep breath of the frosty air, loosened my dagger in its sheath, and looked for a moment up the hill toward the hall, my view of which was blocked from here by some of the outbuildings. While it would have been easier simply to slip the sacks of oats into every home in the village below my vantage point, it would have made it far too dangerous for the folk when the theft was discovered. So we had trucked the oats down to the ship and left for the people of this miserable place barrels of salt pork, discreetly tucked into chimney corners, under stacks of peat, and hidden in chicken coops. The pork came from two districts away, virtually untraceable; the oats we had taken tonight would go to three villages far distant. The neatest thing about the whole operation was that the fat bastard up there couldn't blame anyone in the village, for they were all in his courtyard, munching bones at his summons.

I chuckled, resettled my hood, and followed the barely outlined path to the stables, where I found the two who had laughed about witches sprawled on the soiled hay. They never stirred as I quietly led a huge black gelding out of his stall and appropriated a bridle and saddle from the reeve's tack room.

Before I mounted, I nudged one of the guards with my boot. He didn't rouse much, so I kicked him in the ribs. His eyes snapped open, and he tried to focus. To make it easier for him, I leaned down. 'Bid thy master's daughter my best, would thee?'

He was squinting, and I flipped the cloak over so he could get a glimpse of the Four Spirals embroidered on the back of it. As his eyes widened, I put him out again with a stiff chop to the neck, swung up into the saddle, and rode out into the storm.

The track I was looking for led back up over the shoulder of the hill, skirting the reeve's rock-bordered pasturage. I met no one, which was not surprising on so foul a night. The gelding was fresh and wanted to go quickly to get warm, but I held him to a careful trot on the thick ice. Sometime in that first hour the wind slacked, and the sleet settled into soft and drifting snow. Even with no moon, the snow made it light enough to pick a way.

I came over the ridge down into a corie, a small valley cupped in the palm of the surrounding hill. There was a wood here; the trees, protected by the hill itself from the fiercer winds higher up, found root in the deeper soil that had run off the ridge. Standing timber is rare in the Burren, so this retired Wolfhound soldier had been well-paid for his years of service. I could smell a thread of woodsmoke from his cottage. Slowing the horse to a walk, I went cautiously ahead, drawn sword in my hand, trees sifting snow down on my head.

He would have a dog, of course. When I had ridden as near as I dared, I dismounted and tied the horse to a tree off the path, covering the gelding with my cloak and leaving the black hood slung over a tree branch. This was no place for the Four Spirals; this was not Haunt's work, only my own as the last survivor of Skellig Inishbuffin. I kissed the hilt of my dagger, readied the grappling hook and the square slab of drugged salt pork, and stole down the path through the copse until a clearing opened and the log palisade of the rath lay before me.

I heard the chain rattle before the beast tethered outside in his little kennel hurtled to the full extent of it and began to bark, hackles raised. An angry baying from within the rath made me hastily cut the slab of pork in two. From my safe cover behind the tree trunks, I watched motionlessly as the man came out with a lantern, held it up to peer ineffectually into the darkness and listen intently, then raised his hand to the dog and bade it leave off its howling. The beast slunk towards him to lick his hand, and he drove it to the ground with a curse and threatening gesture. He went back inside and slammed the gate.

I gave it quite a long time, perhaps a half hour, before I pitched the meat to the dog. It began a growl that ended in a puzzled rumble, then a snapping of its jaws told that my pork had gone down well. It did not take long until I could get near enough to throw the second slab over the timber wall. The other dog, no doubt attracted by its fellow's gorging, was already whining anxiously for its morsel. My feet were beginning to numb a bit standing in the snow, and I trotted halfway around the rath and tossed up the grappling hook. When the slight thudding as the prongs found purchase in the sharpened logs aroused no howling, I held my dagger between my teeth and swarmed up the knotted rope.

He'd a neat holding, this retired soldier. Within its protecting wall stood a cottage built of stone and thatched snugly, with an attached shed, possibly for a milk goat. The byre would hold at least two or three cows, or more likely a cow and an ox. The wood on which he made his living was seasoning in long stacks all around the walls. There was one thing more I noticed, a swing hung from the large tree that had been left standing near the cottage to give a little shade in the summer. I had not known that the villain had children, but it was no matter: my skellig folk had had children, too, and the Wolfhounds had showed them no mercy. I left the rope hanging for my escape and walked toward the shed beside the house, trying to ignore the throbbing of the wry bones of my crooked jaw.

When I carefully pushed aside the leather flap that was the door of the shed, I saw that it was, indeed, the nanny's stall. Her head was up, ears pricked, then she began to trample nervously. I picked up the stool and threw it against the wall of the house, following that with the milk bucket, then reached to tweak her bag so that she blatted and kicked. Across the eaves I could hear a hurried stomping into boots and his wife's called question.

I was waiting for him, sword drawn, when he came around the corner of the shed. 'Do you remember what you did at Skellig Inishbuffin, Sergeant?' I asked quietly.

He was still very fast, and Timbertoe's hunch had been right: he'd heard what had been happening to his Wolfhound mates. Desperately he thrust at me with the pike he had armed himself with, but I dodged and the point caught in the rough wooden

8

slabs of the shed. He dropped into a fighting crouch. I went straight in with the sword, intending a clean kill, but the shawled figure of his wife was behind him suddenly and she screamed, both hands to her mouth. Instead of taking him in the throat, my point slashed across his face.

He staggered back, hands coming up to shield himself, and the blood welled between his fingers, black and smoking in the cold air. The wife screamed again, clutching for him, but somehow afraid to touch. My arm drove forward again, and this time the stroke went true. The body stood for a moment before it fell, blood spraying from the severed throat.

The wife retched, crawling away from me, and behind her appeared a boy no older than eight or nine years, with a blanket draped hastily about him, who stared at the twitching thing on the ground, unable to connect it with his father. Then his eyes came up to me. His mouth was open and his eyes were blank. He was so stunned, he couldn't even cry out.

I ran away from his eyes, but I felt them on my back as I galloped the black horse all the way to the sea.

Neddy was waiting when I splashed towards him through the shallows. The horse I turned free with a slap to the flank, then pitched my pack into the leather boat. Even through the steady snow, the cabin boy could see the blood soaking my dark tunic, and he signed a question with hands made clumsy by his long wait in the cold.

'No, none of it's mine,' I answered shortly. 'Sit back, I'll row. Have you got a bead on the ship?'

He pointed. When I squinted, I could make out the lantern. Neddy tapped my arm, offering the leather bottle. He always had one ready for me. 'Drink it yourself, Ned, you must be frozen. I'll get mine aboard,' I told him and began to row strongly, pulling away from that shore and the foul thing I had done.

Timbertoe had the ship rigged and ready. A couple of the lads called banteringly to ask where the hell the booty was, but when they saw my face in the light of the lantern, there was no more said. 'Bring me a bucket of water, would you?' I requested of the boy as I went below to my own small cabin in the bow.

While I was stripping off the sodden clothing, I heard the skipper drop through the companionway hatch and stump up to my door. When I turned he was holding out a brimming mug of the black dwarfish liquor known as flotjin. I reached with one bloodstained hand to take it and drank it off in one long pull. He watched me narrowly, bracing himself on the door framing. 'Are ye all right?'

'Don't mother-hen me! I'm fine!' My hands were shaking though, and his shrewd eyes noted it. When the boy brought the bucket, the skipper told him quietly to pull me a beaker of flotjin, then go find himself a place by the charcoal stove topside. I began to scrub off. 'Did you have any trouble getting back to the ship?' I asked.

'No. Quiet run.' He rubbed his nose. 'One more, ye said. The traitor.'

'Don't look at me that way, Pirate. It's nothing you haven't done yourself.'

Neddy returned with the liquor and set it on my map-making table, then retreated quickly. The skipper said nothing until I had drawn the blue glass bottle out of the drawer of my bunk and laced the flotjin with the tincture of poppy. 'Aye, I've done it a time or two,' he agreed. 'But I never had to drug myself to sleep afterward.'

'Lucky you. You never dived off a sixty-foot cliff and grazed your head on the rocks, either. It isn't the killing, Filthydwarf: it's the pain.' I took a slug of the potion I had made and felt the first familiar numbing of my lips.

He might have pointed out that the pain only came so badly when I had carried out another revenge, but he didn't. 'Sleep well, Giant.'

'I intend to. Timbertoe? Thank Neddy for me, will you? It was a bloody filthy night to wait.'

'Aye, it was at that. Don't take too much of that stuff. Ye have first watch in the morning,' he reminded me maliciously as he grinned and shut the door.

When I was dry, I dressed in my own clothes for warmth, putting the tunic of the Haunt's costume in the bucket to soak. Then I drank a good deal of poppy-spiked flotjin, fell on to my bunk at some point, and lay waiting for sleep. The drug began to work, dulling the pain in my racked head and, as it did, I began to see the play of colors on the rough planking of my cabin wall.

Even if the poppy had not relieved the throbbing headaches, I would have taken it just to see those colors. In fact I did just that sometimes, when I could no longer stand living in a black, white, and gray-shaded world. If there is hell for a painter, it must be color blindness.

And the irony was, I had done it to myself.

Four years previously, intending to find death with my grandfather and all our murdered folk, I had jabbed a drugged needle into my hand and thrown myself from the cliffs into the crashing waters of the place we called the Caldron. But I had woken from my comatose state to the sound of a girl's voice that reminded me of the Swan's wings, and her eyes were as green as the summer sea. I took that memory back into sleep with me. Unfortunately when I woke next, she wasn't there. When I croaked to ask where she'd gone, Timbertoe and the doctor exchanged a look and bade me sleep again. I later asked about her several times, and finally the healer told me quietly that there had been no one there, and of course he was right.

Some weeks later the healer finally gave in to my angry demands, drew off the bandages, and handed me a mirror. I remember a moment of frozen shock, and then a flare of anger at such a cheap trick. I was sure for an instant that the travesty of a human visage staring out at me was painted on the mirror: a joke for the doctor's apprentice, a joke for Timbertoe and his house servants. I opened my mouth to curse them all to the Hag's Embrace, and the gargoyle face in the mirror moved with mine.

Even at this distant remove, nearly a lifetime later, I can still feel my stomach's slow roll as my shaking fingers encountered the sharply crooked jaw just beginning to knit wrongly, then moved to brush the fierce eye whose socket was oddly flattened and sagging under the swelling. And eventually came to rest above – though not touching, I could not bear that final confirmation – the sunken place in my shaved skull.

Timbertoe always said I did not cry out. That may be. The dwarf lied readily enough, but not about this I think, and he *was* there, watching. But whether it escaped my lips or not, a howl of purest agony ripped through the empty skellig of my soul. The echo of it is still bouncing from deserted room to deserted room. I have never blamed the tots who take one look at me and run. I'd have run, too, if I could have.

I overheard the doctor tell Timbertoe the tally of my injuries: I would probably never regain the hearing in my right ear or full sight in that eye, and there would always be a place in my skull where a splinter of either bone or rock protruded. If I was ever hit there, I could easily die. Well, the eye worked well enough, but he was wrong about the ear. I *could* hear out of it. The problem was the sounds I heard weren't audible to anyone else: sometimes just snatches of song heard from afar across some echoing mountain valley, or voices whispering in a twilight of sleep in a language one knew once, but has long since forgotten. Having prenticed with Nestor, I was advanced enough in my healing craft to know this indicated damage to the brain, but as the phantom sounds were not very loud and not continuous I dismissed them as just one more consequence of my stupidity. When they got too disturbing, I'd turn the ear to my pillow, and they would go away. I spent much of those first few months in the dwarf's house lying on my side, staring at a crack in the plastered wall.

To give Timbertoe credit, he stood my convalescence as long as he could. Finally, when it seemed I'd pass the rest of my life in a sickbed, his native irascibility asserted itself. He stumped into my room one day, took a couple of turns up and down the floor as though it were the deck of a ship much too small to hold him, and stopped so abruptly by the bedside that the pegleg skidded a little before he got his balance. I ignored him. It wasn't malice, I just wasn't interested in anything he might have to say.

'Roll over, boy. I'd have a word with ye.' When I didn't move, he reached one massive hand to pluck me by the shoulder and deposit me in a heap on the floor. I did not realize it then, but he had made certain that I would hit the sheepskin rug.

I pushed myself to a sitting position, my head swimming and every bone jarred and aching. It was the first time I'd been upright since I'd jumped from the cliff. I braced myself against the bed and glared up at him.

'Ah, that's better. Always like to see a man's face when I'm about to make him a deal. Now, this is the way it is: we've whiled

12

away the entire summer hunting season nearly, and me crew's getting anxious to go a-pirating. Can't have them anxious, boy – a pirate captain who hangs back from hunting won't be a captain long. Got me reputation to protect, too; there's been some talk already about why I haven't just killed ye and taken that ring you're wearing.'

My eye worked well enough then for him to read me.

He snorted impatiently. 'Relax, ye jackass. I'm already out the price of the damned leech. D'ye think I'd have got him to heal ye up if I meant any treachery?'

'Why did you bother, then? I didn't realize charity was a virtue among filthydwarves,' I croaked, my voice hoarse from disuse.

He grinned savagely. I would come to know that grin well. He meant every square tooth of it, did Timbertoe. The dangerous smile relaxed into his customary scowl. 'Charity be damned. This is business. I had a contract with old Bruchan to give ye sanctuary. He'd settled for it in advance. So your life's bought and paid for.'

You have no idea how high was the price, Dwarf, I thought. The room was steadying around me, and I discovered that it actually felt rather good to sit up, if I could ignore the throbbing. 'What's your point? You've discharged your obligation. Why don't you just go and do whatever pirates do for a good time – burn a town, butcher a few—'

The iron tip of his wooden leg slammed into the floor between my splayed fingers. Instinctively I threw myself to the side and fetched up against the large carved chest which held my medicine bottle and a night candle. My breath came quickly, and I was dizzy again, but I gathered myself for a spring.

The pirate captain sat down upon the edge of the bed, arms folded. 'By His Beard, ye make it bloody hard to believe you're the old man's grandson. He'd more brains in his navel than you've got altogether.'

That stopped me absolutely cold. 'You *knew*?'

'Not until just now.' That damned grin again, but a shrewd gathering of the crow's-feet around his eyes. 'Don't make that mistake again, boy. There's others would sell your life for less than the price of a Tarnikov whore.'

I had no idea what the going rate might be for such companionship – or, indeed, of where Tarnikov might be – but I had been sold once and did not aim to be again, certainly not at a lower price than I'd brought the first time. I looked up at him. 'But you won't betray me, I take it. Why not? It would be good business.'

He had an unnerving laugh, one of those silent ones. His brawny shoulders shook for a moment, then he rubbed his nose, twisted one of the braids of his beard, and regarded me. 'You're a pretty cool one, no mistake. I like that in a lad, so long as it doesn't get in the way.' The smile left his face. 'You want the truth? So then, here it is: I won't betray you because I liked your grandfather, respected him. He'd a way of saying truth, even when it was hard hearing.' The dwarf's back stiffened. 'He was my *friend*, though ye might think it odd to hear a Jarlshof pirate say the word. Staunch mates aren't so easy to come by in my line of work.'

Even then, not knowing him very well, I could see that he had, indeed, told me the truth. I drew my knees up and laced my fingers around them. The chalcedon ring was softly lustrous in the light from the open window, and I looked up from its pearlescent surface to find him regarding me with grim pity that quickly became hard calculation when our eyes met. 'They butchered them, Timbertoe,' I heard myself say.

'Aye. I know. Me men and I weren't faithless, we just were on other business when the message from Bruchan came in. 'Twas over by the time we made Gull's Cove, but we went ashore anyway.' His eyebrows bristled. 'I saw.'

I brushed my eyes on the sleeve of the nightshirt. 'So, what's the deal, pirate?'

'Sail with us. We could use a lad who has no fear of dying.' He understood me better than I had guessed. The corners of his eyes crinkled. 'We've been known to hunt the black ships of the Dinan. Maybe ye'll get lucky and the traitor will be on one of them. What was his name? Cal—?'

'Cathir.' I retained enough of my pickpocket's instincts not to show anything. 'And if I choose not to become a pirate?'

He sniffed thoughtfully. 'Then I'd have to lock ye up every time I left on a voyage, because of course I'd never trust ye to stay out

14

of the cellar – too much danger of my missing the odd chest of
gold coins or whatever – and that would be a bloody nuisance.
I'd pay somebody to come in every day and feed ye, but—' One
shoulder lifted in a shrug. 'They might forget.'

I gave it enough time, then I spat into my palm and held out
my hand.

Timbertoe eyed me under his bushy eyebrows, spat into his
own palm, and we shook.

And so I became a Jarlshof of pirate.

My shipmates never knew much about my past, not even my
true name. To them I was a Burrener refugee named Cru. I was
also a taboo to be broken, because initially there was quite a
lot of talk about my appearance. No one with an obvious
deformity was welcome aboard, unless he'd got the crippled
leg or missing hand from honorable combat, 'honorable' by their
lights meaning a mercenary raid. But I was skilled with weapons,
thanks to Symon, and Timbertoe had a run of particularly rich
pickings during the first year I was with him, so that in time
I became regarded as rather a good-luck charm, and the old
pirate never had any trouble making up a full crew when he
was getting a hunting expedition together. I had my fights,
bought my rounds in the tavern we favored, stood my watches,
and became a better-than-average navigator. That I took spoils
only when we hunted Dinan ships didn't hurt my reputation,
either. There were whispers that I was consumed with a fire
of revenge and speculation that it might have to do with my
injuries. It made a convenient excuse for not participating in
the casual despoiling of coastal villages, which was abhorrent
to me, and besides I had business with the Dinan that initially
only Timbertoe knew about. In time, I was trusted enough to be
made pilot on Timbertoe's ship, the *Inishkerry Gem*. Some wag
'honored' my advancement by sewing a flag with my portrait –
he said it was a proper skull and crossbones, but the resemblance
was close enough that I thrashed him anyway – and Timbertoe
flew it out of grim humor. I suppose it was an affectionate enough
gesture, if you want to look at it that way.

I had made a good enough life with the pirates, and if I was troubled by my own ghosts – or 'walkers' as the dwarves would say – so that I drank more than was perhaps necessary and had black moods, when my mates learned to avoid me, none of this detracted substantially from my standing in the guild. Men who base their every action either on the drive for booty or on maritime superstitions that to the outsider's mind may seem absurd are surprisingly tolerant of other people's quirks.

Besides, I could thrash any one of the blackguards and they knew it.

I was thinking as I watched the colors bloom and swirl across the cabin wall that I could probably expect another fight when they found there was no profit from tonight's granary raid. Well, no matter, I thought languidly. I'd find some way to pay them off, pick up the tab for a whole night's revelry when we were in port, something like that . . . I stretched, comfortable at last, and drifted off to sleep.

I did not know why there was no warning. One moment I was sitting cross-legged on my bunk with the drawing board braced across my knees; the next, planking and timbers were exploding around my head, and a cataract of water drove me across the tiny cabin, smashed me against the bulkhead, and then swept me under.

I cried out and, of course, that was a mistake, but somehow there was the door of my cabin before me. I fought through the brutal current underwater, found the bolt by touch and began to draw it, but before I could get it open, the force of the inrushing water behind me tore the door off its hinges and flung me into the companionway.

I had time to draw one frantic breath before the seawater filled the narrow corridor, bearing me along its crest like a woodchip whisked down a sluice. The door to Timbertoe's cabin wasn't there, but even so I could not get in against the force of the water. The companionway was all wrong: it was angled upwards. Somewhere in my mind, even while my body struggled to find air, a very rational voice said, 'We've been rammed. We're sinking. You'd better get the hatch open, or you'll die.'

I frantically searched for the leather handle, found it, and tried to heave the hatch open, but it wouldn't move. My lungs were already struggling in my chest, but I resolutely braced my feet against the ceiling and put all my weight into a shove that accomplished nothing except to make black dots dance before my eyes and to stun the muscles of my shoulder. In despair I hammered on the hatch with my remaining strength, but realized no one could help me even if they heard, because the framing was skewed. I began to drift, took a breath I was sure would be my last and found a pocket of air instead of water. I sucked desperately, suppressed the panic, and opened my eyes. My face was wedged into a corner, the timbers of which stank marvellously of pine forest. My mind began to clear a bit, and I realized that I was going to have to swim back down the companionway, through my cabin, and try to get out through the hole that must be gaping in the 'Kerry Gem's starboard side. I could not understand where the rest of my shipmates were, and I felt angry and betrayed.

The air was nearly depleted, but I drew as much into my lungs as I could, jackknifed, and swam hard against the current, lesser now than it had been at first, but stiff-going still. I found my cabin, drew myself through the doorway by grasping the sides and eeling through, and felt my way through a tangle of flotsam, going – I hoped – toward the hole. But I could not find it. I began to flail again, like a salmon in a weir, hoping to find a way out, or a pocket of air. Something stabbed deep into my leg, and I reached down to pull out a jagged spear of wood, but then I forgot which direction I had been working in and became convinced that I had turned around. My heartbeat hammered in my head, my lungs would no longer obey, and I began to see bubbles of rainbow color before my staring eyes. I reached to catch them with one nerveless hand and took a breath of seawater.

It wasn't so bad as I had thought it would be, drowning. There was light, for instance. I hadn't expected that. Curiously I watched as the pool of light drew near, as though some watchman on a foggy night approached with a lantern. A voice, too, came closer, echoing a little, probably because of the water. He was chanting, whoever he was, and he'd a good voice, strong, deep. You'd have to have, to sing here.

I sighed, bubbling a little, and the light opened out before me suddenly, as though I had come to some high vista and could see what was beyond a concealing rise of land. I was in another boat, not the *Gem*, yet familiar. We were riding easily before the wind, the dragon prow lifting black and graceful against the sunset. Off our port bow a coastline slowly passed, near enough that I could see the trees. These astonished me. They were not the dwarfed and wind-bitten apples and yews of my own country, but tall trunks curved to the warm breeze, with no leaves except a canopy of fringed vegetation at the very top. A sweet smell, almost overpowering, came from that shore. I breathed deep of it, reveling. 'It's beautiful,' I marvelled.

The singer beside me – a companionable presence though I could not turn to see him fully – broke off his song to laugh a little. 'Aye,' he agreed. ''Tis. And tastes as good as it smells, what's more.'

'What is it?' I asked my guide.

'Thee knows.' His tone was teasing.

I searched my mind. 'Oh. Calan-calan.'

'Indeed.'

We sailed for some little while in silent enjoyment. He handled the tiller skilfully. I could see his hand from time to time as it extended before us to grasp the long oar. A ring winked on his finger, a milky gem set in a silver signet.

'Aye,' he said again in answer to my unspoken speculation. 'Who else would They send to bring thee back over the great sea?'

The sunset had cooled to navy night, and I was all at once a little cold. 'Where does thee take me, my lord?'

'It is not "where", boy. It is "when".'

I did not understand him. 'Is my grandfather there? I'll go gladly if only—'

If he answered me I did not hear him. There was a kind of rushing in my head, and I found myself in a liquid, black world. It was some flotsam that I was sprawled across, and those dipping lights must be stars. I was lying on my back and when I lifted my head a huge black shape was bearing down on me. I heard men crying for help and gutter language answering them in Burrener. 'Die, you bastards!' someone shouted from the black shape, which must be the ship that had rammed us, a Burrener ship. I hitched myself over the edge of my ragged section of planking and entered the cold water without a splash. There was a scream. Probably they had speared some poor wretch from the deck. I began to swim in the direction of the breakers I could hear surging on some shore invisible in the darkness. I hoped for a sand beach, but more likely it would be rock.

When the fin broke the surface right next to me, I bit off the scream that rose in my throat only at the cost of inhaling more seawater. *Don't thrash, you'll only provoke it into attacking!* I forced myself to continue a slow stroke. A shining eye rolled free of the water to inspect me, and a rounded dome of head with a small snout lifted clear. It made a small sound, not unlike a mother cat's, and I felt a gentle bump along my side. Relief flooded through me, and without thinking I reached to stroke the dolphin's smooth head. Aashis' creature stood my touch for an instant, then tossed away and paced me easily, a length to my right. Together we swam slowly away from the wreck and the scavengers who preyed upon it.

My instinct for self-preservation warred with anger and concern for the dwarves I'd left behind, but my leg where I had stabbed it in my shattered cabin wasn't working well at all, and my lungs were burning with seawater. There was nothing I could do alone and unarmed, anyway. Better to hope that some of them were escaping as I was.

I tired quickly and began to lose my clean strokes, chopping at the water and wallowing. Somebody back on that deck must have had a spyglass sweeping the water. 'Hey! One of them's getting away!' a voice shouted. 'Over there!' I was immediately sure he meant me. I hadn't breath for more than a grunt of despair and, to make matters worse, the ends of my sash were impeding my movements.

Before I could grasp what was happening, the dolphin gave a little flip, dived under me, and I felt a tug at my waist. The bloody thing must have seen one end of the sash and was curious to explore what it was. 'Shoo,' I told it feebly and fanned some water with my hand. An arrow whizzed into the sea not an armspan from my head. Aye, it *was* me that bastard look-out had spotted, all right! I gulped a breath and submerged. I couldn't see, but I could feel the water streaming past my face and a steady pull at my waist. The dolphin had hold of my sash and was towing me. I was too tired to marvel at this behavior I had only heard of in old salts' stories. There was a bad moment when I wondered whether it was pulling me back out to sea, but when I surfaced to snatch a breath the voices were further behind me. I relaxed then and trusted my bright-eyed friend.

My bad luck held, though; the attacking ship had put out dories, and they were quartering the area for survivors. I could not understand why they were so persistent and I was very angry, though truth to say, we had done it often enough ourselves. Slaves brought good money, and it is a kind of mercy not to leave even an enemy to drown.

At length, the breakers drew near enough that I could hear the sand hissing down the shingle at the pull of the waves, and that was exactly when a rowboat rocked out of the darkness not a dozen feet away. A long oar slapped the water, and a voice shouted back to the mother ship, 'Here's one!' I dived, the dolphin hauled me sideways right under the boat, and then hurtled toward the shore so fast that I had to hold on to my sash with both hands and squeeze my eyes shut against the stinging bits of shell and rock streaming out with the water from the beach.

I did not know I was in the shallows until my creature dropped the sash, and I coasted in to scrape the sandy bottom with my face. The crashing surf threatened to draw me out again, but I staggered to my feet, dashing the salt water out of my eyes. A few feet out, the dolphin watched. 'Bless thee, brother,' I croaked, careless whether my pursuers heard me. In that one moment I didn't care.

The next instant, the sleek head was gone, and the creak of oarlocks came clearly over the sound of the surf. I staggered heavily toward some rocks just visible through the white streams of water that crashed against them. The boat was lying to just offshore. 'Where'd the whoreson go?' I heard someone say, and there was an incomprehensible murmur in reply. Hugging my rock, I tried to ignore the deep throb in my leg and peer into the darkness inland. After a moment or two, I realized that the land rose sharply, not perhaps in rock cliffs, but certainly in a leap of salt-bitten turf and scree. Shifting to get a better vantage, I was startled to see a steady blue light from the top of the rise.

'He'll be making for the siochla,' one of the men in the rowboat said resignedly, and I grinned in the darkness, slipped to the sand of the beach, and—

The water was real suddenly, stingingly cold, and there was salt in my mouth. Neddy backed a pace at the look I must have given him and quickly signed, *Skipper wants you topside* NOW. He flushed and gestured at my sodden jersey: *Sorry. I couldn't wake you at first.*

I swung my feet over the side of the bunk, grasped the clothes hook on the wall and hauled myself up, suppressing a groan at the effects of the hangover. 'Has the look-out sighted prey?'

He shook a quick negative, his round face unaccustomedly strained, and added another urgent, *Hurry up!*

It was trouble, then. I lurched out of the door of the cabin and groped my way topside.

CHAPTER TWO

When I climbed through the hatch, I saw that the morning's thick curtain of sea smoke dropped an artificial limit to our world not more than two or three hundred yards all around. The cabin boy pointed forward to where Timbertoe and some of the others were grouped in the bow and followed as I ran up to the quarterdeck.

'Way for the pilot!' our bo's'n, old Ries Nyboldson, bellowed as I swarmed up the ladder. The men parted to let me through to the rail, but being much taller than they, I had already spotted the small open boat drifting slowly through streamers of smoke about two hundred yards off our starboard bow. Silently Ries handed me a spyglass.

Timbertoe had his own glass trained on it. 'What d'ye make of her, Giant?'

I studied the boat. Her hull was painted black, and it was new: when she lifted in the rolling swells, I could see no trailing seawrack or barnacles. Slowly I swept the glass down the length of her, noting the neat lines, a limp white pennant at the masthead, a very odd sail shiny even in the gray-white light, and covered oar ports. 'What kind of sail is that?'

'Looks for all the world to be cloth-of-gold,' the skipper answered.

My spyglass came to rest on her stern. 'No rudder.' I lowered the glass, and Timbertoe did the same. We exchanged a glance. 'A funeral ship?' I guessed.

'A funeral ship,' he agreed and rubbed his nose thoughtfully with one broad hand.

I knew exactly what he was thinking. Though rare, ship burials were occasionally practiced by both the Ilyrians and my own Burreners, and sometimes by others as well. One knew of such things from tales. But one knew also the unwritten law of the sea: for one who disturbed such a boat in its passage to the watery halls the curse was virulent and immutable. Already I could sense tension in our own ruffian crew as they stared silently across the water. The flag at our topgallant snapped like a whip, and I saw Timbertoe cast it a glance over his shoulder. The blood-red arrow, proud symbol of the Jarlshof piratical brotherhood, pointed straight toward the funeral ship. Timbertoe's eyebrows went up, he gave a tug to one braid of his woolly beard, and his peg leg scraped the deck as he drew himself up. 'Ah, well, can't hurt just to have a little closer look at her, right?' The thought of gold to that old seadog was like the vapors of a whiskey barrel to a drunk.

I shrugged.

His eyes narrowed dangerously, and he whirled to face the crew. 'Well?' he challenged.

Forty pairs of dark dwarf eyes flicked from their captain to the black-hulled ship. And back to their captain.

I turned and put my back to the rail. 'I agree, Skipper. There can be no harm in looking. I'm curious. We've heard of no notable deaths over there (the Burren is always *over there* to dwarves) or among the rivermen, either.' By which I meant Ilyria. 'But that is plainly a nobleman's funeral boat, and she's riding low in the water.' They knew well enough what I meant. A boat bearing only a single man's body, however big he may be, doesn't displace that much water unless every nook and cranny around the corpse is stuffed with something very heavy. Something like metal. And if the sail was gold, it wasn't likely whoever had sent the dead man on his way had used pig iron for ballast.

They were swayed, though unconvinced. I folded up the telescope with a snap and handed it back to Neddy. 'There's our homeward course to think of, though. We don't need any curses dogging us. How about this? Suppose we lay to, and I'll row over there in the curragh, just to see what's what. Then, if there's any bad luck, it'll come on my head.'

A ripple went through the crew, and Ries nodded to himself. Timbertoe swept his men with a scathing look, spat over the rail, and folded his arms on his chest. 'Suppose ye'll want a 50/50 cut, then.' This was a quarter higher than my usual take.

I eyed him coolly. 'No. I'll want it all.'

A sudden squall of furious voices shouted invective at me. I waited it out. Timbertoe raised a hand for silence, and before he could speak, I added, 'I'll hold all profits for a year. That ought to be time enough for a curse to strike, if it's going to. At the end of a year, if nothing's gone wrong, your split will be a quarter. Take it or leave it.'

He stared at me, then slowly grinned. 'Ye should have been a dwarf, boy. Ye've the proper balls for it.'

The tension drained off in the general approving laugh. I flicked a sign to a couple of the men to lower the landing boat away and put a ladder over the side for me. The dwarves swarmed into the rigging to get a better view. Timbertoe and I turned back to the rail, and under cover of one hand scratching his beard, he asked, 'Ye're not really thinking of boarding her, are ye?'

'Hell, no. Only a jackass would muck about with a funeral boat. I just want to know which king it is.'

He understood immediately. No death boat save a king's would be fitted with a golden sail, and if either Diarmuid ap Gryffin of the Burren or Fergus Fairhand of Ilyria had died, we pirates of Jarlshof could use the information. The disorganization attendant on a king's death would make the country's shipping ripe for the taking with little fear of retaliation. We would, of course, send a funerary tribute to the bereaved court with Jarlshof's most sorrowful compliments to the heir apparent. The guildmaster of pirates would pay well for the news.

The captain nodded his satisfaction and took out his pipe. 'Mind ye don't spend long over there, Giant. I don't much care for lying to like this. The watch spotted that rotten *Wind Courser* in the fog this morning, but she slipped us.'

'You're not worried, surely?' I knew he was and grinned wickedly. 'Come, Timbertoe, you know Brunehilda would never sink you.'

'Not if I sank her first,' he parried evenly, refusing to rise to the bait. He had very nearly sent the swift gray ship of our arch-rival to the bottom two months prior when we'd had the good fortune to round the headland off Mizzenmast Creek and find the dwarfen woman's ship in our sea lane. Brunehilda, as superb a sailor as Timbertoe himself, had escaped, however. We had seen her through the spyglass staring back at us through her own. When she was aware of us watching, the lady admiral made an emphatic obscene gesture. In answer, Timbertoe walked to our rail and casually passed water. Her scream of rage came clearly on the wind as we left her, *Wind Courser* rocking in our wake. Timbertoe had laughed himself into a violent headache that I'd had to dose him for, and had spent the last eight weeks balking at every headland and cove. It was an old story; he and Brunehilda had been hounding each other for years. Nothing personal, just business the talk in the dockside taverns went. I wondered.

'Get into the whoreson curragh, would you?' he now said, irritably. 'Think we've got the whole bleeding day?'

I threw him a salute and trotted aft, taking deep breaths of the icy air to try to clear the fumes of the drugged liquor from my head. They had the boat lowered, and I climbed down the rope ladder to it. One of the men leaned over the rail to call, 'Hey, Pilot, better cover up! Ye don't want that face of yours to throw a fright into the poor dead bugger!'

I suggested what he could do with himself and rowed toward the death boat.

I worked into the rhythm of the low swells with an ease which had become second nature. When I glanced back over my shoulder some moments later, the '*Kerry Gem* was already blurred by mist, the crew just dark spiders against the web of rigging. It was very quiet, the only sounds the creak of the oarlocks, the splash and trickle of water off the blades as I stroked, a slight rippling of the golden sail ahead as the wind backed a point or two and then settled again. A few tendrils of fog curled around me and beaded my bare arms, so that my hands on the oars seemed limned in a soft sheen of light. The black ship was near enough now to see the proud curve of upsweeping bow that gives the type of craft its name, 'dragon-prow', a small twenty-oared boat, graceful and shallow-drafted with every plank of her hull fitted as carefully as the overlapping layers of a green pine cone.

The wind freshened a little, and the black boat began to draw away, her gold sail pregnant with the breeze. I cursed under my breath, lengthening my strokes to make headway on her, and I looked back toward the *Gem* for a moment. 'Come on, you poxy old bastard, bring her up,' I muttered to Timbertoe irritably.

'Don't make me row all the way back, too!' One of my oars skipped over the water, a result of my momentary inattention, and sprayed me with a nice, cold shower. I scuffed the salt water out of my eyes on the shoulder of my jersey, spat disgustedly and bent my back to the rowing. By the Fire, I'd catch that whoring little black bastard of a boat if it was the last thing . . .

A sound, a hum, low, but clear enough that I heard it over everything else, coming from the death ship. The wind in her rope lines, I told myself, but I wasn't convinced: in four years before the mast on some rotten, stormy nights, I had never heard such a sound. It ceased as quickly as it had come. Sweat suddenly sprang on my nape and I cursed myself for a gutless fool. The fog rolled in over the water, and the black hull sailed into the cloud. I tried at the last moment to reverse my direction, but I slid into the wall of gray mist.

The world became a thick and moist realm of dim sight and magnified sound. The water gurgled past the bow of my curragh, the flutter of the other boat's sail became a distinct snap of cloth, and I could even hear her rigging straining a little and the rhythmic knock of the yardarm against the mast as she dipped and curtsied in the waves. Then the hum began again, and I thought there was more to it than the single, low note. My hands clenched on the oars.

I thought of my knife and was just reaching to my sash for it when the sound stopped. A dark shape suddenly loomed up out of the fog and before I could do anything about it, I had bumped into the black hull as neatly as a whale calf coming to its mam.

The funeral ship's rail was higher than my head, and her hull lifted from the water in a graceful outward curve, so as I sat in the curragh I could see nothing of her cargo. For that, I would have to scramble up on to the thwart and brace myself against the death ship's planks. There was a rope coiled in the bow of my boat, and I cast it around the carved spiral of the black ship's bowsprit so that the curragh would be towed along with this drifting wayfarer.

I stowed my oars carefully out of the way, rubbed my hands the length of my jersey to dry them somewhat, and reminded myself that the gulls had probably been at work on him. After what I had seen at the skellig and in the intervening years with dwarfen raiders, the thought didn't bother me much. I stood, gave it a moment to get my balance riding with the waves, and then stepped up on the wooden seat. But in reaching to catch a purchase on the black ship's rail, my hands slipped. Lurching, I barked my shins painfully on the thwart and cracked my head – not on the bad side – on the side of the funeral boat, which seemed to buck suddenly to meet me on the way down. I nearly fell from my dory into the water, but managed to catch myself and throw my weight backward into the boat. I lay half-stunned for a moment, then felt gingerly of my forehead. I brought my fingers away expecting to see blood, but there was none and my shakiness turned immediately to anger. I leapt to my feet, kicked the oars out of the way, and jumped for the rail that arched over my head. The funeral ship shied at my weight, but I was ready for it and hooked one leg over the rail, hauling myself up until I was astride it.

The corpse itself was not visible, and I was surprised at that. I'd thought there would be a bier nailed across the thwarts and the dead man's grave goods heaped about him, his sword by his hand and perhaps the carcass of his favorite hound at his feet. The gold and silver were there as they should be, but not so much as I would have thought, and in barrels rather than chests or coffers of fine wood. There was no ritual meal, though perhaps the gulls had got it, because there was an empty wine cup of horn and silver lying on the decking. I cast an eye up at the golden sail and wondered if some other raider had got there first.

Maybe the breeze had lifted, though I had not registered it, but my eye, traveling up the length of the mast, was attracted by the unfurling pennon of purest white. And as the wind streamed it out, I found myself staring as I had stared once before into the Swan's living black eye. I blinked quickly and when I looked again the flag was only a flag and not so white, the material having faded in the sun to an antiqued ivory and the eye of the swan represented there merely a bead of polished jet that caught a sheen of wet from the fog.

It took me a moment to work up the saliva to spit, but I did, and swung down into the boat. If there were no corpse, there was no curse at boarding a funeral ship, and I wanted to know what had happened here. I gave that flag another glance, though. It was distinctly odd. I had never heard that either king, Diarmuid or Fergus, had any special devotion to the Hag.

I shook my head, discovered that I must have cut myself falling after all, and held my sleeve to my forehead for a moment while I dipped a couple of handfuls from the barrels of gold and silver. This booty I secured in my sash pocket to pay off the lads, before moving down the ship toward the stern. The mast was well-fitted, but the turnings of the oaken deck shoe were of an unusual design, and I studied them for a moment before I realized what had pricked my attention: there were no nails, no iron of any kind. I took a closer look at the planking beneath my feet. Every bit of the joinery was pegged with wooden bungs. This was an old boat, indeed.

I picked up the king's cup and set it right, then moved on.

Just aft of the mast I found another odd thing, a deck prism set into the planking. Now, deck prisms have only one function: to let in light below decks, so that lanterns need not be used during the daylight hours. The flat end of the inverted pyramid is set flush with the deck, and the pointed end extends below to channel and amplify the light, casting a small flood of illumination down into the cargo holds or living quarters. It is a pretty effect sometimes, for the prism rainbows the sunlight, and then sailors call it the Little Magefire. I've heard it called the Frost Giant's Snots, too, but that is only among the uncouth. To find a deck prism here was another indication that someone had adapted this old ship to their purpose rather than building one new. It also meant there was another deck. I looked for the hatch. There wasn't one.

I pressed a hand to my head, winced, and made another search the length of the ship, every inch of the planking, but no hidden spring was released to my probing touch and no hidden trap door swung open. The pennon snapped above my head with a sound like a whip cracking, and I looked up at the jet-bead eye. 'Keeping secrets, are we?' I muttered to the image of the Hag.

I could think of only one more thing to try, so I let myself down on the deck, cupped my hands around the prism to block most of the light, and lowered my head to squint through it. At first I couldn't see much beyond a dim luminescence, but as my eyes adjusted to the effect of the prism's facets, I could begin to make out the dim outline of wooden crosstrees holding up the decking, and a couple of the ship's ribs curving away into darkness on either side. I shifted a little to get a better angle directly below me.

By the Four, he was a king all right! Though his unspoiled face was neither of the ones I had been expecting. He had been cushioned on a bed of what looked to be prize fleeces strewn with flowers now dried, and he was wrapped in a thick dark cloak that may have been royal blue. In his hand was a mighty blade. His chain mail tunic looked gilded, and a crown encircled his brow. Several fine earthenware pots had been grouped about him, and a couple of them had been tossed and broken by some heavy sea. At first I thought it was spices or expensive unguents that had spilled out of them, but then I closed one eye, put the other right on the prism, and saw the single spiral pressed into the earthenware, the design magnified by the glass facets so that for a moment it seemed to fill my sight. I had seen that insignia before. They were broken color pots.

The ship lifted slightly under me through the swell, rolling the corpse a fraction, and I saw his cloak brooch. The Four Spirals engraved in its bronze surface seemed to swirl suddenly before my staring eye as though his chest had risen.

Whether my heart actually stopped, or only seemed to do so, I have no way of knowing, but I sprang up from that deck like a water droplet on a hot griddle. It was well that I was momentarily frozen in my tracks, else I'd have broken a leg falling over the thwart not three inches from my knee.

The deck was gone, the prism was gone, and a bier was nailed across the thwarts. On it the corpse of an old man dressed in the royal checkered pattern of the House of Gryffin lay ravaged by the birds, the stub of a curious thin blade showing between the ribs. Disbelievingly I cast a desperate eye up at the white pennon, and saw that it was white no longer, but showed rather the griffin rampant on a field I knew would be gules, the royal cipher of the Burren.

My head swam. Having poppy dreams when I had taken the medication to induce them and was safely in my bunk was one thing: having waking dreams from the lingering fumes was another. It was the first time it had happened, and I was brushed by a cold touch of dread.

Thinking it might be useful for blackmailing purposes, I had enough presence of mind to wrench free the point of the weapon that had killed King Diarmuid, and I was scrambling for the rail when the boom suddenly swung around, catching me a glancing blow that knocked me clear over my curragh into the waiting sea. The water broke over my poor melon of a head with a sound like the Falls at the Edge of the World. I sank under the cataract, and I think I did not come up again for a while.

Voices gurgled around me. Very disturbing it was, that bubbling echo of sound; I could not get hold of it with my mind. A bad dream lay just over the horizon of the gray fog that filled my head. My forehead began to sting as though I'd fallen into a bee skep. I roused enough to realize I was in the sea and lifted my head from my sodden sleeve, squinting to look around. I must have got hold of one of the oars from my boat, for I was clinging to it, bobbing in the swells, while the sea smoke swirled over the water and angry voices yelled over my head.

'—whoreson funeral ship, I told you!' Timbertoe was roaring. 'No prey of ours – or yours, Brunehilda!'

'I see no other ship but yours, pegleg! If you choose to heave to, and if I just happen to be coming along, that's your problem! Now, send over that ransom, and be quick about it!'

The lady captain sounded immensely satisfied. She must have caught our ship dead to rights, and now she had Timbertoe over a barrel: if he gave her the money, our hunting season would be wiped out; if he didn't, she'd ram him and send the 'Kerry Gem' to the bottom. If she was as confident as she sounded, she must have a perfect attack angle. I wiped the streaming hair out of my eyes and stared until I could just make out the darker gray wall that rose out of the gray fog some distance to my right. I looked left, but could not make out the Gem. As quickly but quietly as possible I began to swim towards Brunehilda's ship. What I planned to do when I got there, I didn't know, but if one of those big ships was going to race down on the other one, I had to get out of the way in any event. So I might as well see what I could see.

When I was near enough to begin to make out shapes lining the *Wind Courser's* rail, I abandoned my overhand stroke, submerged and swam for her stern. My head began to pound immediately, and I tried to surface quietly, but I was too close. A voice called, 'Hoy! What's that?' I waited to hear no more, but jackknifed and followed her planking by touch until I felt the squared corner and knew I was astern of her. My lungs were bursting, but I came up slowly, barely poking my nose and mouth above water. It was all right, though; the ship's flaring aft deck was well over my head and so no one topside could see me. I floated, willing the sickness to pass, and listened carefully.

'Come on, Timbertoe, quit sulking! I've got your nuts in the cracker, old boy, so pay up!'

'Damn it, it's against the rules, and you know it, woman! Article 147 of the Codex Maritima expressly forbids—'

'Nah, nah, if it's 147 you're invoking, where's the flag, then, hey?'

Dwarves! They'd face down a sea serpent together, and then fall out arguing over how many teeth the damn thing had! I swam carefully around to the other side of the ship, reckoning that the attention of everyone aboard would be fixed on the *'Kerry Gem.*

In this, I seemed to have guessed correctly. Better yet, they'd left the drag line over the side. The crews of most ships at sea supplement the dried stores they have aboard with fresh fish and sea-bird meat. The simplest way to accomplish this fishing is to bait several hooks along a line in the morning, toss the line overboard to troll behind the ship, and pull it up at evening. With any luck, you've enough of a catch to supply supper. I wasn't sure the line would hold my weight, but if Brunehilda's crew was as serious about their victuals as ours was, they'd not use any flimsy stuff that was likely to let a couple of fine fish get away. Giving the line an experimental tug, I ascertained that it was firmly secured up there, and also that it seemed reasonably stout. I wiped one hand across my forehead, had to bite my lips to prevent an involuntary cry, and then began to climb. Finally I got one hand hooked over the rail and hung there, gathering my strength before peering up over the side.

I had been right. They were so engrossed in the spectacle unfolding across the water that no one was even looking this way. I slipped over the rail, ran lightly to the shelter of the companionway hatch and caught my breath. Timbertoe and Brunehilda were now yelling about the Rule of Primacy, an obscure clause governing which pirate captain has first crack at a merchantman. Generally it boils down to the one with the biggest ram. Let them argue! I had thought of something with which to budge the lady captain.

Slipping through the hatch, I made my way below. Like most sensible captains, Brunehilda had her pirated cargo well lashed and secured, and as evenly distributed along the length of the ship as possible. With these boats, balance is everything, not only for safety's sake in foul weather, but also for the sake of speed in the hunt. A well-balanced load makes for a ship that doesn't wallow under sail. I could have played hell with the lashings, dumping barrels and bales all over the hold, but that would have taken more time than I had, and also wouldn't have had the impact I was looking for.

Every dwarfen captain has the means to scuttle his or her ship, because if they are cornered by an enemy they must hide the evidence of their piracy, it being a hanging offense in every country. I found the cocks where I expected to, used all my strength to open the two in the bow, ran past the midships ones, and hesitated at the stern. These ships are fairly small and founder quickly. I decided not to do the thing too thoroughly; I didn't really want to sink Brunehilda. She hadn't done anything Timbertoe wouldn't do. This would just give them both something to laugh over in the years to come.

I swarmed up the ladder to the deck, crouching behind the small deckhouse to wait. The bow was already down a degree or two.

Brunehilda's head went up first, and she swung to listen. Even over the end of Timbertoe's insulting bellow, we could all plainly hear the cataract belowdecks. I jumped to the rail, where I balanced by grabbing one of the sheeting lines, and saluted the lady smartly. 'Captain Timbertoe's respects, ma'am. Your bung's open.'

'My wh—?' Then the realization hit her. 'You son of a whore!' She came for me at a dead run, cutlass in hand, but I jumped up and out and treated them all to a beautifully executed somersault which I am not sure they appreciated under the circumstances, and which probably wasn't wise given the state of my head.

I swam hard for the *'Kerry Gem.* Timbertoe had the sheets up and three men leaning from the cargo net to catch my hands as the ship cut past me, and then I was aboard and we were away free and clear. I had to tell what I had done over there at least four times with a full pitcher of ale to each telling and so many slaps to the back that I was sore for days afterward.

Later, after the lads were singing and playing at tiles, Timbertoe went below to his cabin. He lit the lamp, handed me a shot of flotjin from his private store, and settled himself on his bunk with his bad leg elevated on a pillow, a trick I had taught him to ease the phantom throbbing that troubled him sometimes. He silently toasted me with his own glass, and we drank. His dark eyes searched me over the rim. 'So? Who was it?'

My throat suddenly closed as it all came back to me then, and my crooked jaw locked. It did that sometimes, when I was under stress.

'It's all right, Giant, it's all right,' he said companionably. 'Drink up. I've no real interest in dead men, after all. Time enough later. Ye hit your head a mean one, it looks like.'

'Fell,' I managed to mumble.

He snorted. 'I should say you did! What, did he sit up and talk to ye?' The dwarf chuckled into his glass.

I clenched a fist.

Timbertoe shifted to bring his mouth close to the speaking tube and whistled.

'Aye, Skipper,' the helmsman hurriedly answered. 'Holding course for Inishkerry.'

'Belay that order, Pers. Set a new course for Jarlshof. I want to talk to the guildmaster before Brunehilda does.'

'Oh, aye, Skipper. That'd be wise, I don't doubt. By the way, that funeral ship's off our starboard stern now. Whose was it, anyway?'

When he cast me a questioning glance, Timbertoe caught me making the sign. He grunted in amusement. 'I thought ye were the one who wasn't scared of a funeral ship!' he said.

'WHAT?' the helmsman shouted through the tube.

The skipper bristled. 'If I wanted ye to know, ye'd know! Think

I'm going to give away any information to you maggots up there and have one of ye sell it as soon as we get to port? *Get a bloody course laid for Skejfallen!*' He thumbed the cover into place over the tube, and almost immediately we heard rope running through tackle as the sails were trimmed for the new bearing.

I gulped the flotjin. 'Diarmuid. It was Diarmuid ap Gryffin. He'd been done to death.'

Now it was Timbertoe's turn to make the sign, for I'd broken a taboo. Dwarves never, ever, mention the word 'death' at sea. Hurriedly he thrust a finger into his glass and flicked a few drops of the powerful liquor over his shoulder. This is thought to sting the Hag's eyes and make Her look away from you. 'Damnit, boy! Use your bloody head, will ye?' he growled. After a moment to get his breath back, he cleaned the taste of fright out of his mouth with a swallow of the powerful black liquor. 'The Gryffin, eh? Interesting. So old Diarmuid is left with not a son to his name to take the throne after him.' All the royal progeny had managed to kill each other off over the years.

My jaw straightened with an audible click. 'Unless there really is a lost prince,' I suggested, the flotjin beginning to settle my stomach.

'Oh, aye, the Wee Monster Prince.' The skipper chuckled. 'That one's a good tale. Have ye ever painted it?'

'A deformed child, the queen mother who flees her husband's wrath to save the infant's life, the flotsam that comes floating in from their wrecked ship?' I shrugged. 'You couldn't make much money off that one on a fair day. Folk want a funny story.'

He nodded and sipped reflectively. 'Won't those poxy Wolf-hounds have a fine time now? Bloody foxes in the henhouse they'll be.' The crow's-feet at his eyes deepened. 'Maybe ye ought to go over there and press your claim, Giant.' His shoulders shook silently. At my scowl, he swiped at his nose and sighed. 'Ye're as touchy as a bloody king, that's for sure. Well, get some liniment on that head of yours before ye add another scar to your collection.' Raising his voice, he bellowed, 'Neddy! Bring us a bucket of seawater!'

The boy tapped a light acknowledgement on the door, and we heard his footsteps go topside.

I poured myself another to take back to my cabin. 'If the

guildmaster is paying for the information, I get an eighty/twenty split.'

'Don't press your luck, Giant. Seventy/thirty.'

'Fine. Take your own ship through the channel, then.' I leaned casually against the bulkhead. I had him there. The sand bars shifted with every tide.

'Someday I'm going to get hold of that rutter of yours, Pilot, and make a bloody fortune copying the thing.'

I laughed. 'It would do you no good, Filthydwarf. Copy away.'

His eyes narrowed. 'That's what I thought: you've put it in code, haven't ye?'

I didn't answer, but of course I had. Only an idiot would leave his precious log of soundings, landmarks, maps and notes undefended. Mine contained false information, too, in case anyone ever did get hold of it. So I merely made an obscene gesture to which Timbertoe responded with one of his own, and we left it for the time.

Later, after playing some tiles on deck with the men and giving helm directions for the daywatch, I retired to my cabin. The gold and silver I stowed in the secret compartment where my rutter was secured, as I couldn't very well give it to the men now without revealing that I had taken it from a funeral boat. The murder weapon I hid also. Then I got out the ink and recorded in my secret book the previous day's sailing, a task to which I normally should have attended last night. I ruled a new page for today's log, made a notation about Diarmuid's death ship, then hesitated. The blank sheet stared up at me, but I was seeing those broken color pots. No, I decided, I couldn't call myself a decent pilot if I recorded that on this day I had seen my forefather Colin the Mariner, ancient king of Ilyria and Master of Inishbuffin. Not even in a secret journal could I record the hallucination of seeing a man who had been dead for nigh five hundred years.

I closed the book with a snap, stowed it behind its panel, and roughly bandaged the small cut on my forehead. My head was aching, but I did not take any more poppy or flotjin.

CHAPTER THREE

The old city of Skejfallen was a wonder to me. As a boy I had known no community larger than Bhaile ap Boreen, the largest town in our district and the place where Bruchan had purchased me at a fair. After that, I rarely travelled outside the skellig, and when I did, it was to some coastal town where we traded for needed goods. Until I first sailed to the dwarfen capital with Timbertoe, I had never been in a city, and certainly had never experienced anything remotely resembling the crowded, vital bustle of this port which considered itself the navel of the maritime world.

As we rowed towards one of the quays through the crowded traffic of the harbour, Timbertoe hailed old friends and cheerfully shook his fist at old enemies, all the while keeping up a steady stream of unnecessary commands to the helm. This was a matter of pride; the one place you didn't want a docking accident was at Skejfallen, with a crowd of old salts sunning themselves on their benches outside the taverns and the harbormaster himself in his tower as witness.

At Ries Nieboldson's clipped order, the rowers shipped oars and, looking smart, we glided to a space at the pier. I jumped ashore with the bow line and was making fast to the bollard when from the door of the warehouse opposite a voice yelled, 'Get away, or I'll call the watch on ye!'

I cast a look over my shoulder while I went about the business of casting another loop of rope over the wooden piling. A hunched figure seemed catapulted on to the wharf to land just a few feet from me. I had one quick impression of long stringy hair, rough beard, and dirty clothes before the warehouseman followed him into the road to plant a solid kick in the fellow's ribs. Doubtless the ill-favored man was a beggar, and the warehouseman had caught him stealing from whatever cargo was stored inside.

The dwarf on the ground rolled, trying to protect himself, but the guard caught him another kick on the hip. The fellow grunted, then glared up at the warehouseman, who by now had worked himself into a temper. The beggar's lips drew back in a snarl, and his eyes gleamed. 'It's my glass,' he said hoarsely. 'Lord Aashis give it to me up on the mountain.'

'It's Burgher Karlsson's glass now. If ye'd earned some money fishing instead of playing with the goats up there, ye could have paid off your debt. Ye had your chance, so don't come crying poormouth around here, Olin Olafson! You're nothing but a damn bum, and if ye come near here again I'll set the dog on ye!'

'*My* glass.'

'Go home, ye crazy bastard!' The warehouseman lifted the truncheon that he had so far not used.

This would get ugly in a moment. I walked over to the two of them. 'Easy now,' I counseled the warehouseman. 'You don't want to get the watch down on you for thrashing this poor whoreson.'

The fellow's anger would have its out. 'What's it to ye, Burrener?'

I spread my hands as if in a gesture of peace, but I was actually showing him the tattoo on my forearm, the pirates' mark. I had already noted his. 'Nothing. I just don't want to have to appear in the Moot as a witness against you. They'll summon me, sure, if you beat him.'

That registered. He didn't want any trouble with the law. He was very red in the face with anger. 'Look, he hasn't been bothering *you* for a fortnight over some damn glass floats. Every time I turn around, the whoreson's in the door again!'

'Lord Aashis . . .' Olin began.

The warehouseman suddenly snorted. He shook his head and gave me a conspiratorial wink. 'Thinks the Wind gave him some glass net-floats up on top of Barak-Gambrel.' He jerked a thumb in the direction of the skep-shaped mountain that walled in the city on the East.

I didn't like the wink. 'Maybe Aashis did give it to him.'

The fellow laughed. 'What, did ye get dumped on your head, too? They say that's how Olafson—' He swallowed the words as

I turned full to him. 'Well, I didn't mean you're crazy, of course, just because *he* is.'

'Right.'

He fumbled to hang the truncheon from his belt again, then shook a finger at the watching beggar. 'Next time, it's the law for you!' He stomped into the warehouse.

Olin Olafson slowly swung his unstaring gaze to me. I realized that they were not the simpleton's usual blank eyes. In fact, he somehow looked very aware, like a man arrested in the act of listening to some far-off music only he can hear. I stuck out a hand and leaned over to pull him to his feet. 'You want to go carefully around the warehouseman,' I told him. 'Stay away, if you can.'

'It's my glass,' he told me quietly, sounding perfectly rational.

'Well, the law won't agree with you, friend. If the rich man says he owns it, they'll probably give it to him.'

He made a small sound of disgust or pain, I couldn't tell which, and I picked up his hat for him. 'It's mine,' he repeated.

I could see why he'd got on the warehouseman's nerves. 'Fine. It's yours. Here, take this.' I flipped him a bronze farthing from my sash pocket. 'Go buy yourself a pint.'

Olafson cast the farthing on to the ground disdainfully. 'Lord Aashis gave it to me.' A tremor shook him, and for a moment a shining look of exaltation bloomed over his benighted face.

'It's special glass, then,' I murmured in pity.

To my surprise, he gave me one swift look. 'Aye. Very special, very rare. A deck prism for the world. You understand?' He jammed the hat down over his ears and regarded me confidently.

My mind flashed back to the vision I had seen. 'Deck prism?' I questioned, taking a step closer to him.

'Damn it, Giant, we're drifting from the stern!' Timbertoe bellowed from the deck. 'Get the line tied off!'

I turned my head to tell him to hold his water, and when I looked again, Olafson was gone.

As soon as the line was snubbed tight, Timbertoe came down the gangplank. 'What the hell was that all about?' he demanded.

'Just breaking up a quarrel. I figured you wouldn't want to be held up here while the city wardens tried to sort the thing out, probably calling our lads as witnesses.' I didn't want

39

to discuss Olin Olafson and his Aashis glass with my pirate captain.

'Oh. Good thinking,' Timbertoe approved gruffly. 'Come now, step lively. I want to see the guildmaster today, and it's likely he'll keep us cooling our heels a while.' He turned back to the boat. 'Ahoy, there, Nieboldson! You may dismiss the crew, except for the normal deck watch. All hands aboard by the time the tide turns, or we'll sail for home without them.'

'Aye, Skipper. Good luck to ye,' the stout bos'n called back.

Timbertoe gave him an absent salute, and we moved off up the wharfside alley. 'Relax, Skipper,' I told him, sensing his nerves now that we were actually on the way to report. It was no small thing to have attempted the scuttling of another captain's boat. 'It's a clear case of self-defense, and besides, Brunehilda can't possibly have reached the guildmaster before us, even if she was bent on taking you to Moot over the whole thing.'

'Right,' he said. But there was a note of doubt in his voice, explained a moment later when he mused, 'Ye don't suppose he'll hold that bit of trouble last year against us, do ye?'

No, I shouldn't think so, I answered silently. *The bastard made a tidy sum on the pay-off.* There were people all around us in the busy street, however, and one never knows what ears may be listening, so I merely replied, 'No. It was proved the fight was started by the other crew, don't forget, and you paid our half of the damages promptly. I don't think the guildmaster could hold that against you.'

He grunted an amused agreement, and I knew that he, too, was thinking how much the last incident had cost us. There was no help for it, though; any dispute involving members of the piratical guild was referred by custom, if not by law, to the guildmaster. This was an elected title (or, more accurately, a purchased one) of paramount influence and wealth in the social strata of the islands. The honest citizens of Skejfallen, and there were a few, would have been scandalized to know exactly how much of their trade and treaty was manipulated by the head of the pirates' league. If the dwarves could have bent their stiff necks to accept a king, the guildmaster of pirates would have bid pretty fair to wear the crown.

In the four years I had been a member of the guild, the office had been held by a seadog named Sitric Jorgenson, called Sitric Silkenbeard for his most distinguishing characteristic. He had the beard curried every day by two virgins with ivory-and-boar-bristle brushes, the tavern talk said. More power to him, in my opinion, since it must have cost him a pretty penny. Virgins aren't thick on the ground in any port city, and Skejfallen was no exception in that regard.

Besides the beard, Sitric also had the ability to negotiate truces between the most obdurate folk on earth, and the iron will to see his judgments carried out, by his own picked men if need be. He was not to be taken lightly in any regard, and I was curious to meet him as Timbertoe and I walked up from the waterfront through the cobbled streets to the great house set behind its own stout walls on a height overlooking the city.

As we drew near the high wooden gate, ornately carved with nautical scenes, Timbertoe cast a critical eye up at me. 'No smart arse talk, now. The guildmaster's not a one to trifle with.'

I'd like to have told him exactly what the guildmaster could do with himself if he objected to anything I said, but this was important – even I recognized that fact – and we could already hear someone inside coming along to open up, so I merely looked down at him for a moment. I was wearing what Timbertoe referred to as my 'pot', a round, close-fitting helmet of boiled leather with iron bands that criss-crossed over the dangerous place in my head. It had a kind of scarf stitched into it, which I could wind about my neck for protection on cold days, or draw across my face below my eyes to hide my ugly countenance. It had quickly been adopted by many of my pirate mates as a comfortable piece of protective gear which had the added virtue of making identification of any one face on a raid virtually impossible. We had heard that even some of the Wolfhound soldiers had embraced the style. Now I asked, 'Do you want me to cover up?'

'No.' He had the grace to color.

The wicket opened, and a face nearly as ill-favored as my own scowled out at us. 'Name and business,' the doorward demanded gruffly.

The pegleg drew himself up. 'Timbertoe, of the *Inishkerry Gem*, come to speak to the guildmaster about an Article 147 incident.'

'Right. This the other party?'

'No. This is my pilot, Cru dun Gill.' My true name was a closely guarded secret, and there was no need to use it here.

The guildmaster's guard knew enough of the Burren tongue to recognize that Cru meant 'dog' or 'hound', and he probably also knew it is the nickname commonly given to very ugly or deformed people. If he had smiled any more broadly, he'd have split his face. It was all right, though, because it was a kinsman's smile. I wondered how the other combatant had fared. Unless I missed my guess, he'd lost the piece of ear in a savage brawl. 'Right,' the fellow said again. 'Wait here, then. I'll be back directly.' He slammed the wicket shut.

We did not talk while we waited. Some of Timbertoe's edginess had infected me and though I did not look up, I was certain we were observed from the little gatehouse above the arch leading into the estate. Somewhat to my surprise, it was not very long at all before we heard the bolts being drawn, and the gate swung open.

An inner courtyard was before us, paved with well-hewn stones, and the house itself was also built of stone, a grand affair with squared columns and a double door that would easily have admitted a team of horses. More wonderful to me were the windows, no horn or oiled paper covering these, but entirely glazed. I had never seen so much glass in one place before in my life. The stone court and outbuildings might have belonged to a prosperous inn, but those windows marked the guildmaster's wealth as nothing else could have done. Timbertoe and I exchanged a carefully blank glance and followed our ugly guide into the house.

Once in the broad entry hall, we were handed over to another servant. This one was dressed like a pirate, but his blond hair was carefully oiled where mine was a wind-knotted shag. His jersey was clean and showed a Running Knot pattern, a high rank in piratedom, while mine was salt-stiff and only displayed the Anchor Chain, next-to-last rank and about the best I could aspire to without being born a dwarf. His trousers were good wool, woven expertly, while mine were part wool, part bog-cotton, and all itch; and his sash was a bold swag, while my own was faded with sun and salt. He looked like a pirate gone landlubber with soft living. I'd have laid long odds on his having handled a line in a gale any time recently.

'You find something amusing?' he inquired, his voice stiff, but civil.

I was saying 'No, sir,' when Timbertoe's elbow found my wind, and he cut in, 'Ignore it, by your good will, sir. It's a tic. He can't help it with that jaw of his.'

I followed his cue, and let my crooked jaw sag a bit and the weak eye drift half-shut as it did sometimes when I was tired. The fellow looked somewhat mollified. 'Your weapons, please, pirates.' He smiled at our immediate exclamations of protest and made a slight gesture of apology and reassurance. 'A rule of the house, I'm afraid. We who have the guildmaster's safety as our charge feel this precaution is a fair one.'

It did make sense. One didn't become guildmaster without making enemies along the way. Reluctantly, Timbertoe and I drew our daggers and laid them side by side on the polished table top nearby, and both of us knew that we'd better our case by being forthcoming, so we added the boot knives, too, without being specially asked.

The guildmaster's man nodded his satisfaction, but added to me alone, 'I must ask you further to keep your hands very still, sir, as it is clear you are trained at unarmed combat also.'

Give him highest marks, I thought admiringly. He'd noted the calluses on the outside edges of my palms. I gave him a slight bow for answer, and he nodded once more and led us through a doorway, down a corridor, up a stairway, and along a hall to the room where the interview was apparently to take place, the room where, as he had just told me, unseen watchers would hear every word and be alert for the slightest sign of treachery. There he left us with a gesture at the chairs drawn up to the fire.

'Nice house,' Timbertoe commented, hands clasped behind him.

'A palace,' I agreed. He looked sharply at me, but I shrugged as though I didn't know why.

The bronze door latch lifted and Sitric Silkenbeard, encumbered by two lithesome girls – the virgins, no doubt – bumbled into the room. He was huge of girth, extremely red of face, and just now perspiring from the effort of moving three bodies. He seemed surprised to see Timbertoe and me standing there. 'Oh. Oh, yes, the 147,' he realized after a moment. Giving one girl a kiss on the cheek and the other a pinch on the bottom, Sitric ordered, 'Away now, my pretties. Silky has business.'

The brunette had a pretty, practiced, pout and she made good use of it as they obediently swayed out.

The guildmaster looked after them for a moment stroking his flaxen beard. 'Of all life's baubles, jolly girls are surely the loveliest – and the most expensive, eh, lads?'

'Depends on what you want them to do,' I answered, taking good care to block Timbertoe's elbow this time.

Sitric's head snapped to me, and then he let out a huge shout of laughter. 'By His Beard, I guess it does! I like you, Pirate!'

'Same, sir.' I really wished he wouldn't laugh so hard, though, because he was having trouble getting his breath.

He stuck a hand out to my skipper. 'Well, Timbertoe, a bit of trouble you've had, I understand. I'm sure it's nothing we can't sort out pretty quickly. Have a seat, have a seat. Flotjin? No? How about some brandywine, then. This stuff's supposed to be good, got it off one of Brunehilda's shipments last month.'

His opening gambit: *we* hadn't sent him anything last month. I felt myself pricked to irritation at the openness of the jibe.

Timbertoe accepted a glass of amber liquor. 'I can recommend it. She gave me a bottle out of friendship, too. We cracked it open that night, in fact.' He raised the glass in a toast. I smiled inwardly, and waved off the glass Sitric offered me.

The guildmaster nodded a fraction, as if in silent acknowledgement of Timbertoe's parry. He lowered himself into a chair, sipped, made a small sound of appreciation, and waved the glass benignly at the skipper. 'So now, let me hear what has happened to bring you here directly from your boat, without Brunehilda's even being sighted passing the channel marker at the Ledges yet.' If he caught the pegleg's small start of surprise, he gave no indication of it.

His intelligence was first rate. Heliographs, I assumed. Only mirrors could pass a message so quickly. I wondered how many watchers he had stationed along all the seaways.

Timbertoe cleared his throat. 'How did ye know it was Brunehilda we had the trouble with?'

Sitric smiled broadly. 'Who else would have dared to try to hold *you* to ransom, Timbertoe?'

This was flattery of the basest sort, and I could see my old seadog preening a bit, but it was also a very sound piece of reasoning. I reminded myself that despite the luxury with which he surrounded himself, the guildmaster's reputation might be entirely earned.

'Aye. Indeed,' the pegleg agreed. 'Well, to make short work of it, Guildmaster, the way of it was this: we'd hoved to in order to check out a drifting boat. Looked to be a funeral boat to us, and—'

Sitric sat up at that and interrupted. 'You disturbed a funeral ship?' His expression was faintly horrified.

'No, no,' Timbertoe assured him hastily. 'Not *disturbed*. Cru, here, volunteered to row over to it and just have a look-see.'

For the first time I spoke. 'So that we might bring you the information, Guildmaster.'

'Why would I be interested in a funeral ship?'

Timbertoe frowned as I answered, 'For the same reason we were.' I left it hanging there. What kind of idiots did he think us? Of course we wouldn't have approached the black ship without a damned good reason. If the fat fool couldn't figure it out . . .

The guildmaster seemed nonplussed, and Timbertoe looked as though he were about to unscrew his wooden leg and whack me over the head with it. In the silence the sound of the latch lifting was very loud. The magnificently dressed servant who had conducted us here stood in the doorway. He jerked his head at the dwarf sitting across from Timbertoe, and the fellow rose quickly and went out, shutting the door behind himself. The taller dwarf came across the thick carpet to us. 'So Diarmuid ap Gryffin is dead?' he asked, addressing the question to me. And then, of course, I knew.

'Aye, Guildmaster. Murdered.' I made no move to give him the point, which I had discovered upon closer examination was made of bone. If he wanted that, I wanted money first.

He stared and murmured, 'Indeed?' Clasping his hands behind him, he took a thoughtful turn the length of the room and back. 'Was there aught to tell the manner of his death?'

'Aye, sir. There was.'

His eyebrows were so light they were nearly lost against his faded tan, but I saw them climb toward his hairline, and then he laughed. 'What's your price?'

'I'm sure you'll know what's appropriate, sir.'

Sitric's gaze went to Timbertoe. 'You've a savvy pilot, for all he's a Burrener.'

My seadog sniffed. 'Taught him everything he knows.'

The guildmaster smiled slyly. 'Well, now, let me take a shot in the dark. I'd guess you boys found a bone lance or arrowhead in the old fellow. Ah, too bad, no nice bit of coin for that information, though you'll collect for this report of Diarmuid's murder, of course.' He winked at our disappointment and pulled from his pocket a bit of thin rope. His restless fingers began to tie an intricate knot that I recognized as a Puffin's Ladder. 'I'd heard the Wolfhounds were up to some new devilry, and this is the second report of such a death that's come to my ears. It surprises me, though, that those maggot Wolf priests would reach as high as the crown itself.' He took a turn up and down the rug. 'Diarmuid was no sailor. Why would they have sent him off that way? Would you judge it a sea burial with full rites?' he asked me.

I thought back to the brief glimpse I'd had in the course of vaulting for the rail to get the hell off the boat. 'No. A hasty one, I should think. There were no remains of a ritual meal, nor any grave goods, not even his sword. And the coins on his eyes looked like brass farthings, come to think of it, not gold.'

Sitric pulled at his neatly barbered beard, which was not silken at all, being quite a little darker than his hair and thick. 'Not just what you'd expect for a king.' His fingers went on with the sailor's knot in the bit of rope.

Unless no one is supposed to know he's dead, I thought. But I didn't say it, waiting to see what the guildmaster might come up with on his own. 'Apparently your mirrors hadn't told you of this.'

Sitric regarded me expressionlessly. 'If I *had* mirrors to pass information, it would be essential to keeping us safe here in the islands against certain parties who would like very much to make dangerous mischief among us. Naturally, then, I wouldn't take it kindly if rumor about such mirrors began circulating from a careless word over a pint.'

I made him a grin with my crooked mouth. 'Naturally.'

Just to make sure I'd got it, he gave me the benefit of his stare for another long moment. He'd a very good stare, but I had a better one, and Sitric dropped his eyes first. 'Yes. Point taken,' he murmured, 'but we must be careful here, as you have seen.'

Timbertoe determined to get back into the conversation. 'It's a very good ploy, if you'll pardon my saying so, Guildmaster. Having the other fellow pretend to be you, I mean, whilst ye pretend to be his servant.'

Sitric shrugged. 'It's the oldest trick in piratedom, Timbertoe, confusing an enemy by giving him a target too inviting to miss.' His eyes lifted to mine. He was tall for a dwarf; they didn't have to lift far. 'Rather like the Haunt of the Moor does.'

I controlled my face. Timbertoe covered by drinking off the last swallow of his brandy.

The guildmaster smiled, and I thought, *How the hell did he find out? We've never told anyone outside our own crew, and they've been paid to keep their mouths shut.* But obviously they had not been paid enough, and now my secret vengeance against the Wolfhounds was compromised. That being the case, I'd best get Sitric on my side, and fast.

Carefully I said, 'If there were a Haunt of the Moor, he probably wouldn't want stray mirror flashes to rumor his comings and goings.'

Sitric's smile widened. 'Naturally. You may speak freely, incidentally. There are no guards or spies listening behind the draperies.'

I wasn't sure of that, but if there were other listeners the damage was already done, so when Timbertoe shrugged at my raised eyebrow, I folded my arms and asked the Guildmaster of Pirates, 'What use will you make of this news of Diarmuid's death?'

He began pacing again, and I saw the habit for what it was: he'd trod the deck of many a ship in his time. The knot grew under his fingers. 'That depends,' he answered, 'on what the Wolfhounds are up to. Unless they intend a complete revolt, I'd guess their aim is to put a distantly connected royal personage on the throne, some willing puppet who will act as mouthpiece for their archpriest.'

'There's the nephew, Leif Lackwit,' Timbertoe suggested, giving the unfortunate young man his common nickname. 'He'd be the perfect fool.'

'Mm,' Sitric agreed musingly. 'I think our course now is to send an embassy to the Burrener court to inquire after His Majesty's health, feign surprise at the news of his death – they must be saying *something* about it – and perhaps attempt contact with the heir to see if we might be able to work with him on legitimate trade matters . . . and other things.'

'If the Wolfhounds will let your ambassador anywhere near Leif,' I reminded him. 'With King Diarmuid out of the way, I don't doubt they have Lackwit safely on a leash.'

'Even puppies slip the leash from time to time when they see a rabbit,' he suggested lightly. He stuffed the knot in his pocket. 'What will the Haunt do, that's rather the question, isn't it?'

'Oh, I should think he'll find enough to keep busy,' I parried. I liked him, but I did not trust him yet. He could not reveal what he suspected about my identity without posing a threat to his own, but there was much he could do short of that to make our operations very dicey.

Sitric was looking from one to the other of us with narrowed eyes. 'If any mere mortal could advise the Haunt, I would tell him to lie low. His own safety is in jeopardy. I have had reports from several quarters that questions are being asked in nearly every tavern in nearly every port, and always the question is the same: Does a young, red-headed Burrener sail with you, or on any crew you know of?'

I stiffened.

The guildmaster nodded. 'I have sent out a Null Whisper order. No pirate will transgress it, I think you may be assured.'

'I'm in thy debt.'

He waved it off. 'I don't like outsiders meddling in guild business. We pirates value our privacy.'

Timbertoe asked, 'Do your sources tell ye who these prying outsiders are?'

He smiled grimly. 'They wear no Wolf's Head insignia, but I think we can make a guess. They speak atrocious dwarfish, by the way, and that in itself is one reason our folk give them little heed. Burreners are bad enough, but when they can't even speak the language . . .' He shrugged expressively.

I gave him a token rude gesture for his token rude jibe, pirate to pirate, and then took him off-guard. 'And what insignia do *you* wear, Guildmaster? What's your interest in the Haunt of the Moor?'

He reddened under his flaxen beard, but kept his temper. 'Purely business. By using our ports and ships, the Haunt has drawn unwelcome attention to us and our activities. The Dinan will strike us in force unless he's very much more careful than he has been.' He said no more, but seated himself.

I poured myself some of his brandy. 'How much are the Dinan offering for my capture?' I asked him quietly and took a swallow.

'Five hundred gold pieces for your corpse, double that if we deliver you alive,' he answered promptly. Over the sound of Timbertoe's involuntary curse, he added, 'It's quite a compliment, actually: you're worth more than the year's revenue from a middling-sized district.'

Much as he had done earlier, I took a turn up and down his carpet, thinking furiously. Of course he was demanding blackmail to hide my identity, and of course he would know already that neither Timbertoe nor I – nor, indeed, all the pirates of our home port of Inishkerry together – had any hope of matching the blood price.

Timbertoe heaved himself to his feet and cleared his throat. 'Cru's my man,' he said gruffly. 'If it's a thousand in gold, it's a thousand in gold. Have your scribe write up the paper, and I'll sign it, Guildmaster: a tithe on every cargo I raid, from now till however long it takes to pay off Cru's protection.' His voice was stiff, and well it might be: he'd be under bond for the rest of his life.

I forestalled the one magnanimous gesture he'd ever given way to in his life with a quick gesture to Sitric. 'No. No, not that way.' I walked over to them and looked down at the blond dwarf. 'It's not gold you want anyway, is it, Guildmaster?'

He studied his fingernails. 'I certainly wouldn't turn it down, if nothing better were offered.'

'Chalcedons.'

Sitric smiled. 'Yes, I rather thought you might get round to that.' His gaze went to my skipper. 'Timbertoe used to trade in them, I believe, but there's been a regrettable scarcity of them these past few years. I wonder why that might be, old friend.'

To his credit, Timbertoe tried to save the situation for me without revealing that he knew the whereabouts of a mine for the rare gems. 'Got tired of the risks. Too chancy, paying out good money to those thieving packrats from Nabilia.'

The guildmaster chuckled and rose. 'Nabilia, eh? Well, maybe if you put Brunehilda in touch with your packrats, she won't summon you to the Moot.' He gestured away the skipper's start of recollection of our errand. 'I'll do what I can about your 147 incident.' Reaching for the bell that stood on the table, he rang to summon his impostor.

'Do these Burreners with the atrocious accents mention any other identifying characteristics?' I meant my damaged face.

Sitric shook his head as the door opened and the fat dwarf, 'Silky', stood waiting for us. 'Oddly enough, no. A point to your advantage.' He extended a hand, and I shook it. 'Beware the Inishbuffin peninsula, Pirate,' he suddenly said in a voice low enough not to be heard by the impostor at the door. 'Good, stout dwarves say the place is haunted these four years past.' He eyed me. 'But maybe you'd know about that already.'

I returned his look levelly. 'I've heard it.'

He offered the traditional pirate farewell. 'May ye go safe upon the deeps, then.'

'And beat you home to port,' I answered with the ritual phrase.

Sitric smiled and put on his servant's face. 'I'll show you to the door, pirates. It's this way, please.'

As we passed by Silky, I lowered my voice confidentially to ask him, 'Tell me one thing straight, mate: how the hell did ye land this billet?'

'Bit of luck,' he replied straight-faced.

'Wouldn't mind a bit of that kind meself,' Timbertoe allowed under his breath as we followed Sitric down the stairs.

We stopped a moment outside the guildmaster's gates, and I drew the scarf across my face. If foreigners with atrocious accents

were asking in Skejfallen pubs after a red-headed man, then it
was only wise to cover up till I got back aboard the *Gem*. It
was getting on for night, and already the fog had blown in off
Skejfallen harbor as it did near the sea nearly every night at that
time of year. Timbertoe was resettling his boot knife. 'Thanks for
offering to pay my blood money, Skipper.'

He sniffed. 'Didn't think I meant it, did ye?'

I played along. 'Of course not. You'd give the guildmaster your
pledge, then take a long, long time to pay off the tithes. Still, it
was decent of you.'

He set the good foot down and stamped to settle the boot. 'Was,
wasn't it?'

'All right, Filthydwarf, I see what you're driving at – sixty/forty
split next raid, your favor.'

He grinned. 'Right, Giant. Ye know, ye've turned out a decent
lad for all you're a foreigner. Come along now, and we'll tuck in
a pint or two before the tide turns.' We turned down the street
and followed it down from the guildmaster's hill overlooking the
harbor, though in that fog you'd never have known it was there
but for the creaking of a winch and the forlorn clanging of the
bell buoy off the main dock.

Each of us busy with our own thoughts, we did not speak again
for some minutes until the pool of hazy lamplight loomed up
ahead, and the brisk clatter of spoons against trenchers amid a
hubbub of conversation told of the tavern ahead. It was The Top
Gallant, the pub we favored when in this port.

Timbertoe cast an eye up at me to check that my 'pot' was
securely in place. 'Are ye going over to Inishbuffin to get Sitric
his chalcedons?' Neither of us had been back to the scene of the
massacre.

'After I get Cathir tomorrow night.' The skellig where our
former steward had been installed as master was not a long sail
from Inishbuffin, so we could stop there before going home. I
returned to the subject of the chalcedons. 'One maybe. A small
one. If I can find the mine.'

I suppose it was some measure of the respect he held for my
grandfather's memory that he was silent a moment. 'Will ye want
company?'

It was a notably delicate question for a pirate captain, so I gave him back the answer he deserved: 'You only. The crew can lay by for us in Gull's Cove.'

I had not often seen that look of genuine pleasure on his face. After a moment he covered by hawking and spitting. 'Right enough, Giant. Well, come on, boy – the beer doesn't get any better with keeping!'

We found three of our own lads inside, snug by the fire and wading through mutton-and-onion pie. They slid over on the benches for us, dumped some pie on a wooden plate for the captain, and carved a leg of chicken for me. Neddy made a question sign, and I nodded. 'It's all set,' I told them. 'The guildmaster said he'd take care of it.'

Pers wiped gravy off his chin with a dirty hand. 'Old Brunehilda'll be some ripped when she gets to port and finds the deal done without ever her gettin' her piece spoke.'

Timbertoe shrugged. 'I'll think on sending her some kind of little gift to sweeten her up, a keg maybe, pirate to pirate.'

Pers winked. 'Send flowers, Skipper. Wimmen loves them.'

Across the table Harrald snorted. 'Flowers! Any flower that came within twenty feet of old Brunehilda would get frosted, sure!'

The skipper picked a shred of mutton out of his front teeth, regarding him narrowly. 'How do you know, sardine prick?'

Harrald mumbled something and buried himself in his pie. There was assiduous eating for some moments and relief when Timbertoe called for the potboy to bring another pitcher.

When the beer came, it was the landlord himself who brought it. 'There you are, lads, our best, good on a wet night like this one.' He had leaned over the table with his back to the room, and now hiked up his sleeve to show us his tattoo. Not to make our business too obvious, some of the men bared their wrists in the course of reaching across the table for a bit of chicken or a mug, and others put up a hand to scratch a beard or pick a nose so that their cuffs fell free. I pitched my chicken bone on the floor and let him see my snake, the mark I had chosen in a grim jest only I was privy to. He nodded slightly and gathered trenchers and plates to look busy. 'You've new come to port, mates, so ye'd not know. There's a Null Whisper order out.'

Timbertoe and I did not look at each other. Gunnarsson whispered, 'No shit? What's it about, then?'

'Strangers are asking after a young, red-headed Burrener who sails with pirates. By the guildmaster's order, they're to get no answer.' His eyes came up to mine from the tabletop. 'Even if ye know him.'

Such is the danger of the trade that all these men were well-accustomed to guarding their looks. Only the boy Neddy was staring at me wide-eyed, and I saw him jump. I assumed that Timbertoe had found the lad's foot with his wooden stump. I slid a brass penny across the tabletop to the landlord. 'Which none of us does. Thanks for the information, mate.'

He nodded. ''Twas no trouble, Pirate.' Putting the penny in the pocket of his grimy apron, he took away the tray of dirty dishes.

Pers stretched elaborately and yawned. 'I'm for the ship, lads.' He meant that we should get aboard right away.

'Wait,' Timbertoe counselled in an undertone. 'Every pirate in the place knows what the landlord was just telling us. Let's give them no cause to wonder about Cru. Drink your beer; bring out the tiles, Pers, and go find a game, and take Harrald with ye. Neddy, find out what's beyond the alley door, just in case.'

'Wait, Ned. Did you get it?' I asked.

He grinned and winked, then left. Pers and Harrald strolled to an empty bench, making it look very natural, a crew at liberty for a few hours till the tide turned. Timbertoe pulled out his pipe, turned to have a word with a pair of sailors talking across the hearth, and they handed over the checkerboard. 'Come, Giant. Let's have a game.'

We set the pieces on the board. Quietly I said, 'You're trolling.'

'Aye,' he admitted at once. 'Let's see if any foreigners who can't speak dwarfish try to strike up a conversation with any of our lads. They wouldn't approach you or me directly, of course.'

I took the red men and opened. The first few moves of any game between the two of us had become so mechanical that neither of us needed to pay any attention. Covertly, we watched the room. 'Lift the cup, boy, lift the cup. We want the two of us good and drunk when we're seen to stumble out.' That was a good ploy, and I made sure to seem as though I was swilling beer like a man who hasn't seen a keg for a year or so. The skipper did the same, though as a dwarf he wouldn't be expected to be as obviously drunk as I would. He did a convincing job of letting his hand knock some draughts pieces around the board, however, and I cursed him roundly for it. Neddy came back, signing his report. The alley was clear down as far as the wharf, and as nearly as he could tell all of the drunks sprawled in it really were passed out, he relayed innocently. Timbertoe and I did not need to speak of it; we would on no account leave this tavern by the alley door.

I let the skipper win, and we started another game. He ordered the boy to get himself down to the ship and tell Ries to be ready to slip the lines on an instant, then stay aboard and watch for us. Neddy left.

'No foreigners in this lot,' I murmured.

He had noted it as well as I. Everybody in the place except me was a dwarf. If I had been hanging from a yardarm, I would have been no more exposed. Timbetoe hunched a little over the board, relighting his pipe. 'Aye, all dwarves. But not all pirates. Fishermen, most of them, who wouldn't mind finding an extra farthing or two in their nets. Had enough mumming?'

'Let's get out of here,' I agreed.

We stood and made for the door, not forgetting to weave a little. Once outside we went only a little way down the street before ducking into the shelter of a warehouse entrance. The door behind us was padlocked, and the building silent for the night. We waited. Pers and Harrald came along within a moment or two.

Harrald cast a look behind him to check the street. 'It's Cru the Null Whisper's about, isn't it?' he hissed. 'Got to be. There ain't any other red-headed—'

Timbertoe collared him and drove him viciously against the brick wall. 'Shut your poxy face,' he said slowly, 'before your brains leak out. If ye think any damned foreigners are going to mess about with my pilot, think again.'

Pers said, 'We wouldn't, Skipper. Cru's our matey.' Harrald nodded nervously.

I levered myself off the wall. 'Thanks, lads. I'll remember it.

Now, skipper, why don't you all go down to the ship? I'll be along presently.'

He snorted. 'Right, and leave ye here alone, and footpads maybe about!'

'It's the best way. If we have company, they'll hear all of you pass by, and in the fog and dark they may think I'm with you.'

The pegleg tugged a braid. 'Nothing I like much more than being a target for somebody else, Giant.'

I grinned.

'All right, all right, do it your way, then. But I warn you—' He shook a finger at me. 'This is going to cost ye plenty.'

'It always does,' I said indifferently. He growled a curse and led the men out of the doorway. Within paces they were swallowed by the foggy night, but I could hear the scuff of their sea boots and Timbertoe loudly asserting he'd have Pers straddling the bowsprit when we pulled out in the morning if he didn't stop treading on his heel.

I drew my knife and followed my shipmates.

There were two of them, and I nearly missed them in the deeper dark formed by a pile of barrels and a sagging fence of planks. I was creeping along when some freak of hearing in my bad ear brought me a soft whisper. 'That's him, there in the middle. He's hunched over, drunk belike.'

'Are you sure?' They were speaking the Burren tongue with the accent of one of the border districts.

'Didn't we see him leave with the stump-legged one?' That must have settled it, for there was a pause, and then they began to move forward.

I wanted to knock out one and seize the other to put a few questions to him, but they gave me no option to do so: when the first one cleared the mound of barrels, I caught the glint of a blade in his hand. So it had not been mere information they had wanted, after all. They broke into a cat-footed run toward Timbertoe's voice.

I had the advantage of surprise, and I used it to dispatch the rearward man with a quick thrust of my dagger. He dropped like a rock, and I hurdled him and went for the one in the lead. But some sound made him turn his head to look back at his companion, and his reflexes were first-rate. He threw himself to the side as I lunged toward him, whipping up his dagger to take me in the ribs. I twisted away in time, used a foot against the wall of the warehouse for leverage and scissored a kick to his midsection. His breath whooshed out, and the dagger wavered for a moment. I kicked out and sent it spinning from his hand to land some feet away. He stood slightly bent and sucked for air.

'Who sent you?' I demanded harshly in Burrener.

He met my eyes for a moment, then shook his head, and mopped his face on the shoulder of his cloak. At least, that's what I thought his motion meant until he suddenly crumpled to the street, jerked once in a spasm, and lay still. I thought he was shamming, but when I feigned a kick at his groin and he didn't react, I hissed a curse and bent over him quickly. His lips were stained, and there was a reek of bitter almonds. He must have had a phial of poison sewn into the cloak. I cursed again and turned to whistle for Timbertoe and the boys.

That was when the third man hit me.

My helmet took most of the blow, but it was still enough to daze me, and I sprawled over the body of the poisoned man, trying to roll free. A sword sliced the air where my head had been and struck sparks off the cobbles. I had lost my knife, so I swung the hardened edge of my hand and connected where I knew the side of his knee must be. He grunted, the knee caving under him, but he kept hold of the blade and brought his arm back. It was just then that, from the alley opposite, a knife flashed end-over-end to take him through the throat.

I rolled to my feet, crouched for another attack, and whistled our three-note signal to Timbertoe. Far down the street toward the docks there was an answering whistle.

'Show yourself,' I demanded in Burrener to the darkness of the alley mouth while I snatched up the last man's sword. There was no answer. I ducked to the cover of the warehouse door. 'Show yourself!' I repeated in dwarfish. Again, there was no sound from the alley, but I caught just a glimpse of long, stringy hair and a rough beard.

I had my mouth open to call Olin Olafson back when Pers and Harrald came running up the street, knives drawn and cursing the fog. They stopped short when they saw the bodies, then one broke for one side of the street, and the other dived the other way. I put up the sword and stepped out of the doorway. 'Good thinking lads, but there's no need for tactics now.'

Pers slouched out of cover first, whistling softly. 'By His Beard, you've put in a fair old night's work, haven't ye, Pilot?'

I didn't answer. I was using my dagger to cut away the tunic over the right shoulder of the swordsman. Not finding what I was expecting, I did the same to the man who had bitten the poisoned phial. By this time Timbertoe came stumping up, out of breath and out of temper at having missed a fight. 'Dammit, Giant! What—?' Then the import of what I was doing got through to him. 'Are they marked with the Fang?' The Wolfhounds had a small tattoo in the shape of a wolf's tooth inked in the hollow beneath the collarbone.

I sat back on my heels. 'No.'

'Is that poison on that bastard's lips?'

'Yes. They've all got a phial of it sewn into the shoulder of their cloaks.' I had found them in the course of my search.

Like any good pirates, Harrald and Pers had been busy lifting the dead men's purses. Now Pers gasped, 'Bugger me! Look at this, will ye!' His cupped palm was filled to overflowing with silver pieces.

'They were set to pay well for information,' Timbertoe guessed.

'Aye, there's more of it here,' Harrald gloated when he opened the next man's purse.

Pers reached for the third, slashed through the thongs that bound it, and tipped the contents into his hand. 'Piss,' he said disappointedly.

'What's them?' Harrald wondered, peering over his shoulder.

Pers brought the handful of objects to his eyes to be sure. 'Looks like some arrow points. They feel funny, not like metal. Ow, damnit! They're sharp enough, for all that.' Angrily he cast the things away and sucked at the ball of his thumb. I barely heard him, being occupied with searching the corpses for some clue as to who they had been.

A cheerful whistling and the small light of a lantern came from the further end of the alley opposite. 'Scarf it, mates, it's a warden!' Harrald hissed.

Timbertoe reached to his sash pocket. 'To the ship, quick and quiet!' he ordered, already stooping to fit a kind of sock over the end of his wooden leg, a strategem he had long ago devised to dampen the sound in situations like this one.

I sheathed my dagger and dipped a finger into the congealing blood to write the runes for Null Whisper next to the swordsman's body. The first pirate who saw that sign would take the news straight to the guildmaster, while those to whom the signs were unknown would assume that the three had been killed for their purses by thugs who had begun to scrawl graffiti but who had been interrupted by the warden's approach. Either way, we should be covered. As an afterthought, I stooped for a quick look at the points Pers had found. Yes, bone again. I stowed one carefully in my sash.

We were on the pier by the time the warden's tin whistle shrilled, awakening answering toots from all over the city as his fellow watchmen converged to give him help he wouldn't need.

CHAPTER FOUR

We left Skejfallen with the tide. I had it later from Ries that Pers soon felt sick, but didn't say much about it. By the time our very worried bos'n came to fetch me at the turning of the watch, Pers was parching with fever and having trouble catching his breath. I fed him willowbark tea, but it did no good. The cramping started soon after, and soon after that he was dead.

Of course our suspicions went at once to the curious point on which he had pricked his thumb, but as I told Timbertoe, poison usually produces deathly chill, not fever. This was something more like an extremely acute attack of some illness. Timbertoe swore bitterly and claimed letting loose a plague was just the sort of thing Wolfhounds would do. I wondered. Even the Dinan an Lupus couldn't be stupid enough deliberately to spread a plague which might as likely take their own followers as kill anyone else.

We readied Pers' body for his sea burial and after the ritual moments of silence Ries blew his pipe, and the canvas-wrapped body slid down the tilted board to splash into our wake. After that we went to our bunks for what remained of the night. Pirates like to pretend they do not mourn, you see.

I didn't feel tired, however, and lay in my bunk with the events of the past few days whirling through my mind. Eventually I must have dozed, because sometime later a lantern shining in my face woke me at the change of watch. Neddy signed that it was time. He added, *Nice night, eh?* and grinned, gesturing at the lantern, which was swinging wildly in his hand. It was blowing a gale. A nice night, indeed, for my last bit of work as the avenger of Inishbuffin.

I grunted a reply, sipping the tea he had somehow managed to brew on our charcoal stove. It helped calm the butterflies taking wing in my stomach. Even to myself, I had to admit this would be a tough one.

The boy lay out my outfit for the night, a full Wolfhound uniform of black tunic and pants, topped with a black chainmail vest. He put aside the dark cloak and hood, and took the last vital piece of disguise from his sash: an officer's insignia pendant, the bronze Wolf's Head set with ruby eyes. Neddy regarded the ugly thing for a moment, then grimaced and made a sound in his throat that passed for a growl. Knowing his reasons, I poked no fun at him. His look swung to me. *Be careful tonight,* he signed.

'I always am. Besides, with my luck, I'll freeze to death waiting to waylay a courier who's safely between the sheets with a jolly girl at one of the inns along the way on a night like this.' I answered Ned's grin.

This is the last one? he questioned.

'It's the last one I've sworn to kill. But I've been thinking: do you want me to go after the one that—' I had been going to say, 'cut your tongue out', but he'd been not much more than a baby at the time, and I didn't know how raw the memory would be. Timbertoe had told me the bastards had killed his family that night. So now I changed it to, '— did that to you?'

His hands froze as he was laying out my sword belt, but he did not look at me. After a moment, he shook his head once, *No.*

'As you like,' I agreed immediately, sensing that he did not want to be questioned further. I began to dress. 'Is the fake courier's pouch ready?'

Yes. It's warm by the stove, he told me.

'How the hell did you come by an adder at this time of year?'

The boy rasped the harsh forcing of breath that passed for his laugh. *It was sleeping in the pile of turf at The Top Gallant,* he revealed. *The landlord was happy to give it to me, if I'd catch it.*

'I'll bet! And you're sure the damned thing can't get out till the pouch is opened, right?'

One nod, emphatic. He laughed again at the look on my face and pointed to my tattoo. *I thought you liked snakes, Pilot,* he signed.

I pricked myself on the brooch pin, swore, and then reached for my pot helmet. 'Not me, mate,' I told him. 'I can't stand the damned things. This one's for a gift.'

Timbertoe bellowed down the companionway that we were dragging anchor and if I didn't get gone he'd use me for one.

A short time later, much wetter, I made shore in a curragh that despite my best efforts had nearly swamped. 'Get yourself up to that overhang there,' I told the boy. 'There'll be dry driftwood, and you ought to be able to make a fire. Don't worry about anyone's seeing it. On a night like this, nobody but stupid pirates will be at sea to spot it anyway.' He gave me a cheerful salute and strode off in the icy rain.

I surveyed what I could see of the rocky cove and was satisfied that no fisherman's cottage was nearby. Our landing had been unobserved. The road to the skellig should be right up on the crest of the bluffs. It was a good half hour's tricky going but I made the ascent and settled by a boulder to wait for the courier from the capital at Dun Aghadoe. Spies in the employ of the Haunt had watched this place for three years, and I knew the schedule of the Wolfhound fortress as well as their own steward did.

An hour later I was fairly certain the courier would not come, and two hours later I was sure of it. By that time the freezing rain had glazed my clothing so that I crackled when I moved. I only hoped the damned snake was still alive in its pouch. Overcoming my natural resistance, I had gingerly held the courier's pouch inside my cloak, against the chainmail vest, to warm the serpent.

My feet were half-frozen, and I did by accident what I had intended to do anyway: I fell heavily on my side, ripping the black cloak on the rocks. I thought ruefully it might be convincing enough as I limped up the road toward the skellig cursing at the icy footing.

It took another half hour of hard going before I heard the sentry challenge, 'Halt! Who goes there?'

I limped a little closer to the guardhouse, empty palm up to show them.

'Friend! A courier from court! I was thrown, and I lost my horse. Open up, for pity's sake!'

'Stand.'

I did so while someone came out of the postern, sword in hand, to inspect me. He was well-muffled against the cold, wearing a pot helmet and scarf like mine, and like me he had drawn up his dark hood for more warmth. I wished desperately I could tell what color the eyes were in his Wolf's Head pendant. I saw him take note of my courier's pouch with its stamped insignia of the Fang. Warily, he said, 'You're not the regular courier. Where's Ian?'

There was something about the way he said it that alerted me. 'There is no regular courier, as you damned well know, and I don't know any Ian.' I put my hand to my sword hilt, answering his suspicion with my own.

He relaxed. 'Easy, Lieutenant. We're on special alert because of that damned Haunt. There was an incident in the next district last night. Come on up.'

I fell in alongside. 'What happened?'

He recollected he was talking to someone from the capital, and that his master would not thank him for admitting there had been a major strike within his territory. 'Oh, just more thievery. You know how the bastard works.'

'I do, indeed.' Did Cathir also know that the ex-soldier at his isolated rath had been killed? 'He murdered a pensioner over at Watersmeet, where I used to be stationed. Strangled him. Leastwise, we always reckoned it was the Haunt, but we never could prove it, and we never saw hide nor hair of the whoreson.'

He grunted. 'Well, he won't try it anywhere near here, or my lord will have his guts to feed the pigs.'

So they did not know yet.

The Wolfhound led me in through the postern. 'Courier from Dun Aghadoe,' he told his watchmates briskly. 'I'll take him up.'

'Where's your horse, Lieutenant?' One of the others wanted to know.

'Halfway back to his stable, the bastard,' I swore bitterly and drew a laugh from them.

'We'll keep an eye out for him,' the other assured me. 'Maybe he'll catch a whiff of our stables.'

'Thanks, but even if he comes in, he'll be lame, and I need another mount. I'm to take the reply back immediately.'

'Tonight? In this weather?'

I shrugged. 'Orders. Could you have another horse ready for me?'

'Aye, brother.' One of them rose and slung on his cloak.

I answered their salute and followed my guide, who was impatiently shifting his feet. He'd be glad of the occasion to get to the fire in the hall, I'd wager. I'd be glad of it myself, actually.

Our intelligence had been so first-rate that I could easily name the buildings as we passed them. Unlike my own skellig this one had only one outer wall encircling stables, armory, bakehouse, practice yard, and keep. There were no cattle barns, no dormitory or refectory, and no round tower. This was a military skellig, not a community.

When we came into the keep, we had to step carefully around the prone forms snoring in the rushes. The lowest level of Cathir's hall also served as barracks for his men. 'You've a full complement,' I whispered. 'Didn't anybody pull guard duty tonight?'

He laughed a little, quietly. 'Lord Cathir's a good master. Besides, what need is there to stand out on the battlement when you couldn't see your hand in front of your face anyway?' We went up the steep stairs along the left hand wall to the quieter solar. Here the snoring was more genteel. These were the fort's officers, rolled snugly in their cloaks around the two great bronze braziers.

A guard nodded over his pike at the door of the private apartment, but straightened with a snap when he saw me advancing toward him with my escort. He swung a stiff salute for the Dun Aghadoe courier, eying the pouch. 'We hadn't looked for you tonight, with the storm, sir.'

'Well, I made it through. Announce me to my lord, please.'

He hesitated, licking his lips, and his eyes flicked to the man beside me. 'Um, it might be better to wait, sir. His lordship doesn't like to be disturbed once he's retired for the night.'

I drew myself up. He couldn't see my expression behind my scarf, but he could read my eyes well enough. 'Announce me,' I ordered deliberately.

He saluted hastily, leaned his spear against the wall, and tapped timidly at the door, straightening his uniform tunic as he did so.

I chafed my gauntleted hands to cover the slight shaking.

My guide was sharp. 'Still cold, eh, Lieutenant? Would you like a flask to take back with you?'

'That would be wonderful,' I told him honestly. 'Thanks, brother.'

The pikeman bit his lip and rapped a little harder. One of the officers nearby roused briefly, swept his eye over the courier's pouch at my hip, and rolled over. My heart was pounding.

The latch lifted, and he stood there, oily face, crow's-feet, pig eyes: Cathir, who had betrayed us to the archpriest, Jorem. His limp hair was damp. 'I've told you—!' Then he caught sight of my pouch.

'The courier from Dun Aghadoe, my lord,' my guide said unnecessarily.

I found my voice. 'I beg pardon for disturbing your rest, Your Eminence, but the commission with which I am charged would brook no delay.'

He ran both hands back flat through his hair, cast a look over his shoulder, and hesitated.

What would his harlot look like? I had time to wonder before he surrendered to the inevitable and motioned me in.

I took it all in: a large writing table, littered with wax tablets and papers; a good brazier, glowing with peats; the elkskin on the floor; the bed with its carved headboard and footboard, and rug of rabbit fur. The mounded figure under the covers was far too small to be a woman's.

He saw that I had noticed. 'My page,' he said indifferently and held out his hand for the leather bag. I unslung the courier's pouch and handed it to him. 'You may warm yourself, if you wish, Lieutenant,' he said absently, motioning at the brazier. He touched the wick of the honeycomb candle to the embers until it caught, then carried the pouch to the work table. 'Key?' he said over his shoulder.

'Oh, yes. Forgive me, Your Eminence. Here, let me do it: I had a fall, and I'm afraid the lock may have some ice in it. If I hold it at the fire for a moment . . . ?' He waited impatiently while I warmed the leather bag, setting the iron lock nearly right down on the coals. After a moment there was movement inside the bag and an angry hiss, which I covered by stamping my feet as though they were still cold. 'That's got it.' I fitted the key, turned it, and handed the bag to him to open. 'There you go, my lord.'

The Wolfhound set the pouch on the table, pulled up the flap, and reached in.

I had my hand over his mouth to stifle his scream in the split second it took for him to jerk his hand back, drawing the adder with it to strike him again in the belly, where the thin wool of his nightshirt bulged over the table. The serpent

was flung to the floor and shot away into the shadows under
the bed.

Cathir struggled against my hands, butting his head back. I
rapped him sharply just off the point of the chin, enough to stun
him for a few moments, but not enough to keep him from feeling
the effects of the burning venom. His knees sagged long enough
for me to whip the gag I had brought into his mouth and tie it
behind his head. When I was done, his legs would not hold him,
and he sagged to the floor, clutching at his belly with one hand and
desperately flinging the other around, as though he felt the snake
still there. His eyes were wild, and he was pouring sweat.

I crouched to him and unwound my scarf. He didn't get it until
I took the pot helmet off, and my red hair showed. 'I bring thee
greetings from Inishbuffin, Cathir,' I said softly.

For a moment he stilled, staring out of popping eyes. Then he
hunched one leg under him and started to crawl for the door.

I held his naked foot, easily tethering him. His face grew
suffused, and I imagined it would be purpling as the venom
found the humors of his heart. His legs began to jerk, and
I let him go and stood to watch the end. Only when I was
sure, did I remove the gag, stuff it into my belt, and turn to
the bed.

The boy, who could not have been more than ten, was sitting
up, staring with fierce gladness at Cathir's corpse. His hands were
knotting the bedclothes.

I said quietly, 'Somehow, that wasn't as satisfying as I had
thought it would be.' When his eyes found mine, I asked, 'Do
you have the courage to try to get out of here tonight? No! Don't
get off the bed, the snake's under there, and you have no shoes!
Wait a moment, lad.'

'I'm Derry,' he whispered. 'I ain't got no clothes but this. He
said my other ones stank.'

'He would. We'll have to get you some, then.' I was rummaging
in the clothes chest at the foot of the bed and pulled out a dark
robe. When I had hacked off a few feet of it, I tossed it to the
boy, who grabbed it and slipped it on. The neck fell down across
his shoulders, so I laced it quickly with a thong cut from another
garment. A strip of the wool from the hem of the robe served him
well enough for a belt. 'Do you live near here, Derry?'

For the first time, his eyes filled, and he fumbled with the belt. 'They killed me ma and da. Nuncle and Auntie lives across the hill, though, I can go there.'

'All right.' I went to the window and pulled aside the flap. The candle blew out behind me. This keep was not high, but there would still be a drop at the end of it for him, and the ground out there was iron-hard. I lifted him off the bed and sat him on the table. Cathir's soft leather slippers stood by the bed. Gingerly I pulled them near with the poker, checked for the snake, and stuffed them through the boy's belt. 'You'll have to go down barefoot. I don't think you'll be able to feel the rope through these, they're so big. Put them on when you get to the bottom.'

'You got a rope, master?'

I took a breath and flipped the covers on the floor. The straw pallet followed. It was a rope mattress, as I had hoped. I slashed it free of the frame, dancing out of the way of the snake as it wriggled into the corner behind the headboard. I held up the 'cargo net'. 'I have a rope. Come, now, quickly.'

He slipped off the table, eyed the snake's dark shadow, and dashed across the elkskin to me. 'I'll lower you as far as I can, but then you'll have to be brave and jump the rest of the way.'

'I can do it,' he whispered sturdily.

'Good lad. When you get down, put your shoes on, then get to the stable – it's the second building on your right – and wait there for me. I make no promises, Derry. This is going to be very dicey. Do you understand that?'

'All they can do is kill me.' As plainly as if he had spoken it was the implication that he had already suffered far worse than mere death.

'You've a stout heart.' I slung the end of the mattress net out the window, where the wind flapped it against the wall of the keep. 'Over you go.'

He was down that net with an agility that would have done a Jarlshof tar proud. I leaned as far from the window as I could to give him the shortest distance to jump. He looked up at me once, then let go. My heart seemed to stop, but then he was up and crossing the patch of open ground between the keep and the bakehouse.

I turned back to the room with a smile and hastened to pile the straw mattress and bedding back on the empty frame of the bed. Damn the snake or where it went, now. Cathir's body I lugged to throw down on the heap, drawing the rabbitskin quilt up over him, and turning his discolored face to the window wall. He was lying far too close to the floor, but maybe a casual glance would let it pass.

I slung the courier's pouch over my shoulder, shoveled ash to bank down the glow of the brazier, and rewound my scarf about my face. I was drawing up my hood and resettling the pouch when I stepped through the door, and I made sure to block the guard's view into the room with my body while I swung the door closed.

I met the guard's carefully bland look with an equally bland one of my own. 'Goodnight, brother,' I said. 'His Eminence said to tell you he'll require no further service tonight.'

He nodded, relaxing a little, and saluted as I headed through the sleeping officers to the stairs. I hoped to hell he didn't take it into his head to tap on the door and make sure Cathir didn't want anything before he retired.

My guide jumped up from his seat at one of the downstairs braziers. 'They've got a horse saddled for you, Lieutenant,' he whispered, 'and here's the flask.' He pushed the corked leather bottle into my hand.

I clapped him on the shoulder. 'Thanks. Now, where's the stable?'

He led me to it. The big gray gelding twitched his ears at me as I swung up. There was no sign of Derry, and my man was standing at the bridle. 'Would you just hold the door for me?' I requested. 'I don't want the wind to catch it. I've had all the falls I want for this night.'

He chuckled and went to swing open the broad door.

So quickly that even I who was expecting it never saw where he came from, Derry was at my stirrup. I swung him up behind me, felt him burrow under the black cloak, and touched my heel to the gray's side. We trotted briskly past my guide, who was hunched into the protection of his hood, and barely lifted a hand to salute as I went past.

'Draw up your feet!' I told the boy on the way down to the gate, and he did, somehow. They had heard the horse's hooves, and had the gate swinging open for me, so I did not have to rein in.

'Better you than me, brother!' one of them called as I trotted past, and I made him a rude gesture. He was laughing as they winched the gate closed behind us. I felt Derry's head rest between my shoulder blades.

I pushed the gray faster than I should have done, but we made it safely to the small farm some miles away, and I gave him a hand down at the crest of the hill. There was a comfortable smell of peat smoke all around. 'There. You'll want to tell your aunt and uncle to keep you out of the way for a few days. They'll be looking for you, maybe, though I think they'll see quickly enough the fang marks on him and know you couldn't have anything to do with it. If they do find you, just say the messenger who came to His Eminence's room did it, and you saw your chance, so you slipped out when the guard fell asleep. Right?'

He was looking up at me. 'You're the Haunt, aren't you?'

'Maybe. Maybe I'm just a Wolfhound who's sick of it all. Either way, it makes no difference. Go on, lad. Forget me.'

Derry shook his head slowly. 'I won't do that,' he said in a low voice. Then he bolted away down the hill, skidding in his oversized slippers. I heard him laugh before I turned the horse's head and trotted away. I would need no poppy this night, I thought.

'Sanctuary!' I gasped.

The peep hole below the sugan Vanu carved in the heavy wooden gate slid shut, and I could hear the bolts being drawn. The metal screeched a bit, and I surmised that so out of the way a place as this would not have seen much traffic in wayfarers as desperate as I. In the lulls between blasts of the wind blowing strongly here on the heights I could make out the sharp strike of ironshod hooves on the rocky path that led up from the sea. They were coming fast, faster than you would think in the pitch-dark of a full-blown gale. I had by foulest mischance run into an army patrol from the local town, and I was on no road an official courier would have taken. I could not risk being taken back to the barracks for questioning, so of course I'd had to run for it. They'd found my range with one arrow, but nothing worse so far.

I held the tired horse with one hand and felt for the rusted ring imbedded in the mortar beside the gate and used it to haul myself a little straighter. Technically, you had to be inside the gates to claim sanctuary, but some held that holding to the ring was good enough. Somehow, I doubted the men pursuing me would be the clement types. I pulled the scarf closer about my face not to scare anyone, leaned my forehead on the wet stone, and prayed that the door would open before the foremost soldier topped the hill and spurred for the dark walls.

The gate swung inward, and the light of a candle-lantern blazed like a beacon fire. 'Come in,' she urged, reaching to grasp my arm and draw me under the lintel. 'Quickly, now – they're right behind you.'

I stumbled through the portal, handed the gray over to a hunchback man who must be a ward of the witch's, put my back to the door, and together she and I drove it shut even as an angry shout went up and an arrow thrummed into the framing timber beside my head. My rescuer hastily set down the lantern and used both hands to shoot the bolts, while I drew my sword and ducked into the best fighting stance I could manage. It was a moment before I realized there was no need: they couldn't have come through that door even if she had dropped nothing but a bit of stick across it to bar the way. I had made it, I was inside a siochla's gate just as in my dream, and that was that. I wheezed the beginning of a laugh, but it caught in my throat as the stout oak vibrated under a crashing thud. Near at hand I could hear the trampling of a troop of horse, and I guessed that the first man had been so hot behind me that he'd pulled up only just before he would have hit the door himself. That echoing thud had been his horse's hooves striking the gate as it wheeled.

'Pirate,' shouted a voice roughened by anger, 'don't think this will save you!'

We were close enough to the ocean for that to be a reasonable guess on his part. I wiped the rain from my face and hastily improvised. 'You're the one who's sitting with his arse in a puddle, soldier.'

Another thud, lighter this time, probably the hilt of his sword. It would be too dangerous to have them camp outside the walls and wait for me, so I did what any good pirate would do. 'Look boys, it's been fun, but it's time to call it a night, don't you think? I stowed my pack on the way up from the beach. Now, if you'll just go and leave me in peace to bleed all over this nice lady, here, I'll give you directions to find it, and health and good fortune to you. On the other hand, you can stay out there and drown for all I care. Which is it to be?' I took my hand away from the arrow stub in my leg and listened.

She picked up the candle lantern and shook the hem of her robe. I spared her what I hoped was an appropriately grateful glance. Two steady gray eyes measured me and found me wanting. 'Come up to the house. We'll be getting things ready,' she said quietly and left me there, the hunchback soothing the exhausted horse and following her.

From outside came a gutteral exchange. Over the wind, I couldn't distinguish the words. The same voice, raised to me: 'There's probably nothing but an extra cloak and some rotten food in your lousy pack, anyway, Pirate. What kind of fool do you take me for?'

There were several answers to that, but I was by now a little dizzy and needed to end it quickly. 'Would I have hung on to that pack for as long as I did with you chasing me for a bagful of dry underwear and some maggoty biscuit? No, I'm not talking to a fool, I can tell that. Take the pack, and go back to town. I reckon there's enough to buy all of you hot supper and drink, a dry bedplace, and two whores apiece. A word of advice: avoid the tall, horse-faced one with the black hair – she's poxed.' I had never been in this town, but wherever there is an army post, there is a jolly house, and a whore like that. I paused. 'Go on, soldier. Take it. Who's to know?'

'Right enough, Donn, nobody else—' I heard one of his men put in, but the speaker stopped short, no doubt at some threatening look from the leader.

'All right, Pirate. Just supposing – where is it?'

'My hand clenched. Got him, by the Four! 'By the fork there's a big bush of thorn – it stands alone. You know the one I mean?'

'Go on.'

I discovered I was sweating coldly, and my breath was coming in gasps that I was sure they could hear outside. 'Under it.'

'If you're lying, the Wolf will eat your entrails, you whoreson bastard,' he threatened conversationally.

70

'Oh, aye. Your mother suckled a snake, by the way. Good night, soldier.'

Maybe the wind played tricks, but I have always thought I heard him grunt a chuckle. I hope so, I hope he found a little humor, because it was his death I was sending him to. The little hollow under the thorn bush was a fox's den – I'd seen the scat – and when the first man reached in to get the pack that wasn't there, the vixen would attack. Even if she didn't kill the fellow outright by ripping his face open, the sudden scare would cause the horses to shy, and on that narrow path there would be no room to maneuver away from the cliff edge that dropped off to the crashing sea.

A moment later there was the sucking squelch of hooves on the soggy turf as they rode away, and a moment after that I was sitting on the floor of the entryway, shaking like an aspen, and not all from the shock of the wound in my thigh.

Then the hunchbacked man came back with a garden barrow, and I laughed a little hysterically but got on to it anyway. He wheeled me to the cottage, where there was a warm room, some pain and, finally, blessed sleep.

Among the learned they were called Vanui, for the Power they served, but among the common folk the term was siochla, 'wise woman'. It is – not coincidentally – the word for witch.

It was not only in the Burren that their members were to be found, either. They lived among the dwarves on the Jarlshof islands also, and, as I was later to find, were revered among Ilyrians, where they were known as Ritnym's Daughters, or the Green Mantles, for the characteristic garment that distinguished them when they went abroad. Nearly every village or town had its siochla, of a greater or lesser rank depending upon the size and importance of the population whose needs she served. A small holding would be provided for her, usually not much more than an encircling wall enclosing a cottage, a hen coop, an ample garden space with some hives, and perhaps – if her folk could afford it – a shed and cow.

In return for the living thus provided, the siochla was expected to keep her people right with the Power of the Earth. It was the Vanui who made the charms to protect barley field and byre, who delivered the children and buried the dead, who grew healing plants in their gardens and knew the uses of them, even to making a young man fall in love with the right young woman.

Yes, all this, but they were followers of the Hag, let it not be forgot. The charm that could protect, turned awry, could be a deadly snare, and barley went to mold and cattle rotted from the inside. Children, too: a changeling might be left, if the expectant parents had insulted the siochla or her Mistress. And sometimes the fire in a young man's loins was not love, and the witch had done that, too. Indeed, folk had good reason to fear these unmarried and childless women, to speak them fair and think them foul.

No doubt some of the siochlas were little more than village scolds, packed off by a father who could afford no dowry anyway, to learn the bare rudiments of the Vanistic discipline and thereafter to earn themselves a good enough living. These were the 'wise women' everybody knew, the village 'aunties', and to say the truth many of them were simple, decent practicioners of their art. As a boy, I had known a few of them and got no worse than boxed ears and a round cursing when I filched the odd heel of bread that someone had left outside the witch's gate for an offering.

There were other, higher, ranks among them, siochlas of whole districts or cities, of guilds – the piratical brotherhood of Jarlshof had one, and she lived in a handsome demesne above the harbor of Skejfallen – and even of royal households, where she would have her own separate hall and be treated as an honored advisor to the ruler, more influential in the running of the kingdom than the queen. These were Vanui of the highest training and the most accomplishment, though what exactly those accomplishments might be was the subject of mere conjecture to the shepherd, the goose-girl, or, indeed, to the apprentice painter.

On the night that king's patrol surprised me, I saw the blue light from the lantern they hang above their gates and rode toward sanctuary as fast as my tired horse could take me. It was coincidence of a kind my grandfather would have recognized instantly, but I had been a long time away from his gentle wisdom, and I was only glad to reach the wall of the small place that stood on the headland I am not sure I could even find now. No matter. I may not remember the place, but I remember her: Caitlin, the first siochla of rank I ever met.

CHAPTER FIVE

When I woke to the light of full day, I knew at once that too many hours had passed. I lay for some little while licking the remains of the sleep-inducing medication from my lips and wondering what Timbertoe had done when I had not flashed him a light from the appointed spot the previous night. Likely he'd have sent a party ashore to find me. If the king's patrol had gone to the fate I had led them to, they would have come up overdue at their post and a search would be on for them. Further away, his men must have discovered Cathir's death, and they would be out in force, too, though with luck they would have no idea in what direction to look. I should try to move from this safety as soon as possible.

When I turned my head, I discovered that the clothes of my Wolfhound disguise, dried and brushed, were folded on a stool beside the low bed. It was charity, but I cursed under my breath because it meant that she'd stripped me and so, of course, she'd found my grandfather's ring. Normally I carried it secured by a thong inside the pocket of my pirate's sash, but last night I had worn a canvas belt of the kind some merchants wear beneath their robes when they do not want to take the chance of having their pocket picked at a fair. No doubt it was foolish of me to carry such a precious thing everywhere I went, but it was my luck talisman and my amulet, and I could not have defined myself any other way than by knowing I was Bruchan's grandson, Colin Mariner's heir. I could only hope the siochla had not recognized the rare milky gem of the signet for what it was, because if she had, she'd likely demand the ring in payment of my obligation, and there was no way I would – or could – give it up. Maybe I could buy my way out of it, if it was money she wanted.

That was the crux of the problem that faced me now. In claiming sanctuary as I had, I had put myself under obligation to the siochla of this place, and she could claim anything – *anything* – of me

73

in return. The geis, it was called, a solemn debt as binding as a religious vow. My life literally belonged to the Hag until this siochla decided to release me. There were terrible tales of what happened to those who did not fulfill the geis, and I suspected some of them might very well be true. Normally, it does not do to slight the Power who is châtelaine of Under-earth.

But what this poor witch in her out of the way boreen couldn't know was that, after what Vanu had allowed to happen to the folk of the skellig, I couldn't even work up enough interest in the Hag to scorn her, much less fear her, so there wasn't much chance of a curse sticking.

I dressed myself slowly (discovering that the canvas belt was, indeed, empty), tested my balance, and found that I could manage well enough without the aid of the stout walking stick she'd left propped against the stool. With instincts honed by years of living shipboard among pirates, I moved quietly across the small chamber to the door and bent my head to listen.

They were talking very quietly, and I had to strain to hear. A man's voice: '—dead on the beach. The others were taken by the waves last night, I should think. There's no sign of the horses.' So the hunchback wasn't a simpleton.

'They'll have gone back to their own stables,' the siochla said. 'Was there a pack?'

I heard him make no answer. Perhaps he merely shook his head, because the next thing he said sounded like, '—not marked with the Fang, but that courier's pouch is real enough, I'd wager, and so is the pendant.'

'The sword isn't standard issue, though,' she observed shrewdly, 'and the snake tattoo fits if he is a pirate. I've never heard of one pirate going about alone on horseback, though.'

'It was a wild night, good weather for raiding. Maybe he waylaid the courier, stole the clothes as being handy, and was riding back to his landing ship when the troop saw him.'

There was silence for a moment, then she said, 'But there's the ring.'

'And an explanation for it, if he's a pirate.' I heard the scrape of wood against the flagged floor, a chair or stool moving maybe. He'd moved a little away, and his voice was more muffled when he asked, '—anything with the glass?'

'No. There's no sign of pursuit this morning. The barracks looks quiet. They probably think their men were benighted somewhere out on the burren.' The clang of a pot lid. '—too quiet.'

'Shall I see whether Thom or the other lads have heard anything? They're all down at the weir.'

'Yes, that might be best. But be careful, dear.'

I could hear his smile, and his tone was indulgent. 'I always am, ma, you know that. *You* be careful, though: if he is a Wolfhound, he'll have little enough respect for you as a Vanu, and if he's a pirate, even less. I'll be back as soon as I'm able. What's the matter?' he paused to ask.

'I don't know. There's an aura about him.'

'Evil?'

I listened intently. Would she sense the murders I had done? The siochla said hesitantly, 'I'm not sure.'

'You think he's the Haunt, don't you?' It was a statement.

'Oh, I *know* he's the Haunt – trust the tiles to tell me that much, at least – but he's something else as well, something I can't quite read, and that concerns me.'

'The sooner he leaves, the better, then.' The outside door swung open, and his uneven tread went toward the gate.

You're right about that, mate, I thought. I waited long enough that it might seem to her I had been wakened by the hunchback's departure, then lifted the latch, and pulled open the door.

The house was not large, being comprised as nearly as I could tell of the one small bedchamber in which I had been put to sleep and an open room with a hearth and alcove bed. A plain enough place, but the hearth was of good stone, the thatch above my head solid and snug, and the flagged floor dotted with sheepskin rugs. The window was unshuttered just now to the weak southern light, and the bunches of dried herbs in the rafters gave off a rich smell compounded of summer and turf smoke.

She was spinning, the wool bulging from the distaff, and she looked up at me over the twirling cord. 'You'll be hungry. There is soup in the pot, and bread and cheese on the table. Can you manage, or shall I serve you?'

'I can manage very well, mistress, thank you.' I dipped myself some pease soup and carried the bowl to the table, conscious of her silence. The bread was crusty and still warm, and the soup smoked all the way down to my empty stomach. I ate steadily for some time while the stitches in my leg throbbed and the spindle spun a pattern of shadow on the floor.

When I was done I gathered the crumbs and put them on the windowsill for the birds, then washed the bowl from water in the bucket puddling on its slab by the hearth and set it up to dry near the embers, along with the wooden spoon.

'You've good manners for a pirate.'

Given a choice of being taken for a Wolfhound or a pirate, I saw no reason to hedge. 'Thanks,' I answered, straightening and turning from the hearth. Until then, I had not looked full at her, because people did not usually like me to do that out of my ruined face. Though she would have seen it dimly at the gate last night and in sleep, seeing me waking was a different thing, and I needed to gain at least enough of her trust that she would let me go as quickly as her ward wanted.

Now I saw that she was older than I had thought from her voice and the glimpse I had had of her the previous night. Her face was finely molded and her eyes the clear gray of autumn mist, but there were lines of thought or worry in her face, and her ash-brown hair was liberally threaded with white strands that curled resolutely out from their restraining hairpins. Her hands plied their craft deftly, long fingers that once would have been fine, but were now a little swollen with work and rather the worse for wear: even across the room I could see the half-moon bruise under one nail where she had dropped something heavy on it. I took note of those patrician features and the cultured voice, and began to suspect that I had fallen into the hands of no mere village siochla.

The spindle stopped twirling. 'Is there something you would wish to know?' she asked wryly, and I was startled to realize she had been aware of my tally.

'Much,' I admitted, abashed, then inclined my head slightly in apology. 'Thy pardon, mistress.'

I thought there was a flash of interest in those gray eyes, but she only gathered her skirts and rose. 'My name is Caitlin.' She gestured to the open door. 'I thought we might take tea in the garden. The day is better than most lately, and the air healthful.'

I stopped on the threshold, utterly unprepared for the view.

76

Caitlin's holding was set, as I have said, on a hill, and the cottage stood higher than the front gate, so that she had a view straight out to sea. The storm of the previous night had blown in clearing weather, a turn toward the mildness of spring. The sky showed leaden still on the horizon, but that was moving off, and only thin cloud obscured the sun. The sea swirled light and dark over shoal and deeps. Nearer at hand there was a bit of turf dropping steeply to the beach, and closer, the wall protecting a garden still snugged under its winter blanket of salt marsh hay. A few pansies bravely lifted their faces at the borders of the paths, and some early crocus fluttered in the breeze. The rambler cloaking the garden wall was showing healthy red canes, and the espaliered fruit trees were neatly wrapped in sacking to protect them from the cold. I recognized wrinkled pea seeds spilling out from under some of the straw and smiled at the memory of my medicine master Nestor, and Padraig's wife, Nan, arguing about who would have the earliest crop of them. It had been something of a contest between them every year. Jorem's men had destroyed more, so much more, than the lives they had taken. . . .

'It looks odd, I'll grant, but it works,' Caitlin said. 'We have peas by a month or so after Beltane.' She was pouring tea into two bowls on the barrow, which would serve as our table.

'I know. We used to plant them that way, too.' I limped to one of the stools set up against the wall of the house.

She was arrested in the act of pouring the tea. 'Really? Where?'

'The place where I lived when I was a boy. The healer let me hang about sometimes. He did it your way.'

Caitlin had a disconcertingly direct gaze. If I had believed in witches, I would have believed in her. She finished pouring and handed me the tea. I sipped, turning sideways to her so that she could see only my profile, my custom when conversing with folk other than my mates. People found it less awkward.

'You needn't think to spare me. I have seen much worse,' she said quietly. 'Such injuries as yours are not uncommon among quarrymen, or those who make a living gathering sea-bird eggs.'

Too close by half. I changed the subject, gesturing to the spy-glass on its tripod that was set in the midst of the garden. 'Keeping an eye on your townsfolk?' I asked lightly.

Her laugh took me by surprise. I suppose I had expected a delicate, aristocratic titter, but Caitlin had a wonderfully free, full guffaw which drew a smile out of me in response. 'It is useful to let them think so. No, actually I watch the dolphins.'

And the shipping, as I'd heard. She might make a nice tuppence or two keeping the officer down at the post informed as to what flags came and went past her vantage point. It was information of a sort that the king's men always wanted to know.

'Dolphins?' I prompted.

She knew exactly what I was thinking. No fool, this woman. Her voice had gone cold when she answered, 'They're a great deal more interesting than people.'

'Most things are a great deal more interesting than people.'

'Ah, a skeptic. How nice. We needn't beat about the bush, then. You killed those men last night, and you did it deliberately, even after they had conceded you sanctuary. I don't like that.'

It was like being dressed down by my auntie. I hunched one shoulder in a shrug and thumbed my bad ear, which had begun to ring. 'One can't always pick one's supplicants. Your ill luck. Thank you for opening the gate, by the way; it was a bloody awful night to stir from your snug hearthside.'

For a moment I thought she might slap me. Then she looked away, out to sea, and was silent. She was controlling her breathing, I realized, the same relaxation exercise Symon had taught me. My respect climbed another notch. I was fairly sure this was no part of any ordinary siochla's training. But if she held a higher rank, what was she doing here watching dolphins?

Finally, when Caitlin was ready, she drew my ring from a pocket in one fold of her voluminous skirt and laid it on the barrow between us. 'I will ask you a question, one only. Tell me the truth, please. I've small patience with liars.' Before I could avoid her touch, she reached across our rude table and laid one finger over the pulse point in my wrist. She would have the truth, indeed, or she would know it if she did not. I might have flung off her hand, but that would have been churlish. And cowardly.

'Ask, mistress.'

Her eyes were on mine. 'Did you steal this ring?'

I counted ten long beats. I am sure she did, too. 'Yes,' I answered.

The light touch left my wrist, and she straightened, then rose and walked slowly to the middle of the bisecting paths of her garden, where she stood with folded arms and head bent. I watched her and drank off the rest of my tea.

She came back, still with arms folded, and stopped before me. There was a look in her face that made me quickly get up and step away, faltering on my injured leg. 'Were you the one who killed him?' she said.

'Killed who?'

Her lips tightened. 'The Master of Skellig Inishbuffin. It is his ring. *Was* his ring.'

I was taken so off-guard that I could not even try to dissemble.

'Here, sit,' I heard her say through the sound in my ear. When I looked up, she had run lightly to the house. A moment later she returned with an earthenware jug and splashed some in my empty tea bowl. 'Drink, it will steady you.'

I took a swallow. It was potcheen, the potent spirits of country folk all through the Burren.

'Better?'

'Yes, thank you, mistress. Sorry – I must have lost more blood last night than I thought.'

'That's part of it,' she murmured as if to herself and took her own seat. The breeze blew a tendril of hair into her eyes, and she tucked it back absently. 'I knew something had happened back then when my pigeons returned still with my messages unopened. Pirates, or Wolfhounds?'

'Wolfhounds. I'm not one, incidentally. Mistress Caitlin, I'm – it isn't you, I just can't speak of it. There was a massacre.'

'Powers,' she breathed, then softly: 'All of them?'

'All,' I said flatly.

'Except you.' There was no accusation in her voice, only pity.

I gulped potcheen. 'Except me.' My tone was a rebuff.

I could feel her eyes like hands tracing my crooked jaw and the sunken place in my skull that was covered by my rough shag of hair. She would have found it last night in tending me, and I knew she had speculated how I came to be injured like a quarryman or a sea-bird egg hunter. It made me angry to be examined like flawed glass, so I turned the full effect of my gargoyle glare on her. 'What of it? How did you know about my – this ring?'

She smiled a little in the face of my anger. 'The obvious way, of course: I saw it on Bruchan's hand more than once. He was a dear friend and visited when he was journeying about to fairs and storytelling competitions in this district.' Caitlin drank some tea, and there was silence between us. 'Did he give you the ring to hold?' she asked gently.

'I stole it, I told you.' In every way that mattered, I had. Bruchan should have lived; *he* was a worthy heir to the Mariner.

'It's valuable,' she said.

'Looks it.' I hoped I sounded indifferent.

'But you haven't sold it.' She smiled a little, knowing she had me there. Any poor man, especially a slave or bondsman who's been unexpectedly freed by a massacre, knows the worth of bread for today.

I shrugged. 'I didn't want to let it go for a short price, and dwarves don't pay well. I've had to stay with them, so I've kept the ring put by secret-like. Someday I'll get to Dun Aghadoe, maybe, and find a trader who's willing to fork over some decent gold for it.'

I had lied before to many people and got away with it, but this witch sounded my depths. 'Did Symon train you?'

I had answered, 'Yes,' before I saw the trap. She had seen the calluses on my hands, of course. The indentured boys were not taught those tactics. So she knew now that I had been neither slave nor bondsman. I began to sweat, dumped some tea into the bowl to dilute the liquor – I needed clear wits here – and drank. It will tell you something about how skilled she was if I say that even though I had been trained to withstand such techniques as she was using, I did not even perceive that she had me under a compulsion until later.

She shook her head and blew an impatient breath. 'Young man, I told you I did not suffer liars gladly. Now, I could force you to tell me, but I don't think either of us wants to go through that.'

I felt as though I'd been held underwater for a long time. Gritting my teeth, I said, 'It was Master's, as you say. He was good to me, and I didn't want the bastards who murdered him to get it, so I took it and ran. All right?'

And they didn't pursue you?

'I hid.' I had been staring at her defiantly, but it was not until she blinked in surprise and put one hand hastily to her mouth in the manner of one who has said something she shouldn't that I realized her lips had not moved!

'You heard that?' she asked.

At the same moment I gasped, 'By the Four!' and sprang up from my stool, my hand making the sign.

She laughed a little. 'I'm sorry, did I frighten you?' Then, with her finger across her lips deliberately, she added, *I wasn't expecting you'd be able to hear me.*

My breath was caught somewhere down near my stomach, but she was so matter-of-fact about it that I was damned if I'd look like a country bumpkin taken in by a mountebank at a fair, so I uncrossed my fingers and hooked the stool closer to me, pressing my bad ear closed. 'You needn't shout.'

One eyebrow arched. *Thy pardon*, her voice said in my mind at a normal conversational tone. *It usually takes some little time to become attuned to the kenning.*

My breath had found its normal way again, and I realized the sense of compulsion that had been upon me earlier was gone. 'You ensorcelled me, Witch.'

She nodded complacently, unwrapped the teapot from its cozy, and poured some for herself. 'Only a slight truthsaying spell, which didn't altogether work. That in itself told me you were no ordinary pirate. I had to know about the ring, you see, and though I was fairly sure already, I could not risk the possibility of your being a soldier of the King.' She frowned a little handing me the teabowl. 'There is a kind of dark aura about you that troubled me, but now I see it for what it is,' she said quietly, as though thinking aloud.

'Do you?' A bitter smile twisted my lips.

But she waved the question aside and clasped the straw sugan Vanu which hung as a pendant around her neck. 'Those burn scars on your chest: they are from no ordinary fire, are they?'

That was altogether too near the mark. I'd told no one, not even Timbertoe, what had happened at the ancient sanctuary when I painted the Four Powers into the world. For a moment I felt again the lacing Fire that had scourged me as the Dark One had blown past me into the world. I swallowed. 'Are you reading my mind?'

Caitlin shook her head. 'It is not permitted to violate another in such a way,' she answered quietly.

'Just as well,' I growled. 'I doubt you've heard those words before.'

She smiled. 'Oh, my dear boy, you've no idea the words I know.' The siochla chuckled at some private thought and sniffed. Her head went to one side as she regarded me. 'You should not turn your profile to anyone who knew Bruchan.'

Our eyes met.

I hesitated a moment, then picked the ring off the barrow and slipped it on my finger.

'Yes, I thought so,' she said. 'You would be the boy called Aengus.'

'I go by Cru now, lady.'

'The Painter.'

I looked away, out into the garden. 'I have been,' I said carefully.

The witch smiled. 'I'm glad I opened the gate last night, then, even though it was so awful out and so nice near the fire. We thought you lost all those years ago. And now, here you are – in the seventh year, too.'

I was wary of the look in her eye. 'You wit — you Vanui have been looking for me?'

'Yes. Well, I mean, others of the sisters looked for you. I had—' Her eyes flicked away for a moment. 'Tasks of my own.'

Not much will make a man feel less comfortable than the thought that a coven of witches has been looking for him. I made the sign behind my back, covering by scratching. 'Did your sisters send men with bone darts?'

She spilled some tea. 'Bone?'

Was her reaction fright, or guilt? 'And did they kill King Diarmuid with one?'

Fright, no doubt about it. The tea bowl smashed, and her color was bad suddenly, so that I jumped to steady her on the stool and held the potcheen to her lips. She swallowed some, then pushed my arm away. 'How do you know Diarmuid is dead?' she demanded harshly, searching my face. 'There was nothing in the tiles—'

'Then your tiles are deceived, mistress. I saw him with my own eyes. We found his funeral ship drifting in the searoads between Windy Hook and Inishkerry. I boarded it.' She was still pale, and I didn't think she needed to hear the details about how the gulls had cleaned the body down to shreds and bone. 'The point was still in him. I removed it and saved it because I hadn't seen one like it before.' She didn't need to know I was after booty when I'd taken it, either. I pressed her to drink more spirits, and she sipped. 'I am sorry, lady. I didn't know the news would be so ill to you.'

Caitlin's color was coming back, but there was a tremor in her hands, and she was thinking hard, one hand pressed to her mouth, eyes on the shards of the teapot, but I didn't think she was seeing it. She swallowed and put a hand on my arm to let me help her rise, a naturally graceful gesture, as was the way she gathered her worn skirt to step over the shards.

Maybe in that moment of shock she had dropped some spell of concealment that clouded my eyes, or maybe I suddenly realized what would make a patrician siochla with a hunchbacked ward content to watch dolphins. My breath seemed to stop. 'By the Four! You're—!'

'Trapped,' she said very calmly, 'or about to be. They've found us.'

She was looking past my shoulder, out to sea. I swung around. A black ship with a figurehead I recognized even from these heights, a Dinan ship, was nosing into the cove below Caitlin's cottage.

'There's time,' I told her. 'My ship will be waiting a mile or so up the coast.' At least, I hoped fervently that Timbertoe would have gone to the alternate rendezvous. 'I'll get my horse. You and His Highness can outrun them while I lead them the other way: it might be me they're after anyway.' Without pausing to hear her answer, I ran toward the small byre where I could see the gray's ears over the half-door.

'No, wait, there's another way out, and besides, they've already got us flanked. By our Mistress, and Jamie's out there!' She was controlling the panic, but only just, staring up at the troop coming over the crest of the hill above the house.

'Where is he?' I asked urgently. 'I'll go!'

She raised a hand over me in a gesture I had not seen before, but one which made the gooseflesh rise suddenly. 'Get my son to the Vale, Aengus: I charge you with this geis.'

'We'll all go, lady queen, or we'll all die. *Where is he?*'

Caitlin began to point down to the shore – of course, that's where the weir would be, I thought, and damned myself for a fool – but at that moment the front gate swung open, then slammed, and the hunchback dropped the bar across it.

'Mother be thanked!' the woman breathed, then: 'Get my tripod, would you?' She went quickly into the cottage.

I wrenched the thing off its stand, looked up at the mounted troop, which was near enough now to hear their hunting cries above the pounding hooves, and ran down to turn the gray out of the byre, together with the plodding cow. The Wolfhounds would burn the place, I was betting and I didn't want the animals trapped. Jamie flashed me an approving glance, but went straight on by to the house, the breath straining in his twisted lungs from his run up the hill.

By the time I was done the troopers had split neatly into two columns to encircle the boreen. I could see a pennon on the end of a spear tossing above the gate. 'Open, by the archpriest's order!' a voice cried.

I ran for the house, skidded through the door and went into the bedroom to snatch up my helmet, jamming it on my head, and then buckling on my sword belt. My grandfather's ring would have to stay on my hand, as there was no time now to secure it in the canvas belt once more.

When I came out into the main room, Caitlin had her back to me, yet I could see her taking something that glinted from behind a rock she had removed from the hearth. She had flung a cloak around her. Jamie, a pack over his one good shoulder, dragged the nanny across the floor from the shed. Being a stubborn creature, she did not want to go out. He closed the door on her as the same voice shouted from the gate, 'Open, you filthy bitch, or we'll come in after you!'

I drew my sword. Caitlin grabbed a lantern and lit the candle with a small splinter of wood which she drew along the hearth with a brisk motion so that it flared. At the time I thought it was some sort of spell. 'This way,' she said.

A trap door in the floor of the shed was revealed when she

scuffed aside the straw and dung. I grasped the rope handle and pulled it up. A steep flight descended into the darkness, hewn out of the rock. I could hold the stairway, perhaps, unless they used pitch, but there was a surer way. 'Start down my lady, and don't wait for me. I'm going to cover our tracks a bit. It won't take long.' I lifted the stable broom.

I don't know whether she guessed what I would do, but the queen went quickly down, and after a puzzled glance, the 'Monster Prince' went with her. I made sure they were well away, held the broom in the hearth until the twigs caught, and touched the fire to the thatched roof in several places. The bunched herbs helped, as did the tarring from 'the open peat hearth that had coated the straw up there.

Then I ran for the trap door, slammed it closed over me, and stumbled down the stairs by touch.

PART TWO
THE HAG'S EMBRACE

CHAPTER SIX

Timbertoe had a fit, of course. *Never a witch by sea nor a cat by horse,* runs a dwarfish proverb concerning people and things that should not be moved.

He had come himself with some of the crew in the other small landing boat to collect me at the alternate meeting place. I had it from Neddy later that our boat had barely nosed around the hook of land into the little protected cove when the fleet Dinan ship passed by, headed for the beach below Caitlin's cottage. The pegleg had fretted himself into a state of dangerous temper and drunk nearly an entire bottle of flotjin, the emergency cordial stashed aboard each of the landing boats. Neddy and Arni had been dispatched to reconnoiter, and when they worked their way over the hill above the siochla's sanctuary, they'd seen me talking to the witch in the garden. They'd hastened back with the news.

The skipper had cursed all witches (with his fingers making the sign behind his back Neddy said), posted look-outs, and settled to a day's wasted enterprise, figuring that I would make a break for freedom only under cover of night. He would allow no fires, so although the crew had found some tremendous lobsters on the underwater rocks, they had no way to cook them. I gathered they'd done little that day but play at tiles and trim their toenails. They were a surly lot by the time the witch, the hunchback, and I clambered down through the gap in the huge tumbled slabs of rock that led into the cove from the landward side.

I sketched a salute. 'Hoy, Skipper.'

He spat and squinted. 'Hoy, Giant.'

'This is Mistress Caitlin.' I did not introduce Jamie and left them to think he was the witch's property.

Timbertoe sniffed. 'How do?' For him, this was civil.

Beside me the siochla could not have failed to note, as I had, that

89

every man of the crew except Timbertoe had one hand behind his back. There was a lot of signing going on, and Neddy was staring again. Caitlin stepped forward and inclined her head gracefully. 'Pleased to meet you, Captain. Charmed, I'm sure.'

A chuckle got away from him, but he grabbed it by the tail, you might say, and hauled it back to kennel behind his customary scowl. 'My man Cru, there. He is under geis to ye, is he?'

Caitlin passed over my travelling name without even a momentary pause. 'Yes, of course. He claimed sanctuary, after all. The terms of the geis have not yet been imposed,' she lied smoothly.

My seadog nodded slowly, chewing over her words. 'So is he free to go, or what?'

I jumped in with both feet, which was the only way that stood any chance at all with Timbertoe: 'Caitlin is coming with us.' There was no need to say the servant would accompany her.

'She's *what*?' he bellowed over the curses of the crew.

'As a paying customer,' I added.

That was different. Not all pirate profits come from raiding. In fact, a good deal of their business lies in providing sea passage for those who have the money to pay for fast, discreet charters. Caitlin was a woman and a witch, though; that was the sticking point. An unaccompanied woman aboard ship is bad enough by dwarfish reckoning, but a witch is poison.

Caitlin must have known what they were thinking, and she knew, too, that the smoke from the cottage must be clearly visible over the hill. From the purse at her girdle she withdrew a beautiful piece of goldwork encrusted with gems, probably the only bit of queen's jewelry she'd been able to save. 'I can pay,' she said quietly, holding it up.

She shouldn't have to do that, I thought. I covered the jewelry with my hand and stepped to her side. 'I'll stand their fare, Skipper.' I threw a warning glance at the silent crew. 'And don't anybody even *think* about pinching that brooch.' I didn't care what they thought had happened to me at the sanctuary.

The pegleg chewed a braid of his beard and muttered, 'Isn't the fare I'm worried about – it's the magic.'

'I can pay in that, too, if you prefer,' she said serenely.

He made the sign then. 'Thanks, no,' he answered stiffly. 'We get our charms from the guild's witch.'

Caitlin considered a moment. 'Has she given you a Protection Against Witches spell?'

'No, we don't have that one,' he admitted reluctantly, probably thinking he shouldn't reveal the fact.

She looked pleased. 'Then we can do business, hey, Captain?'

He still wasn't easy about it, but in the end a deal was done. She had to make the charm first, naturally; he wouldn't have let her aboard without that provision, since it was as much a guard against Caitlin herself as against any other witch. She took the pouch of crystals from her girdle, selected a light one, and with it made some motions over the captain and crew. Then she took another crystal, spoke some whispered command, and a quick silver light gleamed for a moment above the heads of every man present save me. She nodded. 'It's set, even against me.'

Timbertoe nodded gruffly. 'Thank'ee, mistress.' He gave me a quick glance from under his bushy brows when Caitlin named her destination as the Vale. 'Never been there,' he ventured to say, but she merely assured him that she knew the way, gathered her skirts, and let me help her into the curragh drawn up on the rocky shingle. Jamie followed without meeting anyone's eyes.

The siochla perched herself on a thwart. The men looked to the skipper. 'Is there some problem?' she inquired.

'By the way, Skipper,' I put in as he hesitated, 'this place is going to be swarming with Wolfhounds in a few minutes. I had a bit of trouble, I'm afraid.'

He cursed me roundly and whirled to the boat, clambering in awkwardly. The boys helped me push off the curragh, vaulted in and dived to their oars, being careful not to touch the witch in passing. The hammer clanked, the oars flashed and dipped to catch the water, and we arrowed out of the sheltering cove.

I was in the stern with Timbertoe directly in front of me. Under cover of the slap of the wavelets against the leather hull and the grunts of the rowers, he asked in a low voice, 'Are ye all right, Giant?'

I grinned. 'Never better, Filthydwarf.'

He looked doubtful, but left it for the less cramped quarters of the mother ship. I caught Caitlin's eye and winked. She smiled and said in my mind, *There's no such thing as a Protection Against*

Witches spell, so I gave them a Protection Against Clap spell. Do you think they'll mind?

I laughed and then had to pretend I had a sand flea caught in my throat.

If any look-out aboard the Dinan ship spotted the '*Kerry Gem*', he obviously didn't report it, because the Wolfhound ship was still anchored off Caitlin's cove when we winched the little landing boat aboard our mother ship, ran up the sails, and headed west for Inishbuffin. Despite the urgency, the guildmaster's business came first. My business, now: I owed my own blood price to Sitric, a considerable backlog of booty to the crew and, now, two fares to a place that existed only in legend.

'How's the leg?' he asked, stumping up quietly next to me.

I didn't turn at his approach. 'Well enough. The arrowhead came out cleanly, and the witch is a good seamstress.' We leaned on the rail, and Timbertoe drew out his pipe and tobacco. For a few moments while he struck sparks and drew to get it going, neither of us said anything, watching the two-hundred-foot cliffs draw nearer.

The day was passably clear, and even at this distance some two miles off Inishbuffin peninsula we could see the clouds of seagulls swirling against the gray rock face. I did not realize my hands were clenched on the rail until Timbertoe suddenly said, 'Bugger it. Let's put about and head for home, and tell the guildmaster we couldn't get near the place. Dinan or ghosts or whatever. We can forget about this run to the Vale, too: we don't need the witch's silver, or yours.'

'No.' I straightened. 'No, it's time I went home.'

He drew on the pipe, then said quietly, 'Thought ye'd made a home with us, Giant.'

I stared up where the round tower stood in the pale sunlight above the skellig, the glazing of the roofing slates seeming like the bright surface of quiet water. 'So did I. Until now.' At his silence, I realized how that sounded. 'I didn't mean—'

He waved the pipe abruptly. 'Doesn't matter. I told ye before, 'twas business.' He levered himself off the rail. 'Well, now that you've seen it, d'ye still want the boat to anchor at Gull's Cove, or would ye rather just tie up at the jetty and go up the cliffwalk?'

We could clearly see the steps cut in zig-zagging flights up the cliff; they seemed perfectly sound still.

'No, I . . . let's head for Gull's Cove as we planned. I don't want to go in by the back door with all the men watching.' What I meant was that there is a certain ritual to a homecoming, and I wanted to go in by the front gate, ruined though it was.

Maybe he understood, or maybe he was thinking of that climb and his wooden leg, for he nodded, spat over the rail, and called to Ries to reef the sheets and stand by to lower the curragh. 'Step lively, Giant. Don't much care for lying in this close to shore on a day like this with Wolfhounds looking high and low for you and Princess Charming.'

If he only knew how close the nickname came to the truth! I'd mentioned nothing of Caitlin and Jamie's real reason for flight, but I had told the skipper everything else that had happened: about Cathir and the boy Derry; about being chased by the patrol to the siochla's gate. I couldn't leave her there to suffer at the hands of the Wolfhounds, I pointed out, when they found out she'd given sanctuary to the killer of a powerful Dinan skellig master. Besides, she'd seen my face, and could be forced to tell what she knew. He saw the sense of that.

Just to be prudent, though, he had ordered down our own flag, burgundy background with a white diamond, and run up a copy of Brunehilda's flying greyhound on a black field. This is a common enough tactic to confuse identification, and all pirate captains have a sea chest full of duplicate flags with which to cast blame on their rivals. In this case, it might help us avoid more than a cursory glance if the look-out aboard the Dinan ship back at Caitlin's cove had taken note of the *Inishkerry Gem* flying from our mast. (I will add here that the only complication to this pirate strategem is that if you are conducting a raid under a rival's flag and that rival happens to show up, you are then held to be acting on your rival's behalf, and any spoils become his or her property. It is fair recompense for tarnishing another captain's name. It also comprises half the business of the dwarfish Moot.)

Now as he and I prepared to go ashore I told him, 'A moment. I need a word with the siochla.' He cast his eyes skyward, but nodded.

Caitlin must have heard the relayed order, because even before we had slowed appreciably she came on deck from my cabin. 'Is something wrong?' Her eyes sought out Jamie, who had proved something of a pleasant surprise to our hardened crew. He wasn't a simpleton and though he was forbidden to play tiles (at least they assumed he was forbidden the game, because he served a witch who used such tiles to cast fortunes), he could, and did, play draughts well enough to give Ries, our best player, some real competition. Just now the hunchbacked prince was trying to teach Harrald some strategy, a hopeless effort, as I could have told him.

Wordlessly I pointed behind Caitlin, and she looked over the top of the hatch to the cliffs now no more than sixteen or seventeen boat lengths away. Ries brought us to skillful anchor off the mouth of Gull's Cove. From here she could not see the skellig. I shifted the pack that held a lantern to see our way in the mine, some rope, and other equipment we thought we might need. 'Why did you want me to come here?' I asked. She looked surprised, and I said, 'You heard my orders to the helmsman. If you'd really wanted to go on straight to the Vale, you'd have slapped a spell on this ship.'

The siochla smiled and lowered her eyes. 'It isn't so easy as that. As to why I let you come here—' She looked up at the cliffs. 'I cannot say for certain, but I think there is something for you here.'

'Something about the ring?'

'I don't know. No, truthfully, I don't, despite what you think.' She looked tired in the morning light, the lines around her eyes deepened. 'The tiles are confused on this point: one part of the pattern they make indicates great fortune, or great good; but there is another part.'

'Indicating evil,' I guessed.

'Indicating death.' A line thrummed above our heads, taut in the breeze.

'Come on, Giant!' Timbertoe bellowed. 'We're doing nothing but collecting bird sh—'

'Hold your damned water!' I yelled back irritably. I swung back to look at Caitlin. 'Your tiles could hardly say anything besides death, could they? After what happened here?'

'It isn't a warning of old deaths, Aengus.' She took the bronze sugan Vanu from around her neck and hung it around mine. 'Beware.'

A deathly cold touched my bones, but I smiled for her. 'The most I have to fear is Timbertoe.'

Whatever emanations were coming from the skellig, the impact of them was plainly visible in her eyes, but she matched my tone. 'And that's bad enough, indeed. Go now, and mind you're back before sunset.'

She needn't have told me that. Even in full daylight the place held enough ghosts for me. I nodded, trotted aft to the rope ladder, and climbed down into the curragh where Timbertoe was waiting. 'Give ye a charm, did she?' he rasped, eying the sugan.

'I suppose it made her feel better,' I answered as I pushed us away with an oar against the tight planking of the *Gem*, and then settled to row. Timbertoe loosened his boot knife and drew his cutlass to test the edge against his thumb. It was sharp enough, and he sucked the cut and darted his eyes all over the beach, the rock verge, and the soaring cliffs of Gull's Cove. 'I'm sorry, I had forgotten about the ladders,' I told him. That was why he had suggested the cliffwalk with its carved steps.

'No matter,' he said absently. 'I've done this a time or two before.'

In fact, he had done it a great deal oftener than that. He and my grandfather had been allies in the silent war against the Dinan an Lupus, and Timbertoe had been a frequent visitor, always under the guise of a pirate raider. Bruchan had left him messages on livestock, and the dwarf had carried off an old ewe or cow with no one the wiser, either the skellig folk or the pirate crew. I smiled now as I thought of the two old foxes outsmarting their people.

'No, I don't go up in an Old Maid's Goose, either, so ye can wipe that grin off your face,' he snapped.

I fended us off a rock, backed a little to line us up with the surge of breakers, and shipped oars. 'I didn't think you would.' Not for a moment could I picture him sitting in such a rope sling, like a wet and frightened sailor being taken off a wrecked ship, or a dead drunk dwarf being taken aboard one.

We rode in handily through the surf. I jumped into the tug of foaming water to haul the curragh up on the sand. Here it was that I had once painted the Swan floating on a river I had heard about only in legend, and looked up along an enemy's sword in the fog.

95

'That's good – I've got it,' the dwarf said as he swung over the curragh's gunwale to land on his good foot and take the rope from me. With an easy tug of his powerful shoulders, he hauled the leather boat several feet further up the beach. The tide would turn in about three hours, and it would be depressing to come back and find we'd lost the curragh. Though the crew would see it floating from the *Gem* and come in closer for us, it would be a cold swim out to the mother ship. He straightened and rested his hand on the hilt of his sword, looking up where I was looking at the ladders that in other days had been pegged into the cliff face. 'Few rungs missing,' he noted, 'but I think we can make it.'

'Aye, but I'm going to take the mooring line.' The short length of rope at the curragh's bow might help us over some of the rougher places.

He shrugged. 'If ye think ye need it.'

'Nay, for lowering this pack when we fill it with chalcedons. It'll be too heavy to climb down with.'

Timbertoe's crow's-feet wrinkled, but he didn't quite break a smile. 'Right.' He knew, as I did, that I was on a memorial journey, not a treasure hunt. However, if we found treasure, we certainly wouldn't mind.

I coiled the rope, slung it over one shoulder, and climbed over the few boulders tumbled at the cliff's foot. 'Ready?'

'Always.'

I tested the first ladder, found it sound enough, and began the ascent. I was scarcely up the first stage and resting on the little shelf, when the pirate's head appeared at the level of my feet. 'Winded already?' he needled.

That was the last pause we made. Generally, where rungs had rotted away there were still iron spikes sticking out of the rock to provide a foothold. Only two ladders proved to be unusable for their entire length, and these we were able to skirt with the rope, which, I noticed, Timbertoe used with no further gibes. When I finally hauled myself over the top and flopped on my back to pant a while, I said to the deep sky, 'We leave by the cliffwalk. To hell with the curragh.'

The dwarf heaved his bulk to sit beside me, leaning back on his hands, and trying not to breathe any more loudly than I was. 'By His Beard, that's a bonny view. Always admired it.'

'It was Nestor's favorite place. It restored his heart when he was weary, he said.'

Timbertoe sniffed. 'Would have made a good king, him.' Our physician had been one of Diarmuid's brothers. With a family like that, I could understand why he'd opted for the peaceful life of the skellig. If my grandfather's plans had not gone awry we would have put Nestor on the throne of the Burren, while I became his brother king in Ilyria. I wondered if Nestor would have cursed the fate that took him from this view as much as I had railed against mine. Probably not. He had been a strong man.

I growled a curse at an ant which had pinched my back, and rolled to my feet. 'Come on, Filthydwarf. Let's go stir up some walkers.'

He pitched a small rock out over the pristine cove and followed as I took the well-worn path toward the skellig walls which crowned the headland.

Jorem's men had done the thing completely, give them credit for that. If some weaponsmaster wanted an example of how pillage and slaughter should be carried out, he'd go far before finding one better than this.

Where once there had been a cluster of thatched houses with geese and chickens and small, orderly vegetable plots contained within their low stone walls, there were now only charred corner posts, some mounds of old thatch that had sprouted into strong stands of hay, and thistles that had seeded themselves in the dooryards and taken over, despite the cropping of the wild goats on the peninsula. Those silent reminders were all that was left of the village where the married folk of the skellig had lived, those reminders and the walls that made a patchwork showing where patient men had practiced the arts of husbandry. Not one wall had tumbled down, through fog, sleet, gale, or villainy, for four years. Jorem's army had killed Skellig Inishbuffin, but they could not break its bones.

Timbertoe was watching me out of the corner of his eye, though he pretended to be surveying for a trap door, but he respected my silence and did not speak until I did. 'The entrance to the mine wouldn't have been in the village, anyway,' I told him as he came back from inspecting a tangle of blackberry briars where Padraig's wife had grown her pea patch every year. 'It will have been within the skellig walls somewhere.'

'Aye, I thought so meself.' He squinted around at the ruins. 'Wish I'd thought to bring a bottle. Spot of the old stuff would go down good right now.' His eye had rested, as mine had, on the white tangled mounds at the base of the wall, where the great gates had hung.

Stiffly we moved toward the place where the slaughter had begun.

There was nothing to say, and we did not make small talk. Timbertoe must have been seeing the shin bones, the craniums – some split – with the jaws separated from them, the chines regular as columns, the finger digits fallen from the bones of the wrists. But I was seeing the bodies as I had seen them four years ago, still raw and bleeding, some still warm to my touch when I had stooped to search for a beloved face that was not among these defenders of the gate. In my mind was that day's numbing drizzle of fog and sorrow. I drew a lungful of salt air. 'I should have come back to bury them,' I said.

'One lad, alone, and sore hurt? Nay, there's naught ye could have done to make this – decent.'

'There's a lot one man could have done in four years, if he'd wanted to.' At my feet lay a skull with an arrow through its eye socket. I knew it must be Niall's, our horse master. I bent, pulled the arrow out carefully, and flung it away. Then, without looking any more at the remains, I strode through the breach in the wall where Jorem's army had rammed the gate. Timbertoe followed, being careful not to crush any of the bones with his wooden leg, though it really didn't matter.

I headed for the armory. Timbertoe, stumping quickly to match my strides, asked, 'This the way to Bruchan's quarters? Maybe there'd be a clue amongst his papers?'

'Not yet,' I said shortly. 'There's something I have to get, first.' The practice yard was somewhat as it had been, the sand underfoot, the quintain now sagging from its post, even the knotted ropes still hanging from the wall – though these were frayed with the wind's blowing them constantly against the rough stone. The armory shed, protected from the elements by the walled enclosure, still stood solid, the roof of wooden shakes having shed most of the rain over the years. I went through the door. I had to duck a little now, as Symon had always done. It was the first time in my years with the dwarves that I remember realizing I had grown taller. I'd have been able to look our burly weaponsmaster in the eye now, I reckoned.

And suddenly he was standing there in the dim interior of the shed, biceps bulging from his sleeveless leather jerkin, sword resting casually over his shoulder, the way he always rested between practice bouts. 'You took your time about coming home, for truth, boy. Did you never stop to think there might have been some babies alive in the tower?'

'The d-door was too hot to touch!' I stammered.

'My youngest was up there. Did you see him, Aengus? Did you?'

'Sy, I—' My jaw locked.

Timbertoe came from behind me. 'What d'ye say?'

I saw the weapons rack clear through Symon's body just before he vanished. Sweat trickled under my hair, and my heart pounded.

'What's the matter, Giant?'

I stared at him. 'See him?' My voice came out a garbled croak, indecipherable even to my ears.

The dwarf frowned and glanced around at the sturdy racks, stripped of their weapons, and at the polishing barrel in the corner near the foot-driven whetstone. 'Something's missing that ought to be here, is that it?'

I wiped my face and shook my head uselessly, making an angry gesture of denial. He moved aside as I shouldered past him and lifted out of the way the rack that had held spears. I wasn't sure exactly which stone it was, so I picked a place and starting pressing. I had not done five when there was a click, and the hidden niche was revealed. The amber bottle was there. Symon must have returned it to its hiding place after dipping a pin for Padraig, who had been like a brother to him, and to whom he had sworn to give this secret.

I lifted the bottle carefully, for my hand was still trembling at Symon's spectre. The sugan inked on the label warned in apothecary's notation of a deadly poison.

Timbertoe's eyes were on the bottle. 'Th' Hagges Embrace'?' he questioned, reading it. He looked up to my face. 'That's the stuff ye took, isn't it? The doctor always said there must have been something else besides the head wound to account for why ye couldn't be roused after we fished ye out of the Caldron.'

My law was loosening. 'He was right. It's a drug Nestor discovered.' I cut an end off my sash, wrapped the bottle securely, and stowed it in the pack.

'Done in here?'

'Yes.' He preceded me out of the door, and I paused for a moment to look back. Nothing met my eye but the dust motes we had disturbed, streaming in the light of the single small window. 'Sy?' But he would not answer. I left him to his troubled rest.

'Now to Bruchan's quarters?' Timbertoe questioned as I came out into the sunshine.

'Aye. It's over this way.'

I set the pipe upright, but there was nothing I could do about the severed mouthpiece. The brass bowl had darkened and showed an edge of green rust where the marauders had hacked at it. I hung the candle lantern on the wall sconce, for in this chamber there was no window. Timbertoe lifted some of the slashed strips of the tapestry hanging across one side of the small room, looking for a door behind it, but there was none. He pressed the strips into some sort of alignment and backed off to arm's length, trying to puzzle out what the scene woven there might have been. 'I think it's the Willowsrill,' I said, naming the great river of Ilyria. By its banks, according to the story my grandfather had told me, our ancestor Colin Mariner had met his end, poisoned by his treacherous brother when he returned home to claim the hall that should have been his own. He must have been a bit simple, I'd always thought, to believe any brother would yield up a kingdom after nearly a lifetime of holding it – just because someone showed up with a better claim.

Timbertoe was chuckling.

'What's so funny?' I asked, pulling up one corner of the worn carpet. There was nothing under it but solid timber flooring. I let it flap back and looked across at the dwarf.

'This,' he answered. 'This is the river country, right enough – I recognize the place, even. That's what ye see if ye're standing at the gate of Fergus Fairhand's dun.' He gave it the Burren word, meaning 'fort'. 'But see this?' He smoothed the tapestry and made an oval with his fingertip around the purpled mountains where a rough V-shaped notch showed blue sky beyond the horizon. 'Well, the fellow who made this must never have seen the place, because that notch is over here.' He moved his finger left at least two feet. 'It's the gap that's the only pass in the mountains between the Burren and Ilyria.'

I shrugged, losing interest. 'It doesn't matter. It's still a nice piece of work.'

He nodded as he let the tatters fall. 'Still, all the time it must have taken to weave it, and he gets it wrong.' He chuckled again.

I was piqued, because the tapestry had pleased my grandfather enough to have it hung in his private study where we stood. 'I'm taking it,' I said shortly. 'Maybe somebody skillful with a needle can mend it for me.'

He caught the undercurrent in my voice and helped me get it down. 'Quite a bundle,' he commented as I rolled it and tied it with a piece of the border that had been cut away.

'You won't have to carry it.'

'Damned right!' He pivoted on the wooden leg and left angrily, clunking down the winding stair faster than was prudent.

When he had gone I spent some moments wondering whether this room would be haunted as the armory had been, but nothing appeared in the steady light of the candle lantern. I lifted some of the fragments of stained paper scattered about, the remnants of supply lists. The Master of the skellig must have been looking over accounts at some time immediately before we were attacked. I rifled through the smashed writing case, checked the fireplace flue, and even emptied the basket of still-dry turf. I don't know what I expected, but the place was barren, dead for me. I could detect nothing of my grandfather's presence. I took the lantern and the tapestry and followed the stairway down, carefully stepping around the dark stain on the stone that showed in my memory as a wide and glossy trail of blood. Bruchan was not here.

Timbertoe was sitting on the threshold when I came down the stairs. I put down a hand to haul him to his feet, and he rose, grunting a little. That climb up from Gull's Cove was playing hell with the ruined muscles above his stump, I guessed. 'I'll

101

have Neddy heat us up a couple of tubs of sea water tonight somewhere up the coast,' I said, 'and we can both soak a while.'

'Aye, with the witch watching through that glass of hers, I don't doubt.'

I laughed. 'Well, allow the poor woman that, at least, if she can't take a husband.'

He colored. Dwarves, even pirates, are rather prudish where respectable women are concerned (which may be why when one of them runs amok and commits rape in the heat of a raid, his mates are ashamed enough to pay the guild's witch to make the offering to the Hag for them on their return to Jarlshof). Jolly girls are considered to be a different matter, and fair game for the crudest jests.

'I was thinking the cargo bay might be a good place to try,' the dwarf was suggesting. 'There was a natural cave there once, before it was made bigger for hauling in goods from the jetty, right? If there's a mine, there has to be a cave.'

'Right you are. The stairs go down to it from the corridor off the kitchen, past the round tower, there.'

'Maybe there'll be the odd barrel of ale still lying around,' he ventured.

'Don't get your hopes up, Skipper. The Wolfhounds must have worked up quite a thirst with all their hard work.' So saying I led him around the base of the tower, not glancing up at the door which still firmly closed the tomb. We could not get to the kitchen doorway without passing Gwynt and Alyce, however.

I had not expected that it would all catch up with me there, in the out-of-the way angle between the tower and the wall of the skellig; but as my eyes went to the bones I knew would be there, I had to pretend to drop the tapestry and stoop over it so that Timbertoe should not see me unmanned. I think he guessed, for he said something about looking for that barrel and went into the kitchen and refectory block, leaving me alone in the courtyard where my friend and his sweetheart had committed suicide together rather than be taken.

I choked the silly sounds I was making and fumbled with the knot that bound the tapestry in case the pirate was standing inside the kitchen, watching me; but try as I might I could not stop the tears. These came in a flood I had not known was in me, blurring my eyes so that the pale sunlight struck like a shining lance.

'You couldn't help it, Fat-Lip. It's no blame to you that they were crazy by the time they finally broke their way in. I couldn't get much of what they said, but they were yelling something about a curse.'

The voice was Gwynt's, though I could not see him through the painfully bright curtain between us.

'It *is* my fault, Gwynt,' I told him hoarsely. 'I told them Master was a mage. I thought it would scare them off.'

'Oh . . .' he said.

I heard the condemnation in that falling syllable. My attempt to be clever had convinced the Wolfhounds to obliterate this place in their religious zeal. I shut my eyes. If the curtain cleared, I did not want to see him.

His next words scalded the heart of me. 'Alyce jerked as my knife went in. It hurt her, I think.'

I wanted to tell him that a body will do that when the brain stem is severed, as hers must have been when he'd plunged in his dagger beneath her jawline, just as Symon had taught us to do. But he was echoing away.

His voice came faintly. 'Finian was wrong about it, you know. I heard him that night when you thought I was sleeping. There aren't any flowers here.'

'There must be, Gwynt!' I cried desperately, but he was gone.

My headed pounded cruelly, the bad ear surging with a pulse that stabbed like a stiletto and shrieked like a line just before it snaps in a gale. I rubbed one rough sleeve across my eyes to clear them, staggered to my feet, and made for the welcoming shadow of the kitchen door. There, out of the sun at last, I leaned against the cool wall until I felt steadier, then scrubbed my face on my sleeve. I stuck one finger in my ear to dull the sound and walked past the broken crocks where the cooking oil had stained the flagstones, and the chopping blocks that must have been too heavy to carry away and not worth the trouble of toppling. 'Skipper?' I called.

'Here,' he answered promptly from just around the corner. He came through the archway from the refectory. 'No barrel that I could find, but the cistern is still good. I got us some water.' If he had witnessed what had happened to me in the courtyard, nothing of it showed in his face or manner.

I supped from my hand and splashed some on my face. It was cool and smelled a little dank, but I had drunk worse. 'Thanks. That's good.'

'There's some kind of hatch in the corridor that's fallen through. I figured we could bridge it with one of these benches.'

'That would be the cargo elevator,' I explained. 'We winched a platform up from the floor of the bay down there. It was much easier than trying to carry all the supplies up the stairway.'

We had walked out to the back of the kitchen as I had spoken, and I saw that he was right. I could have stepped across the opening in the floor, but Timbertoe couldn't and to try to jump it with his wooden leg would have been folly. One of the benches from the dining hall quickly made us a bridge, and we followed the corridor past the plundered storerooms to the door leading down.

It was swinging ajar, and I nudged it open gingerly. The stairway was still sound, built as it was of squared timbers fully a handspan thick. I stepped out on to the landing. With the bay doors shut, there was not enough light from the doorway here to reach to the floor, so I lit the lantern once more and we went down. There was an overpowering smell of dead fish and rotted leather, for this was where the skellig's curraghs were racked, and salted fish was stored in barrels so that the damp chill would keep them. The salt had long ago absorbed water out of the humid air, however, so the fish were rotten, and by the lantern's frugal light I could see the molded leather boats. 'I'll try behind the rack,' Timbertoe said. 'Be a good place for a secret door.' He took the spare candle, touched it to the one in the lantern till it flared, and went to investigate.

I stood holding the lantern up to cast a flood of yellow light on the floor at my feet. I looked for a pile of bones with the legs all awry, for I had seen Brother Ruan's body where he had fallen, or had been pushed, from the landing. But there was no skeleton where I expected it. I held the light higher and swept my gaze about the floor. There was a glint of white near the rotted-through staves that had once been the cask set into the floor where he'd kept his lobsters and baits. A jaw grinned there as I approached. I cast about for other remains and found only a piece of skull and a long bone that might have been a femur, and I was puzzled until I realized that all the other corpses I had seen had been picked clean by flocks of birds, but it was rats that had been at work here. My stomach turned. If I'd had any guts at all at the time, I could have hauled him up the stairway when I'd found him, and at least spared him this dismemberment. I touched my hand to my breast in the gesture of respect I had learned here and not used for the past four years.

He was sitting on the edge of the lobster cask, fanning himself with his hood, as if he'd just rowed back from Gull's Cove with a day's catch in his traps. My grandfather's brother, my painting master, smiled.

I smiled back uncertainly. 'Brother Ru?'

'Aye, lad, who else? Now then, thee's solved it?' His thin white hair blew gently in some wind I could not feel.

Solved it? *Damp sand, a stick in my hand, two twinkling blue eyes* . . . 'When thee's solved it to thy satisfaction . . .' I swallowed hard. 'No, master. I still don't know how to paint a teardrop.'

'Hmm, I'd have thought thee might have hit on it by now, thee had such a good start on it. Four years is a long time not to touch the color pots, and I think thee'd best get back to it, we're all waiting for that, thee knows.' He stood as if to leave.

'Don't go, please, master! I can't see the colors, that's why I don't paint! It isn't that I don't want to!'

Brother Ruan shouldered one of his traps. I could see two scuttling claws in it, and my own distorted face. 'Thee was always quick-tongued, boy, but thee never lied to me till now. Thee's afraid to paint, Aengus, even if thee could see the colors.'

Because it was true, the pent-up anger boiled up in waves from my gut, and I hurled the indictment at him: 'You and Bruchan left me without a storyteller, and because of it I botched the painting! I painted this massacre, don't you understand? I made it happen, I let the Wild Fire loose!'

My old painting master bent his head for a moment, then raised his eyes to mine. 'Yes,' he said simply. He reached as if to pat my shoulder in comfort, but restrained himself. 'Poor boy,' he murmured. 'I'm glad it isn't mine to do. Undo, rather, would be the better way to say it, I suppose, considering all. Thee's still the Painter . . . still the Painter . . .'

His voice trailed off, and I found the lantern shattered on the floor, and Timbertoe making the sign behind his candle twenty paces across the floor. 'I saw that one,' he blurted. ''Twas old Ruan, wasn't it?'

'Yes.' I drew a breath. 'Brother Fish-trap isn't pleased with the progress his pupil has made these last years.' I looked over at his darkly shining eyes. 'Could you hear him?'

'No, only you. Fair made me foul myself, it did.'

I bent to retrieve the tapestry and the candle from the broken lantern. 'Come, we're finished here. There's only one other place that makes sense, if the entrance to the mine is inside the skellig.'

He edged around the lobster cask. 'Where?'

'The round tower.'

'But that's where—' He bit off what he had been going to say.

I nodded. 'Hold the candle for me, would you? We'll need all the rope that's left from the elevator, what the rats haven't gnawed, that is.'

In the end, it wasn't as hard as I had thought it would be. I had planned to try casting the rope with the grappling hook up through one of the windows at the top of the tower, hoping to catch it in the webwork of roof timbers inside and climb up that way. If the floors inside had been destroyed in the fire, I would then have dropped the rope down inside the tower and lowered myself to the top of the jumble of burnt timbers. But Timbertoe suggested trying the door first, as the hinges might have rusted enough to force. In this he guessed correctly: the second time I hit the bottom one with the sledgehammer we had improvised from a heavy iron brace, two of the nails sheared off, and after that it was not long until I had it free. The dwarf scrambled up beside me on the platform we had rigged and together we wrenched at the door for all we were worth. Finally the weight on the other side came off. We heard the bar that had been dropped across the door to lock it clunk its way down the unmortared stones to crash on some other wreckage below our height, and the portal I had thought never to cross sagged open before us.

Timbertoe spat into his hands and rubbed them, massaging a bone bruise. 'It's yours to do,' he said gruffly.

Accordingly, I had him lower me on the rope until I stood on a beam which slanted up out of the wreckage. The charred wood still smelled of inferno after all this time, but I realized as I looked about that it must have been the effect of the smoke, not the fire itself, that had caused their deaths – because except for the section of floor directly under the door, much of the timberwork seemed relatively intact.

'See anything?' he called down.

There were few traces of them, the women and the children; birds had nested freely here for years, and the remains had been reduced to bits of bone no larger than the clam shells the gulls dropped against the rocks outside. Still, I hoped even now to find Bruchan, who had dropped back to try to protect them.

'Aengus? D'ye see anything?' the dwarf called again, more sharply.

'Nothing important. I'm going to see if I can get down to the lowest level. There will be a trap door in the floor, I expect.'

And there was.

CHAPTER SEVEN

Timbertoe knotted the rope securely and let himself down to join me on the lowest level of the tower. This would have been where casks of water were stored, and where the privy scuppers channeled wastes to the outside through underground wooden conduits. No doubt the huge water barrels had been an effective cover for the trap door. But Jorem's men had found the chinks outside where the scuppers joined the pipes and had poured pitch in to flood the stone floor where the dwarf and I now crouched. Then a flaming splinter had ignited the pitch, the noisome smoke had been drawn up the tower like a chimney, and by the time the water barrels had burnt through and burst, the fire had got hold of the woodwork of the stairway. The confined space still reeked of it.

Timbertoe spat the taste of it out of his throat and regarded the open hole in the floor where the trap door's hatch had burnt away. To his credit, he did not say it, but neither would he meet my eyes.

There had been a way out, but Bruchan had let them all die.

A cold knot compounded of fury and shame grew in me. I sat back on my heels. 'Well, now we know why we couldn't find his body.'

'Ye don't know for sure. He could be up there.' He jerked his chin at the tower above our heads. 'Likely he'd have been guarding the door, and that section of flooring has fallen—'

'Don't make excuses.' He fell silent, and I lit the candles. 'Let's go find some chalcedons, Filthydwarf. Might as well finish stripping the place.'

As I moved to swing down into the tunnel, the skipper suddenly put one broad hand on my arm, staying me. His fingers bit with the anger he was holding in check. 'Your grandfather was a staunch mate o' mine, boy, and I say don't judge till ye know.'

I jerked my arm out of his grasp and jumped down into the tunnel. For a moment I thought he would not follow, but then he handed down the pack. 'The tapestry, too,' I said neutrally. 'We may not be coming back this way.' He threw it down, passed down some rubbish which I arranged into a step in case we did have to return, and then he swung through as though going belowdecks. I led us off.

The going was easy, the tunnel smoothly hollowed out of the rock of Inishbuffin peninsula and shored with timber. Almost immediately we came upon a torch in a bracket. This I lifted down and managed to light. It was damp and smoked, but gave us more illumination than we'd had. I passed the extinguished candle back to Timbertoe to replace in the pack. We might need it somewhere further on. 'Good work, this,' the dwarf observed of the hollowed rock.

I nodded. 'It must have taken an age.'

A few paces further on, a flight of steps descended for some time. 'We'll be in the Hag's Realm, much more of this,' Timbertoe muttered, awkwardly hopping down the steps on his good foot with both hands braced against the walls on either side.

I smiled grimly, and we went slowly down.

I had been seeing them for some time, but at first took it to be natural coloration in the stone of the steps. At the last step, however, where the flight met a small landing with a door, there could be no doubt: a pattern of dark spots was spattered there. Bruchan *had* passed this way, then. I had stopped to lower the torch to see the bloodstains, and now I glanced back. Timbertoe had noted them, too. For the only time in all the time I knew him, the dwarf suddenly said, 'Me leg hurts.' His lips tightened. 'Can we get on with it?'

I stepped over the last stair without treading on it, lifted the latch, and pushed open the door.

'Bugger me!' the skipper breathed.

I had once jokingly said to my grandfather that the chalcedon mine under the skellig about which he had told me must make him the richest man in all the Burren, maybe all the world. I had not guessed the half of it.

As carefully ordered as any goodwife's root cellar, the treasury of Inishbuffin gave back our torch's feeble light in a myriad sparks. I heard the dwarf draw a breath. I think it was the first either of us had taken. 'What colors?' I asked. He stumped past me to lay a hand on each tray as he enumerated them: amethyst, aquamarine, emerald, sapphire and, rarer than these, the lustrous garnet and ruby shades, all pearled with the gem's distinctive milky cast. There were trays of them, rough-cut to free them from the rock in which they had been imbedded, and polished to judge their color. The trays were sorted by color, by size and grade, apparently, and there were barrels containing the nodes straight from the mine, uncut as yet. A bronze tripod of oil lamps hung over the work table in the middle of the room, where a clutter of cutting and polishing tools and some nodes in clamps showed that the work had gone on nearly to the time of the attack. Opposite us was another door, which must lead into the mine itself.

'And this isn't all of it,' I said. 'The mine isn't worked out yet, obviously.' I gestured at the nodes.

He rubbed his nose. 'I've a nice ship for sale, for the right price.'

I laughed, and the sound ran around the room, echoing. 'I'll buy a fleet and make you skipper of it all, how's that?'

'What's the split?'

'Seventy-five/twenty-five.'

'My favor, or yours?'

I gave him a look. 'What do you think?'

'No good.' He folded his arms, started to spit, and recollected that he oughtn't to damage the merchandise.

I walked into the room and fingered the contents of several trays, working my way around the work table. I picked up a couple of tools idly, examined them, and set them down. I had made him wait long enough, I judged. 'All right, then. How about—' I met his eye and said quietly, 'Sixty/forty.' That was partnership wages. I owed him that, I reckoned.

He looked surprised, but covered. 'Decent of ye. I accept.' He spat in his hand and stuck it out to me.

I matched him, and we shook over the table. 'Now, one more thing: pick yourself out a stone.'

His shoulders squared, and he frowned. 'I don't take charity from nobody, giant. What d'ye want to give me a stone for? I keep telling ye, your life was bought and paid for!'

'I know. This is for Bruchan. Because you were his staunch mate.'

He looked away for a moment. 'Right enough,' he said at last. Licking his lips, he began fingering through the trays, as I was doing.

I searched in a couple of trays Timbertoe had named for a small stone, medium grade, of blue or green cast, and found one that looked right. I tapped Timbertoe's arm. 'Would you say this is worth a thousand gold?'

He hefted it thoughtfully, held it up to the torchlight, and nodded. 'Near enough. Sitric will be satisfied with it for certain.'

I put it in my sash pocket. 'He'll ask you where the mine is,' I warned.

Now the skipper did spit. It was answer enough. We picked out gems to take away with us, just a pouchful, as we didn't want to make it too obvious we knew where a hoard of the things was. It should be ample to get our fleet started. I gave it to Timbertoe to carry, and he tucked it down the front of his leather vest. Though there was no need, he showed me the stone he had picked for himself, a small emerald chalcedon of excellent quality.

I threw it back into a tray, took down a ruby gem of exceptional purity, as big as a walnut, and slapped it into his broad palm. 'I said take a stone, not a mucking pebble.'

'Look funny in me ear,' he said, but his hand closed around it quickly enough when I made as if to take it back. He swung up the pack and headed for the door.

'No, Timbertoe.' When he turned inquiringly, I indicated the other door.

'Want to see your mine, do ye?' he asked, knowing full well that wasn't it.

'Aye. We might as well, as long as we're here.'

'As long as we're here,' he agreed.

Beyond the door, the narrow confines of the tunnel leapt up and away into a huge cavern, a natural one apparently, with further passages showing as dark openings all around us. Two picks leaned by the door, and shovels, and a barrow was tipped up against the rough wall. Bruchan and Ruan had been the only ones who had known about the mine, he had told me.

'Look here, Giant,' Timbertoe said behind me.

As I turned, he pointed to the back of the door. I lowered the torch to see clearly. On the back of the door, where you would put a hand to shove it shut, there was a handprint, stained dark. 'He must have been surprised in his study, wounded, and made it to the round tower, after which the door was barred by the women,' I speculated. 'Probably they bandaged him: that would explain why there were no stains in the tunnel or on the first part of the stairs.'

Timbertoe nodded. 'And coming down the stairs opened the wound again.' He pulled at his braided beard. 'He was going someplace,' he mused, 'not just hiding. The tunnel would have done well enough for that. He didn't stop in the treasury, either, else there'd have been a big stain, plain to see.'

I closed the door behind us. 'There's another way out, obviously. I'd bet this cave system meets the sea cliffs somewhere on the peninsula.'

The dwarf cast a wary look up at the dripping roof and at the honeycombed passageways that opened all around. 'Body could get lost in here and be years trying to find the way out.' A moment later he looked startled as the ominous import of what he had said hit him, and his eyes swung to meet mine.

'I suppose so. Come, let's follow the trail he left.'

There had been torches in the mine itself. I had to try a couple of them before we could get one to light, and with this we supplemented the wavering illumination afforded by the one we had brought, which was now beginning to fail. Timbertoe gathered a few more as we went along, just for good measure. The one thing we could not risk was being left in the dark.

The trail led past the workings of the mine, where rich nodes fairly popped out of the deposits, and into the network of caverns and passages. Except for the main cavern, we saw no more chalcedons but the blood spatters were thick enough. He must have been hemorraging by this time. 'Have you got any sense of direction left?' I asked Timbertoe over my shoulder.

He shook his head. 'The tunnel and stairs angled east, down the hill of the skellig, that's clear enough, else we'd have hit the ocean cliffs pretty quickly. But now I'm turned about, for sure.'

'Well, there's no cave opening from Gull's Beach, of that I'm certain, so I'd guess we're headed north now, toward the Caldron.

That was sea water, and obviously fed from underneath. It rose and fell with the tides. Maybe this connects—'

'Nay, Giant,' he objected. 'Ye just said yourself the Caldron connects with sea water. If this place ran on to it, the whole place would be flooded.'

'These caves could be above the level of the Caldron's water,' I reasoned. 'We may not be very far underground at all.'

'I can't feel any air currents.'

'Nor can I, but the torches are reasonably steady, so the air is fresh enough.' I cast a glance back at him. 'How is the leg?'

'Fine,' he lied. 'How's yours?'

'Fine,' I lied.

Not long after that, the passage narrowed again, and there was evidence that the natural formation had been enlarged to make a walkable tunnel. I lifted my head. 'Air.'

'Aye. Felt it. We're coming to an opening, my guess.'

The tunnel took an abrupt right turn, on the other side of which the floor became paved with sand. Or rather it had been paved. Now the sand was scuffed to the bare rock below, furrowed in places, blurred with footprints, and stained black. In the midst of it all were the bones of my grandfather, the rotted gray cloak on top showing he had lain there face down. One hand was outflung, still clutching a fragment of black cloth, the other was trapped under him, and the back of his skull was cracked.

Timbertoe was examining the footprints. 'This must have been your grandfather. I recollect the skellig folk always wore those flat-soled boots ye made here.' His finger moved to describe a heeled boot. 'But this was someone else.'

There had been that thin thread of fresher air. 'Let's see what's further up here.' He followed me as I walked on, my eyes on the floor. 'Bruchan didn't make it this far. There's no blood.'

'Aye. But Heel-Boots never made it out.' The prints of the stranger went only one way, toward the place where they had fought.

I don't know how long it had been just below the surface of my mind, but suddenly I broke into a run, my torch streaming behind me. I heard Timbertoe shout a question, but I did not answer. The tunnel took another sharp bend, and I had to duck under a low lintel. The floor of perfect sand opened before me,

114

swirled with colors that made no picture, because the Wind in his fury had blown them awry. The alabaster bowl that should have held sweet oil and a moss wick was to my right; the vaulted barrel ceiling above my head by thirty feet was still sound; and a tumble of rock blocked the passageway out, the trap that was supposed to have caught Jorem and didn't.

My grandfather, dripping his life away, had struggled to meet me at the ancient temple, knowing I could not paint the story properly without guidance. He had not taken the women and children with him because he suspected what terrible power would be unleashed here and would not expose them to it. But it had already been too late by the time he had reached the turn of the tunnel back there, because the Door had already been opened to the Fire through my painting and Jorem, his priest, was looking for a way out of the blocked sanctuary. Bruchan must have run straight into him.

I had fallen to one knee. Now I raised my head to the dwarf, who stood under the lintel marked with the leaf, the sign of the Hag. 'You were right, Timbertoe. I should not have judged him till I knew.'

'Who was Heel-Boots, then?'

'Jorem. I thought I'd caught him when the entranceway caved in, but the trap must have sprung prematurely, or he was thrown clear into the apse here.' My mouth twisted. 'Another clever trick that didn't work.'

He came softly into the ancient shrine to the Four. 'There's an air channel up above somewhere?'

I nodded, running a trickle of the multicolored sand from my fingers. 'The window for the sun shaft at Kindlefest.' On the winter day when the Fickle Friend began to regain his strength, the rising sun cast its first light down the small channel in the roof of the temple. I knew where Timbertoe's thoughts had gone. 'No, Jorem didn't get out that way.'

'But he didn't follow the bloodstains out,' the dwarf said. 'The round tower would still have been on fire, and anyway, if that bastard had ever got to the treasury, there'd be nothing left in it.' He looked around the sanctuary. 'He must have slipped off into one of the chasms. No tears there.'

I rose slowly to my feet, dusting my hands, surprised at

the venom in his tone. 'I didn't know you knew His Grace so well.'

For a moment I thought he would say no more. Then he rasped, 'Know how I lost this foot?'

I nodded. Everybody in the fleet knew.

'No, not that codswollop about the innkeeper's daughter and him coming in with an axe. That's just—' He waved vaguely. 'A story. Something to amuse the lads.' The dwarf looked away. 'I was just a young sprat like you at the time, just starting out in the pirate trade. One day me and some of my mates got caught on a raid over here. Well, the local folk were all for stretching our necks for us right then and there, but their lord had just got hit up for more peasants to send to the slave mines, so he had the idea to send us instead.' He sniffed. 'Couldn't blame the man for that, did right by his own folk.'

The torch in his hand wavered in the slight draught from the window shaft. He looked into it for a moment, then continued. 'If ye wanted a taste of the Hag's Realm, Giant, that mine would be it, right enough. And what made it worse was this whoreson of an overseer.'

'Jorem?' I guessed.

'Aye, the pointed-toothed bastard. He enjoyed it, ye could tell.' Timbertoe cleared his throat. 'There was a young fellow chained across from me in the kennel – that's what the guards used to call it – who was simple, but he was strong as an ox, so he lasted. One day when they came through to feed us, an extra bit of bread fell out of the sack in the middle of the cell, and the gaoler didn't notice. Well, I was hungry enough, but poor Tommy used to forget to eat his sometimes and the rats would get it first, so I kicked it over to him and told him to eat it quick.'

His head went down. 'He always did as he was bid, Tommy. Jorem came down the aisle to unlock us and get us out to work, and there was young Tom, a hunk of bread in each hand, and him shoving it in his mouth just as quick as he could. Jorem beat hell out of him. Used a truncheon loaded with lead. I stripped my wrists raw on the chains, but it was no good – I couldn't get free, of course. So when Jorem finally stepped back away from the body, I kicked the bugger for all I was worth. Aye, smile if ye want, but it was worth it, all the same.'

'So he had them take off your foot.'

He nodded. 'Said if I didn't know the proper use for it, I could do without it.' He shook with his silent laugh. 'After that they set me to hauling the ore buckets up to the surface. Didn't need two good legs for that, only me arms.'

That explained his massive shoulders, broad even by dwarfish standards. 'I'm sorry, Skipper. I had no idea.'

Timbertoe sighed abruptly. 'Naught to be sorry for. I escaped from there alive, that's all that matters.' He eyed me. 'I'd just as soon the story didn't get told again, if ye take my meaning.'

'No fear there.' I gave him a wink in the torchlight. 'It's not half as interesting as the version about the innkeeper's daughter.'

He rasped a chuckle, and we both roused ourselves for the return trip to the world above. I gave a last look around at the shrine.

'Peaceful,' he commented. Then he seemed to recollect that my grandfather's remains lay just beyond the entrance to the Hag's niche, for he added, 'In spite of . . . everything.'

'It's empty, Timbertoe. There's nothing here any more.' The presences had gone with Bruchan's guardianship of them, I supposed. There was no sense that this was a hallowed place. 'Help me gather his bones, would you? I don't want him to lie alone here in the dark.'

'Be an honor.'

We went back up the sand-floored tunnel, and now that we knew better what we were looking at, the story told by the trampled sand was clear. Timbertoe lit another of his hoarded torches while I stripped off my jersey and knotted the sleeves to make a sack. Caitlin's bronze sugan was cold against my skin, and I wondered how she had fared all day amongst our rough crew. Very likely she had them all scared to jelly by now. My mind returned to the work at hand. Despite myself, my hand trembled as I carefully cleared away the tatters of the cloak. The spearpoint was still lodged in the rib it had driven into his lung.

'That will have been the wound he got on the stairs up to his study,' I told Timbertoe, who was stooping over my shoulder, holding the light.

'Aye. 'Twas a wonder he could stay on his feet all this way. Must have tried to fight Jorem off with the torch, eh?'

117

The stump of it showed through the shoulder blades that had fallen in on top of it. 'Maybe,' I answered, 'or maybe he deliberately flung himself down on the torch to douse the only light so Jorem couldn't find his way out with it.' While I spoke, I had been pulling the spearhead gently out of the tangle and casting it aside. In doing so, I jostled aside the bones of his right shoulder and revealed the hand that had been trapped under him as he fell.

Somehow he had scribed a single spiral in the sand.

My head snapped up like a look-out's that sights a reef only feet from the bow. 'By the Swan!' I scrambled to my feet, grabbed the torch from the dwarf, and ran back down to the shrine to be sure.

The color pots of Colin Mariner with which I had painted the Powers into the world four years ago, and which I had left scattered on the floor of the ancient sanctuary, were gone.

I know that I stared at the sand floor for some time before I was aware of Timbertoe's voice.

'—whoreson hell's the matter with ye, Giant?'

Drawing a deep breath, I told him, 'Jorem got the color pots. Bruchan must have seen them in Jorem's arms, so he deliberately smothered the torch with his body to prevent the Wolfpriest from following the bloodstains back to the round tower.'

'And then the bugger swung in the dark—'

'Kicked more likely. Bruchan was already down.'

'Aye. Kicked his head in.' He rubbed his nose. We were silent for a moment, then we began collecting my grandfather's bones. It was not a job you make small talk over. At last I picked up the skull and placed it gently in the improvised sack.

Timbertoe got up with a sigh of relief. 'Won't be sorry to get out of here.'

I did not look at him. 'Go back to the ship, Skipper. I have to stay a while longer. I'll signal you when I'm ready.'

He misunderstood. 'I'd like to help ye bury him.'

'And so you shall. But I've got to find Jorem's body and the color pots first, even if I have to climb to the bottom of this peninsula to do it, and even if they're broken when I get there.'

The dwarf stared, then wiped a hand across his mouth. 'Why?'

'Because Bruchan died to keep them safe. I keep his ring: I should keep the pots, too.'

He eyed me, his hand going absently to resettle the pouch of gems I had given him to carry, and then it dropped to his sash pocket to check that the ruby chalcedon was still secure. 'All right. I wouldn't mind seeing Jorem's bones, anyway.'

I met his troubled gaze. 'It must be getting on for late afternoon, Timbertoe. You'd better go topside and hail the boat.'

He knew what I meant, having seen Ruan's ghost himself, but he merely said impatiently, 'Come on, come on. Two can search quicker than one, and if ye do have to climb down some hole after the wretched things, I can haul ye back up.'

'I've only got the mooring line from the curragh.' We had left the long length of rope tied in the round tower.

'Then ye'd better hope he didn't fall too far, hadn't ye, Giant?'

I gave that the answer it deserved and stood up with the sack. We made our way past the sharp corner and back out into the network of the caverns. I noted the dwarf had his dagger in his hand for the first time that day and smiled grimly.

'Well, ghosts can't cross iron, they say,' he rasped defensively. 'I reckoned your grandfather and the other skellig men wouldn't hurt me, but if Jorem's about, I'd as soon not give him a clear shot at me.'

'Aye,' I agreed. 'You wouldn't be much good with *no* feet.'

He kicked me playfully in the arse with the pegleg, and that was exactly when a sudden clear, cold blast of air blew out the torch.

Instinctively we grasped for each other, then swung into defensive stance, backs together, daggers in hand. The utter blackness was almost palpable. He was breathing heavily. I could barely hear him over my heart. 'See anything?' Timbertoe asked hoarsely after a moment of tense waiting.

'No.'

'Bugger that son-of-a-whoring torch!'

'It's right here by my foot, I can feel it,' I told him.

His voice sounded nearly normal when he said, 'And I've got my firedog with me, so we're all right.' I felt him relax a little and turn around. There was a rustle of cloth. 'Where's your hand?'

I stuck both out, and we managed to find each other. I recognized the shape of the iron ring and its flint striker. 'Got it.' Crouching I felt for the torch head and managed to burn my finger on the still-hot pitch. I hissed a curse, struck the flint and iron together, and hoped a spark would catch. None did.

He had seen the flurry of sparks as well as I and now voiced my own thought: 'No good. We need tinder.'

In the minute while we racked our brains, it seemed to get much colder. Fear was doing its work very well, and Caitlin's words came back to me. The tiles had predicted the great good of finding the treasury. Would the second part come true as well? *It is not a warning of old deaths, Aengus.*

'Let me try,' the dwarf said abruptly and reached for the irondog just as I redoubled my efforts to strike a spark. Our hands crashed together, and the iron ring flew out of my fingers. We heard it strike the rock wall beside us, then ricochet away to jingle its way down a long, long fall. It landed with a bright metallic clink that echoed a bit, then died.

After a moment, Timbertoe cleared his throat. 'Got the flint still? Try your dagger with it.'

'I've already got it in my hand.' I scraped some sparks, but it was no use, they weren't hot enough to ignite the pitch.

'Codswollop.' I could hear him scratching. 'Be right handy if your old gent there could get himself up and show us the way out.' He snorted. 'Wouldn't ye know it? The one ghost we could have used is the one we don't see.' I think he was laughing.

Actually I was desperately hoping for the same thing. I felt for the wall to steady myself and gingerly stood up.

'What are ye doing?' the skipper asked.

'Trying to fray some rope. Maybe the strands will flare enough to get the torch going.'

'Good thinking. I'll try for the can – What the hell is that?' he asked at the same moment that my eyes, adjusted now to the perfect darkness, first picked up the dim spots of light forming a path that stretched away from us.

'An exit made for just such emergencies as this, maybe,' I speculated. 'I'm going to see whether I can get to the first spot.'

'Careful. Could light the way to a nice, neat trap.' He put a hand through one strap of the pack as much to haul me back if I started to slip as to guide himself.

We shuffled toward the first dot. I caught the illumination on my hand. 'Air holes to the surface, I think. The tunnel from the shrine was marked with the Leaf. Probably this goes to Swan Pool.'

Timbertoe spat into the darkness. 'Then the Wolfhound got out,' he said flatly.

'With my color pots.' I had not been tired till then.

The tunnel did, indeed, lead to the small freshwater pool where the women of the skellig had once held private observances to their Power. I had seen the Hag in her guise as the beautiful Swan, floating among the dark reeds once. The music of her wings had given me strength enough to save Gwynt's life.

I was saying as much over my shoulder to Timbertoe as we ascended the short flight of steps up from the tunnel. There was a small door which must, I thought, be cleverly hidden on the other side, possibly by a stand of the blackberries that had grown near the pool. I thrust it open.

The entire day had wheeled by. The sun was low behind the skellig which crowned its high ground three miles away over the rocky landscape. From here, it looked as it always had.

I looked down at Timbertoe. 'We could light a torch and go back through the mine to come up nearer the cliffs.'

He shook his head. 'Feels good to be above ground. But I'd suggest waiting to bury Bruchan.'

It's hard to tell when a dwarf is being wry, but I was pretty sure of it then. 'I don't think he'd mind spending one more night aboard your ship, Skipper.'

It was a long walk with the night coming on and Timbertoe not able to go very quickly with his leg. We had to be watchful for bog pools, particularly when we got to the other side of the rutted cart track that had been the main road up the peninsula to the skellig. I had seen a man sink in one and did not relish the thought of becoming a victim of the same kind of death myself. The sea air was cold against my bare chest and back, and the jersey with my grandfather's bones rattled disturbingly at each step. I wished I could have spared him this final indignity.

'Damnit!' Timbertoe finally exploded. 'Can't ye do something about that clicking?'

I stopped, shifting the sack, and opened my mouth to tell him to hold his water. The rattling came again. *From behind us.*

Our hands made the sign at the same instant. 'Company,' my old seadog said.

'Aye. A walker.'

Another rattle came from our left. 'More than one,' he said calmly. 'Piss off!' he suddenly shouted. 'Go back to sleep!' We scanned the thin turf, the rocks casting long shadows, the treacherous flats that looked like firm ground, but weren't. Nothing out there moved, not even the wind.

Though the day had been clear, mist suddenly seeped up out of the ground, or perhaps it rolled in off the sea that we could hear at our backs over a mile of bogland. In the time it took to exchange one glance and draw our daggers hilts-up, the chill gray was up to our shins. 'Run for it, Giant,' he said quietly.

'Codswollop,' I answered. 'We'll go together.'

I tied the sack containing the bones at my waist, put the bottle of Hag's Embrace and the chalcedon that was my blood payment to Sitric in my sash pocket, and pitched away the leather pack and tapestry. Timbertoe drew his cutlass. We put our backs to each other and began to crab sideways toward the sea. The mist was at our knees.

As the sun sank too swiftly toward the horizon of the cliffs, we could begin to see them: here the shadow of an arm gripping a lance, there a smashed and bloody helm turning on an unseen neck, and with nothing but black where the eyes should have been. The rattle and click of them all sounded like some gigantic game of tiles.

'They're waiting till nightfall,' I observed.

'Seems that way.'

The mist had reached his thigh, and the sun was a mere rind over the black cliffs. I reached back and grasped his shoulder, and we turned and ran.

For perhaps twice a hundred yards we went well enough, though at every step the dwarf was jarred cruelly when his pegleg thudded off the rock. Then we ran a splashing step, tried to skid to a halt, and nearly made it, but not quite quickly enough. The sucking bog was up to my knees before I hurled myself backward on to the solid shelf. Timbertoe landed beside me, straining to pull his wooden leg out of the squelching mud. He got it free, was up more quickly even than I, and we probed for the edge with his cutlass until we were around the pool. The rattling had stopped while we had fought the bog, or perhaps I just had not had time to hear it, but now it began again. The dwarf was waist-deep in the fog; the sun was down behind the cliffs, though the sky still glowed; we were near enough to feel the salt kiss of the sea, but had no hope of reaching it.

We went on at a quick walk, all we could manage and probe before us, too. A murmur of sound rose under the rattling now: voices, bloodless and thin, yelling through the veil for our living blood. The sky above us was cooling to twilight. A gray arrow, hissing as it came, buried itself in the mist by my knee.

Timbertoe panted, 'D'ye think their weapons can—'

A sword swept out of the graying air, and the dwarf parried it, sparks striking, then caught it on his guard and flicked the dwarfen blade around to sever the unseen wrist. There was a shriek over our heads, and the walker's blade spun into the blanket of mist, shrivelling as it fell. A lance whistled past my ear, so close I could feel the icy draught of it, and then they were everywhere.

'Take my dagger, too!' he said urgently. 'You'll need both.' I slipped it out of his sash and whirled to deflect a blade that was descending on his broad back. The shock of it sent splinters of pain up my arm, but I managed to hold on to the dagger, and whipped with my other hand toward where his groin would have been if he had been a living man. I heard him curse, I heard that plainly, and then his mist joined with the blanket that was at my waist.

'It's no good, we can't hold them all off!' Timbertoe said hoarsely.

An arrow whizzed between us. 'Give me the sack of gems,' I said urgently.

He thought I was going to leave him, I could see it in his eyes when he turned his head. Then, jaw set, he pulled the pouch from his vest and threw it at me. A sword nearly got to his ribs, but he backhanded a blow that knocked it wide and slashed for the head. There was a hiss, and the gray helm fell into the fog.

I slit the pouch and spilled a few of the gems into my hand. Now I took the first my fingers found, a chalcedon as big as an acorn, and threw it in a high arc behind us. At which, for an instant, the rattling stopped. A blade froze motionless an arm's length from my heart. In the evening sky a single star gleamed.

I ducked under the blade, thrust in my dagger, and spun away from the withering shape. The dwarf was beside me and we ran, heedless of the bog pools. If we had to stop again, we would die. We knew that.

In the rattling behind us there was snarling like that of a wolf pack disputing over a kill. The miserable bastards were as greedy in death as they had been in life. We could begin to hear the breakers booming on the beach.

But, of course, it did not hold them for long and their strength was waxing with the settling of night over the burren, while the day had been too long for Timbertoe and me. I threw another gem over my shoulder.

'—get you, and take it all, you bastard,' a voice said clearly close behind, and its owner struck a sideswipe blow off my pot helmet with a spear, so that I staggered. He followed with the spear shaft held like a quarter stave, slamming it down between my shoulder blades. Timbertoe was there suddenly, his flashing cutlass the last thing I saw before I pitched forward into the thick fog. Breathless and instinctively trying to break my fall with my hands, I splashed into a bog pool.

Even as the sucking mud tried to pull me under, I fought my face above the dank surface, fighting the instinct to thrash. It is the thrashing, the desperate fight, that makes the bog swallow its victims so quickly. If one can manage to float quietly, there is a hope of paddling gently to the side. So I had heard.

I spat the rotten mold out of my mouth, but I could do nothing about my eyes, and the sack tied at my waist was dragging me down. Panic nearly seized me.

'GIANT?' Timbertoe bellowed somewhere above me.

'*Stay back*, by the Powers! It's a bog hole!' The yell to warn him had cost me: my left arm slipped under, and I could not get it free. And if I worked at the knot at my waist, the motion might be enough to sink me.

'Hold on – I've got my sash.'

'Save yourself, Skipper.'

'No, we've got some time. I threw my ruby. There's a whoreson old fight going on amongst 'em, by the sounds of it. Keep talking boy, keep talking.'

'I'll get you ten rubies, Filthydwarf. And a leg carved of pure ivory.'

'Look some flash, wouldn't it? Now, here's the sash.'

Locked behind my mask of thick slime, I could only listen for it. Something may have broken the surface of the pool to my right, I thought. 'No,' I reported. 'Cast it more to your ri – no, left. Your left.'

'Left it is. Like casting for salmon with a net made of spiderweb, this is. Right enough, fish, here ye are again.'

I felt it, felt it tail across my outstretched right hand. I grabbed convulsively, but it was gone, and I only just got my hand free again as I sank in past my shoulders. 'Bad luck. You had it over my hand, but I missed my grip on it. I'm afraid I'm pretty far in now, Skipper.' I had tried to keep my voice steady, but he must have heard the terror.

'A little more left, then, and we'll have ye safely landed. Have ye got a hand free?'

'Yes.'

'Good lad. Steady on, now, here it comes.'

Something sodden, slimy, and gloriously stinking of wet wool slapped me in the face. I forced myself to move very, very carefully, and my hand closed around it. 'Don't move yet, Timbertoe. I've got it, but I have to wind it around my wrist.'

'Aye, lad, holding course.' His voice was freighted with relief.

I drew the sash up to wipe at my eyes and was able to get enough of the stuff off to squint. Then I did the best I could to wind a one-handed knot around my wrist and hand. 'All right. Pull.'

The sash snapped straight, throwing off clods of muck, and I turned my head, fist clenched on my lifeline. I began to move slowly through the ooze, the wound sash cutting cruelly into the bones of my wrist. Just as I thought I couldn't take the wrenching any more, my submerged left shoulder struck ground. 'I'm at the side. Help me out, by the Four!' I was eeling forward on one elbow, trying to pull my hand out of the tangle of sash and get a knee to solid ground.

Above me I heard Timbertoe grunt, and then he dropped the sash, and his hands came down through the fog to find my shoulders and pull me free. I dropped my head to the sparse grass and stones and kissed the earth.

'Boy?' His voice was strained. 'Can ye get up?'

'Here, old friend, I'm here.' I got my feet under me and stood. Only his face was visible above the level of the fog and that was hard to see, for the night had all but come. Nevertheless I stooped to give him a one-armed hug, clearly surprising him, because he stiffened, stood it for a moment, and then put me off. I swung to peer toward the sound of furious scuffling and snarling behind us.

'Aengus, I'm hit,' he said, and then he dropped into the floating fog.

I found him by touch and managed to turn him. He groaned as my fingers brushed the protruding stub. It felt like a slim lance head, and it had taken him in the right thigh. I couldn't tell how much of the slickness was the bog muck from my hand, and how much was his blood, but there was a lot of it, so a vein or artery was severed. The sash was all I had to work with, and I quickly tied it above the wound, knotting it tightly. 'Timbertoe, can you speak?'

'Aye. Drink, too, if I had it.' The words were right, but the weak tone was all wrong.

I ducked as a gray arrow streaked over our heads.

'Go on,' he said after a moment. 'It's in the bone. I can't walk.'

'Garn, it's a scratch, Filthydwarf,' I lied. 'Let's try to get you up.'

'Get out of it, Pilot!'

A spear stuck, quivering, not a yard away. The dark army was finding our range. They'd be on us with swords directly. 'I won't leave you. Your bad luck, Filthydwarf: you're going to have to die with me for company.'

'Anything but that,' he rasped, then gathered himself and

lurched up, weaving on my arm. We began to move slowly around the bog hole. The sack of bones dragged at my waist, and I kicked it out of the way at every step, not even thinking what was in it. I could pay it no heed in my urgency.

My charge staggered, and I took a firmer grip on him. The stars above were mockingly, painfully beautiful. They had been that way the night I carried Gwynt by Swan Pool. Timbertoe was much heavier. I could not carry him, and neither of us had our weapons left. I cast a look back, and confusedly thought I was seeing swarms of fireflies at first, but then I realized that they were eyes. After that, I did not look back again, but I could hear those behind me rapidly closing the gap.

Timbertoe's bad leg went suddenly, the muscles out of control. I leaned him half over me and dragged him for yards, straining for breath. A sword lifted before us, gray against the night sky, and started its flashing descending arc.

Suddenly she went over us, graceful neck stretched toward the sea, and the wind a sweet music in her wings. I stood stock-still while the gray sword withered above my head, barely noticed. I had nearly convinced myself in those four years that I had dreamed those wings, that music, but she had been real then. She was real now. Strength flooded me, and a kind of rarified happiness. I got Timbertoe under both arms, pitched him across my back, and started after the Swan.

She circled, slanting low across my path, and then – as she had done on that other night – led me surely across the starlit burren. I knew the walkers were all around, but their eyes were no more than distant harbor lights, and their fangs only the faintest pricks of cockleburrs. And so we went down to the sea.

CHAPTER EIGHT

I had it from Ries later that the crew had waited for us through that long day with mounting impatience which, as sunset neared, turned first to anxiety and then, with the rising fog, to dread. That there were unnatural things in this fog which shrouded only the land and stopped at the cliffline as abruptly as if it had been cut with a knife, they did not need the witch to tell them. Looking up once from honing his dagger, Harrald had seen, or thought he had seen, pale flames shooting from the windows of the round tower, and Ries himself had watched through the spyglass as three specters slung another's limp form from the high wall to be swallowed by the heaving breakers.

Caitlin had held a low-voiced colloquy with the hunchback, then tucked up her skirts, climbed into the remaining curragh, and challenged someone to come with her. When the men looked to Jamie, the quiet man had shook his head, and the lads had mentally saluted the witch's savvy: they would have pulled up anchor and sailed, but the mysterious woman's servant would prevent it, probably with her spells to help him subdue the pirates. The setting sun had cast a gleam as red as blood on her face, Ries said, and the men were afraid.

Then Neddy, his hands visibly shaking, had uprooted himself from the deck hatch where he had been crouched and got into the boat with her. He signed the crew to lower them away, and they did. The murmured opinion among them as the pirates watched the boat draw away was that of them all, the boy could best be spared. The witch could take care of herself, and was nothing to them. They made everything ready to sail, which Jamie allowed, then settled silently to wait. They would give the witch and the boy half an hour, no more, they told him uneasily: night was falling, and though it is commonly known that walkers cannot cross water, they did not feel it prudent to

129

test the lore. He told them quietly they would stay as long as necessary.

I confirmed the next part of the tale with Neddy, because it was difficult to credit, and I thought Ries might have been trying to make more of it than was really there. According to Ned, he and Caitlin had rowed into Gull's Cove, and she had told him to let the curragh drift, but on no account to land it unless she told him to do so. The tide was ebbing, the sand shore plainly visible in the twilight. Our boat was drawn up above the high-water mark, but there was no sign of us. Caitlin had muttered, Neddy said, and scanned the cliffs above. They had listened, hearing a faint, far-off clamor of what sounded to the boy like seagulls, but Caitlin may have known more, for she was very pale.

They waited a long time. The stars came out, and the phosphorescence of the water breaking over the rocks guided Neddy as he fended his way through with an oar, sometimes having to back water to keep the curragh from beaching. The siochla had her head in her hands. The boy wanted to tell her that the mother ship would leave them, but he didn't think she could read his signs anyway, so he did not disturb her.

At some time in the night the boy came to, staring awake over his oars to realize that they had beached, and the witch had jumped into the surf. He stood up and gave her what passed for his yell, a croupy-sounding forcing of air over the stump of his tongue, but she paid him no heed. Cursing fluently in his head, Neddy splashed ashore, drew up the boat, and went after her.

Caitlin had seen me – or more likely heard me – coming down the beach from the rocky point which arched around the cove opposite the skellig. Ned was fleeter than she and was at her elbow when Timbertoe and I came out of the night. At first the boy did not recognize us: we were all dark, he explained, and he thought he was looking at a hunchbacked walker. He made the sign against evil and pulled his dagger, but Caitlin stepped forward to meet us.

Timbertoe was slung across my back, unconscious, and I was shuffling at no more than a child's pace, head down, making for the curragh we had left that morning.

Neddy belted his knife and grabbed to help me with the skipper. I suddenly seemed to come to life, giving the boy a vicious shove and swinging my arm to bring my hand in a knife-edged blow toward his ducking neck. But Caitlin spoke a soft word – Neddy couldn't hear what it was – and I raised my head and looked at her for a long moment, though no expression came or went across my features. After that I let them help me with Timbertoe.

Somehow we got him into the curragh she and Neddy had come in, being careful not to touch the wounds which were discovered in shifting him off my shoulders. And then Caitlin turned to me. I was standing on the shore, black with mire and bleeding from a dozen different places, and I was staring up in the direction of the skellig, though even in daylight I could not have seen it from such a distance. Caitlin then said quietly, 'Come, Aengus. Get in the boat. There is no more to do here tonight.'

But I turned instead to the beach, walked a few steps on the sand (at which the siochla stood anxiously and seemed ready to go after me), and then fell to one knee. Neddy said he strained to see what I was doing but Caitlin looked for a moment, then went to sit in the bow and hold Timbertoe's head. A few moments later I came to the boat, stepped into it, and sat staring woodenly past the boy.

Ned pushed us off into the water and bent to his rowing. According to him, I collapsed off the seat and lay unconscious in the bottom of the boat before it had cleared the cove. He said he jumped to my aid, but the witch told him to let me be and, after making sure that I was still breathing, he sat down again. She told him to row as if all the walkers in the Hag's Realm were after him. Ned took her literally, picked up the oars, and pulled for dear life.

He had not expected the *Inishkerry Gem* still to be there, but it was – with running lights showing fore and aft, the red and green lanterns giving him a steady mark to row for. When the curragh came nearer the ship, Ned saw that all the sails were up, the starlight softly illuminating the sheets swollen with the night's wind. But the ship was dead in the water, straining like a dray horse trying to move a load too heavy to budge. There were cries of fear on deck as the curragh was sighted slowly approaching, but the witch hailed the ship across the water and told them to stand by to take us aboard. When the crew was sure the boat contained only the people it should, men came down the cargo net to help.

Ries had not liked taking orders from the siochla, but with me down she was the only healer aboard, so they did as she said. The sack made out of my jersey was left on deck, after they had discovered what was in it. I was washed, the curious striped wounds on my legs and chest laved with some ointment from the witch's pack, and put to sleep in my bunk. I did not wake. One of the married men said he wished he had that easy a time with his kids.

They carried Timbertoe to his cabin, where, according to the bos'n, the witch stripped the pegleg as matter-of-factly as if he'd been an ear of maize for the pot, examining the striped wounds briefly, then carefully probing at the stub that was crusted with blood. She snatched her hand away, though Timbertoe did not make a sound, and Ries, who was holding the lantern for her, did not understand why until she washed some of the blood away and he realized the thing was made of bone. The witch and her hunchback exchanged a glance but said nothing and, shortly after, Jamie went back on deck, leaving Caitlin to be assisted by Neddy and Ries while he relayed news to the men and generally made himself useful trimming the sails and relieving Harrald on the steering board from time to time.

It fair made him sick to watch the operation, the old bos'n confessed, but he had to admit the siochla seemed to know her business. The lance head broke, the tip remaining in the thigh bone and, as Timbertoe had already lost so much blood from the nicked artery, Caitlin elected to close the wound and hand him over to more skilled healers at the Vale.

Afterward the witch bathed the dwarf, annointed the other wounds as mine had been treated, and left her critically wounded patient for a short time to see to me. Ries kept watch over Timbertoe, changing the bandage pads where the blood welled up through the sutures until at last the sluggish trickle congealed, and he barked at Neddy in a tone reminiscent of the skipper's own to fetch more blankets.

For the remainder of the night, the ship, freed of the restraint Caitlin had put upon it, ran with the westering wind. The men gathered in the stern at the steering board with mugs of flotjin and a hedge of iron daggers stuck in the decking all around, just in case something had slipped aboard with us. No one would go near the sack of bones to sling it off the deck into the water, though nearly everybody agreed it should be done. Neddy was fed too much liquor and plied with questions about what had happened on the beach.

It is a fact that to the end of their days, the men who were aboard the *Inishkerry Gem* that night reckoned the whole experience one of the great adventures of their lives and spoke pridefully of how their captain and pilot had braved an army of walkers to steal a treasure out of the haunted skellig, for they had found Sitric's chalcedon and my grandfather's ring in my sash when cleaning me up. The small amber bottle they ignored, after sniffing it.

Be sure the story grew in the telling over many mugs in many pubs in many ports, and the legend of How the Pegleg and the Giant of Inishkerry Screwed the Walkers became a stock tale for wandering storytellers and their painters to perform at fairs. I heard it myself many times under other more respectable titles and once King Beod, who knew the truth and was possessed of a great sense of mischief, bade me paint it for the assembled nobles in his wartime headquarters at Caer Ronin. I did the painting for him and captured something of the true nature of the experience, I think, for when I was done the young men were pale in the torchlight and the king himself was making the sign. I was never asked to paint it again.

Neddy cast me a sidelong look as he signed me the end of the night's record, I remember. I asked him quietly what else there was to tell. The boy looked away, began to sign something then changed his mind and motioned, *I didn't know you were a painter.* Though I remembered nothing of it, I think I knew he was going to tell me what he had seen just before he rowed us around the jut of land separating the cove from the open sea: there on the sand, glowing softly with some silvered light that may have been starlight or may have been its own, the Swan I had sketched watched our departure with bright and living eyes.

That part of the tale never found its way into the pub stories.

I woke an hour before sundown the next day to a flash of cold and stinging pain. Some sort of strangled protest must have come out of me, because Harrald's nervous eyes and garlic breath were suddenly in my line of vision. 'Sorry, Pilot!' he gasped. 'The witch said to do it!' A sponge dripped in his hand.

'What the mucking hell—?' I got up as far as my elbows and realized I was alive, certainly, and in one piece, relatively.

'She said the salt water'd do them stripes o'yours good, honest she did!'

Maybe, but salt in a raw wound is not comfortable and I had so much hide stripped off my chest, I looked as if I had been flogged before the mast. I must have glared at him, because he backed off and let me fight my way to a sitting position. He wiped his nose on his sleeve and gestured with the sponge. 'What kind o' weapons did them walkers use, anyway?'

'Teeth, I think,' I answered absently, having some dark nightmare memory of fangs, and eyes flickering in the fog. His mouth went wry and for a moment his hand crept toward the bucket out of sight under my bunk for sickness. 'How is Timbertoe?' I demanded, suddenly remembering.

'He ain't good. The witch is with him, has been all night and day. Neddy's been in and out of the cabin, fetching water and such. He says the skipper hasn't roused at all.'

I swung my feet over the side of the bunk. 'Where are my clothes?'

He snorted. 'There weren't much of 'em left, Pilot. We kept your sash, but pitched the pants.' He cleared his throat uneasily. 'Your jersey's on deck, but I'd rather not fetch it, if it's all the same to ye. And you're not supposed to be up and about yet, anyway, the witch says.'

I got my feet on the floor and braced for a moment, then lurched for the cabin door.

'All right, all right! Don't go out there nekkid in front of her!' he blurted. 'Here, then. Which do ye want?'

I turned carefully. He had flung up the lid of my sea chest. It was packed with trousers, jerseys and vests, most of them clean, apparently. 'What's this?' I asked. 'Did you scum go on a raid while the skipper and I were nearly done to death up there?'

'No, no. The mates just, well, they all wanted to give something, y'know.'

I got it then. They all wanted to be able to boast that I had borrowed a pair of pants or a shirt, and bled walker stripes all over it. If I hadn't hurt so much I would have laughed. I picked out a shirt I recognized as one of Ries', which would be broad and short on me, cooling my wounds, and a pair of dark loose trousers of Neddy's since he was the only other long-legged man on the ship. Then, since Harrald's eyes were disappointed, I said, 'Let me borrow your sash till mine is dry, will you?'

He lit up like a lantern.

A few moments later I went along to the captain's cabin, bracing my hands against the companionway and shuffling like an aged landlubber. At my light tap, Neddy opened the door. He made a delighted gesture, stepped aside to admit me, and shut the door in Harrald's inquisitive face. Caitlin looked up, her expression lightening. She vacated the stool for me. My knees were suddenly so weak, I let her do it. 'How is he?'

People in his state can hear sometimes, they say, so instead of replying aloud, the siochla said in my mind, *Failing, I'm afraid, though he is putting up a strong fight.*

'Neddy, would you mind asking Jamie to let us have some tea?' I requested to get the lad out of the cabin. When he had left, I reached with my good hand to take one of Timbertoe's limp and cold ones. 'Come on, you're not going to earn those ruby chalcedons this way, Filthydwarf,' I said to the still, gray face. 'And who the hell else am I going to get to skipper my fleet, hey?'

Caitlin put a hand on my shoulder, saying nothing.

I mastered my face and looked up at her. 'It got the artery?' At her nod, I asked, 'What kind of point was it? I couldn't see much in the dark, but it felt odd.'

It was bone. I saved it. Look. From a piece of linen lying on the small table she unwrapped the long tapered shape, jagged where the point was broken. In the dimness of the porthole's light it seemed to shine dully with some evil influence. Caitlin handled it gingerly through the cloth, not letting her fingers touch it. 'Is it like the other you saw?' She did not mention Diarmuid, and neither did I.

'Exactly. But the men who attacked me in Skejfallen used something like this, and they weren't walkers.'

'Perhaps the servants of the Wolf have some commerce with the dead,' she mused.

135

'Is such a thing possible?'

She flashed me a glance. 'Oh, yes.'

I didn't ask how she knew. Everyone in the Burren knew the rumours that the siochlas spoke to the dead through their Mistress; if the women could do it, I wouldn't put it past the Wolfhounds to try.

Caitlin made to seat herself on the floor, but I wouldn't allow it, changing seats with her instead. 'Tell me,' she said then.

'A moment. We're sailing for the Vale, I presume.' At her nod, I asked, 'Will your healers there be able to save him?'

She did not try to comfort me with empty hope. *I don't know. I think not, he lost so much blood.* Aloud she said for Timbertoe's benefit, 'I feel sure of it. Let him sleep now, and tell me what happened back there.'

So I swallowed and began. Jamie came in shortly afterwards with tea and a nodded greeting to me. He handed a mug to his mother, and to me, and then he leaned on the captain's desk to listen. I told it all, even about the chalcedon mine. The prince's eyes widened in the light of the lamp he had lit as the cabin darkened, but there was no predatory interest there as I read him.

Caitlin was the first to stir. 'I think the sisters at the Vale would be honoured to have Bruchan interred there, if you would allow it,' she said softly.

'Only temporarily. When I'm done with Jorem, I'm taking my grandfather back. I've got a lot of work to do at the skellig. There's much to be mended.'

She did not seem at all surprised at my resolve to get the color pots back. I suppose she thought for a painter that would be a natural urge, and she could not know I was color blind. She must have heard the brittleness in my voice, though, for she said as though it were a continuation of a thought, 'And he alone of all the principal people of your skellig days did not appear?'

'I didn't see Padraig or Fin, either.'

'But you needed to see Bruchan.'

She had my measure there. I looked away.

'I think it's as well you collected his bones and brought them out of there with you,' the siochla said reflectively.

'Why?'

The sugan on her breast caught some stray gleam from the dying sun outside the porthole. For a moment I thought she would not answer, but then she said cautiously, 'Aengus, we . . . there are ways of journeying to the borders of Mistress' Realm. Sometimes our loved ones who have gone on before us may meet us there, and we may have speech with them.'

Gooseflesh poxed my skin. Behind my back, I made the sign. 'And Bruchan's bones may raise him, you mean?'

'Yes.'

'Then there's a chance I can get the storyteller back!' I did not realize I had spoken the thought aloud until she nodded. My hand shook, and I covered it by clutching the tea bowl. Immediately the possibility that I might be able, finally, to do the right painting to lay to rest my skellig folk burned in my mind. The fact that Jorem was alive and had the color pots seemed a mere trivial nuisance. I would get the pots. I would paint what Bruchan, that magnificent storyteller, dictated. I would be Aengus the Painter once more.

Caitlin was holding up one hand at the hope she must have seen blazing in my face. 'I say only that it is possible, but I make no promise.'

'Will they have the power at the Vale to do it, even if – if Bruchan doesn't want to see me?' That thought had belatedly occured to me, the heavy weight of guilt descending on me once more. Surely my grandfather would hold me responsible for the deaths of all our people, and just as surely he would never have approved of the revenge I took in their name.

'The Maid of the Vale, Ritnym's Daughter, is greatest among us in wisdom of the Mistress. If anyone can find Bruchan's spirit, it will be she. In fact, I am summoned to attend her.' That was news to the hunchback, too, because his dark eyes swung to her.

'Summoned? I thought you were fleeing the king's men.'

'I was, when we left the cottage. But last night, waiting for you, I heard the call go out for all siochlas above a certain rank to make their way home to the Vale.' *The voice can be used at great distances by those of highest rank.*

'I see. How far is it? I've no rutter for the Vale.'

'Oh, only a day or so.'

I stared. 'That's impossible,' I said flatly. 'We pirates know every inch of the coast from the Isles of Wyvin to—'

'The Vale is difficult to find if one does not know the way,' she interrupted, smiling slyly.

'Ah. Magic.'

She shrugged, but would not say.

My eyes went to Timbertoe. 'A day is a long time, sometimes.'

'Tis a lifetime, sometimes.

I hauled myself to my feet and stepped to the door. The cabin boy, half-asleep, was sitting outside it. 'Neddy, where's the stuff from my sash?' He signed that it was in the bottom of my sea trunk. Nobody would touch it, he hastened to add. 'You recollect a small amber bottle?' He nodded. 'Fetch it, and by the Four, be careful with it.'

When he was gone, I told Caitlin about the Hag's Embrace.

Harrald sidled up to me where I stood with the sounding line in my hand as far in the bow as I could get. Though Caitlin had assured me the bearings she had given me were accurate, I didn't like the thought of a place that could suddenly appear nearly under the bowsprit without anyone being the wiser until the keel was ripped open and you found yourself drinking a lot of seawater. So I was tossing the leaded line every few minutes. Even a magical place must have shoals around it, I reasoned.

'Say, Pilot, what's the news with the skipper? How come ye won't let nobody get a glimpse of him but Neddy and yeself?'

'Harrald, if Timbertoe woke up and found you gawping at him, he'd punch your nose in, and you'd spend the rest of your life eating your own snots.' I swung the sounding line. No bottom. He sidled away more quickly than he'd come.

As I pulled the line in I heard her light footsteps behind me. I glanced back. 'How is he?' I barely mouthed it, mindful of the eyes all over the boat.

Caitlin clasped the pin in her cloak and brought the hood up around her head, for there was a brisk wind and the morning haze had not completely lifted. *I have no idea.* Aloud she said, 'Sleeping, still,' so she had seen the men's heads turn to us. At her words, one of them resumed whittling at a piece of ivory, and another sighed and cast out the fishing line to troll behind us.

'That's good – he needs it,' I said, playing out the charade. Actually, there was a very real chance that the pegleg was dead.

If he'd been a healthy man when we'd given him the drug, there would be no question: discovered by Nestor, the drug counterfeited death, causing no detectible heartbeat or motion of the lungs. Its effects lasted for only twelve hours and left no lasting damage. I had taken it once myself and given it to Jorem as part of a ruse to persuade his army to break off its attack on the skellig and withdraw, so I trusted what Symon had told me about it. However, to give it to a man who was already dying . . . I had tried to decrease the dosage, but when the dwarf shuddered and the breath left him with an explosive sigh, I had shaken so much that Caitlin had reached for the bottle to rescue it.

That had been at the turning of the watch early last night. Timbertoe should have wakened when the dawn watch came on two hours ago, but he had not. I had stayed by his bunk as long as I could stand to, and then I came topside to swing the line and tell myself I was doing something useful. Caitlin said something quick about the coma's possibly being extended if the patient were already unconscious when given the drug, but I did not wait to hear it.

Now I forestalled anything else she might say about it. 'If your bearings are right, we're near the Vale now.'

'Do you think to tell with that line?' she asked, clearly amused, as she leaned on the rail. The wind brought the red to her cheeks, stripping years off her countenance. The old tales of her were true: she must have been quite beautiful when Diarmuid had taken her to be his queen.

'No, it's a way of fishing. You plunk the flounder on the head with it.' I was rewarded with her laugh. The strain of the previous day and night lightened in her eyes a little. I hauled in the line. 'Well, they're not biting today, I guess. Enough of that for now. Have you eaten?'

'Thank you, yes. Neddy is a most attentive host.'

I stood beside her at the rail and sniffed deep. For mariners this is often a way to tell whether they are approaching land. Now that I was paying attention, there was a faint hint of rotten egg.

She must have seen my nose wrinkle. 'It's part of the magic,' she said lightly.

'What, is your siochla place built on an abandoned rookery? Phew!'

'It's not so bad when one's in the Vale itself. It doesn't happen very often, and when it does the wind blows it out to sea.'

I got an image of darkness streaked with red rock running and fountains of sparks that blew up into a night sky. 'A fire mountain.'

She looked startled and gave me a sharp glance. 'I should have known I couldn't keep it from you, Painter. Tell me, can you see any of the rest of the Vale?'

After a moment of blankness against the sand floor of my mind, I replied, 'No.'

She tucked back a strand of hair that had blown loose and said tartly, 'Good.' I got the impression it would spoil her pleasure if she hadn't the chance to show it to me first, so after that I did not try to see it in my mind.

Jamie came to join us, and I wondered what he must be feeling so near a place where, perhaps for the first time in his life, he would be safe and acknowledged a prince. His weathered face was as broad as any countryman's, but there was a light in his eye one doesn't often see where men are strapped to the wheel of unending toil with no hope of something better. I made sure none of the crew was close enough to hear and murmured, 'It will be good to be beyond the Wolfhounds' reach, Your Highness.'

He smiled a little at my use of his title. 'Aye,' he replied. 'I'm happy for Mother.' After a moment, he sighed. 'It doesn't smell like home, though, does it?'

Having just come from Inishbuffin's salt wind and bog, I knew exactly what he meant. 'No, and there will be early lambs this year, I'm thinking. Will one of your neighbors bring them in for you?' It did not seem odd to discuss such a thing. He was a man of the land, as I had been in my skellig days. As Bruchan had taught me a king should be, I suddenly remembered.

We stood in the bow, peering into the haze ahead.

About a quarter of an hour later, Caitlin told me, 'You'll want your men to stand by now.'

I turned to Ries, who was watching from his post at the helm, and made the closed-fist straight up. He yelled the order. 'All hands, stand by to make port!'

Heads jerked up, and I saw the crew darting looks to all points, then confusedly leaning to ask a mate what was going on, since no land was visible. In the crow's nest the look-out leaned down to shout, 'Bos'n, there ain't no—'

And then, in the blinking of an eye, we had broken through the sulphur haze to lighter water under our keel. We were racing between the outstretched arms of a wide harbor with the fire mountain rising conical to our right, a terraced height to our left, and the Vale itself straight off our bow behind the tall masts of a sleek barque that blocked the sea lane not a hundred yards distant. We were going to pile it up.

'Into the rigging, into the rigging, damn you!' Ries was yelling, while the helmsman stared open-mouthed.

I was already jumping for the yards of the mainsail, which were tied off on cleats at the midship rails, one to either side. 'Duck!' I yelled over my shoulder to Caitlin and James as I slashed at the line and cut it free. Somebody did the same on the starboard side, and the yards of canvas flapped wildly, held now only by the topmast yardarm; but without that swell of sail to catch the wind, the *Gem* slowed dramatically, driven forward only by the small triangular sheet at the bow and her own momentum.

I went up the rungs of the aftdeck ladder to help Ries lean on the timber of the huge tiller. Straining in every muscle, we fought the steering board, while the masts of the other ship loomed before us. We could see some of their crew jumping from the starboard rail, and others, their faces contorted in the curses they were yelling, scrambling back to be away from the point of impact. It flashed through my mind that Neddy could never get Timbertoe out of his bunk without help.

Then, very slowly, the *Gem* answered her helm. We slewed past the other ship at not much more than the width of my cabin, and wallowed toward the docks.

'Whoreson pirates!' shouted a voice filled with outrage from the steering deck of the other ship.

'Get your damn arse out of the channel, then!' I yelled back. 'What do you think this is, your own private bathtub?'

'This is the *Crown Prince*, you imbecil!'

I glanced to their flag, which did indeed show a crown against a white field. Posh name for a ship. 'And this is the *Inishkerry Gem* out of Jarlshof, bound for the Vale! Next time, get out of our way, or we'll run you down!'

'You tell him, Pilot!' Ries growled.

Whatever else I might have told him was forestalled when Caitlin motioned toward the dock. 'Head for the anchorage on the left, Bos'n.'

'Aye, Pilot. I've got her now, thanks.'

I jumped down the ladder to the main deck. Caitlin met me, and I twitted her, 'Your bearings were a little off, mistress. Next time you pilot a boat in, try to give them enough warning of the harbor so they don't get killed.'

'I'm sorry. We must have had more wind at our backs last night than I thought. That was a nice piece of seamanship,' she added.

I spat the taste of fear out of my mouth. 'Thanks. I always like to make a dashing entrance to a strange port.'

Jamie laughed. His mother smiled, and she and I went below to check on the skipper.

Neddy had stayed at his post in the cabin, though he was white as a sheet, having heard Ries' frantic bellow ordering the men to the rigging and having felt the peculiar heeling of the boat. If there is anything a sailor fears, it is being trapped belowdecks in a wrecked ship.

'Relax, Ned. We're almost at the docks,' I told him. He stepped aside to make room for us beside the bunk. Timbertoe looked dead to me. I touched a finger to where the pulse should have been in his throat, but he was as cold as a winter sea and if his heart still beat, I could detect nothing of it.

'I have sent already for a litter from the house of healing,' Caitlin said, looking down at the pegleg.

'You—? Oh. Right. Will it take long for them to come?'

'No, they will be on the dock to meet us. The hospital is the large building on the low hill just right of the harbor. At least that *used* to be the hospital, though perhaps they've built a new one. I have not returned to the Vale for nigh thirty-five years.' Her voice had fallen, and the blood in her cheeks raised by the wind was fading. I saw that there was none of the relief I had expected at her arrival in this sanctuary. Indeed, she seemed strained in a way she had not been when we'd seen the Dinan ship sail into the cove below her cottage.

'You left your training to become Diarmuid's wife,' I guessed, 'and things were said because of it.'

If she minded my presumption, she did not retort. 'It is permitted, sometimes, for Vanui except the Maid to marry – but it is looked upon as a lapse.'

'And so, for this supposed transgression of yours, my lady, the siochlas would not give shelter to your son when you fled at the king's oaths? Where is the sisterliness in that?'

She bit her lip, suppressing a smile. 'You're a sweet boy, Aengus, but you're very young still.'

I felt about six, and my cheeks grew hot. I have always had an infuriating tendency to flush. To change the subject, I cleared my throat and nodded at Timbertoe's still form. 'Folk say your siochla healers use magic.'

'Folk would say that, wouldn't they?' Her glance crossed mine briefly as she straightened from placing a hand on the dwarf's chest.

'I'd like to go with him, Caitlin.'

'Certainly. We will see him up to the hospital, and then we are both requested to go to the Motherhouse. It seems the Maid knows you're here. She says to bid you welcome.' Caitlin extended her hand. 'Welcome, then, traveller, and may you find here the answers that you seek.' She held my hand for a moment. 'That's the traditional Vanu greeting.'

'I have enough questions, surely. Neddy, can you get me a pot from one of the other men? I lost mine, and I don't want to startle any of the ladies ashore.'

By the time he was back with one, we were at the docks. Caitlin and I went ashore, but James stayed on the *Gem* with the pirates for company. Until the queen knew how he would be received, she had no intention of subjecting her son to unwelcome attention, she explained briefly as the litter bearing the skipper was carried from the deck by four strong orderlies.

It would be easier to paint it for you – the Vale as I got my first good look at it from the terrace of the great house of healing where Caitlin and I waited for the siochla in charge of Timbertoe's case to finish her examination of him. Though the season in the Burren, scarcely a day's sail away, was still making up its mind whether it would be spring or remain winter, here there was a warm breeze and bright sun, and things were blooming that I should not have expected to see for a good two months more. I would have to add the colors to my painting on hearsay, but Caitlin had a good eye, and in any event I could imagine the shades.

In the foreground I would lay down deep navy water, shoaling to bottle green as it met the shore, and dotted with ships that swung at anchor, their flags snapping in the breeze. Ships of lands I had never even heard of. Then, beyond the harbor, I would show you slopes climbing to meet a high rampart of hill, a rim wall that rose on the south to cup the Vale. Those slopes were clothed with orchards and groves, and I would paint them brown and ash-gray and white for the trunks, and above them the canopies of leaves would be rounded shapes of loden, lime, and beech with heavy boughs laden with pink and white blossoms, for the Vale was blessed with good weather, or perhaps the siochlas made it so.

To the right of the harbor, I would sketch a sprinkle of village, well-built of whitewashed stone, with red clay tiles to roof the houses. I would have to pull out all my brightest colors to paint the windowboxes adorning each cottage: cascades of lemon yellow, coral, and violet blue – with here and there a bright splash of scarlet. It would be fun to do those flowers, and it would give you a true picture of the place, for the Vanui were gardeners without peer and early fragrant blooms were everywhere, even on the stables.

Next, behind the village and still further right, the open Vale itself: the saddle of low land which swung to connect the orchards with the vineyards on the fertile slopes of the fire mountain. Here I would need to mix new colors, I think, to do even a semblance of justice to the checkerboard pattern of fields, the planting and care of which was one of the principal works of the Vanui. Here were propagated nearly all varieties of grain, vegetable, fruit, or flower useful for medicine, food, or beauty. The siochlas sent out their workers to collect seeds and cuttings from all the known world – and even from places which are but fables to commoner folk – to study the plants and find what uses might be made of them, for the Mistress they served was the Power of Earth, and these flowers, fruits, nuts, and berries, her children. Just now the food and grain crops were still young, but I might take the liberty of painting those fields as they would be at midsummer, white for camomile, clear blue for flax, ruby for tea berry, and greens so varied the eye would refuse to see them individually and would run them all into one sweep of verdant carpet.

Like a castle surrounded by its cultivated lands, the main buildings of the Vanui community would appear in the midst of the painted patchwork of fields, set on a knoll so perfectly domed in shape that you would recognize instantly it was not a natural feature of the landscape. But in this you would be wrong, as I was wrong when I first saw it. The little round hill was the boss of the Vale's brooch, green with lawn kept carefully mown. If I were painting the scene larger, you might get a hint of the other face of the Power they served, for I would suggest the entrances, many and black-doored, to the crypts that honeycombed the hill.

I would not paint the fire mountain, for it would be behind you as you stood looking at my picture, and since it was on the northward side no shadow of its cone would appear in the scene.

Lastly, at the very bottom border of the painting, I would add the round leaves and perky, hooded shapes of the potted nasturtiums I was looking at when the siochla healer came out on to the terrace and told us Timbertoe was alive.

You would pardon it, I hope, if a sprinkle of golden sand from the flowers suddenly leaped to tinge the navy water of the harbor.

I upset the stool getting up, and an elderly woman, gowned in bedclothes and leaning on the arm of a man I took to be her son, smiled kindly as they passed. 'You're sure?' I demanded of the doctor, a siochla named Neilan.

She was unruffled at my tone. 'Oh, yes.'

'But there's no sign—'

'None that you could detect with the naked eye or ear.' The tall, angular woman with singularly clear skin smiled and pulled from the pocket of the apron she wore over her robe a crooked shape that I recognized as a ram's horn. 'But I can hear his heart with this. He lives, I assure you, though I will not make you any false promises: he is very near death.' She spoke quietly, with compassion. I could see she was trying to tell what was in my face behind the scarf of my helmet.

'Can you save him, mistress?'

'It is with the Lady. We will try. The broken point still in the bone troubles me.' She turned to Caitlin. 'You have given him a new drug, I understand, sister?'

It was one of the things we had hurriedly told the nurse who was waiting to receive us in the hospital portico when we'd arrived. Caitlin explained now its properties and effects and, as nearly as we could tell, the dosage I had administered.

'Actually, *I* gave the dwarf the drug, mistress,' I said when she was done. 'I prenticed with a healer in a skellig, and the Hag's Embrace was my idea. I don't want Mistress Caitlin blamed if . . .'

'I see,' the healer said, looking from one of us to the other. 'Then neither of you knows what the drug is distilled from?'

'No.'

'Hmm, that's a pity. It appears to have useful properties. Well, then.' Neilan stuck her hands in the pockets of her apron. 'We shall adopt the safer course of not administering stimulants which may war with this new drug. There are other medications against infection which may safely be given, however.'

'How?' I asked. 'With him stiff as rigor, there's no hope of getting a potion into his mouth or, er, the other end, either.'

'I have instruments to manage that.'

I studied my interlocked fingers for a moment. 'Haven't you any magic that can save him, mistress, beyond the medicine?'

She looked at me for a long moment. Then her eyes flicked to Caitlin, and I knew that some message had passed between them. 'As to that, what can be done is already begun.'

Caitlin touched my arm. 'Come, Aengus. Let him sleep.'

I asked the doctor, 'May I return later to keep watch?'

'Of course. Come and go as you please, as long as you do not disturb the other patients. Incidentally, you should have those stripes of yours dressed.'

I looked down at Ries' shirt to see crimson blotting through it in some places. I must have ripped them open again in the exertion to avoid hitting that ship in the harbor. 'I'll do that, mistress. Thank you.'

She nodded, grasped Caitlin's hand briefly with a warm and personal smile, and went back into the hospital. She was not of an age to have known the queen when Caitlin trained here, but

146

it was clear to me that the healer knew her story and did not hold circumstances against her.

Caitlin and I walked toward the flight of stairs that led from the terrace to the main entrance. A harsh croaking caw startled me, and my hand jumped as I saw the raven flap overhead. The shock of seeing the Hag's familiar here while the skipper fought for his life hit me like an icy wave crashing against a seawall.

Caitlin's cool fingers came across my wrist to break off the sign I was making. 'We don't do that here. Come. She's waiting.'

I cast an angry glance at the black bird winging over the harbor through the gulls, rewound the scarf across my face and wished I could make myself look more presentable to meet the witch of all the witches, the Maid of the Vale.

CHAPTER NINE

At the head of the steps a man whom I supposed a servant awaited us, smiling. He was silver-haired with an unlined face and pale eyes, and he was dressed in robes of some lightweight material, softly lustrous. The silver torque about his neck gleamed in the sun as he advanced out of the shade of the Motherhouse to meet us. 'Give you warm welcome, Mistress Caitlin.' He'd a rich voice, a singer's voice.

The queen was plainly delighted to see him, for she grasped both his hands in an affectionate squeeze. 'Thank you, Eril.' She drew me forward. 'This is our guest, Aengus.' I knew why she'd made haste to introduce me: without my name, he might have thought I was the 'Monster Prince'.

I stuck my hand out to him, but he was bowing, so after a muddled moment I did the same. He looked shocked for a fleeting instant, but then nodded gracefully. 'We have looked for your arrival, my lord. Allow me to extend our sympathy for the grievous injury to your friend the dwarf.'

Now, he had certainly seen my bloodstained jersey and ill-fitting pants, together with my pirate's sash and the pot helmet, so although I appreciated the words about Timbertoe, I was nettled at the 'my lord'. Wishing for a drink, I rejoined shortly, 'Thanks. And it's "Pilot". That's my rank.'

He inclined his head. 'As you will, sir. Pilot.'

Caitlin may have sent something to his mind, because his brow, which had knit a little at my tone, suddenly smoothed and he nodded slightly to her. She said to me, 'Lord Eril Silverstar is Eldest of the Yoriandirkin, the folk with whom we share the Vale, and chiefest of the Maid's councilors.' *And he's never met a Jarlshof tar before. Try to make it a nice experience, will you?*

There might be rich trading here in the future, that was a consideration. I brought my hand to my breast in the skellig's gesture of respect. 'Thy pardon, sir. I'm afraid I am somewhat out of my depth here.'

Eril smiled, a gentle relaxing of his unlined face. 'It is no matter, Pilot. The water is not deep.' Even through the concealing scarf, he must have read my sudden grin. He beckoned us with a gesture. 'The Maid awaits you in her garden.'

For the first time, Caitlin faltered. 'Her garden?'

'Indeed, my lady.' His glance flicked to me, then returned to the siochla. 'She wanted to see you both the moment you were finished at the house of healing, and just now she has taken the hour of leisure to work in her garden.' He extended a hand to indicate the way with a wave and bowed us onward.

'What's the matter?' I murmured to Caitlin as we walked through a cool colonnade.

'The Maid's garden is in the private portion of the house, that's all.' She glanced up at me and smiled a little shamefacedly. 'I suppose I had been dreading having to brave everyone's eyes in the council hall, but this will be a very private meeting. I don't know whether to be relieved or not. I do not know the current Maid personally, and I have brought Jamie here without her invitation. It will be . . . awkward.'

'There's a pirate proverb: If you're going to drown anyway, ye might as well drink deep and be satisfied once.' I gave her my arm as I had seen mummers do at fairs when they were mocking the nobility. For all I knew, it might have been actual court etiquette.

The queen smiled, put her hand on my arm, and we promenaded after the Yoriandir lord through linked courtyards where bees simmered in the herbs and the wind came off the harbor smelling lightly of salt. Caitlin pointed out to me arched entrances leading to the scriptorium and library, the great hall where the siochla council met to entertain embassies or petitioners from foreign courts, guest quarters for such visitors, and many workrooms where seeds were dried and stored. This was just the public portion of the vast, rambling structure. The mistresses' quarters and the temple were beyond a wall further up the slope, she told me, and that way visitors were not ordinarily permitted to go.

I suppose if I had been familiar with the place it would not have seemed a long way from the entrance to the low wall which marked the separation of the Motherhouse precincts. Here Eril nodded to one of his mates who was evidently the door ward, and the latter swung open the ironwork gate after a sharp glance at me. We passed through and immediately the feeling was different. I understood why when I glanced around at the one-storied ell with its individual cells, each with its flowerbox, at the lime-trunked apple trees, the shady arbor, and the line of hedges with washing drying in the sun. The part of the Motherhouse lower on the knoll was for show; this part was for the women's private lives. A cat twined about my feet as we halted for a moment for Eril to blow some sort of signal on a small silver whistle he pulled from his pocket. Caitlin, who had unpinned and removed her cloak, lay it across Eril's arm and smoothed her hair, explaining, 'Men are not usually allowed inside the cloister. The whistle is to let the sisters know someone is here.' Out of the corner of my eye, I saw a linen shift hastily plucked off the laundry hedge and tucked behind the skirts of a stout woman who stared for a moment, then whisked through a door. Thereafter, I kept my eyes guarded as much as I could, though my natural curiosity was urging me to look around. I did not realize Eril had withdrawn until Caitlin gestured me on.

Crowning the hillside at the highest point inside the precinct walls was a mosaic façade showing an intertwined extravagance of fruit, flower, and leaf, with a wide, dark entrance which must give on to the crypts. This would be the temple to the Hag, I surmised. At first I thought we were headed for it, and I was about to tell Caitlin I'd rather not go in if it was all the same to her, but then we veered right on a gravelled path lined with stone lanterns unlit at this midday hour. This we followed through a grove of resinous-smelling pine, and came suddenly around a curve of the path to find ourselves in an open garden above the Vale, bordered with low stone walls. In the midst of it was a snug cottage, thatched and built of stone given a lime wash, with the bee skep on its bench and smoke trickling the smell of new bread into the sea breeze. A small pool reflected the sky, two white swans paddling complacently. It was as homely a place as I have ever seen, but hardly what I had expected for the leader of the Vanui.

Caitlin dropped my arm and called toward the woman who stooped half-hidden behind a clump of blue sage, 'Mistress, we are here.'

There are moments which forever afterward remain frozen in one's memory, bright-edged and charged. For me, this was one of them. The siochla bending to the flowers straightened, stepped to cast on to the compost the spent blossoms she had been deadheading, and turned. Across the neat beds and the pumphead trickling water our eyes met. Eyes green as the summer sea, peaches in her cheeks, hair as shiny and black as a wet seal, she stood there: the girl I had seen in the pauses of my coma four years previously. Rose, the girl Timbertoe had told me never existed at all. 'That old bas—' I started to swear incredulously, and my crooked jaw locked.

Neither of the women had heard. Rose was saying quietly in answer to Caitlin's hail, 'I know. I heard the whistle.' She dusted the dirt from her hands on the apron she wore over her white robe, and I became aware that beside me Caitlin had fallen into a deep reverence, head bowed to the much younger woman. If Rose was at all surprised that I did not make her any sign of respect, she did not show it; indeed, her eyes began to twinkle as I stared. 'There's tea and bread. It isn't much, but it might hold a Jarlshof tar till supper.'

She approached to raise Caitlin with a sisterly kiss of greeting. 'It is an honor to have you back among us, lady. The Vale lost a jewel in Mother's crown when you were shunned. Though I cannot undo the past, I would propose we try to lay it to rest. Be welcome indeed, and Prince James with you, and give no thought to the priests of the Wolf. I don't.'

The two women were much alike, I thought as Caitlin's eyes brimmed and Rose comforted her for a moment. Both had the same clear, direct glance, and the same grace of person, and both were strong. I had seen Caitlin's strength, and I could sense Rose's in a certain tilt of her head and in her speech. But where the queen's beauty had mostly mellowed to the kind of textured loveliness some older women have, the Maid of the Vale was still very young and without doubt the most bewitching woman I ever met, and I do not intend that as a pun.

It was not just her raven hair, tied back just now with a scarf, or the dark brows that tilted over heavily lashed eyes, not the blood springing healthily in her cheek, or the sheen of her lips, or form sweetly ripe. This was part of her allure, but only part. There was intelligence and pride, too, and perhaps most endearing, a certain wild and unbroken dangerousness, like a tabby who reminds you with one swipe of a ripping claw that she is, after all, only putting up with your pretense of owning her. Rose was altogether intriguing.

She stood arm-in-arm with Caitlin, and then gave a hand to me, looking into my eyes above the scarf. 'It is my honor to welcome you, my lord of Inishbuffin, though I wish we might have met under more pleasant circumstances.'

I thought she did not know me, and disappointment cut as keenly as a knife. *Again*, I tried to get through my still-locked jaw to tell her that I knew her, oh, I knew her, but only a distorted grunt came out.

Her eyes softened. *I'm sorry, I didn't know the jaw hadn't healed cleanly.* So she did recognize me! 'I'm sorry,' she repeated aloud for Caitlin's benefit. 'Do you think you could manage the tea, at least?'

Belatedly I made her the skellig's sign of respect. 'It's no matter, lady, it doesn't happen much,' I said, the painful creak as my jaw straightened an audible click over the drip of the pump. 'And the bread and tea sound wonderful.' I gestured at my stained clothing. 'Thy pardon for my appearance.'

'They are honest clothes, my lord, but we'll find you some others later.' *I would appreciate your not mentioning our previous meeting to anyone.*

I gave her a nod. Now, after the first shock of seeing her again, my sense was returning and with it a crushing disappointment. Just my luck. Wouldn't you know I'd do something as stupid as get my heart in a flutter over a woman who was vowed to the Hag? Behind my mask, I smiled bitterly.

'—grandfather well. He was a welcomed guest here, and we were sorrowed at his passing,' she was saying when we stepped inside the cottage, which was like any other well-kept home.

She looked no older than I was, and to my knowledge Bruchan hadn't made a trip here while I'd been at the skellig. So if she remembered him, she must have been only a girl at the time of his last visit. She was speaking on behalf of the Vanui, then. I glanced at Caitlin. 'And so was I, lady. So much so, in fact, that I have only just gone back to Inishbuffin to seek his resting place.'

She had been leaning, reaching to take the iron water-kettle off the fire. Now she suddenly snatched back her hand and whirled full to me. 'By our Lady! You went *there*!'

She had heard tales of the ghosts that haunted the place, then; that was my immediate thought. 'Aye, lady. Yesterday.'

'*Yesterday!*' Rose's eyes went to my bloodstained jersey. 'Then Timbertoe was hurt by *walkers*?'

As I nodded, the older siochla unhooked the purse at her girdle. 'I saved the weapon to show you, Mistress,' she said. 'You should know that Aengus has seen these in the hands of Wolfhounds, incidentally. I have good cause to believe on his authority that my hus— that Diarmuid ap Gryffin was killed with one not long ago.' She had carefully drawn the lance head from her purse and now held it on her palm, a fold of cloth between the bone and her skin.

The Head of the siochlas went white so suddenly I thought she was going to faint, but she threw up her hand in the sign of protection against the Hag that Caitlin had told me they did not make here. 'Drop it!' she gasped.

Caitlin dropped the thing hurriedly on the floor. Hard as the beaten and swept earth was, the jagged edge stuck upright, and the lance head quivered in the shaft of sunlight from the open door. Then it began to tilt toward Rose, for all the world like a serpent questing its head back and forth to find the range of its victim.

Rose abruptly gestured toward it, making a fist, and for a moment a pure white light glowed through her skin so that the veins showed delicate as tracery in alabaster. Then a stream of that cool light leapt from her fist to the walker's lance head and, in the space of a heartbeat, burnt it to powered ash.

My bad ear was ringing like chimed crystal, and my head pulsed with pressure while flashes of rainbowed light shot across the sand floor of my mind to show a woman. It was this woman but not this woman, lying in a bed richly draped with a white velvet pall encrusted with blue-green stones in the shape of a rose, in a room that, I thought, bent around her and began to shrink, and my heart was riven because I knew that the queen was dead.

'Aengus, drink this. Come, drink it,' a voice was saying through the chiming.

I could not see, but I groped out blindly, and she set the cup in my hand and guided it to my lips. The stuff was sweet as almond cake, cool as well water, and it cleansed the fear from my mind and sickness from my lips. The chiming dulled and became the tinkle of wind bells outside her window. 'Thanks,' I said thickly. 'It's all right now.'

Her hand left my wrist. I blinked several times to clear the last of the blurriness and took in the empty cottage and the small pile of ash on the floor. My pot lay on the table. 'I sent Caitlin away,' she said quietly. 'I've put an injunction on her to say nothing of what happened, at least until after the council meeting tonight. I'd rather you were presented to them at the proper time, and in the proper way.'

I wiped a hand over my face and reached for the bowl of tea that steamed on the table before me. 'You have a ring like mine.'

She smiled. 'Say rather that *you* have a ring like *mine*, and you will be closer the mark.'

I sipped. 'I can't do—' I gestured to the burnt cinders. 'That with mine.' There was a question in my voice which hung in the air until I looked at her over the rim of the bowl.

'Yes, you can.'

Some of the tea sloshed on to the table.

'It is not the ring which has the power, Aengus. It is you, yourself. The chalcedon only focuses it. It is the stone's unique property. You can sometimes hear a humming or ringing, can you not, or a kind of music?'

'Yes, but I thought it was because of what I did to my head.'

She fetched a rag from the wash bucket and mopped the table. 'The injury may have forced your brain to some other kind of hearing to replace what you lost in that ear. At any rate—' She pitched the rag into the bucket and began slicing the round loaf on the board before me. 'You and I seem to be the only people who can hear the music of their own aura.' She drew the crock of butter toward her and thickly plastered the bread, smiling

155

at some secret remembrance. 'It's how I was chosen Ritnym's Daughter, in fact.'

I got a scene of her, younger, black pigtails flying and mouth open in a terrified shriek, racing out of what seemed to be a dark sanctuary where a stone set in gold had suddenly flared against the altar stone. The sands dissolved.

She was sitting across the table from me, head a little cocked, studying me intently. 'Is it Sight?' she asked.

'I don't know. A couple of times I've seen pictures, sands making paintings in my mind, and I know what I'm seeing exists, or has happened.'

Rose nodded thoughtfully. 'And do you ever paint things that then come true?'

Thinking of the woman in the funeral bed, I answered, 'I hope not.' But, strictly speaking, I had not painted her. Then, my brain still slow, I looked up.

'You mean when I paint with the ring on? I've only ever done it once.' I looked away from her eyes. 'And that was a disaster.'

'Will you allow me to ken what happened from your mind?'

No, I would not do that, because at the end of the story she would look up through a haze of drugged pain and see herself as I had seen her. I cleared my throat. 'I'll sketch it for you. The charcoal from your fire will do.'

So I ground some peat charcoal between my hands and began to paint Ritnym's fair form, clad in robe and girdle of straw sugans and standing in her springtime garden, a welcoming smile on her lips. And the deep, wise eyes of Aashis of the Wind, with his porpoises and streaking stars, and his tower of crystal at the edge of the world sea; and Tychanor the Warm Fire – young mischievous, lord of the sun in his high Valley where the sunmill turned in the thousand greens and the hundred yellows that were the Meadows of Morning.

I hesitated, crushed blackest charcoal, and swiftly drew a grinning wolf's head with behind it fire . . .

I got no further. Rose's foot came down to rub out that part of the painting. When I looked up she was rigid. 'You painted the Wild Fire as well?' She shook her head, staring at me now as had others who only saw my gargoyle face. 'Oh, Aengus, how could you?' she breathed.

156

'It is not possible to leave Him out, my lady. His power—'

'Is evil, and you have loosed it into the world!'

I rose to my feet. 'I painted the Powers as they appeared to me.' My voice was cold with trying to hold the fury in check. 'Maybe I didn't do it well, and maybe the painting would have been different if Bruchan had been there to tell the story. But you cannot have sunlight without shadow, and you cannot have the Three without the One who opposes them. My grandfather believed that.'

'And he suffers for his belief now.'

My head began to pound. How dare she presume to judge him! I did not trust myself. 'I'm going down to the hospital.' I grabbed my pot from the table.

'Painter!'

I would not face her, my hands shaking with anger as I rewrapped my scarf. 'The next time you have anything to say to me about my grandfather, you'd better be sure you know what you're talking about. He was a good man, the best either of us has ever known, I'll wager. Don't you dare tell me he's not at peace in the Hag's Embrace, Witch, because no man ever deserved it more.' I took a step from her threshold.

'Aengus, he's not there.'

I turned to find her clasping the gold sugan at her throat. She met my eyes steadily. 'Your gift is to see pictures. Mine is to hear voices, voices from beyond the Gate. I ken the dead, Aengus. That is why I am Ritnym's Daughter, because I can hear the Lady and those in her gardens.' That tallied with what Caitlin had said on the boat. She came to me and looked up to meet my glowering, and now fearful, eyes. 'And what I hear is screaming and cries for help from the dead, who say the Mistress is gone.'

I knew what she was going to say with dread certainty.

'The gardens are laid waste, Painter, and the Dark One reigns there now. You gave him no realm in your painting, nothing to confine him, so he took what he wanted. He is lord of Death and my Lady is gone, where I do not know, but your grandfather has gone with her. Did you not know that the Master of Skellig Inishbuffin has been the Lady's Lord Protector since Colin, who was her consort? And that the Mariner was brought here to die of the poison his treacherous brother gave him, but lived by the Lady's grace, though he was never the same man again?'

I was struck to stone.

'No, I thought that might be news to you,' she murmured.

The vision or dream came back to me. 'And when he died, you put him on a boat and gave him a mariner's funeral, sending him off in a high-prowed ship, black, with a Swan pennant over his head.'

Her lips parted a little. 'No. He was not dead when he went aboard that boat, Painter. But he could no longer bear the weakness of his body, so the Reverend Daughter of the place at that time gave him what he wished: a boat with a single sail, enough food and water for one last meal, and no rudder.'

That was not the end of the story as Bruchan had told it to me, as it had come down to Colin's wife and small son from the lips of Macguiggan the Bold, the Mariner's loyal captain and friend, but I could understand the lie, and I could understand the disgust at the body that had betrayed him and which had impelled the Mariner to choose suicide rather than live a shadow of his former self. I could understand that very well.

With a silent gesture, she invited me back to the table. 'Now, Caitlin has kenned a report of her suspicion that you are the Haunt we have heard so much about, and I assume that's why the Wolfhounds chased you to her sanctuary?'

I explained a little of it, but about my private revenge I told her nothing. She didn't seem the sort to understand murder, so I simply told her there was a young boy being abused by the master of that skellig, and I went in to get him. Then she asked about the bone points, which brought up Diarmuid and the stalkers in the alley at Skejfallen and the guildmaster. 'So I went to Inishbuffin partly to get a chalcedon to pay the bugger off so he won't turn me in for the reward, but mostly . . . well, to go home. I found the treasury, but we had to throw all the gems at the walkers to draw them off us long enough to make it out. The Swan came and led me back to the boat.' I finished the tea, now quite cool but still good, and watched her. She was thinking. 'Lady, what are these bone points? I can understand their power in the hands of real walkers, but why have the Wolfhounds adopted them?'

She looked up briefly, then returned her gaze to the table top. 'To explain that, you must know what walkers are, Aengus.' The Maid of the Vale gathered her thoughts. 'When folk die, their shades normally turn their steps toward Mother's Realm, a turning as natural as a flower following the sun. But sometimes the shade becomes confused, or simply refuses to leave this world, and then folk call them ghosts, walkers, or the Old Folk because they do not want to give them the power of a name.' She saved a hand slightly. 'Whatever they are called, the essential thing for us to understand about them is that they are not quite living and not truly dead. We Vanui have a special charge to try to bring these unfortunates to Mother's Realm, and thus I in particular try to talk to them and see if I can set them at peace.' Her eyes came up to me. 'But, because they are between Earth-Above and Earth-Below, their mortal remains have unusual and frightening powers. If a walker's bones should come in contact with a living person's, not only will the living person die, but his own shade will be unable to find Mother's Garden and so it will become a walker, too.'

I know I had gone pale. 'Timbertoe!'

Rose reached then to take my hand. 'No! We will not let him go that way, not by all the blossoms in the Vale, I swear it! Even now, the fight goes on for his life, believe me!' She dropped my hand and sat back. 'Believe me,' she repeated.

I did, but my blood still ran cold with dread. 'By the Four, poor Pers,' I murmured. 'And King Diarmuid, even that old fox.'

'Ah, there is something else at work in the king's case, as well as this business of making new walkers. This is the seventh year, after all.'

'Three times now I have heard the same phrase, once from Brother Ruan's shade, once from Caitlin, and now here. Do I guess correctly that the seventh year refers to something special about this year's Vanu's Eve ritual?' The feast of the dead was the only thing I could think of that was celebrated only once in seven years.

'Indeed. You have attended Vanu's Eve in the past?'

'As a boy, at the big town in our district. The only things I really remember about the last one are the bonfires, the wild colors of the caskets, and being beaten by a man who thought I was trying to pinch his offering.'

She smiled a little. 'Were you?'

'Of course. We were hungry, and I figured the dead didn't need the loaves.' That would have been the year before I went with Bruchan to live at the skellig, the last year with my father, when he was drinking so much.

Rose laughed, then suddenly sobered as though she recollected something. 'Then you know something of the meaning behind the dark festivities of that night, but unless you have been to Cnoch Aneil on Vanu's Eve you could not know all of it.'

My hand jumped to make the sign. 'Folk don't go to Cnoch Aneil. It's the Hag's Threshold. To set foot on that mountain brings death.'

She smiled. 'Except that on Vanu's Eve in the seventh year, the Maid of the Vale ascends the mountain and performs there the most sacred of our rites. It is not normally permitted to speak of it, but for Colin's heir I think I may suspend the rules this once.

'The most ancient holy place we know is under the summit of that hill, a vast tomb, if you will. No plan or map of it exists, of course, but we know that it has two entrances and a way clear through the maze that links the two of them, if the Maid can find it. And find it she must, because on Vanu's Eve she goes into that underground crypt with no lantern or light, accompanied by the king, or a stand-in for him. Usually this is a painter, since part of the ritual involves the making of three paintings. She journeys to the Gate of Mother's Garden, and the next day, on Mother's Morning, she returns. She must come forth from the other end of the maze, bringing Mother's gift of Spring to Earth-Above. We symbolize it with a seed, usually a bean. The Maid gives the seed to the king, who gives it to his people. By that sign folk know that the Gate between Earth-Above and Earth-Below has been opened once more for their departed loved ones to pass to Mother's Embrace and be reborn.'

'And if the Maid can't find her way out?'

Only the sound of the wind chimes broke the silence. After a moment she answered, 'Then there is a new Maid for the next seven years, and Earth-Above limps along without Mother's blessing until the ritual is completed.'

'The Maid who climbed Cnoch Aneil seven years ago didn't make it through the maze, did she? And this being the seventh year – no, the fourteenth – you believe the power that sustains the earth has grown weak. That's why this winter has been such a fierce one, and last summer's harvest was poor.'

Rose nodded. 'And why, if the ritual is not completed this year, there will be famine.'

Even stripped of its ritual significance, her assessment was an accurate one. From the misery I had seen as the Haunt, I knew she was right. If the Burren did not have a good harvest, many, many people would die.

She rose from her seat at the table and went to take a piece of paper from a stool by the fire. 'Now look you,' she said, returning to put the paper before me, 'how the Wolfpriest thinks to play his hand.'

Jorem's writing. I recognized it at once from the letters we had intercepted from him to his spy Cathir at Skellig Inishbuffin. I tilted the letter to the light of the window and read:

From His Grace Jorem, Servant of the Flame, Regent of the Burren, to the Maid of the Vale, Greetings in the Name of the Wolf.

You will have heard by now our grievous news, Reverend Daughter, and we know you mourn with us the loss of His Majesty, King Diarmuid. But by the Wolf's providence, we have a strong heir to the Gryffin throne, the late king's nephew, Lord Leif ap Gryffin.

It has come to our attention the Vale has long rumored one nearer in blood to Diarmuid still lives. I refer, of course, to the peasants' stories about the Monster Prince. Please be advised, dear lady, that we would take it most ill if the Vale sought to promote the ascendency of any other person. In fact, I would venture to suggest the lives of your sisters in this land might be in danger from certain factions who would certainly not tolerate what they would view as unconscionable interference in our affairs.

I feel sure you will bear this in mind when making your decision not to conduct any rites on Cnoch Aneil this Vanu's Eve. In plain, we want none of your siochla magic here.

We are convinced your mind will be as one with ours on
this matter.

I looked up from the letter. 'So every siochla in the Burren is a
hostage against the possibility you would come out of the crypt
and give the seed to James.'

'Exactly.'

'Whoreson bastard.' I regarded her. 'Can the ritual be performed anywhere else? Here, for instance?'

'Sometimes it has been done at Croagh Raven, but that is not
for the making of a king. Only Mother's Gate at Cnoch Aneil
above Dun Aghadoe is strong enough for the kind of power we
need to summon this year.'

'You'll tell him you won't do it, of course, and then try to sneak
in. It's the only way.'

'I can't just sneak in, Aengus. The people have to know I'm
coming so they can bring their relatives' caskets for the rite. No,
I'm afraid His Grace will be disappointed. There will be a Vanu's
Eve ritual this year. I have already written to tell him so, and my
sisters are even now spreading the word amongst the folk of the
Burren.'

I stared. 'He'll execute as many siochlas as he can find. You
know that.'

Her lovely face was set. 'Yes. And the terrible part is that it
will mean nothing in the end. I cannot open the Gate. I told you,
Mother is not in her Garden. The Dark One is there. All those
spirits waiting for the Hag's Embrace would be consigned to his
instead, and he would never let them be reborn. As Maid of the
Vale, I cannot do that, not until I'm sure Mother's Realm is freed.'

'Is there a ritual for that, too?'

'No, no ritual. This has never happened before. But we have a
Painter who, as you just told me—' She gestured to my charcoal
sketch on her floor. 'Knows what the Realm should look like, and
may be able to restore it with the Consort's ring and his color
pots. Will you come to Cnoch Aneil with me?' She misunderstood
the sudden sick look on my face. 'For I do believe you are Colin's
own hands returned to us, Aengus, despite what I said. The fact
you could empower the Fire by your painting in the temple
proves—'

I held up a hand. 'Rose, I have something to tell you. I'm sorry to dash your hopes, but I can't paint.'

'But you—' She nodded at the sketch, puzzled.

'That was only sketching. I couldn't use the color pots even if I had them: I'm color blind.'

She was rigid, then she sank into her chair, her gaze touching my crooked face and sliding over to the sunken place on my head. 'Mother bless you,' she whispered. 'How can you stand it?'

'I try not to think about it,' I replied shortly. 'So, if I can help any other way, I'll do it, but you can't count on me for painting, my lady.'

She blinked and looked away. 'We have very skilled healers here. Maybe . . .'

'After so long? Not likely. The splinter embedded in my brain will stay there, and it's no one's fault but my own.' She was silent, and I could see she was biting her lip. I couldn't stand her pity. 'There is another thing I don't think you've considered. If you don't do the ritual, how will you raise Jamie to be King?'

'I cannot give him Mother's blessing without the ritual, Aengus, but I can make him a king, Lady willing.' She left it there.

'You would need an army to do that.'

Unexpectedly she smiled. 'I have one.'

'Eril's people? No doubt they are loyal, but—'

'No, the Yoriandirkin are our personal guards here in the Vale, but their protection is not of a martial nature, and, anyway, they are far too few to launch a war.' She got up then, and went to bank the fire with ashes, for the time of the evening meal was drawing closer. With the council after that, it would be late when she came back to her cottage for sleep. At least, that is why I thought she had gone to busy herself with poker and shovel. 'We have allies, however, powerful ones some of them.' She put a heap of ash on the peat and said no more.

I felt it like a sword stroke. 'The Ilyrians.' She did not answer, nor did she have to do so. 'You're going to give my country to the River Men.'

Rose did look up then. 'Certainly not. When the Wolfhounds are broken, we will put Prince James on the throne.'

'Ah, yes, the Monster Prince.' My voice was harsh. 'Do you

163

seriously believe Fergus Fairhand of Ilyria will conquer us and then hand the crown over?'

She stood dusting her hands, and her chin lifted. 'That is exactly what I think.' A sly smile touched her lips. 'I have him under a geis.'

I snorted. 'And his heir, what's his name, Beod? The Burren would make a nice principality for him, wouldn't it?'

Her eyes slid past me to the window with its view of the harbor and the terraces on the other side. 'Beod will accept James's pledge of fealty to him as overlord. Beyond that, he will take this war as a special obligation out of the devotion he has for . . . the Mistress.'

That might have been what he'd told her, but I'd wager he was in it for the spoils. My poor Burren was going to be ripped apart. 'The cure looks to be as bad as the ailment.'

Her eyes flashed. 'What would you have me do, then?'

I stood and put the chair carefully back under the table, picking up my pot once more. 'I'd turn the bloody Wolfhounds' own magic against them, keep your Ilyrians on a leash, and send one man in to kill Jorem.'

She shook her head slightly. 'Too late, I'm afraid. The invasion forces are already gathering. In fact, this council meeting tonight is to solemnize the pact. And, anyway, you can't do it alone, Aengus.'

'No, but the Haunt and I can do it together, and in such a way that Jamie will have something left to call a kingdom.' I jammed the pot on my head, adjusted the scarf, and asked, 'Will you speak to the council on my behalf, lady?'

'The Master of Skellig Inishbuffin is a member of the council. You'll have the chance to present your plan to them yourself, but I warn you: they are a difficult group to convince.'

'So are pirates, and you'd be amazed at some of the things I've talked them into. I'll see you after your banquet, then. I'll be with Timbertoe.'

'Word would have come to us if there had been a change in his condition. Let him be.'

She still didn't get it, so I gestured to my face and asked pointedly, 'Look: would you want to face this across the board at some posh dinner?'

Rose looked surprised, and I knew that in just one afternoon she had learned to accept my countenance, to be untroubled by my face. She raised one brow. 'Well, I fully intend that you should be beside me at meal, my lord of Inishbuffin, and the rest of the guests can go hungry if their stomachs are so delicate. You must be presented to them *sometime* and at least at the banquet they'll have their food to attend to.'

'But—'

'Yes, we've got something for you to wear, too, so you needn't use that for an excuse. In fact Eril is waiting for you in the pine grove to take you to your quarters.'

I rubbed my nose, a gesture I had picked up from Timbertoe. 'And my mates? Are they going to be treated fine, as well?'

That stopped her for a moment. Then she said, 'I'll have word sent out to your ship immediately that your captain holds his own and that the crew is welcomed ashore, if they wish to come.'

'Dare to come is more like it. They're probably sure by now that the skipper and I are both spellbound. But they're a hardy lot, and where there's food involved, I think they'll brave it.' I added, 'And have your messenger tell them something from me: I will personally see to them if anybody pinches anything. Aye, you may laugh, Mistress Rose, but you'd better nail down your silver. Pirates have come to the Vale!'

As it turned out, the pirates had the better evening.

Eril escorted me back through the Motherhouse precincts and indicated we should turn into an atrium, where the silver-haired lord led me past a pink flowering tree with weeping branches. 'These are the quarters my lady directed to be prepared for you, Pilot. The bath house is just across the courtyard, and I am asked to help you make ready. I hope you find everything satisfactory?'

The three rooms were bigger than most houses. 'Yes. Grand,' I managed to say.

After that, things went rather quickly. I got a bath and haircut – if I was going to be the main attraction at the bloody banquet, I was going to give them an eyeful – and a siochla appeared to bandage my stripes with some unguent that felt wonderfully soothing and smelled of hazel. She left, and I dressed. The linen shirt was soft as a cloud against my skin, and to wear over it

Eril gave me a robe he told me was deep blue wool, the color of a summer's night, with the blazon of a white swan stitched on the right breast, the insignia of the Protector of the Vale. He added a wide tooled belt, gilded and studded with stones that I hoped, for my dwarfish mates' sakes, were only glass. I knew they weren't though. I added a small gold eating dagger, then he nodded me toward the bronze mirror.

I saw a tall king with his hand on his hilt, a set jaw and fierce eyes, one of which drooped a little.

'You are requested to wear your ring, Pilot,' the Eldest told me.

One part of my mind told me I should resent being managed for all the world like a puppet in some Fair day show, but the other half of my self was feeling a bittersweet satisfaction: in another time, in another place, I might have looked like this. I smiled into the mirror, and I shouldn't have done that. Gargoyles should never grin.

'All right, Eril. If you can get me a mug of ale, I can probably get through this night.'

And he did get me the ale which was, incidentally, the best I have ever tasted, before I had to brave the huge hall. Feeling a little more comfortable and with him for escort, I stepped through the doors carved with a rose motif.

Up to that night the largest room I'd ever been in was our refectory at the skellig, but this hall of the Vanui would easily have made three times the size of it. And where our dining hall had been a simple stone-walled room filled with sturdy benches and tables, this was designed to vie with royal halls – as befitted the stature and importance of the siochlas and of the Mistress they served.

So the tables were gleaming with silver flagons and gold plates, and glass goblets were set ready at each seat. The lighting came from oil lamps on the tables themselves, and candle chandeliers down the middle of the hall, and braziers glowed under them to take the night's small chill out of the air. Rich floral tapestries rippled slightly against the walls, though in my opinion none of them could match my friend Finian's work. The room was full of people, most of them standing with goblets in their hands around the braziers or around the upper table where Rose, gowned in white and wearing a golden circlet on which was fastened a golden sugan Vanu, sat to bid them formal welcome. She smiled, and held out a hand for a portly man in ridiculously elaborate robes to kiss the Mother's ring. While he bent, she looked up and our eyes met across the whole length of the hall.

A woman's voice, well-modulated and carrying, was raised at my elbow to herald my arrival. 'Reverend Daughter, I announce Aengus, the Master of Inishbuffin and Lord Protector of the Vale.' The herald dropped into a deep curtsey and held it.

I mentally gave a hitch to my sash and went forward. She awaited me standing, which I have since learned is a mark of singular distinction in any royal hall. When I stood before her, I brought my hand to my breast. 'Give you good evening, Mistress.' That must not have been correct form, because someone nearby sniffed audibly. However, Rose extended the ring and I kissed it while her merry voice told me, *The clothes do you justice, my lord. Ah, you've worn the ring, I see. Excellent. That will begin to dawn on people shortly, unless I miss my guess.*

I wished I could have kenned, too. I'd like to have known who she expected might notice Colin's ring, and why. Certainly they were all staring enough, but I didn't think many were looking at the ring.

She was saying, 'We welcome you most heartily, Your Eminence. We hope your injuries have been attended?'

She knew they had, so I was puzzled, but replied, 'Aye, lady, Reverend Daughter.'

I began to get some sense of what she was doing when she casually swept the assembled guests and raised her voice slightly. 'My lord was attacked by walkers yesterday, and bears their stripes.'

The effect was rather as though lightning had struck nearby, and I saw more than one hand make the sign that was not made here. Very subtly, one or two of the guests moved a little away from me.

'Walkers? Where?' asked a voice behind me that I thought seemed familiar somehow.

'At Inishbuffin,' Rose said, and I turned to see who had asked.

'You!' he exclaimed.

Bugger me, he *was* the Crown Prince. I recognized his voice from this morning's near accident in the harbor, but I knew his face from the same dreaming coma wherein I had woken to Rose's voice above me: Beod, Prince of Ilyria.

'Hullo,' I said to the angry eyes the color of woodsmoke. 'How's your bathtub toy?'

CHAPTER TEN

If it had not been the Mother's hall, he'd have swung at me, Beod laughingly confided to me some years later, and I, with equal humor, told him I'd have broken him in half if he'd tried. Both of us were being quite truthful, actually.

But Rose threw oil on the storm waters. 'One of my sisters has been at fault, I am afraid, Your Highness: the bearings she gave His Eminence were a little off, and the vapors that hide the Vale threw off his crew's reckoning. My apologies to you both, my lords, for the scare. Come, may I join your hands in friendship?' The voice of her kenning was clipped: *He's a council member, and you'll have foul weather all the way home if you don't shake his hand, I swear it.*

I don't know what she told *him*, but at her firm grasp on our wrists, Beod and I clasped hands. The tall, rather heavy-set young man had been bred to a noble lifestyle with its rules of order and realized that as a prince he was outranked – at least in this hall – by the one who had the title Lord Protector of the Vale, so it was Beod who spoke first. 'Then it was only your extraordinary seamanship that saved us worse than a scare. My apologies, my lord.' His handsome face strained into a smile.

'It's naught. We weren't quite as sharp about the rigging as we could have been. Sorry.' I matched his smile, but of course on me the effect was somewhat nightmarish. I heard some intakes of breath around us.

If he was at all discomfited by that grin, he betrayed it by no sign. He'd steady nerves, I'll give him that. We broke off the handshake.

Rose seemed relieved, having envisioned the possibility of a donnybrook before the first dish was on the table, no doubt. 'You have not been presented, my lords.' She indicated him with a smile. 'This is His Highness Beod Mac Fergus, Prince of Ilyria.'

169

Remember you've never seen him before, she kenned. 'And this, as you have heard, is His Eminence, Aengus of Inishbuffin.'

We did a creditable bit of mumming. On his part, it probably wasn't much of a sham. Though he may have known the title I held, I doubt he recognized anything of the countenance he had last seen swathed in heavy bandages on a boat somewhere between Inishbuffin peninsula and the island of Inishkerry. I wondered what he'd been doing there.

He inclined his head to me, and I to him. Beod looked to Rose. A message passed from her to him, and his smile became genuine. 'You really ought to lift the magic when there's a ceremony, Reverend Daughter, else your guests will be swimming ashore.' From the assembled guests at this end of the hall there was a polite titter.

The siochla smiled a little and seated herself once more. 'You'll be relieved to hear I did finally remember it this afternoon, Your Highness. I will remember sooner next time, I promise. Perhaps we might even arrange swans to guide you in after this.'

I joined the laugh and studied the fellow who would one day hold the throne that should have been my own. Rose turned to greet a late arrival, and some of the assembled folk returned to their own interrupted conversations. From the tone of it, I was pretty sure they were talking about me.

Beod cast back his cloak with its border of gold and set his thumbs in his belt. Now that we were no longer the center of attention, he lifted an eyebrow and said conversationally, 'That's an interesting retinue you travel with.'

Dwarfen pirates, he meant. 'I'll tell them you said so. They thought your lot was pretty interesting too.' If he was smart, he'd not let us catch him at open sea with that pretty boat of his. It was just a friendly warning.

A flicker of amazement went across his face. I don't think people were in the habit of threatening him, at least not openly. Then he laughed. 'By the Powers, I'd like to cross swords with you some day. That would be a wager worth playing.'

I knew intuitively that the practice of arms was all sport to him: he had not killed a man yet, neither in battle, nor in heated argument. Ilyria must be a very peaceful place. We were of an age, perhaps twenty, but I was years older than Beod was. Still, he had meant no harm, so I gave him a reply in the same tone. 'That depends on how much gold you're willing to part with.'

He laughed again. Rose, who must have been keeping an ear cocked to us, said smoothly, 'There will possibly be an opportunity for a demonstration of your skills, my lords, at some day in the future. For now, let me enjoin you to remember the peace of Mother's sanctuary. We are all friends here.'

Women, I have found, do not understand this business of a man's taking the measure of another man. Neither Beod nor I by this time had any intention of coming to blows; it is the verbal engagement that establishes what sort of fellow the other is. Women size each other up too, I believe, but they compare the size of stitches in a hem, or the cobwebs that lace together the roof rafters. It is a much more subtle measure, and a more accurate one.

Beod made Rose a bow, then tapped me on the arm. 'Come, Your Eminence. Let us lift a cup together at least, if we must forego other pleasures.' I saluted Rose, and he led me toward a long table where prentice siochlas waited to pour drinks for the guests. 'What will you have?' he asked, waving a hand at the board full of glass bottles.

'Flotjin, if they've got it,' I answered absently, half-turned to scan the crowd. Most of them had found something else to look at besides me now, at last. Across the hall, Caitlin, attired in a new robe, her hair dressed with a lace veil, was talking with a distinguished-looking lady her own age. They shared what looked to be a fond laugh. When the queen looked up, I caught her eye and made a slight palms-up shrug together with a look around the hall. *Where's Jamie?* She shook her head, one finger across her lips. So the prince was not to be mentioned.

I was mulling the reasons for that when a familiar voice said quietly beside me, 'Try the gold-seal flotjin. I recommend it highly.'

I turned too quickly for my skinwalker stripes. 'Guildmaster!'

Sitric nodded familiarly to Beod and cautioned me in a low voice, 'I don't use that title here, if you please. It might make things difficult for the Maid if her other guests knew. Here I am just a glass merchant called Eomer Edvaardson.'

He had made no attempt to keep Beod from overhearing, so they knew each other. Behind my glass, I said, 'I've got something for you back on the ship.'

'It cost you dearly, apparently. I've been to see Timbertoe, but they wouldn't let me in.'

On my other side Beod turned his back to the room. 'What's this? I'd heard nothing about the old fellow's being hurt!' I wondered at the concern he was showing and explained briefly about the walker's lance head. I did not mention the Hag's Embrace. His face was clouded and serious when I had finished. 'That is hard news.'

'The siochla got most of it out, and he's still alive,' I said. 'Don't haul down the flag for him yet.' The flotjin burned my throat. 'I wouldn't think the Crown Prince of Ilyria would have much to do with a pirate seadog like Timbertoe.'

'I wouldn't think the Master of Inishbuffin would, either.' He made no move to tell me what his business with the skipper was, so I didn't reveal mine.

Sitric smiled behind his dark blond beard. 'So many secrets, eh, mates? I wonder how the Maid manages to hold them all in her head. What do you suppose the dear young woman has up her velvet sleeve tonight?' He spoke indulgently, as of some spoiled niece.

Voices from the dead that would curdle your blood, Silkenbeard, I thought. My ire had risen at his tone. 'Maybe she has a few Null Whisper orders of her own to put out, Glass Merchant. It's her hall; let her turn over the first tile.'

He straightened a sleeve. 'We're all her tiles, Pilot, and she'll turn us all over before she's through. Her Mistress is no respecter of men's lives. Think on that.'

The guildmaster took a glass and sauntered off casually.

I eyed Beod sidelong. His jaw, which had corded, relaxed. He had not liked Sitric's comment, either. 'This council of the Maid's,' I said. 'Is he a member?'

'Yes. And usually the dissenting vote.' The young prince glanced at me and half smiled. 'As you could probably guess without being told.'

'Give a dwarf a chance, and he'll say you nay every time.' I refilled my glass and we strolled away from the table. People wanted libations, but were holding off coming near me, I could tell. 'Are all these folk here at the Mistress Rose's behest?'

'Oh, no. Some have come with petitions, some in fulfillment of a geis put on them by the siochla of their own town or guild, some with rare seeds or plants to donate to the Vale's collection. This feast is a monthly affair to coincide with the public ritual for Vanu at the temple. The council meets during these feasts to obscure our true purpose. One never knows what eyes may be watching.'

'Even here?'

'Especially here. Nowhere else do men of all lands come and go so freely. For this reason, it is an excellent place to listen.'

'It's also a very good place to keep your mouth shut, then,' I muttered.

We had stopped in a corner, near an open window looking out to the harbor. I could see the lantern at the *Inishkerry Gem's* bow amongst all the others; ours had a pane of glass missing from one side of the red lantern, so the light was startlingly two-toned. It looked quiet down there. My thoughts went to the hospital. I shouldn't be floundering about at this feast like a fish out of water, I thought. I should be down there, with Timbertoe. Some mate should be sitting with him.

But then a trumpet blew, startling me, and dinner was announced. I drank off my flotjin for courage. The guests began drifting to the tables. She had put me at the head table to one side of her with Beod to the other. I had to remind myself to keep my head up. The king in the mirror was the part I had to play.

I have no doubt the dinner of grain and vegetable dishes was excellent, but I would have been better served by the rough fare at some dockside tavern. The food was too richly seasoned, the hall a little too warm for one used to an open deck, and the wine an unpleasant mix with the flotjin and ale I had already drunk. The eyes were what I was chiefly aware of, eyes that wanted to see whether a gargoyle could eat without slobbering. In consequence, I ate very little and hated it all. Rose asked once if something was wrong and I lied and told her merely that I was used to short rations and her bread had been enough. She gave me a glance that told me she knew exactly what I felt, but she did not ken me anything and did not press me to make conversation, for which I was grateful.

The only thing of note that happened is that once I looked up idly and found a man dressed in the clothes of a middling wealthy burgher and his wife beside him looking at me. As I met their eyes, she ducked her mouth into her hand, and then made me a little wave, timidly, and patted the bench beside her. They wanted the novelty, I suppose. Thoroughly disgusted, I took a huge draught of wine. *Codswollop on all these pop-eyed bastards!* I thought forcefully. Beside me Rose's head jerked up, and every siochla in the hall swung to look at me. After a startled instant, they covered smoothly and returned to their service at the tables, though I saw one of the sisters, an awkward girl no more than fifteen, jam her hand over her mouth and give me a merry glance. And by the doors at the foot of the hall Eril was smiling.

Very good, I must say. Rose sounded amused. *Normally it takes a deal of time to get that much volume.*

That was the first time I used the kenning to my knowledge, and I think it may have been the effect of the spirits I had drunk at least in part, because it took me a while after that night to learn to use it as a regular thing. No doubt Colin's ring, recognizing the powerful emanations of the Vale, was focusing my thoughts whether I willed it or not.

At length the eating was over. The Maid gave me her hand, and it took me only a moment to realize I was supposed to escort her out, probably to the temple for the ritual that would conclude the public observances. I groaned inwardly. At this rate, it would be the middle of the bloody midnight watch before we got to the council meeting.

Our route this time did not intrude upon the private section of the Motherhouse. Instead we exited the hall by a side door and followed a torchlit path then swung above the siochlas' living quarters to approach the temple from the right along a broad, marble paved avenue. The night was moonlit, and the mosaic vines on the façade seemed to twine forbiddingly. I did not want to go into this shrine of the Hag but Rose's hand was still on my arm, and I was not Lord Protector of the Vale for nothing, so I took a breath and escorted her under the arched door.

It was dark inside, which I had expected, and warm, which I had not. Somehow I had thought it would be danker, smelling of mold, dead as a bog hole. As my eyes adjusted I perceived a silvered light coming from somewhere ahead. The short tunnel or entryway we were in led to it. Here the tunnel did not crowd one into a crouch, as did the one leading to the skellig's ancient sanctuary; here the tunnel was wide enough to accomodate many people at once.

We came into the antechamber, and here the warmth of the tunnel became noticably hotter. An acrid fume hung in the air which the inflowing draught from the entry did nothing to dispel. There was glassy black rock underfoot which leapt to surround us in a womb of mirrored darkness, silvered by the ghostly white light of the moon shining down some unseen window shaft and in the middle of the moonlight shaft was the altar of polished white stone and on that altar was a skull garlanded with a sugan crown.

No, I did not want to be here.

This was not the same Power whose music had twice entranced me to allow me to do things I should not have been able to do. This was not the Power with the silver hair and face as young as my own waiting on her island with the water lilies about her feet, with the flowers of her Realm blowing soft about her. This, I prayed, was not the Power my grandfather had gone to in death.

This was the Power against whom one made the sign, the Hag châtelaine of the earthly charnel house, Ritnym's other self, as necessary as winter to spring, as decay to rebirth, but fearful to men in the dark of death or doubt.

Now Rose took up the mask of the Mother from the altar, a split visage, her own lovely young face forming the bottom half, and a skull doming over her forehead with its white bone and blank eye sockets. I suppressed a shudder to see her so changed. The acrid atmosphere became heavier as incense smoked on the altar, and possibly there was a mild drug in it, for I felt the glossy black walls fall away into void, and I could not look away from the altar.

She was there suddenly, the Hag, a spectral dark shape cowled in some manner of rough cloth. One bony hand lifted to point into the crowd behind me.

'Mother, my daughter?' a woman's voice behind me quavered.

The Hag's hand dropped, and there was tense silence. Suddenly a little girl's piping voice came out of that cowl: 'Mommy, don't be sad any more. It's all right. I and my puppy just went into the forest to chase a bad old crow away from Daddy's corn.'

I was aware of the woman's cry as she recognized that voice. Two siochlas stepped forward from the wall to help her out of the shrine. The Hag's hand lifted again, and, 'Mistress, I'd have my wife speak, if ye please,' a man called, his voice betraying the dread that his matter-of-fact words tried to mask.

The incense cloud thickened. 'Och, Harry, 'twas a son, a braw little boy. I'm sorry, dear.'

I think the bereaved husband may simply have folded to the floor, because he made no outcry, but I heard the sound of someone falling. Siochlas stepped forward to get him.

Again the hand, and the woman requesting someone named Malcolm. This time the voice from within the cowl was a man's, rough with anger. 'Damnit woman, I told ye that man o'yours would kill us both someday, but no, ye had to keep coming round. And now you're still bothering me! *Leave me be!*'

'But I love you!' the unfaithful wife cried after him. Her voice echoed in the temple, gradually to be silenced by the darkness.

The bony hand lifted, pointing at me. 'Painter. Come to me,' said the Hag's own voice, a sibilant whisper, like a snake curled as close as one's chin.

My lungs coiled in a knot, and I fought for a breath. 'No,' I croaked.

'Come, Painter. I will have you sooner or later,' she whispered, and bog water filled my mouth, the sucking mud pulling me down, and I could not get free.

'No,' I gasped as my head went under and I thrashed.

'For ever, Painter. My Brother wills it so. Come to me.' Her hand reached out to squeeze my heart and the pain went through me like the lashing of skinwalker stripes, like lightning against the sky, like . . . chiming crystal.

For an instant, blue sky showing through the black clouds. 'There is another color pot, grandson! Thee must go back to Inish—' His words broke off abruptly, and then there came a strangled cry of mingled fear and pain such as I knew he had never made in life, not even at the end of it. Filled with horror I tried to give him light in that everlasting dark. I knew the ring on my finger was blazing like a torch, but I could not send it to where he was. Yet for an instant, a mote of time, I could see. Dead men's bones were knee deep on the plain that stretched away into limitless distance, tangled with sere leaves and vegetation, all withered to brittle skeletons. In that moment

176

my heart thudded like a coffin struck with a shovel and I saw color in that dead place: the soft gray of his robe, and his mismatched brown and blue eyes, his face looking as it had looked in life with the healthful blood springing under the black and silver beard, a mighty blade chanting the language of swords in his hand. But again he gave that awful cry and my stunned gaze fell to the creatures that battened on his stripped flesh that were getting in past his faltering guard, their gnawing fangs devouring him even as I watched – while behind him the Lady of Earth lay still and silent where she had fallen.

I sprang toward them at full speed, clutching for the dagger at my belt, thinking I could at least draw a few of the walkers off and go down to death together with him. Two of the walkers were aware of me now and leapt for me, their long-nailed bones clutching. I drove forward to meet them, and the obsidian wall of the cavern struck me in the side of the head.

I became aware of the incense, of the glassy floor under my throbbing cheek, and of the screams and shouts I had not heard till then except as the moans of the dead. A voice echoing in the sacred precincts shouted, 'Treachery!' and someone stumbled over me. There were running feet all around suddenly. 'Get a light!' the same voice, a man's voice used to giving orders, yelled. I put a hand to my head because I wasn't sure whether it was bursting in half – it certainly felt like it – and rolled up on to an elbow.

At first I thought I had been struck blind, had lost what sight I had left, and panic made my stomach lurch warningly. Almost immediately, however, I knew that the silvered moonlight in the Hall of the Dead was only cut off by the silhouettes of the men and women who were running past. Another of the fleeing figures crashed into me, scrambled up without a word, and hurled himself once more toward the outgoing tunnel. If I stayed on the floor, I would be trampled. I found the wall behind me with one hand, and by using it to brace myself was able to get up.

It was Beod's voice shouting, 'Get out of the way, damn you! Move!' The crowd surged as though some force had pushed it from behind, and he broke through, roughly shoving the frightened worshipers aside, trying to work his way to the entrance. He saw me braced against the wall and reached one arm to grab me and pull me along with him, crying, 'Help me move these fools! Oh, Powers, it's too late already, I know it!'

Beod thrust the stout burgher one way, I threw his pop-eyed wife another, and we were in the tunnel where we ran with the stream of people. 'I saw you go for them, you were the only one who did. How did you know they were there? I saw nothing but cowled figures, like any other pilgrims, the bastards!' He spoke on one breath and did not wait for my answer as we crashed through the crowd milling around the outside entrance. '*Eril!*' His hoarse shout rang with frustration. He grasped my arm once more. 'Come! The paddocks are this way!'

A jet of pure ice-water shot through my veins. 'Where is Rose?'

Even running, he stared. Then he must have seen the trickling blood that I could feel as a warm drip down the side of my head. 'They got her!'

The memory of pain gripped my heart. 'Walkers?' I gasped, the vision spilling over into the waking world.

'No, these were real enough – even through the fumes of the temple I could tell that. They'll be headed for the harbor.' We vaulted a stile and I raced after him through neat beds of flowers toward a low block of buildings that must be the stables. I tried not to step on too many of the plants, but Beod seemed to know the place well and never hesitated as he sprinted for the black square of door. Anxious nickers greeted us, and one stallion, alarmed by the two running figures, kicked out at the solid wall of his stall. 'Where the hell are the Yoriandirkin?' I heard him wondering as we made haste to bridle the first two horses we came to.

'Ready?' he asked short moments later, swinging to the back of a huge gelding that looked black to me.

'Right,' I answered, gathering the reins, and he was out of the stable and flying down the hill before I'd even vaulted to my mare's back. I dug in my heels and raced after him toward the harbor. If the attackers who had taken Rose were afoot, we stood a good chance of catching up with them before they could get to the boat that must be standing ready for them. If they were already on it and rowing out to their ship among the others in the harbor, I'd whistle up my lads on the *Inishkerry Gem*. Either way, we'd have them.

Ahead of me Beod rode as though he were born to the back of a horse, the cloak streaming behind him. I saw his gauntleted hand shoot out, pointing right. 'Fire!' he shouted back to me.

I followed his pointing finger and saw why the Yoriandirkin had been so few to guard their mistress at the temple. The arboretum was on fire. I could see running figures crossing in front of the flames. They must be hauling water up the slope. Also, a small troop of horses was headed for the temple. They must have realized that there was some trouble, and the off-duty men were galloping to help. They were going the wrong way, though; there was no one left to catch at the temple. I whistled to attract their attention. 'Hoy! To the harbor!' I swept my arm to show them, and they must have seen the prince and me on our two horses streaking toward the sea in the moonlight, because they wheeled and followed us.

I urged on my mare, trying to catch up with Beod. She put her head down and lengthened her stride, and the gap between us closed while the fields flashed by to either side. We were just at the outskirts of the village. I heard a cock crow rustily, startled from his roost by the thudding hooves maybe, and down the lane someone stepped out of his door into the road, scratching his head sleepily and looking for the riders who had disturbed his slumber. 'Back in your house, idiot!' the prince of Ilyria yelled at him without checking his horse, and the cottager jumped for his doorway. When I passed a moment later a look of blank shock was still on the fellow's face as he clung to the frame. We cleared the cottages and broke out on to the beach, reining in momentarily to take in the situation.

There were two boatloads of them, one still drawn up on the shingle, the other already well away and speeding out into the harbor with flashing oars. The thought went through my mind that there were more of them than were really necessary to abduct one woman, but no doubt they had expected more resistance from the Yoriandirkin guards. I could see Beod's jeweled dagger catch the moonlight as he drew it, and then he clapped heels to his horse and went straight for the Wolfhounds caught on the beach. I ran my mare a little past the knot of them, then came around to catch them from the other side, dropping the reins and drawing my boot knife into my left hand as my dagger was already in my right. I leapt from the mare's back into the knot of them, for a horse is no good in the kind of fighting I like best.

I nearly cut the hand off the first of the hooded men who came for me, then used his body as a momentary shield to attend to a sword that was thrust toward my vitals. Slashing the left-hand dagger across the swordsman's face, I spun, both blades scything. I didn't hit anything, but two of the hooded men threw themselves backwards as the silver flashed toward their eyes, and this cleared a place for me to use my feet. I dropped one with a kick that took him in the groin, and slammed the right-hand dagger up to the hilt into the other's belly. He folded over my arm, trapping it for an instant as I tried to wrest the dagger loose. A sword struck out for my chest, but I pulled the falling body into the attacker, and he was thrown off enough that the blade only burned past my shoulder. I was cut, I could feel it for an instant, but then I had to let go of my right-hand dagger to get ready because the swordsman, his eyes grimly glinting in the hood, whipped his sword back and brought it sweeping toward my head. I brought my left arm up sluggishly because of the wound, and he'd have had me if at that moment an arrow hadn't taken him in the back. The attacker jerked, the sword flew out of his grasping hands, and he fell. I snatched up the sword, and only then realized there were no more of them.

I straightened, grounded the blade, and leaned on it, panting and looking for the source of the arrow. Far back, too far for me to credit the shot, was a single archer among the Yoriandirkin troop. The feeling was coming back into my left arm, and I glanced down. A slash, but not very deep, I judged. I blew and looked to Beod. He was covered with blood, standing dazed and motionless in the midst of the men we had killed.

I jumped to him. 'Where are you hurt?'

'No, it's not mine,' he said slowly. 'It's his.' He nudged a body with his foot, and then stood staring down at the pool that had seeped into the sand from the slashed throat.

In a flash I remembered my intuition back in the banquet hall. No, he had not killed before this night, and without Symon's lesson to prepare him, he had not expected it to be so bad. gripped his forearm hard. 'Come on, Prince. The work's not ove yet.' His eyes came up to me, but I didn't wait to see what migh be in them. Time for ghosts and regrets later. I whirled to look for the other boat and spotted it about midway across the water apparently headed for a fast-looking ship with her sails already running up the lanyards. I cupped my hands to my mouth and put as much breath behind the shout as I had left. 'Hoy, *Kerry Gem*, stand off and block the harbor!' My yell rolled over the water. I stooped to pitch the sword and a dagger into the boat the attackers would have used. 'Get in,' I said to Beod. He woke from his daze as I heaved the dory into the water, and he splashed the few steps to catch up with it, jumping awkwardly over the side. 'Can you row?' I asked.

'No. Sorry.' It cost him something to admit that, I could tell by the way his eyes followed the boat out there and the clench of his hands.

'All right, sit still then and keep me on line for my ship. It's the one with the hole in the red lantern.'

'The one moored beneath the hospital?'

'Aye.'

'Right. Got it.' He scrambled to a thwart and twitched his cloak out of the way as I picked up the oars, which were already fitted to the oarlocks, and put my back in it.

'You did well,' I told him between sweeps. 'My compliments to your weaponsmaster.'

He glanced back at me, then resumed his steady gaze to track the fleeing boat of the Wolfhounds. 'How did you know?'

I strained at the oars. 'Because when I killed my first one, I puked for a week.' I didn't tell him the first thing I'd killed was a sheep.

His shoulders moved briefly. I couldn't tell whether he had laughed, or felt the urge to vomit. 'You took care of four of them.'

'I've had more practice at it. The Burren's a wild place, Ilyrian, and then I took up with pirates.'

He looked at me then. 'Who *are* you?'

'Ah, I didn't think you recognized me.' I left off rowing for a moment to yell once more, 'Hoy, pirates! Damnit, block the bleeding harbor!' I'd have thought one of the blackguards could've stayed awake, even if they'd been ashore for dinner and a chance to look around.

Although no acknowledgement came from my ship, my shouts had by now roused some of the other crews. I stared at the pirate ship, rocking peacefully in the moonlight with nary a man to be seen on deck. I think that was when I knew it first.

'We've drifted right a little,' Beod reported, sighting for the *Gem*, then as I did not resume rowing, he turned to look at me. 'What's the matter? What are you waiting for? They're getting away!' The Wolfhounds' boat had made it to the sleek mother ship, and I saw the men going up a net waiting for them over the side. Some dark, heavy bundle went up slung over the last man's shoulder, and as soon as he had climbed over the rail, the ship's sails popped open with a report that echoed over the water like a lightning strike. The dark ship slid at increasing speed for the neck of the harbor.

I dipped one oar, leaned on it, and brought the dory about. If I had rowed steadily before, I was a man possessed now, and I had the incoming tide to help me, whereas the black ship had to make way against it. Beod rocked the boat as he lurched to his feet. 'Sit down or I'll knock you over the side!' I told him.

'But, damnit, man—!'

'She's not on that ship,' I said. 'They'll be going over the fire mountain. That ship out there is only to block the harbor so there can't be any pursuit. Didn't you wonder why we came so close to catching them with the headstart they'd had from the temple?'

He was quick, he caught it on the first telling, and after that he was as grim as death. When we neared shore, he yelled, 'Eril, is that you?'

'Nay, Your Highness, 'tis I, Dlietrian.'

'Dlietrian, is there a landing place on the other side of the mountain?'

'Indeed, lord, but the way up from it is steep and winding, so—'

Beod cut across his words, all urgency. 'That's the way they've taken your mistress. Ride, by the Powers, catch them before they make the boat!'

I suppose it was too hard for the Yoriandir on shore to believe, since he could plainly see the ship out there racing for the harbor mouth. The troop started to move, but it was at a confused walk.

Beod cursed them, but by then we were shooting through the shallows. As one, we jumped from the dory. The prince pulled his man bodily from the saddle. I gave mine the option to jump and took the moment while he did so to snatch up the other sword that had been left on the sand, as Beod had taken the first one. Then I mounted, clapped the horse on the flanks with the side of it, and pounded after the Ilyrian. He was holding back a little, waiting for me this time. 'I'll get Rose, you take the Wolfhounds. If there are only five or six of them, you won't need any help from me!' His teeth gleamed. Some men are like that: when their blood is up, they can make jokes. Now that he was blooded, Beod of Ilyria was beginning to show what kind of a fighting man he could really be.

I wasn't that cold, but I made him a grin. 'Right!'

Then we dug in and flung ourselves up the road that wound past the hospital to continue up over the shoulder of the fire mountain. Behind us we could hear the hoofbeats of the troop. Dlietrian must have decided we might know what we were about, or perhaps he realized he could do nothing from shore against attackers that had fled by ship.

We left the lights of the torches bobbing along the avenue from the Motherhouse knoll to the shorefront and even the soft lanterns of the hospital below us. The road, little more than a path through the terraces here, was regular and well-maintained for the sake of the carts that would take the grape harvest down to the Vale to the winery, but it was a fair grade and before long our horses were laboring a little. 'Beod, they can't be on foot,' I called up to him.

'Just what I was thinking. They must have had accomplices waiting when they brought her out of the shrine. Pull up a moment!' He had seen the droppings, as I had, and swung down to examine them. 'Still steaming,' he reported with satisfaction. 'Let's go.'

I put my hand down on his reins. 'Wait. Let's get over there into the terrace. That way if they have somebody watching behind, we won't be standing out against the moon when we crest the pass.'

But it wouldn't have mattered anyway, as we saw when we got to the top of the mountain's shoulder. Below us, too far away by minutes, a boat was rowing from the small jetty out to the mother ship standing two hundred yards or so off shore. We reined in and sat watching as the curragh nosed into the bigger ship's shadow, and the shore party climbed up the nets and on board. This time there was no doubt in my mind: a man mounted slowly, two limp arms swaying down his back as he climbed. Rose's hair was flying around her as he swung her over the rail into the hands that waited to catch her.

'Powers, they've got her. They'll kill her.' Beod's voice was hushed and flat. His horse blew gustily and tossed its head, sidling toward the grassy verge of the road, but he checked it roughly, unconscious I think of anything save that limp form.

'No. They could have done that in the temple tonight. No, they'll force her into a ritual on Vanu's Eve to make their puppet the king, but they'll never let her anywhere near Cnoch Aneil for a real rite. Afterwards, though . . . I fear for her.' Beod's horse curvetted nervously; he must have jerked suddenly on the reins, and I saw there was sweat on his face. It became clear to me then. 'I knew there must be a reason you two were together when I saw you on Timbertoe's ship. As long ago as that?'

'I don't know what you're talking about.'

'Dwarves do a lot of charter work, and their silence can be bought. For what it's worth, I've sailed with him for four years, and he's never given me the slightest inkling. In fact he told me I had dreamed it.'

He still did not look at me, but he answered, 'The penalty for the Maid who takes a lover is death. Did you know that?'

My own horse shuffled its feet and champed the bit. 'No, but I could have guessed. This cult is an old one.'

He straightened and sighed. 'If she were free, I would make her my queen when the time comes. But she was vowed to Vanu from birth.' The Ilyrian's eyes, dark in the night, met mine. 'Do you see?'

I saw that she could not love me, if not because of her duties as Maid, then because her heart was already given to this handsome fellow who had killed for her tonight and was now in an agony that she would be mistreated by her captors. He would have swum all the way to Dun Aghadoe, if he could have, to spare her. The fact that I would have done the same would never occur either to Beod or to Rose.

My head began to thrum with the headache that, despite the liquor, had not hit me till then, and I turned my horse back toward the lights of the Vale. 'Yes. I see.' Then I jammed in my heels and let the wind of the gallop dry my own sweat.

We met Dlietrian's troop only a little way down the road, and Beod explained briefly what had happened. The Yoriandir pointed. The black ship had, indeed, blocked the harbor mouth, standing just outside and holding station to ram any boat that might try to pursue the ship bearing Rose. 'Are the dwarfen pirates ashore?' I asked him.

He didn't know, having only raced after us without taking much time to note what was going on in the village. We cantered down past the hospital, took the main track along the beach, and trotted up to the large crowd milling on the shore. Most of the pilgrims were bewildered and frightened still, having gathered that the Maid had been abducted, having seen old Eril's hacked body just down from the main entrance of the temple, and now finding the bodies around the curragh. Among them my pirates stood, still half-drunk on the rations provided by the hospitality of the Vale, and not quite daring in this crowd to rifle the bodies for booty.

'Garn, that ain't the pilot,' I heard Ries saying to Harrald in a voice that said Harrald was mad to have thought so.

I rode through the people and tossed the reins to Dlietrian while I slid down and went to turn over the first corpse I came to. 'Bos'n, how is it that everybody's ashore in a foreign port?' I called sharply.

Harrald held on to Ries for support, and they both stared. *'Told ye,'* Gunnarson said, vindicated.

Ries thrust him off, leaving him weaving, and approached me wide-eyed. Our old bos'n found his voice. 'It's all right, Pilot,' he was saying as I tugged off the black hood of the attacker, and slashed at the material of the tight-fitting tunic to get his right shoulder free. Tattooed in the hollow of his collarbone I found the Fang. Ries bent to catch my eye over the corpse. 'It's all right,' he repeated. 'I left Neddy aboard, he didn't want a drink, and besides, what's to worry in the Vale?'

The next second my hand knotted in the front of his jersey, and I threw him into the boat. 'All of you, in, and row, damn you!'

I think Dlietrian read my urgency better than my mates did, for he gestured quickly to his troop, and several of them raced their horses up the beach to the dock to launch another boat. Beod caught my arm. 'What?'

'I'll be back ashore in a little. A favor, if you would: check on Timbertoe. I think these bastards were after the Maid, but there's the off-chance they got wind that the Ha— that I was here. I don't know whether they knew the dwarf was in the hospital up there. And send people to see whether Caitlin and James are all right.'

His eyes widened. He glanced once at the *Gem*, nodded, and swung to the gelding's back. We launched the curragh with a flying shove, Ries growled Harrald to the oars with him, and we sped out toward our ship, arriving only a few boat-lengths before the Yoriandirkin without a word having been spoken.

I didn't wait for a ladder I knew the boy would not be throwing down; instead I jumped for the anchor line and went up hand-over-hand, clambered aboard, and looked sharply the length of the deck. Nothing was to be seen, so I headed for the companionway hatch and tossed down the ladder as I went by. Taking the lighted lamp that swung by the hatch, I went below.

I was prepared for blood, was steeled for it. I quickly flung open the door to the captain's cabin first, but Neddy was not there, and nothing was amiss. I backed out and went along to my own cabin, pausing only a moment to take a breath before I opened it.

He must have run down here to try to hold the door against them, but it hadn't worked. I stepped over the boy's body and made sure they had not found my secret compartment. The bottle of Hag's Embrace together with Sitric's chalcedon and my rutter were untouched. That fact, together with the unrifled state of the ship, convinced me that they had not known the Haunt was about. Probably poor Ned had seen the hooded figures headed for the beach, and they had spotted him watching. 'Ries,' I asked over my shoulder, 'has that ship cleared off the harbor mouth yet?'

He spoke something to one of the other men and a moment later the answer was relayed back down from the deck: the Wolfhounds' ship was just getting under way now. The channel was clear.

The bos'n was stone-cold sober now, his eyes guilty and angry. 'Poor lad,' he breathed. 'I swear I never looked for trouble here, Pilot, else I never would have—' But it was useless to defend his judgment now. He hitched at his sash. 'I'll get the men in the rigging, shall I, Pilot? That ship looked fast, but—'

'Yes, stand by to sail. And Ries, tell the mates: there's a chalcedon in it for every manjack of them if you catch that ship.'

He snorted at the outrageousness of it, saw my eye, and slowly took in my fine clothes and the jeweled belt. I don't know what he thought had happened to me in the witches' Vale, but I could see him straightening up mentally. 'Aye, sir, I'll tell 'em.' He spun for the door.

'Ries, I'll want rowers to take me ashore.'

'Very good, Pilot. We'll wait on ye.'

'No.' I shook my head slowly. 'I won't be going with you. I have business here. I want you to take the ship out and chase them. If you can catch that ship, sink it, but don't go after the other boat that will be sailing ahead of it.' The Wolfhounds would kill her rather than allow her rescue.

'What the hell happened here tonight, Pilot?'

'Wolfhounds. They got the Maid of the Vale.'

'Be a nice reward in it, belike, if we could get her back,' he speculated.

'Not as much as the chalcedons you'll earn for getting the bastards that got our little mate.'

Ries rubbed his chin, quickly concluded I was right about the chalcedons, and went topside. I heard him order rowers into the curragh and all hands to prepare to sail. I took the articles from my secret hiding-place, tucked them in the neck of my fine shirt, which was by now a little worse for wear, and went on deck.

Beod met me at the dock, knowing nothing of the slain boy. 'I've seen the queen and prince, and they never even saw the attackers. The old fellow is awake!' he called as we bumped against the bollards. He stood with the reins wrapped around his wrist, the bloody sword forgotten in his other hand, grinning. 'What exactly *is* codswollop?'

CHAPTER ELEVEN

Dlietrian held my horse's reins while I turned for a last word with the dwarves in the curragh. 'All right, back out to the ship, and nip quick.'

Harrald and Arni exchanged looks. 'Ye're not coming with us, Pilot?' Harrald asked.

'Not this trip. I've business here tonight, and you'll be back by mid-morning. Tell Ries to keep a sharp eye out for the shoal waters off Seal Point.'

'But how will we get back into this here port without a pilot?' Harrald worried. 'We damn near piled it up the first time – on account of some landlubber what had his ship—' His eyes were on Beod, and he'd recognized him obviously.

'Stop. There's no time. Bos'n's waiting. You won't have any trouble coming back in this time; there'll be no magic to hide the Vale. Straight out, straight back. It's an easy job, with booty in it.'

Their ears perked up at that. Arni nudged Harrald with his elbow, and picked up his oar. But Harrald was looking up at me on the dock. 'Does this mean ye ain't a pirate any more, Pilot? Found some grander friends, have ye?'

Amongst dwarves there is only one way to deal with an insinuation like that. I jumped into the boat, and before he had time to make it to his feet, smashed him in the mouth and knocked him over the thwarts. 'I'm more pirate than you'll ever be, you little maggot. Get the hell out to the ship!'

He glared up at me. 'Where's me sash, then? Ye don't need it with them fancy clothes, and I can't keep me britches up without me sash!'

I unbuckled the leather belt studded with rubies and dropped it on his chest. 'There. Now—' I stuck my fists on my hips and leaned to say sardonically, 'If you can fight off the other lads,

189

you can keep it.' I gave him my best gargoyle grin. 'Have a nice voyage, Harrald.' Arni was already eying the treasure.

I stepped up on to the dock. 'Speed well. Tell Ries to keep the flotjin locked up.'

'Aye, Pilot,' Arni agreed, though both of us knew that was the first thing they'd be into, and they rocked away from the dock.

Dlietrian looked askance at me. 'Is it thus in the dwarf islands, sir?'

'No, they were a bit off stride tonight. Thanks,' I added as he gave me a leg up.

He stood looking after the boat thoughtfully. 'They are rough, indeed. But doughty fighters, I have heard.'

'True enough. They have no archers, though.'

I had intended it as a compliment to his skill, but he merely looked up at me with an unreadable expression. 'Neither do we Yoriandirkin,' he finally said, and let go of the bridle, stepping back as Beod nudged his horse to a walk.

'Word was brought while you were out on your boat,' the prince told me: 'The council is gathering in our usual place to plan our strategy. Needless to say, we had counted on having Rose here when we attacked the Burren, and need to rethink. They wait only for you and me.'

'They can wait a few minutes longer. I'm going to see Timbertoe.'

We had been riding side by side. Now he drew rein. 'Aengus, there is something you should know.'

'I know, I know. The council doesn't have the foggiest idea who I am, or why I should be in on its deliberations. Rose explained that to me; she was to present me tonight,' I said impatiently.

'The council knows more of you than you think. No, that isn't what I was going to say.' He fidgeted with something on one of his gauntlets, looked away, then looked back at me. 'Just don't be too surprised when you see him, that's all,' he said quietly.

I frowned. 'He's weak. You can't expect the old rascal to be himself till he's had three or four pints of flotjin.' The Ilyrian did not smile. A knot grew in my stomach.

'Aengus, they had to take his other leg.'

I still remember I could hear the waves shushing on the beach behind us, and the sound somewhere far-off of a door closing.

'Thanks for telling me. Where will I find you when I'm done?'

'Dlietrian will wait for you.' Awkwardly he leaned for a moment to grip my arm, then wheeled and trotted back to order the Yoriandir to attend me. I went up to see Timbertoe.

A dwarfen siochla, not the healer but one of her assistants, I guessed, met me as I came up the stairs of the terrace. I waved her off. 'I already know.'

'Mistress Neilan says to tell you she regretted the necessity, but the captain would have died otherwise. You were in the service, sir, and it is not permitted to interrupt the Speaking.' She was anxious, her hands fumbling with the ends of her sleeves. 'You'll be brief, I hope, sir? He should sleep, but he won't take the draught.'

I could not afford this anger; Timbertoe would read me like a book, and besides, the siochlas had only done what Nestor would have. I stopped. 'Put it in flotjin, Auntie. He'll take it then.' She was sniffing doubtfully when I left her and went in.

What words could I say to him?

I took it all in: his white face, stark in the tangle of sweat-soaked hair; the crisp white sheet that mounded in the moonlight over one leg to mid-shin and lay impossibly flat below the other hip; the two dark eyes watching me cross the threshold. I went to one knee beside the bed and took one of his cold hands in mine, thumb around thumb, pirate to pirate, and neither of us said anything for a moment.

Then he eyed me glassily and nodded a bit. 'Told yer grandfather I'd see ye a bloody king someday, I did. Ye look some flash in them togs.'

'Miss me sash,' I told him. 'Me pants are falling down.' He could not laugh, but one side of his mouth bunched in a smile. Encouraged, I pursued the joking mood. 'Ye've got to stop swearing in here, Skipper. These aunties will be corrupted. They don't even know what codswollop is.'

'Well, fine. If they don't like it, then they can cut out me bloody tongue, too, while they're at it.'

He spoke so lightly you might have thought he was joking, but I knew what was in his eyes. I'd seen it a hundred times in my shaving glass. 'Is that why you won't take the sleeping draught?'

He closed his eyes. 'Man never knows what he's going to lose next, falling asleep here.' While I was trying to think of something to say, he asked quietly, 'Did you know they were going to do it?'

'No. I didn't find out until a little while ago. There's been . . . some trouble here tonight, and I was giving them a hand with it.'

His head moved against the pillow, nodding, and he sighed. 'Didn't think so. Didn't think me giant would have let them at me.'

'Timbertoe—'

'—toes,' he shot back so quickly I was stunned. I knew now what he had seen in me all these years, and that gave me a clue about how to treat him.

I leaned over. 'It'll be Timber Pecker if ye don't open your eyes and look at me.'

He was still my old seadog. He started to laugh. I had to hold him against the pain, but he growled, 'Piss off, Giant. I don't need a bloody nursemaid.'

I don't know whether she had been listening just outside the door, but she decided that was as good a moment as any to come back in, cup in hand. She nodded to me, and I reached back for the potion laced with flotjin. 'Mother's milk, Skipper. Open up.' I swirled the cup under his nose so he'd get a good whiff of it.

A little brightness came into his eye, but he asked warily, 'Something else in it, too, ain't there?'

I did not lie to him. 'It's against the pain, Dwarf. No shame to that.'

He snorted. 'Pain! Nay, I had pain *last* time I lost a leg. This was easy, I'll give the witches that much. They were gentle about it, put me to sleep first. Not with an axe. Chop and it's gone.' He was beginning to wander and that scared me.

'Timbertoe, look at me. That's better. Always like to see a man's face when I'm about to make him a deal.' He recognized the words, giving me a sour mouth. 'The head siochla told me there's surgery they can do on my head. It may give me back colors, no guarantees. Or—' I paused. Well, there really was no need to say what the 'or' was. Even through the loss of blood and the weakness, he was sharp enough to know what it meant to me to be offered that slim hope, no matter the cost. He was watching me. I put the cup in his hand and held it braced there. 'Now, here's the deal, Filthydwarf: I'll let these witches cut my head open, if you'll drink this off and stop thinking about a shaving knife.'

We stared at each other. 'Right,' he said at last. 'What does the captain of a fleet have to do but sit on his arse in the warehouse all day, counting up the booty, anyway? Don't need legs for that. Meantime, while I'm looking to our many business ventures, ye'll wander from king's court to king's court, the greatest painter of the day, making pictures and pinching the odd bauble or two. How's that?'

'Garn! I'm going to be sitting on my arse right next to ye, making sure the tally is right!' I spat into my palm, and held my hand out to him.

He couldn't spit, but he made the gesture of it and grasped my hand weakly.

'Are ye scared, boy?' he asked quietly.

'Shitless. You?'

He fingered for a braid of his beard, but the siochlas had combed it all out. 'Nay, not a bit. Help me drink this bilgewater, will ye?'

Dlietrian conducted me back toward the Motherhouse. The night was quiet once more, the stars bright overhead, the tide turned down on the strand so that now the waves could be heard clearly at their high-water mark on the sea wall. I gestured across at the arboretum. 'How bad was the damage?'

'I have not been home again yet, sir, but I understand from others that it was mostly a stand of evergreens that was set afire. The trees are sore hurt, but we hope to begin reseeding tomorrow. The chief danger now is the embers, and we have set watch on them, you may be sure.'

Our horses clopped up the avenue leading straight through the fields toward the knoll. 'How is it that you're an archer, Dlietrian? I thought your folk did not kill game for meat, or engage in warfare.'

'Both those things are true, my lord. It is forbidden us to take life. Mother gives her earth as equally to us as to the animal folk. And it is certainly abomination to kill a person.'

'It cost you much, then, to save my life tonight, and I have not even thanked you properly for it. I'm sorry. What is the penalty you face now?'

He looked momentarily surprised. 'There is no penalty, lord. There has never been the crime before. I . . . I suppose I ought to go away,' he said uncertainly.

The affair was none of mine, really, and I shouldn't put my oar in, but he had made himself an outcast among his own folk for my sake, so I told him, 'If you want my opinion, mate, I think the Vale is going to need all the archers it can get. There are far more wolves than there are lambs in the world.'

His intelligent eyes turned back to me. 'I heard what happened to your skellig. Master Bruchan was a man of peace, yet I do not think he was less dear to Mother because he was accomplished in the arts of war also. Thus for some time now I have tried to make myself ready to defend the Vale, in case the Dark One should point his minions toward us someday. It was not a popular decision, and it will be less so now. I will be shunned.'

There was something about his cadence and the timbre of his voice. 'Surely your folk would miss your stories if you went away.'

The night was full of crickets. *I should have known the Lord Protector of the Vale would know his own folk,* he kenned, and smiled. *Perhaps I may have the honor of telling a story before you one day, my lord, though my skill is small.*

'And perhaps I'll have the honor of painting it,' I said to pay him back a little for the peace he had sacrificed. *If I ever paint again.*

I did not intend to ken it, thinking only of the surgery I must undergo, but as he led me under the gatehouse, Dlietrian's silver voice said in my mind, *You will, my lord. The trees have said so.*

At the time I thought he said 'leaves', and I was amused that the siochlas were not the only ones in the Vale who dabbled in soothsaying by reading the pattern in the bottom of a tea bowl. Their gardeners did it, too.

'I don't like it,' Sitric said flatly. He threw a fire-stick into the brass bowl on the table, sprang to his feet, and began to pace as he smoked.

Beod and I exchanged a glance, and the Ilyrian smiled a little.
The dissenting vote, as usual, was coming from the guildmaster.
'We must keep to the plan, despite her capture. Now more than
ever, in fact,' my Ilyrian friend repeated. We were meeting in the
smaller room off the siochlas' large, chapter meeting room. This, I
understood from Dlietrian, was called the privy council room and
the assemblage of people in it, the privy council. I hadn't known
what to expect when he'd swung open the door for me. For all
I knew of privy councils, we could all have been meeting in a
two-holer.

But it was a normal room, to my relief, hearth at one end,
shuttered windows, one long table down the middle of it, the
carved chair that must ordinarily be for the Maid at one end
under a tapestry showing a rose, her personal seal, I guessed. In
the comfortable chairs drawn up to the table were an assortment
of people as different in aspect and costume as could be imagined,
but all with a common stamp of authority and knowledge. I
could well picture Bruchan among them, but I was distinctly
uncomfortable.

Beside me Beod – here as his father's emissary – was at his
ease, his manner indicating clearly that he had been brought up
to secret meetings where taxes were discussed, kings' daughters
were brokered off, war strategy was made. He'd probably been
made to sit through his father's privy councils since he was
old enough to keep an intelligent conversation, or to keep his
mouth shut, which ever the occasion demanded. I envied him
his aplomb.

Sitric had left his seat next to my Ilyrian friend on the other
side, the last on our edge of the table. Across from us ranged
three faces I was to come to know well. Furthest down from me
was the middle-aged or rather older Burrener woman who had
talked with Caitlin in the banquet hall earlier tonight. She was tall
even when sitting, dressed in widow's weeds, a white coif under
a black mantle hiding her hair. She had sharp eyes, as though she
took the sum of a person at a glance, but her mouth was kind
and her voice pleasant. She was Lady Sive Mac Maille, widow of
Brandon Mac Maille, with whose death my friend Gwynt had been
charged during the time of his service at court in Dun Aghadoe.
The charge had been false, the death of the powerful Burrener lord

an assassination, not an accident of my friend's horseshoeing. For Brandon Mac Maille was a follower of the Four, as our skellig folk had been, and an outspoken voice against the growing power of the Wolf cult. He was also the direct descendant of Macguiggan the Bold, my ancestor Colin Mariner's loyal captain, And Lady Sive obviously knew it, for she treated me with the respect her husband's family had accorded my grandfather even though I was no more than a boy really, and our families had not been bound for hundreds of years. Still, she was prepared to give me full partnership in the deliberations of this council so long as I proved not to be some hot-headed youth who would wreck all their carefully laid plans. Years later, when she was an old woman and I in my own middle age, Sive confided that she felt she'd got her murdered son Owen back when she met me. I took that as a great compliment.

In the middle of the table on that side lounged at his ease the most extravagantly robed man I had ever met outside some mummer's fantasy of what a king would look like. His name as he pronounced it in his own language was an unrepeatable amalgam of Ilyrian and some other tongue that had a lot of shushes and vowels in it. Seeing my confusion, he smiled with startlingly white teeth and told me I could call him Ja-Solem. He wore not breeches, tunic and cloak, nor even the robe and high boots I was familiar with, but rather a flowing white robe: long, elaborately worked with a wide border of what Beod later confirmed to me was gold thread and beads of amber to match the color of the over-robe. This had a long tasseled hood attached to it, lined with more of the same white material as his robe. But it was not his robes that intrigued me so much as the way he wore them, with dash and a fine air of mystery, as though he might suddenly whip a magic treasure lamp out of one of those billowing sleeves. Though older, he was in his way as handsome as Beod, and I could tell the Ilyrian didn't like Ja-Solem much. There was a sister, Beod told me afterwards, whom Ja-Solem wanted to marry off to him, and Beod's father had entertained Ja-Solem's emissary when he'd come to pay a call. He was from Shimarron, a land south of Ilyria, and knew much of the Wolfhounds' doings in the mountain country that was the border between them.

The last member of the council was the most surprising to me. I

had lived among dwarves and thought they were a short people,
but this fellow would have been small even by their standards. In
truth, at first I thought him a dwarfen freak and told myself sternly
not to make the little fellow feel worse by staring. I knew what
it was like to be looked at that way. But Comfrey Lichen was, it
turned out, of a race distinct from the dwarves. Nowadays Ilyrians
call them Littlemen or even Teazles, but Comfrey told me that his
people simply referred to themselves as 'the Folk'. They lived in
mountain country; where, he did not say, and I did not get the
chance to ask that night. He certainly did not have the dwarfish
temperament, this small, light-haired man: several times I found
myself chuckling at some turn of phrase or jest, and not one of
them was dirty.

As I have said, Rose herself would have rounded out the mem-
bership of the council. In later years we added other members, but
that was with the future. On this night, we sat in the middle of
a dark Vale and tried to think how we could avert the travesty of
the kingmaking ritual as Jorem planned it. Well, it was the other
five who deliberated. I already knew what I was going to do.

Finally Lady Sive smiled down the table to me. 'Our painter
has been quiet. What is he thinking, I wonder?'

'I am thinking, madam, that all the talk of this council has been
of mustering a large army, of a flotilla of dwarfen shipping to take
it to Dun Aghadoe, of a secondary force running up through the
gaps in the mountain country. Now, I am used to somewhat
plainer talk, and I hope you will forgive me if I ask a plain
question. Why?'

Sitric clenched his teeth on his pipe stem and said through
them, 'You have a better idea, I take it?'

'That depends on the intentions of this gathering. If your aim is
conquest of the Burren, I have nothing more to say other than that
none of you, except Lady Sive, Prince James – who, by the way, I
am astonished not to find here – or myself has the right to consider
such a thing. My country is not for carving, gentlemen.'

Ja-Solem's teeth showed. 'Our young friend is forthright.'

Beod, caught between our still very new respect for each other
and his father's orders, reddened, a slow flush that spread up from
his collar. 'There are considerations beyond the . . . personal ones,
Your Eminence.' So we were back to being formal. 'Aside from

the fact that this vermin Wolfhound has now stolen away the Maid of the Vale, he has for some time harassed our border provinces. In time, as he has plainly shown, he intends to expand the borders of the Barr— the Burren, excuse me.' He had been going to give it the Ilyrian word, but switched to mine, a delicate diplomatic gesture that subtly acknowledged my right to protest. He turned to look full at me. 'Would you have us let him get away with that?'

I waved a hand. 'It's done all the time, isn't it? I mean, that's what kings do: chase each other back and forth across borders. And only the folk of the border country suffer for it because you, my lords, don't have to live there.' Lady Sive leaned back in her chair, folded her hands in her lap, and smiled.

There were no smiles anywhere else in the room, though Comfrey's face showed none of the irritation of the others. He was looking at me, head cocked to one side, as some folk watch a storyteller at a seisun. The little man broke the silence. 'And what would you do instead, Aengus?'

So I explained it to them. When I was done, Ja-Solem nodded. 'I like it,' he said. 'It is simple and subtle, like a fine dagger.'

Beod was staring, all his court etiquette forgotten. 'You're mad! It will never work! And even if he doesn't kill you straight off, there's no way you and Rose—! A *painting*? You'd risk her death and your own for a *painting*?'

The Ilyrian had no idea. His was even then a brilliant military mind, as I had realized listening to the strategy he had planned that night, but he had no understanding of the things beyond the realm of ordinary daily experience. I have since found this a general trait of the Ilyrian people: their genius is all for building and ordering, while ours was all for making song and story. If he came upon a ear of wheat in the road, the Ilyrian would stoop to pick it up, hull it between his hands as he walked along, and munch the kernels. A Burrener would retreat back the way he had come, recognizing that the Reaper would soon be back to collect the one he'd missed.

I looked around at them. 'Bring a force. I don't say there won't be work for them to do in paralyzing the rest of the Wolfhound soldiers. Bring a pirate armada, especially, to cut off Dun Aghadoe from the sea. But leave the Haunt free to act; I'm much more skilled at this sort of work than your troops are. No offense, but it's the truth.'

'Call the vote,' Sive moved. 'All in favor of Aengus' plan?'

In the end, Beod was the only one who voted against me. I asked, 'Will you lead your troops in, nevertheless, to secure the Cnoch?'

He sighed and nodded. 'It is the oath of the council to support its resolutions. On my father's behalf, I am authorized to commit our forces to the plan.' He met my eye. 'You may safely trust that part of your scheme, at least.'

'I never doubted it. May I leave you, the guildmaster, and Ja-Solem here to coordinate your parts, then?' I gave a grin to my co-conspirators. 'I have to go and get my head examined.'

'I'll say!' Sitric muttered as I left.

'Here,' she said, 'and here, I think.' Neilan's light touch probed the sunken place in my skull. 'Yes,' she said to herself. 'That ought to do it.'

I watched the sun beginning to illumine the harbor behind her. It would be rose and lavender, I thought, the color showing mostly in the caplets of the waves, the rest still the deep, quiet blue of night waters. 'Have you done anything like this surgery before, mistress?'

'Yes, once. Turn your head this way, please.'

She hadn't reassured me with a case history. The other patient had died, then. Her probing touch found the place, and my hand shot out to grip her forearm and push her away. Momentarily my head swam, then I swallowed and released her. 'Sorry.'

'No, it's quite all right.' She put her hands in her apron pockets and regarded me where I sat on a stool in her consulting room. 'There is a fragment in there, no doubt of it, whether of rock or of bone I can't tell, of course, but that isn't important. And if you can feel it when I press it, then it is at least somewhat free to move.'

'The skull bone hasn't closed around it, you mean?'

'Well, it's closed, but not, I think, to a normal thickness.' She smiled. 'That will help.' *Easier to cut*, she meant. She pulled her hands out of her apron and sat down in the chair on the other side of the table littered with wax tablets, instruments, and stoppered apothecary jars. 'Now, I know that you have been trained in medicine, so: what can I answer for you?'

I needed to stretch, so I got up and walked to the window, where I leaned on the casement and looked back at her. 'Mistress, if you had a chalcedon mine, would you bet it on this operation's succeeding?'

'No.' No hesitation, no apology, no hedging. I liked that. 'I think I can give you reasonable assurance of surviving the procedure,' she continued, 'and I believe removing that fragment will relieve pressure and perhaps make it possible for your sight to heal itself. But frankly, most of the knowledge we have of the brain comes from observing head injuries: a blow to this area produces these effects, and so on. It seems reasonable to suppose that if you had color vision before the injury, and now have none, that fragment may very well be the reason. But I am not at all certain of that. It is a chance, no more.' She was uncannily like Nestor. I think that was one reason I trusted her. The other was Timbertoe's wound. If she could save him from a walker's bone point, even at the cost of amputation, I was willing to trust her skill.

She was giving me time to work through it all. 'When can we do it?' I asked.

'How about tomorrow?'

'How about today?'

The siochla laughed a little, not unkindly. 'I know you want to get it over with, but there are one or two preparations to make first. I want to give you something to build up the humors of your blood a little against shock, and then, of course, we must also wait until your body has rid itself completely of the flotjin and the drug you have been taking regularly. Poppy?'

Her tone was neutral, but I was unnerved that her examination had uncovered my secret. 'A tincture,' I confirmed. 'It . . . I . . . sometimes when I can't stand it any more, the poppy gives me colors, if only in dreams.' I kept my head up.

'You know its deleterious effects.' Neilan didn't seek to blame, she only wanted to know if I knew how dangerous the stuff was.

'Yes. After a time, one can't break free of it.'

'Are you in that stage yet? Tell me honestly, please. I cannot make allowance for it in my calculations, otherwise, and an error could be fatal.'

I folded my arms across my chest. 'I think so. Early in the stage, anyway. I don't need it every day, or anything like that, but every once in a while I have a craving for the dreams, and then I take the poppy several times over the course of two or three days.'

She nodded. 'And how long has it been since your last episode?'

I mentally reckoned it out on my fingers. I was coming off one the day we'd found Diarmuid's death ship. 'Five days since I last took any.'

'Hmm. And in these days, have you experienced any itching or a sensation that your skin was crawling, or other symptoms – hallucinations, for example?'

Deep waters. Was the vision in the temple last night an hallucination, or a vision? Drug, or part of what made me an instrument of the Powers? The siochla was watching me, and, reckoning she must know something of these matters because some of her sisters were Sighted, I answered, 'I saw something the morning after my last dose, but I do not know whether to call it an hallucination. And last night in the Hall of the Dead I saw something else, mistress, but I do not think it was a poppy effect. I think it was a true Seeing.'

'Yes, I heard something of that. I had an intuition you might be one of the gifted ones. I haven't a shred of it myself, but I know how it takes some of my friends.' She smiled briefly. 'You have my sympathy.'

'Thanks.'

She struck her hands on her knees briskly and got up. 'Well, I think we are both as nearly ready as we need be, then. I'll want you to spend the night here for dosing, and then we'll begin an hour or so after dawn when the light is nice and strong. We should be finished before noon, though you'll sleep a good while longer than that, of course.' My mouth was suddenly dry, and my palms were sweating. She saw, because she came to me and took one of my hands in both her own. 'You have courage to run this risk for the Reverend Daughter. I admire that, and I will do my best to see it is rewarded, I promise you.'

'Thank you. Would you do me a favor?'

'Of course.'

'Would you dip your knife in brandy wine and also wash out the incision with it?'

201

'Ah, your healer knew that one, did he? I'm glad he taught you well. So many healers refuse to follow a few simple precautions. Have no fear: we clean everything very carefully.'

That was the only piece of advice I could give from my own experience with Nestor, so I nodded and headed for the door. 'Would you tell Timbertoe that I'll be in to play him a round of draughts a little later?'

'Oh, would you? Sister Gwen needs the break, frankly.'

I chuckled and gave her the salute of the skellig. Then I left the hospital and spent most of the day avoiding company, wandering wherever the will took me, past seafront and village, under the canopy of the arboretum's leaves, through the heavily perfumed pathwork of the Vale, up past the vinyards to where the salt air smelled of pine at the crest of the fire mountain and the sea stretched into the distance. If this was to be my last day of sight, I wanted to store my memory with as many beauties as I could.

Then, when the sun sank below the rim wall to the South, I mounted the slope to the house of healing and went in. There was a message for me with the portress: my pirates had returned to the harbor, and they had not caught up with Neddy's murderers.

She gave me the cup to drink. I put it aside for the moment. 'I'd like a word with the skipper alone, if you don't mind, first.' The siochla nurse left, pulling the door quietly closed behind her. They had put us both in the same room, though the surgery would be performed elsewhere. Last night while we had played draughts had not seemed the time, but it could not be put off longer now. 'Timbertoe, if things don't go well, the chalcedon mine is yours – if you don't mind having somebody take you in there in spite of the walkers.'

He didn't try to argue. 'I'll go in the daytime, in future.'

'My grandfather's ring goes to Rose, if Beod can get her out of Dun Aghadoe alive. If not, keep that too, and don't tell a soul you've got it, ever. Then, last, I want you to give a chalcedon to Pegeen,' I said, naming my Burrener jolly girl.

His eyes widened, but he nodded, then rubbed his nose. 'Go to sleep, Pilot. Ye're talking rot. Gwennie, me broad-bottomed beauty, get in here and knock this lad out!' he called to the nurse. I grinned and reached for the cup. Auntie came in flushed as a turkey wattle and threatening to leave him stranded without a chamber pot if he didn't stop making light of her.

He turned his head to wink at me, and that was the last thing I remember.

It was dark, and the ship rocked gently under me. 'Aengus?' a woman's voice called softly. 'Can you squeeze my hand?'

The breeze must be freshening, because the boat was rocking more, and I could begin to hear water trickling. By the Four, we'd sprung a leak! 'No, lie still,' her voice said above me, vaguely familiar, but what was she doing on the ship? Don't move, please, there are sandbags round your head.' Her voice was soothing, but made no sense. 'Squeeze my hand. Ah, excellent. And can you speak?'

'Tell the helm to trim. We're taking on water.'

She must have thought I'd asked for water. 'Here's the cup. Feel the rim? Sip.'

It was cool, but there was an unpleasant bitterness to it.

'I know. Awful, isn't it? Go back to sleep now.'

'We're rocking.'

'Go to sleep, Aengus.' A bit of inspiration. 'Captain Timbertoe has things well in hand.'

'Oh,' I said, and I slept.

The next time I woke was very sudden, and to great pain. I moaned and put a hand up in the darkness to press my shattered head. A cool touch gently caught my wrist, then held my hand. 'Don't touch. I'll give you something for the pain in a moment. Your eyes are bandaged, so don't be alarmed that you can't see anything. Are you still dizzy?'

'No,' I managed to say, but had to bite my lip.

'Wiggle your toes, please. Good. Here's the urinal: can you go?' I could and did. 'Fine. Good man. Sister, the potion, please?' She must have turned her head; her voice swung a little away from me.

'How did it go?' I said between my teeth.

'Marvellously.' Relief flooded through me. 'I'll tell you all about it later. Here, drink.' This was something different, sweet, smooth in the throat. 'Sleep some more, now. You'll find you can.'

I groped for her hand and grasped it. 'Thank you.'

She touched my cheek gently. 'Sleep.'

After that it was waking to either her voice or Auntie Gwen's, and sometimes the bitter cup and sometimes the sweet one, while Timbertoe rasped at them in the background not to forget this or that until Auntie finally told him very gently but very firmly that she thought she knew her business well enough without direction from somebody who made his living robbing other folk. I smiled and went lightly back to sleep. The pain was never again too much to manage, and the incision didn't infect at all, a tribute to the siochla's skill.

I think several days had passed by the time I was able to stay awake long enough without needing a draught to be able to talk much. Mistress Neilan came and sat down by me, her robe smelling of sunshine and lavender. As promised, she spent some time telling me in detail about the surgery, knowing my training would make me curious. It had been a fragment of my own cranium, she confirmed, which was a stroke of luck because if it had been rock there would have been much more danger of infection when the evil humors around the foreign substance were let out into the air. She had cut a small disc out of my skull, removed it to get at the sliver, cut that free, and then put the disc back into place. (I noticed Timbertoe had gone very quiet. That was a bit too detailed for his liking, I'd have wagered.) There was swelling, but no more than expected, and my reflexes and sensations were normal. 'So,' she concluded, 'the first part of the work has gone well. You've been a model patient, I might add, unlike some others I could name but won't.' There was a sniff from the other bed.

'How long before the bandages come off my eyes?'

She was a moment answering, and I could not tell if this was merely a pause to reckon, or if there might be reluctance to tell me. 'I think we'll give it another week or so. By then, the blood from the surgery should begin to be absorbed, and the swelling will reduce somewhat, relieving some pressure. Yes. I think we may try in a week.'

Powers, it was an eternity, that week! Timbertoe told every ribald story he could remember (that in itself took the better

part of three days and two nights), and once Ries came to see
me – the only delegate from the crew allowed in. I wasn't to have
too many visitors, he told me from the doorway, afraid he'd do
something wrong if he came into the room. The lads all missed
me, he said, and drank a cup to my good health every night, and
another to the skipper's. And one to poor Neddy. We'd a tight
crew, it sounded like.

Beod saw me before he left to sail home on the *Crown Prince*.
We would see each other again at Cnoch Aneil, he said, and we
gripped wrists. He was uncomfortable with the bandages and the
smells, I could tell.

Lady Sive took it all quite calmly on her several visits, and won
Timbertoe's heart completely by playing draughts against him
and winning only half the games. He'd finally got an opponent
of his own caliber, he reckoned, and I think he really believed it.
On the day she was to sail for home, she stooped close while the
dwarf was chuckling and packing the wooden men back in the
box. 'Aengus, regardless what comes, I want you to know there is
a place for you at my holding of Caer Civeen. Come home to the
Burren if you can.' Her hand patted my shoulder and she went
out, her gown rustling on the stone floor.

Her hands made several passes around my head, unwinding the
bandage. At each pass, the light through my eyelids grew and I
told her so. 'Good,' she murmured. 'That's good. Keep them
closed now when the bandage comes off: there's still a layer of
lint padding to get off.'

My nails were biting into my palms, and I had begun to sweat.
The headache came back, not severe, but a steady throb. I didn't
mention that.

Her cool fingers prised gently at the lint bandage over my eyes.
'There. Slowly, now.'

I had to grip my knees and wait a moment for the courage. Then
I slowly cracked open my eyelids. Light lanced in and I ducked
into Auntie's supporting arm, hissed and, shading my eyes this
time, tried it again.

The first thing I saw was the white sheet, pulled up over my
updrawn knees where I sat in the bed. The next thing I saw was
Timbertoe, dressed in a light hospital shift of some bleached stuff,

balancing at the foot of my bed on his pegleg and a crutch. And he was black-haired, gray-faced, gray-armed, white-gowned. 'Hullo, Skipper!'

His face, thinner than I remembered, broke into a cautious smile. 'Hell of a first sight, eh? Can ye see any colors?'

I strained, I willed to see those dead grays flicker into living colors. 'No, not a damned thing,' I said finally, and then disgraced myself by pulling free of the siochlas' gentle hands, putting my head down on my knees, and crying.

CHAPTER TWELVE

Don't give up hope. That is what all healers tell you after they know damned well there's no reason to go on hoping. Neilan told me the same thing a couple of times after the bandages came off until I told her rather more sharply than I should have done to leave off nattering and go tend some sick people. After that, she did not come to see me again for several days, but she did something exquisitely cruel: she sent Jamie in to see me.

The hunchback came at least once a day, sometimes oftener, and we talked of the Burren, of mending nets and shearing sheep, of the best cuttings of peat we had ever known and the worst storms. He was very alone in the midst of the self-assured siochlas and mourning Yoriandirkin.

One afternoon Neilan came back in, asked if I was done being petulant, and when I said I thought so, set about to remove the sutures. He was a very likeable fellow and would make a brilliant king, she agreed, because he knew what it was to be a common man. No, the odds that he would live to old age were not good at all because of his crippling condition. Yes, he knew it. Then she rebandaged me. The air was fine, she said. How about trying the terrace?

The sun, which shone here so much more than in the Burren that it still surprised me, sparkled off the waves in the harbor. I could see Yoriandirkin busy at setting out pine seedlings in the arboretum on the other side. A bee hummed about the nasturtium pot.

'How soon will I be able to travel, Neilan?'

'The bone will take some time to knit, as you know, and I won't discharge you until you're fit. A minimum of three weeks more; five would be better.' Two weeks would have to do. Vanu's Eve was just over a fortnight away. She must have known what I was thinking because she looked over a tea bowl at me. 'Wear your helmet when you leave, would you? I'll feel a little better for it.'

'Just for you. I don't think I can promise to have it on all the time, though.' I grinned at the worry in her face. 'I'll try to duck, if it comes to that.'

The siochla healer started to say something but shut her mouth on it and went back into the hospital. Both of us knew that a blow would open the healing bone again and possibly push the disc into my brain, so there was no need for warnings.

Over the next couple of weeks, I allowed my body to heal itself, walking as much as I was able, finally swimming and running. The throbbing in my head gradually diminished, though the tenderness at the site of the incision itself remained, of course. That could not be expected to heal for quite some time longer. I tested whether I could still trust my reflexes in using weapons, and worked at once more toughening my hands with the unarmed combat that Symon had taught me. James was fascinated by my skill at weapons, having never had the advantage of training with a weaponsmaster. He confided that he felt people would be disappointed in a king who could not handle a sword. I looked at him over the blade I was sharpening. 'You'll have captains aplenty, sire, to handle the swords. It's justice and mercy folk look for in a king and there they will not be disappointed, I think.'

'Aengus, I don't know how to be a king. Mother's tried to teach me enough bearing and manners to get by amongst well-bred company but, truth to tell, I'm a very simple man.'

'Then you will be a very simple king.' I grinned. 'That's the only good kind, eh, neighbor?'

His look lightened. 'If I could give the whole military side of it over to someone like you, I think I might be able to manage the rest.' Suddenly, struck by the idea, he looked at me straightly. 'Will you be my captain, as a favor? I don't know what the proper reward for such duty is, but—'

'The reward for such duty is the duty itself.' Colin Mariner had served King Dilin of the Burren. On impulse, I held my sword out to him across my palms. 'Command me, sire.'

He looked surprised but, then, recalling what his mother must have taught him in boyhood, he took the sword in his big rough hands, tapped me on the shoulders with it, and gave it back to me. 'I accept your service and count you my sworn man from this day, as I am your sworn leige, to both our honors. May there be perfect understanding between us for ever.'

I kissed the hilt of my sword and sheathed it.

His eyes were shining and he seemed to stand straighter. 'Thanks. That's a relief. Inishbuffin will always be yours, if that was on your mind; I'm not after the chalcedons.' He laughed a little. 'But I suppose we ought to worry about this business at Cnoch Aneil before we figure out how to hold the Burren once we've got it.'

'Aye, and there's great risk in it for you. I'm sorry, I couldn't think of any other way to do it.'

'I understand there wouldn't have been any part in it at all left for me if it hadn't been for your voice speaking on my behalf.' That bit of news would have come by way of Lady Mac Maille, I guessed. 'I'll remember that, Aengus.'

I waved away his gratitude. 'I saw you hurling slingstones this morning. It's a weapon I've never mastered. Would you mind showing me how you get that flat spin on them?'

I never was as good with a sling as Jamie was, but I taught him a little swordwork. A week later the message came from Sitric that all other preparations had been made. His spies had confirmed Rose was held at Dun Aghadoe, and a proclamation had gone forth from the regents' council, headed by His Grace Jorem, that the Hag's Embrace festival would take place with the favor of the Maid of the Vale's presence ten days hence in Dun Aghadoe. It was time to move.

Ries, and Harrald – who sported a monstrously swollen nose and no jeweled belt – leaned on the oars in the curragh, watching. The crew had had nearly three weeks to get used to the sight of Timbertoe's empty pant leg and the crutch, but it was still painful for everyone concerned to witness him trying to get himself down into the boat. And he was angry with his weakness, which made it worse. But he was as tough as boiled mutton and he would have to learn to make his way with his condition, so I left him to it, and turned to James. 'Now, the boats Ja-Solem sent will be a little slower than us, so it will be nooning the day after tomorrow when you arrive at Skejfallen. Stay hidden aboard your ship until I get word to you. We have to make sure, first.' In the council meeting we had decided there would be a small group of men waiting for the queen and prince. Instead of a password, they would show their tattooed forearms, and the royal party would have directions to look for a light-colored mate with a porpoise for his tattoo. On so important a mission, Sitric himself would be present at the dockside to make sure Caitlin and Jamie's arrival was covered, and the dwarves with him would be members of his picked guildsmen. The small emerald chalcedon was ample payment, he'd smiled, for this personal service.

But that wasn't exactly how it would go. I'd seen to that. My years as the Haunt had taught me a certain way of doing things.

The prince turned his head to glance out at Ja-Solem's boats, bobbing at anchor in the darkness of the harbor. The robes of his disguise fluttered, and he put an absent hand up to the earring that distinguished Shimarrat men. He and the queen would remain costumed until they were safely behind doors in Skejfallen. The council had felt it likely the Dinan watchers, and there were sure to be watchers, would be looking for the prince and his siochla mother aboard a dwarfen ship, and we had chosen Ilyrian ships as having the best chance of getting through unmolested, but unknown to them I had changed Jamie's party to Ja-Solem's ships. If they were stopped and boarded by Wolfhounds, the flowing robes would help to hide Jamie's crippled back, and the master of the foreign crew had taught him to say some words in the language. I was pretty sure I knew what the words must mean. It was what I'd have told a Dinan patrol that boarded my boat.

At my shoulder, Dlietrian seemed at ease in his robes. I had spoken with the council, and the Yoriandir archer had found a niche with the small retinue that would accompany Jamie. All of us turned as Caitlin came down the dock, accompanied by an honor guard of Yoriandirkin. Jamie heaved a sigh of relief that they could finally get under way and clambered down into the waiting boat.

Caitlin gathered the skirts of her costume, but lingered a moment. The moment stretched. 'You have turned my life upside down, Aengus, but I'm still glad I opened the gate that night, though the fire was so snug and the night so nasty. Goodbye until Cnoch Aneil. May the Lady look after you.'

'And you, mistress.'

Timbertoe hissed impatiently from our curragh. I gave her the salute of the Vale and handed her down to Dlietrian. Then I landed in our boat with a jump that nearly pitched the old seadog overboard, which is where he belonged, I told him, if he couldn't shut up and let a fellow see a siochla off properly, and Ries and Harrald rowed for the ship.

Shortly after the pegleg had been swung aboard in an Old Maid's Goose, we hoisted the mainsail and tacked for the open sea. I got out my rutter, made the calculations, and gave bearings for Inishbuffin. Then I went to my cramped cabin, drew the blue bottle out of its drawer, and poured myself a liberal dose. Since the operation hadn't worked anyway, there was no point in denying myself, I reasoned. I swallowed the drugged flotjin with the guilty sense that Neilan was looking over my shoulder, disapproval in her calm eyes. Bugger it. I stretched on my bunk, watched the colors float for a while, and then slept as I had not slept for weeks, for all the siochla's potions.

In the forenoon we sighted the peninsula through the cold rain that had begun falling nearly as soon as we left the Vale. There was something unnatural in that, Ries said darkly, clouds everywhere else but over the witches' garden. Magic, I told him, and ordered that he drop anchor a couple of hundred yards off the Inishbuffin jetty. Walkers can't cross water, they say. The bos'n was happy enough to comply, never once suggesting that they should take me all the way in to the pier.

Timbertoe was braced against the rail when I went aft to climb into the landing boat. 'No sunshine, Pilot.'

'No, but it's not so dark, and I'll be back in an hour.'

'Don't like the thought of ye going back in there alone.' He was keeping an eye on the battlements, lest any apparition should loose another bone lance from up there. It was a measure of his nerve that he dared to stand topside at all.

'Just be ready to pick me up again.' I had a long rope in my pack, and I intended to come down that cliff face like a bead on a string if I had to escape quickly, no messing about with the stairs cut into the cliff.

'All right. Straight in, straight out! Don't make me have to come rescue ye.'

I made him an obsene gesture, took up the oars, and rowed in. Half the crew were watching in fascination, and half were crouched behind the companionway hatch. The skin between my shoulder blades twitched as I tied up the boat, shouldered the pack, and started to make my way up the stairs. The treads were slimed with bird droppings, but easier than the ladders at Gull's Cove had been. It did not take me long to reach the top of the cliff. Giving a jaunty wave to my mates that belied the flutters in my stomach, I took the landward path around the skellig wall to the front, where the gates had stood.

I could sense presences, but nothing untoward happened when I picked a careful way amongst the remains and entered the skellig. I kept my knife in my hand, nevertheless, and walked quickly, chin on my shoulder to look behind me much of the time. There was a sudden flurry in the grass near my feet, and I jumped, dagger already starting forward, but it was only a fieldmouse frightened by my clumsy feet. It was the first live thing besides birds that I had seen at Skellig Inishbuffin. 'Thy pardon, wee brother,' I murmured, smiling. 'Thee's proof against walkers, I see. Lucky thee.'

I went up through the second gate, then made my way into the complex of the skellig itself. Once I thought I heard a stealthy clicking behind me and swung around quickly, but nothing was to be seen. It must have been a rat, I told myself, but the fear started to gnaw at the back of my mind. I had wanted to go along to the apothecary and see whether Nestor's shade might appear to me, but decided against it and went straight to the round tower.

The ramshackle platform Timbertoe and I had made to climb up to the door was still in place, and I didn't want to make an open invitation to some other foolhardy marauder, so I knocked it all down again and instead slung up the grappling hook. When it caught on something inside, I pulled myself up, then left the hook where it was, but hauled up the rope to lower myself inside the burnt-out tower. I had my hand on the rope ready to slide down when a sound outside made me freeze. There was definitely something in the courtyard below the tower. My breath came fast. If it caught me inside the tunnels . . . *Piss off, you son of a whore!* I kenned to it, and the sound ceased.

I slid down the rope. Now I took the lantern from the pack and lit it, tucking the firesticks I had brought from the Vale in my sash in case the candle went out for any reason. An extra candle was in the pack, and I should be able to find it by touch even in the dark. I left the extra rope alone for now.

The tunnel and stairs to the treasury were not so long as I remembered, possibly because I wasn't having to pace myself by Timbertoe's slow gait this time, and I was soon filling the small pouch I had brought for the purpose. Though I couldn't see the colors of the stones, I remembered what trays were the rarer shades, and I knew in which one I had found Sitric's emerald. I took another ruby chalcedon, easily as big as the first, for Timbertoe; some smaller, less precious green shades for the crew; one that I thought might be a garnet for Neddy's mother; a very faceted sapphire for sweet Peggeen; and one out of a tray that looked as though it might be somewhere between a ruby and a pink for Neilan. As a siochla the wealth it represented would mean little to her, but I felt I owed a debt there. Then I took random fistfuls to finance the fleet and have some left over for myself. Lastly I walked to one of the baskets containing unworked nodes and took a huge one, just for curiosity's sake, which I tucked in the pack, along with the pouch when I had tied the drawstring. Taking another few stones to tuck in my waistband should I need to hurl them at pursuing walkers, I picked up the lantern once more and headed through the mine into the caverns.

At once the fear returned tenfold. I had not realized how utterly silent it was here and, without Timbertoe behind me, I was only too conscious of the sound of my footfalls breaking the heavy weight of the dark into echoes that bounced alarmingly from near to far and back again. I kept walking steadily, though I was only just this side of terror.

I stopped for a moment to lean with the lantern and be sure of the bloodstains that marked the route, *and the footsteps kept coming.*

How I did not let a strangled yell escape me I do not know, because the lantern in my hand shook so violently I nearly unseated the candle from its small cup. I turned to face the thing with my dagger drawn. Far back in the darkness I had come through there was a momentary gleam of light, but it was not the gray shadow of an apparition, nor the bright evil of its weapons. It was an ordinary candle.

I was nearly sick with sudden relief and had my mouth open to yell a hail to whomever Timbertoe had sent ashore looking for me when reason returned in a cold flood. No pirate would have kept coming beyond that treasury, and Timbertoe was not such a fool as to send a couple of them with explicit directions to find their way through the mine and caverns. If he had sent them, they would have been instructed to hail me from the trap door in the round tower, or at most from the mine cavern if he'd sent someone he really trusted like Ries. But there had been no hail, and whoever it was was staying well back.

I blew out my candle and waited in a shallow niche off to the side.

He, or they, followed the bloodstains as I had done and the lantern was well-shielded, affording a very small light, most of it directed straight down. '—a corner somewhere up ahead, likely,' a voice was whispering as they approached my hiding place.

'Hope the bastard hasn't fallen down a shaft. We'll be under the lash for sure if he's managed to kill himself.'

'Rather go under the lash than face His Grace.'

There was a grunt of agreement. They passed by without discovering me: two of them, black hoods cast back in the darkness to listen, amulets of the Wolf's head.

I had my knife in the rearward one and had dumped him over into the chasm on the other side of the path before the leader even realized his mate had suddenly stopped walking. He never really had a chance to deflect the chop that felled him at my feet. The lantern smashed and the light was snuffed, so I carefully felt my way back into the niche and retrieved my own lantern. The bright flare of the firestick got the wick caught in a moment, and by the lantern's light I stripped the uniform off the second man I had killed. I reasoned it was unlikely that only two men had been set to watch the skellig, so I had more topside to deal with. Quickly I dressed as a Brother of the Fang, rolled the corpse into the chasm to follow his friend in case any more of them came this way, and went on toward the temple, hurrying now as quickly as I dared for the sake of Timbertoe and the lads. If fortune favored us, this was a troop that had come overland on horses and hidden in the skellig. If not, then the pirates were out there fighting a Dinan ship, and they had been caught with not much water to work with between the *Gem* and the cliff face.

The scuffed sand and some odd bits of bone, together with the tattered remnants of my grandfather's robe were undisturbed, so the troop topside had not found the Swan Pool entrance and come down here. I whispered a reassurance to Bruchan's spirit, as though in that awful tortured state where he fought the walkers he could hear it, and drew back the cloth to retrieve the color pot. The significance of the spiral he had scrawled in his moment of death had finally occured to me while I had lain thinking in the bandaged darkness of the Vale. I brushed carefully until I uncovered the terracotta pot he had struggled to bring me. It still lay where he had left it, and it was intact, the seal unbroken. Whatever else he might do with the rest of the Mariner's set, Jorem would not get this one. I tucked it carefully in my pack, patted my grandfather's robe, and rose to my feet.

Then I had a thought.

The troop up there couldn't possibly have overnighted in the skellig, or they would have suffered the same fate as Timbertoe and I nearly had. No doubt, however, they had heard the rumors along with everybody in the Burren. I looked down at my grandfather's moldy remnant of a robe.

It was a hard thing, and I had to swallow my gorge once or twice, but finally I had it slung on as well as possible, with the black Dinan hood drawn over my head. I went into the temple, this time making the gesture of respect to the Four, and ducked under the lintel of the Fickle Friend. 'Thy pardon, my lord, but the need is great,' I murmured to him as I took up the divided dish, powder on one side, oil – just a small seep of it left – still on the other. I dusted Bruchan's robe thoroughly with the powder and added some on the Dinan hood as well, mostly to the back of it as I didn't want the stuff around my face. Then, holding the dish with the oil at arm's length and the candle in the other hand, well away from it, I bowed a little. 'Thy help in this, lord, would be appreciated, if the sunmill can spare thee a moment.'

I had not intended to be flippant – indeed, I was more serious than I had been the first time I had seen Tychanor the Warm in this small chamber – and I was shaken by the laugh that ran around the walls, a young man's laugh of great good humor. I bowed again and backed out of the shrine.

This time I did not go out by way of the Swan Pool, since I had to be as near our ship as possible to have any hope of getting out of this situation with my skin intact. There would, of course, be a troop waiting either in the round tower, or just outside it for their men to return with the prisoner.

I made my last preparation at the place where I had killed them: I scraped some lampblack off the shards of the Wolfhounds' lantern and darkened my face and hands as well as I could. In dim light, with fear already eating at them, maybe they would see not more than eyes within a black hood and fisted stumps for hands, one of which held what was obviously a ritual dish. That, together with the hunched back that the pack under my grandfather's robe gave me, ought to help things along nicely. I would ditch the lantern as soon as I heard anything up ahead.

I was becoming familiar with the mines, but everything looks different when you reverse your steps, so I still had to follow the blood trail. I had a bad moment when it occured to me that if there had been more of them sent down into the tunnel, they might be in the mine or treasury, but there really was nothing for it but to go on. When I got into the mine itself, I wrapped a fold of robe around most of the lantern and went across the cavern with as little light showing as possible. I listened at the treasury door, but heard nothing, so I left the lantern outside and whipped around the door frame. Nothing. They had sent only two men; probably the poor bastards had been picked by lot. I retrieved the lantern and shut the doors to the treasury behind me, then began to mount the stairs, stepping carefully not to make any sound which might warn someone up there.

I made it to the top of the steps without incident. From here, I could feel my way along the tunnel wall, so I snuffed the lantern and left it. Shortly after, I began to see dim light where the trap door let a little illumination down into the tunnel. This would be the hardest part, because whoever was up there would have nowhere to run, and in the confined area even a ghost like me might take a mortal hurt from a desperate man's knife. So I gave plenty of warning.

With the haft of my dagger I began tapping very quietly on the tunnel wall, walking slowly toward the square of light that marked the trap door.

'—so I says, How the hell am I supposed to believe it's my kid with you whoring around like . . . What's that?'

'What's what?'

'That, damn you, listen! See?'

Tap, tap. I added a scuff now, one foot dragging longer.

'Hullo, Harry? Will, is that you? Did you get him?' one of them called.

Tap. Scuff. Tap. To this I added my fingernails scraping on the stone, since I was close enough to think they might hear it now.

Now it sounded as though they might both have got to their feet up there; something else, too: a sword chiming from its sheath. 'Damnit, Will, you bastard! I'll run you through if you don't quit frigging around! *Harry, answer me!*'

It was all I could do not to laugh, but white teeth would give it away, and besides I had to do this next very quickly. I stooped to put the ritual oil bowl out of harm's way, left the dagger as well, and limbered my hands. *Scuff.* Fingernails. Gnashed my teeth together.

'By Beldis, what the hell—?'

I took a running couple of steps, hit the pile of rubble that Timbertoe and I had left for a step, grabbed the first ankle I found, and dragged the soldier back down into the tunnel with me. The heel of my hand found the point in the back of his neck, and he was unconscious by the time I let him slump to the floor. I didn't have the heart to kill him. The other man had let out an inarticulate cry of fear, and I had been aware of the scurry of his booted feet amongst the charred timbers up there. Unless I missed my guess, he was climbing out as fast as mortal terror could propel him.

That was fine with me, I let him do it, giving him nothing but silence below, which would work on his nerves more powerfully than any sound could have done. I marked his boots scrambling up the inner wall of the tower. He was hauling himself up on the rope and being very quick about it. He started to bellow when he got his head even with the door, I judged. *'Walkers!'* Then his voice was gone abruptly, and I realized he had jumped from the doorway to the courtyard twenty feet below. He was one frightened man!

There was a lot of commotion out there, but I couldn't tell clearly what was going on because the stone walls were so thick. I heard a horse's hooves, though, striking off the stone court, and that told me this was a land-based troop. Better and better.

Grinning to myself I retrieved my dagger and the oil dish and climbed up through the square hole of the trap door. Smart arse, I thought to myself. That soldier hadn't been too terrified to think of twitching the rope up with him. I had no way to climb out except the long rope with the grappling hook in my pack, and that would make a noise clanging off the timbers of the ruined stair. Then I tilted my head back to study the remnants of the staircase that had once gone from floor to floor of the tower. *Yes*, I thought.

It was tricky in places, and I had to do it quickly or lose the advantage of surprise. The troopers were still in the courtyard, milling, shouting questions and answers. A quick look as I went up showed one of them on the ground, hands clamped to his knee, grimacing in pain while his fellows crowded around and the officer tried to make some sense of it. The same glance told me that a couple of them had bows slung over their shoulders. I didn't like that.

Finally I emerged through the opening of the stair on the topmost storey of the round tower, beneath the fretwork of roof timbers. The floor was still good here, no flame having climbed this far, though everything was blackened with smoke where it wasn't whitened with bird droppings. I startled a lone seagull, preening on the deep stone sill of one of the four open windows that faced in the four directions. Possibly I could have let myself down by my long rope on the other side of the tower from the Wolfhound troop, but at any moment one of them could have rounded the tower and seen me, so I hooked the grappling iron securely, slung the rope over on that side, and left my escape for the moment. Now to drive these vermin out of my skellig! I sheathed my dagger and picked up the dish of oil.

When I appeared full in the window, it took a couple of moments for one of them to see me, because they were watching the door two storeys below. The rainy wind was blowing the robes nicely, and I stood back just a little so it couldn't hit my face under the roof. 'There!' one of them cried and flung up a pointing finger. I had their undivided attention in less than two heartbeats.

They were either very brave, too stupid to be imaginative, or mortally terrified, because not one of them moved except the man with the broken leg, who very sensibly lurched to his unhurt leg with the help of a mate's cloak and began trying to haul himself into a saddle, babbling that he had told them so.

We stared at each other.

Then one man broke, running for his horse, and that started the whole knot of them moving, hands flung up in the sign against the Hag. The officer, who stood with drawn sword, roared, 'Hold! Hold, damn you!' He must have got through to a couple, because they turned at bay against their horses, but they did not mount, and no horse was yet under spur for the gates. The rest made a trampling group behind them.

I stared down at the officer. A tough nut, this one. He was peering with narrowed eyes, trying to see something that would tell him one way or the other whether this thing in the window was alive, or not. If he sent a flanking maneuver around the base of the tower, I'd have to race back down into the mine and try for the Swan Pool, with the whole lot of them following me this time, I was sure.

Get thee gone, I told him coldly in his mind.

He flinched, ducking away as though from a heavy blow, but he didn't break. He held up his sword in front of him for the protection of the iron and straightened. 'Begone yourself, wight,' he said harshly, forcing out the words. 'We want no trouble with you. It's the live one we're after.'

Behind him, his men were now reining in their horses to listen to him, though they had not heard my kenning to him. This time I put as much anger into it as I could and roared the mental words: *Arise, brothers and sisters! Arise, and avenge the master!*

The troopers all heard it. Horses reared at the sudden sawing at the reins, several men cried out in fear, and one soldier slumped from his saddle in a dead faint. The officer backed a couple of paces, sword up, then stopped. A trooper spurred for the gates, and the man with the broken leg rode awkwardly after him.

Damn the man. This was getting dicey.

Last ploy. I raised the dish in my left hand, pointed first at the men below, and then at the ritual vessel. *We will drink your blood,* I kenned to them all.

By some freak, the wind dropped suddenly, as though holding its breath, and the nervous pawing of the horses stopped for a moment. It was utterly quiet, except for the sound of the gulls and the water surging against the cliffs below the skellig. Then we all heard it: rattling, rattling from the gate, from the refectory and kitchens, from the workshop block, from the stables, all converging on this one spot.

As though a spell upon them had snapped, the troopers pulled their horses roughly around and nearly rode each other down trying to get to the gates. The officer's nerve still didn't desert him, though. He moved toward his horse, but deliberately, as if even now he thought one steady Wolfhound could stand down all the heretic ghosts there ever were. He swung into the saddle, checked his horse when it began to walk after the others, and again stared up.

The fellow was tiresome, honestly. *Thy time has come, Wolf's whelp,* I kenned. *Thus I come to take you NOW!* On the word, I dashed the oil from the dish over the powered robes I wore. There was a bright flare which died to be replaced by thick, white smoke coiling up from the robes and carried streaming by the wind through the window.

When I could see through the smoke, he was halfway to the gate.

Before the sound of his mount's pounding hooves had left the courtyard, I had the hood off and was smothering the smoke. The stuff was lethal if inhaled. My eyes burned, and I leaned out of the window on the opposite side from the way they had gone to wash my face under the rain coming off the roof, wetting the hood and slapping at Bruchan's robe. After a moment, there was little left of the smoke. Four years of damp in the untended temple had seeped into the powder grains enough to make me relatively safe. I inhaled some of the cold sea wind and listened. The rattling had stopped. Maybe they would let one man through.

I climbed down into the tower once more to collect the rope dangling at the door. Then I went lightly up, lowered myself on the long rope from the window to the top of the skellig wall that met it on the seaward side, and leaned from the parapet to give a wave to the pirate ship, though I did not raise my voice to hall it in case the sound should carry down the hill toward the troopers. I had fixed the shorter length of rope to let myself down over the skellig wall facing the direction of Gull's Cove when the laughter first came from the kitchen, then from the foot of the tower here on this side, then in many voices from around the skellig, bubbling up like a spring welling from the earth. There was nothing of malice in the sound and, knowing them now, I was not afraid.

The skellig folk had risen at my call, and now they laughed with me at the ruse which had sent the killers from our midst. I paused with my hand on the rope. *I thank thee, brothers and sisters. I would stop for a seisum with thee, but am bound on our business and cannot tarry. I will return if I may to make the fire and see thee at thy well-earned rest. Wait for me, and wait for the Master.*

Faint but clear I heard Symon's voice: *Aye, Aengus, we'll wait. Do thee go safe to make the painting.*

I can't see the colors, Sy. The Powers took my colors away. But I'll do what I can for thee and thy bairns, I promise. Rest a while.

Then I let myself down over the wall and trotted for the cliff walk.

The *Gem* was waiting, though Timbertoe had had to draw his cutlass and stand over the anchor chain, or they'd have had it hauled up and been a mile downwind by now. When they were finally convinced that the thing under the blackened face and grave-stained tatters was only me, I had help getting the curragh aboard, though a couple of them were making the sign against the Hag when they thought I couldn't see. I nodded to Timbertoe, and he called for sails and rudder to take us out.

When we were finally underway, I stripped off the disguise, swilled my hands and face in a bucket of seawater, and unbuckled the pack without removing from it the pouch of gems. I would

221

take that out later, and let it be known I'd acquired it at the Vale, so as to throw them off thinking it came from the skellig, else the treasury would not have been safe very long.

I drew out the color pot, my heart racing at finally seeing this one color so crucial that my grandfather had died trying to bring it to me. The wax seal yielded to my dagger point. Timbertoe was over my shoulder. I handed up the clay pot. 'What color?'

The dwarf steadied himself on his crutch and his pegleg and carefully removed the lid. He looked, brought it closer to his eyes and looked again. Then he glanced around at the watching crew and put it back in my hand.

It was empty.

'Sorry, Giant,' he said gruffly and stumped away, flapping a hand at the crew to take them with him.

Timbertoe was at the rail when we made port at Skejfallen. I was out of sight in the companionway. I had had plenty of time on the way from the skellig to do some thinking, and I had explained it to the lads, who at first were disbelieving, and then a murderous light had awakened in their eyes. They had made it look good for the guildmaster's heliographs on the way in, even though we didn't know how much his watchers could see at night, and they'd have to wait till dawn to pass the message anyway. The burgundy flag with its gem of white was lowered to half-mast, and the crew went about the business of docking silently, as though they had lost a mate nobody was mentioning.

'Got him,' Timbertoe said quietly. 'Warehouseman across the way there is watching us like an osprey.'

'There may be more of them,' I reminded him.

Ries passed the hatch. 'There's another smoking a pipe outside the pub up the street.'

We waited. 'There goes the warehouseman,' Timbertoe reported with satisfaction a few minutes later. 'Off to bring his master the news and collect his coin, the whoreson. Your foreign friend's ships are at the next dock down, by the way.'

'How many ships?' I questioned urgently.

Under cover of striking a spark into his pipe, he turned his back to the fellow watching from the pub. 'Two. Don't see any sign of the third one, the one flagged with the crown.'

'How about the Shimarrat ship? Can you see her?'

'Oh, aye. Right next to us, she is, all safe.'

'Send somebody to find out the gossip about the *Crown*, and another to Brunehilda with your message.'

Ries was dispatched to the pub, ostensibly to bring back a bucket of stew for the men's supper. To any observers, it would appear the crew was staying aboard, which would have been the natural course if we had indeed lost a man on the voyage from the Vale and had not yet returned to our home port at Inishkerry. Our bos'n returned with the stew and the news: the *Crown Prince* had been attacked by Dinan ships and sent to the bottom. The men in the pub were drinking toasts to the Wolfhounds, for it was thought the Ilyrian prince might have been aboard, and the Ilyrians were no allies of Jarlshof.

Actually, Beod should be about at the Gap with his troops now, and Jorem's net had missed James, too, as we confirmed with the master of the Shimarrat ship next to us when the second spy had left his post at the pub.

We waited impatiently for Arni to return with Brunehilda's reply. When it came in the affirmative, Timbertoe gave a hitch to his sash. 'All right, lads, by ones and twos, now, and meet in the barrel yard down the lane from The Top Gallant. Quick!' The ship emptied rapidly, the men scattering to take roundabout routes through the alleys.

Timbertoe and I went ashore after ̇ had secured the color pot and the gems. My grandfather's ring I wore, and my grappling hook was slung over my shoulder. I went in first, left the guard on the door spitting curses behind his gag, and opened the gate to the lads. We crossed the stone-paved court soundlessly in our wetted-down seaboots, Harrald and Arni carrying the skipper between them. The great door was not bolted. Evidently he felt secure enough with his spies and his thugs. We slipped in like fog.

I glanced back to make sure everybody was in. The pirates were looking about with amazement. I snapped my fingers softly. No time for wool-gathering. They nodded, daggers gleaming in their hands. I motioned to Harrald and Arni, and they set Timbertoe down. These three would hold the door clear for the rest of us. Then, two by two, I sent them searching through the house. Ries took with me upstairs.

We surprised the impostor dallying with the girls before the fire in the room where Sitric had told me the Wolfhounds had set a price on my head, a price which I now knew had been carefully negotiated between himself and Jorem. 'Raise an alarm, and you're a dead man,' I told Silky. 'I've nothing against you or the girls. Be quiet and you'll come out of this all right.'

He had the good sense to sit still, and so did the girls. 'Now, now, old lad,' he said. 'Ye can't be expecting to get away with pinching anything from the guildmaster himself.' I was busily lashing him in the chair while Ries did the same for the girls, who were remarkably unconcerned about the ropes, only balking at the gags.

'Don't puff me lips all up,' the brunette warned.

Ries told her what she could kiss to make the swelling come down, but I hissed a warning to shut up and get on with it. 'Now,' I said to Silky with the gag in my hand. 'Where is he?'

He met my eye. 'Don't believe I can tell ye that, mate. I've took his gold all these years, after all.'

I was irritated, but not surprised. It was a fair enough answer. I gagged him, then reached into my sash pocket and made as if I'd withdrawn something small, which I leaned to tuck into Silky's sash. 'If you see him before I do, give him this for me, would you?' I hadn't actually put anything in the dwarf's pocket at all. Drawing Ries close, I put my mouth close to his ear. 'There's a secret door in this room somewhere. My guess is he's watching. Gesture like you're asking me if we should go upstairs.'

The old bos'n was a fair mummer. I nodded to his 'question', and we went out of the room, quietly closing the door behind us. I gestured Ries to go up the flight, making some very slight noise, and then to return silently. Two of the other lads were coming up the stairs, and I made them an urgent motion to freeze. They did, and Ries was back beside me when I went through the door.

Sitric was stooping to get whatever he thought I had left in Silky's sash, completely deaf to the noises of entreaty coming from the girls. The narrow door to the spying gallery stood open beside the fireplace. I caught him just as he reached it and dropped him with a fist to the kidney.

He was no good for several minutes and by the time he was, our lads had secured the house, though we were sure

there must be more of them around in the out buildings. I
had taken the opportunity while Sitric was retching to have
a look in the gallery. Even if this were the only treasury he
had in that house, and I didn't think it was, the guildmaster
was a very wealthy dwarf, and most of it was blood money,
blackmail, or tax of the members of the guild. Also he had a
table back there with tablets and stacks of coins on it. He'd
probably been doing his accounts when we'd broken in and
secured Silky and the girls. I glanced over them and found what
I wanted.

When I came out of the hidden room, Sitric was in a chair,
bent backward with a hand jammed to his back, trying to stop
the spasms. His light hair was stuck to his head with sweat. I
dropped the scroll with Jorem's seal in his lap, and with it his
own reply, a detailed account of our battle plans. He regarded
the scrolls for a moment, then looked up at me. 'Business.' He
grimaced a smile.

'So is this, my personal business as well as the council's. You've
betrayed me twice, Guildmaster: once on the night your h:.._'ings
were supposed to kill me off outside The Top Gallant, and again
when you alerted Jorem to the fact I'd be returning to Inishbuffin
to get the last color pot.'

With my having the proof in my hand in the form of the letter
from the Wolfhound, Sitric made no denial. 'You were never a
real pirate, Burrener.'

Ries went for him, and I had to hurl him back bodily. 'That's
what he wants, Bos'n – to go quickly! Don't do it!'

That brought old Ries out of it with a cold shudder of restraint.
Aye, Pilot. I was forgetting meself. It's yours to do.'

'No, it's the guild's to do, and I have no doubt they'll enjoy
t. This bastard has been fattening himself on all the mates
or years.' I looked down at the flaxen-haired dwarf in the
hair.

Sitric did what I was betting he would. 'It isn't too late to send
nother message to Jorem, a diversionary message, perhaps.' He
ept his head up. 'I'd be willing to do that.'

I pretended disgust. 'At what price? I won't waste another
emstone on you—'

He went for the only deal there was: 'I'll take free passage on a ship, any ship, bound for any port, and I'll swear never to come back.'

But there was the small matter of a young cabin boy. I locked eyes with him. 'No good. You owe us a death for a death, Guildmaster, and by the Four, you're going to pay your tab. The Moot is gathering at The Top Gallant right now, in fact.' If he had been pale before, he was absolutely ashen now. 'But here's the deal: you write a message to my dictation, and send it out by birds or mirrors, whatever you would normally do with urgent news for your kennel mate over in Dun Aghadoe. In return—' I pulled a needle annointed with Hag's Embrace, a lethal dose, from my sash. 'I'll give you an easy going when the time comes. This is poisoned.'

'How do I know I can trust your word for it?'

I spat in my palm and held out my hand to him. '*I've* never betrayed a mate.'

His eyes flicked from Ries to me to Silky. He bit the inside of his cheek to keep from betraying fear. Finally, after a long moment, he spat in his palm and we shook.

I looked down at Silky. 'Can we count on your witness in the Moot?'

No questions, no deal-cutting here, only one emphatic nod, eyes smoldering over the gag as he stared at Sitric. Betrayal of a pirate by another pirate, let alone by the guildmaster, is a heinous offense.

'Untie him, Bos'n, would you? Leave the girls, though.' There was no accurate way to tell where their sympathies lay. I'd send someone to see to them later.

Writing the message didn't take long, and Sitric's hand was steady enough that the script matched his normal handwriting, as I verified by a quick look at his accounts. 'Allow me to point out this is mad. Even if Jorem diverts a large part of his army to Croagh Raven, you can't possibly think he'll leave Cnoch Aneil unguarded. You'll be captured, and the Wolfhounds will most certainly execute you as one of the highlights of the festival. You'll never get anywhere near the Maid.'

'My worry.'

'You have James somewhere safely in hiding, I presume.'

'Presume what you like. On your feet.'

226

For the first time, he showed his fear, but I hauled him to his feet and quickly gagged him to insure his silence on the way out, in case any of his men were about.

The Top Gallant was packed with pirates. The air was already thick with smoke, but no one was drinking. The landlord had closed the tavern. A pirate himself, he wanted everyone there to be focused on the matter before the Moot. Dwarves were sitting on the bar, squeezed in on the benches, thickly crowded on the stairs leading up to the jolly girls' chambers, and there was very little room to move on the floor of the pub itself. Despite the rainy night, the room was already too warm by the time Timbertoe and I walked in with Sitric. Instantly, there was utter silence.

All those eyes took in Timbertoe's empty pant leg, and there were winces on some faces before the guild swung their attention to me. To my red hair. To my Burrener height. As clearly as if they had kenned it, I heard. *Bugger me, it's him the Null Whisper order was about!*

Brunehilda rose from one of the room's few chairs and advanced to meet us, signing her people on the doors to lock them. Guild business was about to be conducted, and we wanted no inquisitive fishermen to come bumbling in. Her look went frankly to the skipper's tucked-up trouser leg, and out of the corner of my eye I saw him holding his breath. The lady captain cocked an eyebrow and said proudly, 'Leave it to you to try to kick the shit out of a walker, Timbertoe.'

The pirates roared with laughter. The two captains grasped hands, thumb around thumb, pirate to pirate. Under cover of the laughing, Brunehilda asked, 'The bastards didn't get anything higher than that, did they?'

My seadog blushed, but answered in the same tone, 'I told them you'd be after them if they did.'

She wrinkled her nose when she laughed, an unexpectedly charming touch that made her seem all at once as wholesome as a milkmaid. Then she looked up at me and tapped my chest with one sturdy finger. 'I've business with *you* yet, junior, so don't get too chummy!'

'Aye, madam,' I assured her gravely as she reached to take

the end of Sitric's tether and lead him to the middle of the tavern. I stayed by the door while Timbertoe stumped after them.

Timbertoe set the case out fairly and concisely. The scrolls were passed around as evidence, and Silky added some damning bits of information about the guildmaster's double-dealings against the pirates themselves through the years. What he had to say was no surprise to anyone; indeed, the sort of game Sitric had played was fair enough by pirate standards. But the letters could not be ignored, and with them the implication that Sitric had betrayed not only me, but also the guild itself to the Wolfhounds. Brunehilda voiced the opinion that the damned Dinan probably had a map of every harbor on the Jarlshof islands, and a full description of every pirate.

When they took Sitric's gag off and ordered him to respond to the charges, he refused. After that, the vote was a foregone conclusion. He was sentenced to death by keelhauling and given into my custody to carry out the sentence.

I thanked the mates with a nod, then, as the landlord opened his mouth to sing out that the bar was open, I held up a hand, tattoo exposed. This signal means that the pirate wished to speak in the Moot. When they had settled once more to hear me, I slowly drew a pouch out of my sash and walked to a table, where I casually set the pouch down. Every eye was on it.

Leaving it unopened under Timbertoe's watchful eye, I looked around the room. 'Mates, you all know now who I am, no less the pirate Cru than the Haunt of the Moor, and it's on behalf of both my countries – the one in which I was born, and the one that welcomed me when I had to leave the Burren – that I speak now. Captain Brunehilda is right. This bastard has sold us out six times over.' There was a growl at that, and if looks could have killed, Sitric would have been a dead dwarf. 'So I say, let Jarlshof strike a blow back. If we don't help these other folk to get the Wolfhounds now, we'll only have to go up against them by ourselves later.'

I gave them time to consider this, watching the nods, the unwilling agreement. When I judged the time was right, I walked to the pouch, opened it, and spilled the chalcedon across the table. 'I'm hiring shipping, pirates. Anybody interested?'

Nearly everyone, it seemed from the gaping mouths and tattooed arms shooting into the air all around.

'Wait a bloody minute!' Brunehilda yelled, climbing on a bench to rise up above those on their feet.

I groaned inwardly. I'd almost had them.

The lady captain stuck her fists on her hips. 'What's this fleet to do, hey?'

'Seal off the waters around Dun Aghadoe so the Dinan can't escape by sea. Whatever you capture, you keep. When it's over, you can harry every damned one of them to the bottom if you want to. For a picked band of mates, there will be other work. They'll be individually paid, on this scale.' I waved a hand at the chalcedons.

Brunehilda pursed her lips. 'Those are dangerous waters, Pilot.' It wasn't just the disturbing closeness of the dun itself; the waters surrounding it were a notorious graveyard for unwary mariners.

'Aye, madam, that's why I don't trust the River Men to do it.'

The pirates snorted and laughed a bit. Brunehilda nodded. 'Seems to me we'd need some kind of captain of this fleet. We pirates ain't worked together before, not like this.' She swept a look around the wary faces. 'Now, all of ye know there's no love lost between this fellow and me, but I'm willing to say I've never known a better sailor than him. I vote we make Timbertoe our guildmaster.'

It was what I'd hoped for, but I was astonished that the suggestion came from Brunehilda herself. I glanced at Timbertoe. His mouth was open. I nudged him, and he shut it hastily and tried to look as though he'd expected this all along.

After a moment in which they tugged their beards or scratched their heads, their eyes went once more to the gems. Our lads and Brunehilda's were on their feet roaring, and then, as one, that whole bloody tavern stood up and applauded. The master of the *Inishkerry Gem* was elected to the office with no dissenting votes at all.

Under cover of it, I leaned close to his ear to ask, 'When's the wedding?'

'Don't spoil a good thing, is what I say,' he muttered, pulling himself up on my arm. He whistled piercingly to settle them, took a tiny chalcedon from the table and tossed it to the landlord, proclaiming, 'That ought to settle everybody's tab, Norni!'

'Bugger me, I guess so!' the awed tavern-keeper agreed.

'Break us out the ale and flotjin, then, and let's get down to work. Pilot, sketch us out a map of this place on the floor, here. Show us what ye want us to do.'

Within an hour it was all set as far as the fleet was concerned. The picked group I took upstairs to talk privately while the party got underway in earnest.

Through it all Sitric was left sitting bound to the chair, and not one word was spoken to him. He might have been a post. When we pirates of the *Gem* finally left the tavern to begin our solitary journey, we dragged him with us. Later that night, somewhere between Skejfallen Light and the Burren coast, Sitric Silkenbeard drank a lot of water.

I did give him the needle.

CHAPTER THIRTEEN

When he left me on the beach three days before Vanu's Eve the skipper cast an eye up at Cnoch Aneil, its top hidden in the low ceiling of rain clouds, and made the sign. 'How the hell will ye find it?'

I made him some sort of answer about looking for a path, but the truth was I had no idea myself. He snorted, shrugged, and barked at the lads to row for the ship, unconsciously fingering the ends of the new sash that marked his rank, and already squinting through the weather, looking for Dinan ships so close to Dun Aghadoe.

When the curragh had disappeared into the driving rain, I squinted up at the dark mountain. It was not so high, this cnoch, but it seemed to dominate the inland plain and coast. Most of my country's settlements are clustered along a narrow band of shoreline, for without the resources provided by the sea, there is not much living in the burren. But for a ten-mile stretch on either side of Cnoch Aneil, there is to be found not one fishing village, not one peat digging, not even any solitary shepherd's hut. It is not a place the living go.

Except for once every seventh year.

Then the folk come to the hallowed hill, to the gateway of the Hag's Realm, bringing with them the washed and annointed bones of lost loved ones. The sarcophagi containing the bones, which are carved and ornamented with much care in fanciful shapes and the brightest colors the family can afford to make or purchase, are committed to a huge pyre at midnight on Vanu's Eve, and the fire is kept burning until the Maid comes forth from her Mother's Embrace the next morning, bearing the seed that brings Spring.

In the old days, our stories say, the king made the journey with the Maid, to be her defender against the demons in the dark. But kings now are not the heroes they once were, and so for lifetimes now an unfortunate painter had taken the king's place, to live or die in the tomb with the Maid while the king himself remained to receive the bean seed from the siochla's hand if she completed the maze successfully, or to lead the sorrowful people away from the cnoch if she did not. Either way, the king lived.

Aware of the mounting desperation among the common folk in this Year of the Bad Fire, Jorem would find a way to prevent Rose from doing the Vanu's Eve ritual on this mountain, I was sure, since for his purposes it was essential that no other Power besides his own Wolf legitimize Leif. When the Hag refused her seed down in the festival field outside the walls of Dun Aghadoe, it would be a sign to all that Vanu was an enemy, and thus the frightened folk would turn to the only Power strong enough to overcome Her. The Wolf would reign uncontested in the Burren, and, of course, the only person who could hear the Wolf was his archpriest, Jorem. It was as tidy a bit of malfeasance as I have ever encountered.

I was bound to drive a hole in the keel of his plan if I could. If nothing else, I was prepared to die and take him with me, but if possible I would set aside my personal vengeance to see that Rose did not go down to the dark alone. I shouldered my pack and began to climb the mountain of death, listening above the rain for the rattle of walkers' bones, making for the flat alp that stuck out like a projecting knee about two-thirds of the way up Cnoch Aneil. This was normally the place of the pyre, the place where the king and his retinue would camp, the place where, for the days and nights of the Hag's Embrace ritual, folk from all over the country would congregate in a darkly festive spirit to tend the fire and wait for the Maid's return. Later, if the rite were successful, there would be joyful merrymaking. That's how it would have gone in a normal seventh-year ritual.

The main entrance to the labyrinth should be reached by a road or at least a broad path from the fire field, since the Maid was ritually escorted to the Gateway on Vanu's Eve by her siochla attendants, the king and his honor guard, and such dignitaries and folk as chose to make the climb on foot to the summit of the cnoch. Once I had found the main entrance, I would scout for the labyrinth's exit to make my preparations. I reckoned I'd have a day, no more to foil Jorem's plan. There was only one logical thing to do: go down into the maze *before Vanu's Eve*, mark the way through the labyrinth, then steal Rose and the color pots out from under his nose. No wonder Timbertoe had laughed when I'd told him.

Even three days before Vanu's Eve, I had left it nearly too late. The guards were already in place. I avoided a couple of two-man patrols doing bored and wet sweeps of the mountain faces, and climbed up the back of the cnoch, boulder to concealing boulder. It took more time than I wanted to give it and, with the maze to face, that was one thing I couldn't afford. At length I came across the brow of the hill and found the entrance to the Hag's Embrace guarded by a patrol huddling around their fire and playing tiles, not five feet from the rectangular opening in the little lawn. I could just glimpse the top steps of the flight that led downward. They were not happy with the duty, not at all, nor with the unrelenting cloud that prevented them from seeing even as far as the pyre field. But the cover worked both ways: if they could not see their mates below, then no one could see them. A leather flask was making the rounds of their circle.

I bit my lip. I could wait till dark and try to get past them somehow to get down those steps, but that would eat up precious hours. I retreated and began to look for the exit.

I couldn't find one, though I crossed and recrossed the summit and the slopes of Cnoch Aneil all that day, coming perilously close to the roving patrols. Darkness came early, and I crouched in the streaming rain, cursing the soldiers around their fire. I ate some of the bread and cheese I'd brought with me, drank some water, and thought about it and the more I thought, the more obvious it became: the entrance and the exit had to be the same. The maze must form a loop.

I grinned to myself in the darkness, a hazy plan forming. Rose and I would go a little way into the entrance of the maze, far enough that our light would not be seen from the well, paint the paintings as well as possible with her telling me the colors as I took out the pots, settle ourselves as comfortably as possible and wait until we judged it time. Then we'd re-emerge from the Hag's Embrace, bean seed in hand, and hope to find James there with his escort of dwarves. We'd never need to pick a way through the maze. First, though, I still had to get the damned pack into the entranceway.

I made sure my sodden scarf was well-wrapped and shrugged deeper into my dripping cloak. Then I dug out of the pack the piece of paper I had written aboard the *Gem* and checked to be sure Jorem's wax seal, lifted from his letter to Sitric, was still glued neatly in place. Preparations complete, I stepped out into the road and walked right up to the guards' fire. 'At ease,' I said.

They sank back down, hiding the bottle, but not quite quick enough to whisk all the tiles out of sight. I gave the Thistle a pointed glance but said, 'I'm relieved to find you men alert. His Grace was most specific about that.' I nodded toward the steps. 'I assume you've checked that.'

The pitch that had been poured on their fire snapped a little, and one of the men nudged a stick of wood further into it with his toe. 'Checked it, sir?' the sergeant asked. 'For what?'

Good question. I snorted as though disgusted at his incompetence. 'A torch, and be quick about it. I want to get down to supper in town after this.' One of the other men had a light going by this time and waved me courteously toward the steps.

I held out my hand for the torch. 'No need for you to leave the fire. I won't be a moment, just long enough to be able to say I saw everything for myself.'

'It's no problem, sir,' the young soldier said brightly, probably thinking to curry favor with the messenger of the archpriest.

I shook my head. 'No, you'll just get cold all over again, and I don't have to sit out by this fire half the night. Stay.'

He handed me the torch. Breathing an inward sigh of relief I left them on their haunches around the fire and went down the stone steps. As I got to the bottom, my stomach did a turn. I hadn't expected a gate. The iron bars were rusted, but not seriously so, and the space between them was too narrow to admit the pack. I held up the torch to peer in and saw a rough floor and an impression of dripping stone. Feverishly unstrapped the satchel, groped for the all-important ring and color pot, and leaned to drop them as far inside the opening a I could do without tossing them. I was afraid to break the clay

'Everything all right, Lieutenant?'

I blocked his sight of the open pack with my cloak. 'Look

234

fine.' I had the pack securely under my arm, and the sergeant was waiting for me. I couldn't throw the rope or the bone lance head in, and there was not the remotest chance of exploring the maze, even if they had the key, without their knowing, so I climbed back up and handed him the torch. 'Continue to keep a sharp watch, now.' I paused and turned back to the group around the fire. 'Oh, by the way, not a word of this to your relief. I plan to pay them a little visit in the middle of their hours, too, just to see they're on their toes.'

'As you will, sir,' the sergeant said.

This was a calculated risk. I didn't want word to get back to the camp that a lieutenant on His Grace's business had gone up to inspect the gate. These men might tip the other watch off, but there would be no mention made of the incident in camp until at least the next day, as they waited to see what I would do.

I went off down the road, but when I judged they could no longer hear my footsteps, I left the road once more and picked a way in the darkening fog over the cnoch. Though I'd rather have stayed on Cnoch Aneil until Vanu's Eve, every time that I had to dodge a patrol shortened my chances of going unnoticed. So I worked my way off the mountain, up the valley a way, and found a place in the open burren where a jumble of boulders formed a kind of rough, unroofed hut. There I settled to wait for the train of pilgrims to begin arriving.

With the coming of twilight on Vanu's Eve the celebration bonfires opened like eyes all over the narrow river valley that at Dun Aghadoe tumbles out of the highland moor and circles the base of Cnoch Aneil to meet the sea. Even from the height above the walled town where we stopped to wrap my horse's hooves, we could hear the thin skirl of the pipes and the thud of the bodhrun. Beside me Beod was peering from the back of his own horse, which was standing head down, exhausted. It had been a grueling two day ride from the border with a picked cohort of men, but not an impossible one. Their charge had been to destroy the signal beacons on the chain of hill running to the capital from the borders. Ja-Solem's men were doing the same as they came up on a flanking movement from the South. 'The gates of the town are still open,' the Ilyrian noted.

'They'll stay that way,' I answered, tying a knot to secure the last hoof covering of leather. 'If he won't allow the ritual on Cnoch Aneil, Jorem will at least have to let the folk come to the festival here in Dun Aghadoe. People will be coming to town with their sarcophagi right up till the ritual at midnight.'

His nose wrinkled a little. 'It's an odd way to honor your dead, digging them up every seventh year to burn like so much rubbish.'

'We don't have as much fallow ground as you do. We can't afford to squander it for graveyards. Ashes take less room.' I pulled down a stirrup and tested the girth. 'That's the practical end of it. The ritual reason is so that the spirits of the dead can go free of the last of their mortal remains and pass through the Hag's Embrace into their new lives.'

'And the sacrifice of the king is to keep the Hag busy with a new consort for seven years, eh? By the Powers, I'm glad we don't do the spring festival this way at home! Bloody savages!'

I paused with the reins in my hand while my horse lipped the peak of the black hood curiously. 'There are no savages here except Jorem and his Wolfhounds, Beod. See that your men remember that. The scything of the king hasn't been done the way Jorem plans it tonight for over a hundred years.'

I think he blushed. At any rate, his skin darkened in the failing light. 'What is usually done, then?'

'We dress a barley-straw scarecrow in crown and finery, and scythe that to be thrown on the fire. You do the same thing, I have heard.'

'That's true. I didn't know that's what it meant, though.'

'Don't be so quick to judge my folk, Prince. We're poor, but not stupid.' I swung into the saddle and settled the pack on my shoulder. 'Besides,' I grinned under the hood, 'for stupidity, you'd go far to find a crown prince riding four hours in advance of his column.'

He'd heard my smile. He might have turned aside my teasing with a joke, but with disarming simplicity he said, 'I couldn't stay away if there was a chance I could help her.'

I could understand the nerves that had his big frame strung tight as a bow. 'Just hold the gate and get the siochlas clear. That will be enough.'

'We'll be waiting for you, never fear. My column will be here by then, and Ja-Solem will be holding the pass at the head of the valley. Your dwarves will have James here, no doubt, by the time you want him.'

'They will. There's booty in it.'

After that, we waited, the horses fidgeting while the dusk deepened to night here in the valley, though the high end of the pass was still brushed with a stray gleam of light. Suddenly, from the hillock opposite our vantage, a fiery circle spun in the darkness, a double-ended torch twirled to make a signal. Beod pointed. 'There it is.'

'Aye. So the lads have taken out those vermin Wolfhounds in their skellig for us. There will be no reinforcements from there, at any rate.'

'They're probably all down in town enjoying your heathen festival, anyway,' the Ilyrian prince said, needling.

'Probably, but if I know my folk, most of the crowd is three-parts drunk already. Let's hope the fellows in the guardhouse have sneaked some of the ale, too. Well, here's to luck.' I leaned, and he shook my hand, then reined back when his horse would have followed mine. 'Look for me at the witching hour!' I called back softly.

I think he said something unbecoming his station, and then rode my sable horse toward Dun Aghadoe, leather-wrapped hooves making a soft thudding drum in the night. Near the last end of the river, out of sight a half mile from the gatehouse, pulled off the road and waited. As I had said to Beod, folk would be coming from the burren into town all the hours of this evening.

Not many minutes later the rumble of heavy wooden wheels and the snorting breath of an ox drew slowly nearer. I made sure of my pot helmet under the black hood and walked my horse out to block the road. When the small torchlit procession – one family and their cart loaded with a sarcophagus in the shape of a small ing – appeared around the bend, I was right in front of them. 'Good Vanu's Eve,' I bid them civilly.

The wife on the seat beside her husband clutched his arm, then shrilled sharply, 'Children! On the cart! *Right now!*' The boy playing the tin whistle swallowed a note, stared, then jumped for the side of the wagon, while his sister peered under the ox's neck at me for a moment, then whirled and scrambled up by her father.

The man raised the whip, the only weapon he had. 'Clear off, you!'

I raised one gauntleted hand, palm up. 'Thee's misunderstood me, sir. I mean thy family no harm. I merely wished to offer thee gold in exchange for a favor.'

The moment when the thought hit them was obvious. The wife put her mouth to his ear to whisper something, but he was already nodding and waving her off. 'Turn around.'

I smiled inside the hood and pulled my horse's head around. It was the back of the cloak they wanted to see, the four flowing spirals embroidered there as a blazon.

'By the Old Girl herself! It's the Haunt!' the boy said excitedly, ducking his father's cuff for the mild epithet.

'Are ye really him?' the man asked directly.

'I am.'

He pulled uncertainly at his beard, then put the whip back in its socket. 'Blessings, then. Good Vanu's Eve to ye.'

'Thank thee.' The boy and girl were agog, and the wife no less frankly staring. 'As I said, sir, I'd ask a favor. Would dare something for a gold farthing?'

The wife's shawl went to her mouth. 'Against them up there?' he asked, indicating the fortress ahead with a jerk of his rough beard.

'Aye, truly, and against their foul practice tonight.'

He thought about it, eying me. 'I've got the family to think of, is all.'

'I understand thy concern, but I cannot promise there will be no danger for them. What place in the land is safe, when it comes to that? These are chancy times.' I sat my sidling horse quietly. 'If thee'd make them somewhat less chancy, I'd suggest thee and thy family stop a moment for a rest break, going off into the burren here for two or three moments. Thee needs do no more, and thy cart will be here safe when thee returns to it.' I took the coin from my belt and flipped it to him.

His hand caught it out of the air automatically, while he thought it through. Then he looked at the coin in his hand as if wondering how it got there. His eyes came back to mine, and he cleared his throat. 'I suppose we ne'er saw ye, right?'

'Right. Haste, please, good sir. Another cart approaches.'

That must have decided him, because he jerked his head toward the walled field to our right, and the children spilled over the side, poised on the wall for a moment, then disappeared. His wife followed. 'What did ye want done with your horse?' he asked as he got down.

'Don't trouble thyself. I'll take care of him.' We could hear singing from the other wagon coming up behind us. 'Right. Luck, then,' he said, and vanished over the wall.

I threw myself off my horse, ran to the single wooden pole that barred the lefthand field, and turned the sable gelding into it with a slap to the flank, replacing the pole. Then I vaulted over the side of the wagon, heaved aside the ornate lid of the casket, and let myself down into the tangle of bones as carefully as I could, scraping a hollow for my body and holding the pack on my chest. The aromatic herbs and sweet oil didn't do much toward masking the charnel stench, but I lay back and slid the cover over me.

He gave me a good long time, for which I uncharitably cursed him now that I was hidden. The other cart pulled up behind to eye the workmanship of the t'ing casket and see why it might have been left sitting in the middle of the road. 'Hullo!' someone from it called. 'Would ye mind going on?'

My host's family came back over the wall, mounting the cart once more. 'Sorry,' the man called.

'Making room for the ale, eh, neighbor?'

'Aye, it'll be a long night. Get on up, now, Buttercup.' The whip cracked, and the cart jerked into motion, shifting the end of a bone under my chin. I nearly gagged, but managed to swallow. To get my mind off it, I began one of the meditations Symon had taught me for steadying one's nerves. The casket lid shifted little. 'Leave it be, Keri!' the man said sharply. 'Billy, play your pipe.'

The boy wasn't a bad piper, and he soon had the folk in the other cart beating a drum and following his song and so we arrived at the gates as two carts travelling in company, which made the guards less interested than they might have been in the lone group of four people. My man barely slowed, then was apparently waved through without any of the soldiers even setting foot on the cart. The other family followed us.

'I'm going to pull off behind the big tent,' my man called, ostensibly to the other fellow, but probably to let me know. 'I don't think we'll get closer than that. My boy and I can carry ours from there.'

'Ours is too heavy for that. Bye, neighbor! Maybe if I see ye, we can tuck in a pint or two!'

'I'll look for ye, then! Good Vanu's Eve!' my host said. There was a chorus of farewells, and then only the background noise of the festival as we wound through the streets, which he seemed to know very well. A few minutes later the ox snorted to a stop. My man cleared his throat. 'Think we'll go claim us a place for the casket before you and I carry her up to the field, Billy. Come on, wife, come on, Keri. Your grandmother will rest a while.'

I heard them jump down to the ground, then it was quiet. I counted two minutes of heartbeats to give them time to get well away, then cautiously slid the lid open a crack. The wet night air felt wonderful, but I resisted the urge to bolt upright out of the welter of bones. Carefully I peered over the edge of the carved casket. For a moment, just a moment, I thought I saw a gleam of red paint in the collar of carved flowers around the t'ing's neck, but then I blinked and dark gray took its place in the dim reflection of the firelight in the field beyond. I looked around.

The nearest person was a man standing with his back to me some twenty yards away. He was watching the grotesque figure on stilts who wove around the field, pelting the festival goers with handfuls of chestnuts and apples amidst much good-natured whistling and jeering. To be hit with a chestnut was good luck, with a wormy apple, bad; so there was dodging this way and that as people tried to guess which sort of missile the stilted figure was aiming at them.

I slipped out of the wagon, already loosening my cloak pin a. I crouched. Quickly I turned the cloak inside out, so that to al appearances it was now an ordinary black cloak, then cast back the black hood to rest on the shoulders of it. My scarf I drew across my face, and the hated Wolf's Head amulet I drew outside the neck of my dark tunic. The Haunt had become a lieutenant of Wolfhounds once more.

Loosening my sword in its scabbard, I let myself fall into the unconscious measured cadence of a soldier as I walked to the edge of the crowd to get my bearings.

The huge open field beneath the foot of the fortress would ordinarily have been used as the practice ground for the king's men-at-arms, but tonight it was the site of the festival. The stack of oil-soaked logs dominated the center of the field, decorated with straw sugans of every size, stuffed into the chinks of the logs. The planked platform for the sacrificed king already was nailed atop the pyre. For now the Vanu fire was dark, but dotted about the rest of the field were smaller campfires to roast potatoes and mull ale, and give enough light to help folk forget they were not on Cnoch Aneil. Vendors wandered through the crowd, or hawked their sweet cakes and loaves from stalls set up along the edges of the field. There was music, too, and the usual dancing, but to my eyes and ears, the gaiety was strained. I caught more than one or two glances up at the platform where no barleyman lay on the planks tonight, and I guessed most of the people who had come for the Vanu's Eve ritual would have been anywhere else if they had dared, but that their obligation to see their loved ones free made them unwilling captives to Jorem's perversion. Personally I was glad my dear ones lay under the clean rain miles away.

I nudged through the crowd to look down the length of the field. There was a raised platform there with woven mats hung at the sides to provide some protection from the chill wind blowing up from the sea. Over it flew the Gryffin and, on a slightly lower standard, the Wolf's Head. The pavilion was brightly lit with streaming torches, and three high chairs were set there, occupied by two men and a woman. I dodged a chestnut that suddenly came at me, causing a laugh, then slowly began to work my way toward the pavilion.

Rose was set between a young man with buck teeth and poor kin, whom I presumed at once to be Leif the Lackwit, and Jorem. My first thought was that the Wolfpriest had some sort of headdress on, but then I realized that his hair, which fell to his shoulders now, had gone completely white. That much my design of springing the tunnel to trap him had done, apparently. He must have been terrified down there alone, sealed in a tomb. I felt satisfaction at the thought.

The Maid of the Vale looked to be attended as befit her rank, but the benches full of nobles and their wives were set a little apart from her, so that she could not have easy speech with anyone save Jorem or his puppet, Leif. The cohort drawn up around the platform, evidence of the archpriest's awareness that not everyone in the field was pleased with the turn the ritual would take, was unmoving and disciplined. There was no horn of ale passing from hand to hand there.

But at a little remove from the royal pavilion stood another platform, this one hung with wildly gaudy banners and flags, some showing the sugan Vanu, some with the symbol of a grinning skull surmounted by a crown. In the open space below the pavilion, acrobats tumbled and flew, jesters screeched raucous obscenities, jugglers tossed clay skulls to each other, and vendors tossed their finest wares up on to the pavilion floor – all of this to entertain the King of the Dead, the criminal who would die in the King's place at midnight.

I could see him: a bandy-legged fellow, squat, missing teeth, with a kind of ferocious energy about him, draped in a cloak of woven straw, wearing a tin crown. He was clutching a chicken leg in one hand and an ale horn in the other, and laughing at the jesters until the tears ran down his face. While I watched, he emptied the horn at one long pull and held out his hand for another, which a soldier – one of the 'honor' cohort around him – supplied immediately. Perhaps to make him biddable, or maybe out of common human decency, his guards were trying to get him stupefied with drink, and it seemed to be working. He took another bite of chicken, threw the bone down into the crowd, and lurched to his feet to hurry behind a curtain at the rear of the pavilion with a woman who looked as if she might have been another of the carved sarcophagi.

An elbow found my ribs, and I turned to find another Wolf-hound soldier grinning 'They're giving the poor bugger a good send-off, anyway. He'll have anything he wants these next few hours. Well, leastwise, most anything.' He took a look around and lowered his voice. 'I doubt they'd give him the Maid of the

Vale if he asked for her, though you can't tell. His Grace is in a fey mood tonight.'

'I've been on patrol, just got back. Tell me: what did the King of the Dead do to get himself picked for the honors?'

'Tavern fight. Killed another fellow over a game of tiles.' He shook his head, laughing a little, his eyes on the pavilion where the rear curtain was quivering now. 'Lost the pot on that one, I'd say.' He sniffed. 'Say, no offense, brother, but you're pretty strong.'

'I know. Sorry. They've had me down at the gate, checking the caskets as they're brought through.' He made a sound of commiseration. 'I've got to keep moving. I can't even stand myself,' I told him with a sketched salute as I moved toward Rose's pavilion once more. The talkative one made no attempt to follow me.

I skirted several groups of mourners gathered around their small campfires, putting last-minute decorations on their ornate caskets and chatting about how bad the winter had been, and wondering how they could stretch their precious stores of seed grain. Nearly everyone wore a sugan Vanu pinned to their clothing.

I crossed to the place below the royal pavilion where the storytelling competition was going on. Just now, a teller with a clear tenor voice was relating the story of the Thief of Knockmuldowney, a comic tale often chosen for this night because the thief, a cocky young lad named Jack, tries to steal apples from a witch's orchard in the belief that they will grant him magical wishes, one of which is to gain the king's daughter. The painter had done a good job of capturing the exact mixture of surprise and fear on Jack's face when he discovered the apples had turned to balls of horse manure in his breeches pocket, and the witch was on to his scheme. I couldn't tell how skilled this painter was with colors, but his sketching was first rate. He wore painter's robe of honor, and I surmised he must be Jorem's man, the one who would paint the ritual story just before the sacrifice of the 'king' later that night. I craned for a look at the pots he was using and was outraged and vaguely sickened to find the colors of Colin Mariner used to limn horse apples.

Before I moved off, I looked up to Rose, rigid beneath the fur wrap that had been draped over her shoulders. Now that I was closer, I could see how pale she was. Very quietly I kenned, *Good Vanu's Eve, my lady.*

I saw her breath stop a moment, then resume. Mastering the impulse to raise her head, she sent back, *You're absolutely mad to be here, and I absolutely love you for it.*

I didn't dare allow myself to take her words seriously. Lightly I kenned, *Courage. Don't be surprised at anything that happens.*

Aengus, be careful. This Wolfpriest is insane, but he's no fool.

That makes one of us who isn't. I'm going to get Colin's color pots and free your sisters, so you'll have to endure this a while longer, I sent. *Be ready to ride just before they kill the King of the Dead. I'll be there when you need me.*

Somehow, I never doubted that. She lifted her head a little and smiled. If anyone was watching it would have seemed an entirely natural reaction to the story of poor Jack, but I knew that smile of gratitude and relief was for me, and my heart did what every bard says it can do, and every healer knows is impossible. I side with the bards on the matter of hearts leaping.

Now for the pots.

I waited for a break in the competition, while the sweepers were at work brushing away his picture. The court storyteller and Jorem's painter exchanged a laugh over something, then the storyteller wandered off into the crowd, probably to get himself a pint. The painter finished strapping the satchel, hefted it, and started around behind the royal platform. I let him come toward me, then lurched to meet him, giving every evidence of having had too much to drink. We collided hard enough that I was able to make sure he went down in a swirl of robes.

'Sorry, brother!' When he got his orientation back, I was leaning to help him up and hand his satchel to him.

'Damnit!' he flared. 'Damn drunken lout! Don't you know His Grace could have you to the mines for drinking tonight!'

'Ah, sir, ye won't report me, will ye? I know; I stink, don't I? They had me down to the gate, going through the caskets, that's why I took a nip, sir, just to clear it out of my throat, ye might say.'

He'd unstrapped the satchel to check the pots. They were whole, and each was marked with a spiral. Somewhat mollified he gave me a wave. 'Get yourself away from here, soldier, and don't by the Fire get yourself into any more trouble.'

'Thank ye, sir. Think I'll just go stand down by the King of the Dead's place, there.'

He nodded briskly, waited for me to step aside, and when I did, went past holding his nose.

I slipped around to the other side of the pavilion and melted back into the crowd. Guards were posted around the field, of course, but people were coming and going to answer calls of nature. I slung the satchel out of sight beneath my cloak, made as if I were one of those people, and walked past near enough that one of the guards threw a salute. 'Nice night, eh?' I asked ironically, and he grunted in the rain, shuffling his cold feet, the spear propped against his shoulder. I walked on, left it long enough, and walked back. 'Like a relief?' I asked.

'Oh, aye, brother, thanks!' he said gratefully, handing me the spear and making for the river at something only just short of a trot. 'Thanks,' he said again when he came back. 'Shouldn't have had those pickled eels, I guess.'

I laughed a little, sympathetically, and handed him back his spear. 'I just got back in off patrol. Thought I heard there were supposed to be a bunch of those dirty witches burned here tonight. Where are they?'

He was expansive, anxious to pay off the good turn I had done him. 'Oh, they'll be bringing them down soon enough from the sun. His Grace didn't want them here too soon. Ye never know what mischief a witch can make.'

I nodded, beating my hands together for warmth. 'Aye, at mess was beside the fellow – let's see, Eomer was it? – who's in charge of them up there, and he said there's a couple of them he wouldn't trust with his back turned.'

He was nodding. 'Owen's his name, and I agree. In fact, that's why they took their index fingers off, first thing. So they can't cast a spell, you know,' he said as I stared.

I clenched my hand on my belt to keep from killing him, he'd said it so matter-of-factly. After a moment, I drew a breath. 'Well, got to get back to the field. See you around.'

In fact, though, I did not go back to the festival. Instead I headed for the stable of the barracks. It was just where our

dwarfish maps of the town had shown it, and left unguarded.
Probably the man on duty had seen the chance to enjoy a pint
or two with no one the wiser. Here I undid my belt pouch and
sought the needle and the drug that I carried there. When I was
ready, I palmed the needle, and waited by the door.

Not long after, the sound of hooves thudding the mud of the
broad track leading up through the town to the dun reached me.
I watched him trot past, ran up behind him, and thrust with
the needle into his thigh, grabbing for the reins to keep the
horse from bolting. The soldier pitched over into the street.
I quickly turned the horse into the stable for a moment and
returned to drag the unconscious man inside. From the pouch
at his belt I took folded orders with Jorem's seal, then swung up
on his horse.

I trotted to the gates of the dun itself, where I found three men
on duty. 'Time, is it, Lieutenant?' one of them said as I waved
the orders.

'Aye. Where's Owen?'

'Down there with them, belike. Shall we get the troop out,
then?'

I flung the reins to one of the men. 'Aye. Have the men muster
here in the courtyard, then march out in two columns. We'll put
the witches between lines of our men. Wait for us at the end of
the drawbridge. I'll go down and let Owen know.'

The more senior of the men saluted, jerked his head in the
direction of the dun, and one of his men trotted away to gather
the troops.

I followed him inside the tallish central keep closely enough
that he gestured back at me and told the doorward, 'We're on His
Grace's business, Tydwal. Sound the bell to gather the brothers,
would you?'

The large open room which formed this first level of the keep
was ablaze with torches as servants raked up the old rushes and
put down fresh ones. The king's hearth hounds were having a
grand time chasing down the rats and mice dislodged by the
cleaning. In the middle of the room the steward was bellowing
and a scared-looking kennelboy was trying to call the dogs to
heel. I'd wager that with the amount of blood already fouling
the rushes, most of the dun's men-at-arms would have elected

to sleep in the stables tonight rather than here in their customary place. I swept a look around. 'Tydwal, where's Owen? I don't see him.'

The ward of the door turned from yanking on the bell rope. 'Why, he's downstairs, sir. Would you want me to fetch him for you?'

'No, but we may need some help with the witches. Come along.' I gestured him to precede me. We crossed through the mess, kicking aside a couple of the dogs on the way, and went out at a door in the righthand wall. From there he led me around to the back of the keep and through a shed built on the side of it. Before we reached the stairs I dropped him with a blow to the back of the neck and finished it with my dagger. Even unconscious as he was, he still jerked when my blade went in, and I was reminded sharply of what Gwynt had said about Alyce. Maybe this man had had a child, and a swing in his yard, too. My head began to ache, and I wished for some poppy.

'Owen?' I called down the stair.

'Aye?'

'Time to bring out the witches. I've got the orders here, if you want to see them. His Grace said you'd probably ask for them.' When his head cleared the level of the shed floor, I kicked him viciously, dragged the body up the rest of the stairs, and rolled him out of the way, covering both bodies with some sacking after had taken the keys from his belt. I cleaned my knife hurriedly and went down to the dungeon.

The siochlas had heard my words. Their eyes were wide, and the chains clanked as some of them stood up in the filthy straw. Their poor, mangled hands were wrapped in strips torn from their own clothing and I could smell rot. Some of them must be quite ill. There was only one way to reassure those deathly pale faces.

Mistresses, I am a friend. Make no sound, please. Can anyone answer me in kenning? I wanted to know if there were any siochlas of rank among them.

I heard gasps, but there was no other reaction for a moment. Then a mental voice said, *I am Noreen. What man uses the kenning?*

I am Aengus of Inishbuffin, Mistress Noreen, Lord Protector of the

Vale. I've come to get you out of here, but we need haste and perfect silence. I began unlocking the chains. 'I've told them to muster their troop outside the drawbridge, and they're doing that now. They expect to see your gaoler and I march you out there in a couple of minutes, so we need as much quickness as you can muster. Can anyone use her hands well enough to unlock the chains?' I whispered.

'I can, I think. I'm Noreen,' one of the younger women told me. When I gave her the key, she grasped it between thumb and middle finger, fumbled it into the next sister's locked manacles, and twisted. Tears of pain sprang to her eyes, but she made no outcry and went immediately to the next prisoner.

'When you are all free, go upstairs and wait in the shed. Take a length of chain with you, and if anyone comes in that door without kenning first, slug him with the chain. I mean it: one shout, and we're all dead.'

'No fear there, master,' an old woman told me. 'Noreen will do it.' She nodded and smiled, and others did, too.

'Ah, Mistress Noreen is your firebrand, eh?' I asked, taking the moment to ease them. 'Maybe I'd better have her go out and open the postern, then, to let in our friends. Don't be surprised when you see them, ladies. They're pirates, but as trusty a lot for this business as were ever hired. They'll take you to a boat and get you to safety.'

There was murmuring at that, but nothing to attract the attention of the guards. Noreen looked back at me. *And the Maid of the Vale? Will you get her to a ship, too, my lord?*

No. Our purpose is not to escape, but to do the ritual on Cnoch Aneil free of the fear that the Wolfhounds will harm all of you. Hurry, now, please.

She nodded busily, and I left them to slip out of the shed. The postern was nearly opposite, not more than thirty feet away. I glanced up to the battlement, but could see no watch up there. I hunched into my cloak and strode quickly, purposefully to the door, as though checking that it was secure. The bolts were oiled since this door led out on to the river itself and was used to bring supplies off barges into the dun. I opened it quietly.

Arni and his men were waiting. We clasped hands briefly, but no word was exchanged. The pirates flooded into the fortress noiseless in their wetted seaboots, pairs of them splitting off in the darkness to go to their jobs. I shut the gate, but pushed the bolts through only enough to keep the door from swinging open and betraying us to the watch.

When I got to the shed, I paused briefly to ken an identification of myself before I stepped inside. Noreen began to ken a question, but I held up a hand. Head bent at the door, I listened until a soft two-note whistle floated down from the top of the keep.

Beckoning to the women, I led the way to the postern, opened it again, and handed them into the care of the second group of pirates. We loaded them aboard what looked to be a Shimarrat ship, flying a trading flag, which waited at the dock. Within moments, the siochlas were all taken aboard, the anchor was slipped, and the boat was floating downriver, the sails beginning to billow.

Leaving the postern open this time – the top of the keep was secured for our side, as the whistle had informed me – I slipped around the keep and surveyed the courtyard. I could see the gatewards still in their guardhouse. I stepped around in through the door of the keep and nearly died on the end of a pirate's cutlass before I remembered the password. 'Codswollop, damnit!' In the dimness of the one torch they'd left unextinguished, I recognized one of Brunehilda's men. 'What's the hold-up?' I asked him.

'The Ilyrians haven't showed up,' he whispered hoarsely.

'Didn't you see them from the river?'

'Couldn't see your own hand out there tonight, mate.'

I swore savagely. 'We have to go on, we're committed now. Where's Arni?'

'Down by the gatehouse. He and his lads are just waiting for something to be done about that lot out front.'

'Send someone to tell him to go ahead. Get that damn gate dropped and yell out that the witches cursed it. Act like you're trying to winch it back up. It'll take them a few minutes to figure out, with any luck at all. By that time, it won't matter. Give me couple of minutes to get clear.'

'Aye. Luck, Pilot. May ye go safe upon the deeps.'

'And beat you home to port.' I dashed for the postern with one of his men behind me to secure it once more

Once outside, I followed the river bank until I was clear of the muttering double column of foot troops, then cut across to the stable. The dark horse's ears shot up when I came for him at a run, and he shied, but I caught the reins, jumped into the saddle and streaked for the field. Behind me I could hear the crash of the iron gate as it slammed down to bar the entrance of the dun and then questioning shouts from the troops outside.

About halfway to the field another rider came galloping toward me. Jorem must have grown impatient and posted another messenger. I had no time for subtlety. My sword rang out of its scabbard.

I do not know whether he saw the blade flash up, or whether he suspected some treachery from the first, but he was armed with a lance. I tried to deflect the head of it and succeeded to the extent that it missed skewering me, and ripped instead through the leather satchel of color pots, spilling them into the street. Through the shock of the thud of the spearhead along my ribs I heard the earthenware shattering under our horses' hooves as we circled. I had the advantage of having my sword already in my hand, and there was a moment while he dropped the spear shaft and clawed at his scabbard when he was unprotected. My blade crashed down on his helm and bit deep into his shoulder near the neck. When he fell, I wasn't quick enough to catch his horse.

I flung myself to the road and tried vainly to gather up the shards, but it was pointless: the sands were spilled, the colors ground into the mud. Not one pot was left whole. Bile was in my mouth suddenly, and I spat with sick despair. There would be no painting on Cnoch Aneil tonight. Above me, from the direction of the dun, there came the sound of swords clashing, and below, from the field, the piping and drum that signalled the procession around the field had begun. There was nothing for it but to go on.

Hissing at the pain in my side I hastily flung off the black hood, drew the pendant off and pitched it into the dark, then reversed the cloak so that the blazon of spirals showed. I remounted and galloped for the field. *Rose*, I kenned desperately, not knowing whether she could hear me, *make Jorem start the ritual!*

Near the horse picket I stopped at a small family consisting of an elderly lady, a middle-aged man who was apparently her son and a boy that must have been the grandson. 'Good Vanu's Eve, neighbors. May I have that sugan, grandmother?'

'What for?' the man asked, frowning up at me as he squatted to quench their campfire.

I drew the cloak around, letting them see the blazon of spirals. 'Because I haven't one, neighbor, and would not go against these vermin without the favor of the Swan, tonight of all nights.'

The woman, quicker-witted than her son, reached to tuck the sugan into my hand, patting it. 'Lady bless ye, sir.'

'Thank thee, grandmother, I hope so. If thee'd do one favor more, go across to that family there and whisper to them that the Haunt is here.'

The boy, flushed with excitement, jumped up and was away in a scuffle of sandals against the hard earth. I nodded to them and made my way through the back of the crowd around this side of the field, undoing the pouch at my belt to pick out the bone point. The campfires were being extinguished, the torchlit procession winding intricately about the field with Rose at its head. It would come to an end with the marchers drawing close to the King of the Dead's pavilion, where the evening would take its final macabre form. Once, I had to walk the horse around a couple of Wolfhounds, but most of them seemed as riveted on the condemned man's pavilion as the rest of the crowd, and I was not stopped.

The drums and pipe had abruptly ceased, and in the tense darkness Jorem's voice from the tavern fighter's platform rolled out over the crowd in the opening words of the travesty of a Vanu's Eve ceremony. 'The hour is come to open the gates! Let the king's blood be spilt for his people!'

The usual cheer that would have greeted the words was reduced to a thin, ragged groan.

'Halt! Who goes there?' one of the guards facing me challenged in a low voice, not wanting to ruin the effect of the ritual taking place out front. He was trying to see whether I was wearing a pendant. I did not rein in, only waving him off as though I had perfect right to be there. His hand strayed to his sword hilt.

Jorem's voice once more, louder, as though overriding the emotion of the crowd: 'This is the king.' He would be pointing the hapless criminal, who, with any luck, was beyond caring.

The guard had his sword drawn now and was starting toward me, while to either side his fellows were beginning to realize that I was not one of them.

'Does anyone challenge him?' the Wolfpriest shouted confidently.

I spun the sword out of the guard's hand with a kick, crashed through the ring of his fellows, and brought the horse to a plunging halt before the platform.

I was facing Jorem, not three feet away. 'I do,' I said clearly. My arm whipped forward with the bone point, and I heard him gasp. Then Rose leapt into my arms, I slapped the horse's flank, and the Maid of the Vale lit the pyre with her ring as we broke through the ring of stunned soldiers and raced for Cnoch Aneil.

CHAPTER FOURTEEN

'How badly are you wounded?' she asked.

She must have heard me sucking for air every time my horse's hooves hit. 'I got pinked along the ribs with a spear. Be all right if I were on a ship instead of a horse.' I didn't mention that the jouncing wasn't doing my skull any good, either.

'You got the sisters safely away, I assume?'

There would be time, later, to tell her about the index fingers. 'All tucked aboard a pirate ship by this time.'

'Will the town gate be held against us?'

'I don't know. Beod's men are supposed to be there. We'll find out soon enough.'

She nodded and said no more, but I saw her fist clench on the ring. She didn't ask where mine was; perhaps she thought I was wearing it under the gauntlet.

The gates of the town loomed up, dark, no torches burning. I slowed the horse to a trot toward them, then stopped. No challenge rang out. I could hear the charge of the troops gaining on us from the fire field. 'Hoy, the gate!' I shouted.

'Codswollop!' came the relieved answer.

I spurred for the dark entryway. Ja-Solem's brilliant smile flashed, and I hung on the rein for a moment to tell him, 'Our lads hold the dun, but there's a foul-up somewhere. Beod's men never showed!'

'They had to come across the river!' he answered. 'But it's all right now – I've just had a message! We've brought up your horse, too! Get out of the way, now!'

Rose and I cantered through the gates and between the troops who were massed outside and ready to pour through to set a line of bows and pikes. A young soldier in the Shimarrat flowing robes brought my horse, heaved me into the saddle, and then we were off again, going faster now that the horses were not burdened with two riders.

We raced across the bridge over the river and out into the open Burren. Between Dun Aghadoe and the rise of the cnoch, we discovered why Beod's troops had been late. It had been a sharp skirmish, apparently, for quite a number of dead, both Wolfhound and Ilyrian, were strewn on the ill-kept road. I wondered if this might not be the troop that had been sent to Croagh Raven. Why, then, had they returned before Vanu's Eve was over? Though I was puzzled about it, it really was of no importance now that Beod's men were in Dun Aghadoe.

Our horses hit the inclined slopes of the cnoch and settled to a heavy canter. Rose's hood had fallen back in the wind of the ride, but she looked comfortable as she caught my eye. 'We're supposed to climb this on our knees!'

I had to tell her. 'We're *on* our knees, my lady. The operation didn't work, and the color pots were broken tonight.'

She reined in. Our horses stood blowing in the rainy night air. 'You knew you couldn't paint? Yet you risked all to come get me?'

I pulled my cloak closer over the burning wound in my side. 'The pyre down there was for you, Rose,' I said quietly. 'The Wolfpriest was going to get rid of the witch of all the witches on Vanu's Eve. His zeal would never have let you even begin the Mistress's ritual. Think: if all he wanted was to prevent the kingmaking ritual on Cnoch Aneil, why didn't his Wolfhounds simply kill you the night they raided the Vale? Why take you prisoner, if not for some deeper cause? And the only cause that interests Jorem is making the Wolf paramount in the Burren.' She knew it now. I saw it in her eyes.

Rose looked up toward the crest of the hallowed mountain. 'Then, somehow, we must make certain the Mistress triumphs.'

'You'll still attempt the ritual?'

'If you'll still come with me into the crypt.'

I didn't tell her I had already tried to go into it to no avail. 'I will.' Neither of us spoke again until we reached the crest where the corpses of the guards sprawled about the entrance. Beod's troops had taken care of that detail before running into the battle below. I'd have thought he'd have left guards of his own posted, but he must have thought Cnoch Aneil itself would be enough deterrent on Vanu's Eve.

I held her horse while Rose climbed down. She made at once for the stairs, and I followed. At the bottom, rather than taking out a key, she simply touched the lock with her ring, spoke some word I didn't catch, and the gate swung open. My ear was ringing, and I winced, thumbing it. 'Hold up a moment, my lady. I left something here earlier.' Stooping quickly, I felt for the pot and the ring, and my heart bounded when I recognized the shapes of them by touch.

'What—?' she started to ask.

The sudden flare of torchlight at the head of the flight made us both squeeze our eyes shut. Some instinct deeper than awareness made me hide the pot in a fold of my cloak and palm the ring while above us an ironic voice said, 'Pickpocket, you disappoint me.'

My belly cramped, and I squinted up at him. Rose had never known him, but I had, and I should have realized in that split second down in the pyre field. I hadn't killed Jorem: I'd killed his double. He must have picked up the ploy from Sitric.

The Wolfpriest still had the most pointed canines of any man had ever known. His smile was maddening. 'Now, now, Reverend Daughter mustn't take it that way. Don't think to set me alight with that ring of yours, by the way, dear girl.' He peered and danced his own hand before our eyes. I couldn't see the color of the gem, but I could see the ring. 'You'd not care for the result, I do assure you. Take it like your stoic young friend. It's all a game, really.' He tossed down a leather bottle. 'Flotjin and poppy. I understand you like it. Take it, you'll want it before the night is over.'

'How long have you known?' I asked him, staring at the flask, then looking up at him once more.

'That you survived the purge of the skellig? Oh, I knew that immediately. You see—' He pulled aside the neck of his tunic to show me the burn scars. 'I, too, have been touched by the Fire. And, as they say, like calls to like. The Master will have you for his own, pickpocket.'

I gritted my teeth. 'Not bloody likely.'

He showed his teeth again. 'He will, and soon. And while

you're enjoying the Hag's Embrace, I'll be up here putting things to rights. It shouldn't be very hard – your friends have very cleverly cut themselves off from reinforcements. Such marvellous tactics!' He laughed. 'Good Vanu's Eve to you both!'

He was still laughing when I shot out my fist, and my grandfather's ring woke to rainbowed fire. I very nearly caught him with it, but out of the space where he had been arrowed, a bone dagger took me through the ring hand and quenched my light with pain so intense it was as if my hand were caught in a potter's kiln. I heard myself scream.

Nearly mindless with agony I was hardly aware that Rose shouted something and then she was pulling me away into the darkness as I caught at the neck of the bottle and they levered the mountainside down to fill in the stairwell.

'Aengus? Come, dear, wake up. Please!'

My lips were numb with poppy, and colors spiralled away up into the dark sand background. 'I'm dead, Rose, I'm dead. It's a bone point. I'll be a walker.'

Her hand was cool on my forehead. 'And if you become a walker, and I am left here alone, alive? What happens then?'

She knew, and I was suddenly angry. 'Then you use your damned ring to wither me, or whatever it will do to a walker!' A deeper panic surfaced suddenly. 'Why the hell did you give me the drug? For all you knew, he might have poisoned it!' Actually, I knew even as I said it there was no poison – other than the drug itself – in the bottle. Jorem wouldn't have been so merciful.

'I sipped it first, of course. There was no danger, and if we're to have any chance at all, we have to keep you on your feet, don't we? Here, another tiny sip, and then we must move if you're able.'

I clamped down the hysteria rising in me, because she was right, and she had not intended to ignite my lust for the poppy. But the one dose I'd had was begging for more to follow it. I swallowed as she held the bottle to my lips, then replied to her little tug on my good hand. 'What's the point? There's no exit to this place.'

'Of course there is,' she answered quickly.

'Well, I looked all over this whoreson mountain for it, and I couldn't find it.'

Her hand clasped my arm so suddenly I gasped and tried to roll away from her touch. 'You must have seen the circle of standing stones.'

'Oh, aye, but . . .' But there had been tumbled stone heaped in the midst of them. I'd thought that was odd even at the time, and now its significance stopped my breath. When I could speak again, I whispered, 'He's filled in that stair, too, the bastard.' My heart began to thump. Poison, or fear? I wondered.

Her voice was shaken, but controlled. 'Then we must hope either that we can find another way out, or that Beod and the others can win through and open a passage for us. Meanwhile we must have something to keep us from madness. Come, let's begin the ritual. I have your color pot. Here's my hand.'

I let her pull me to my feet, which felt curiously spongy, as though I were slogging about in seaboots several sizes too big. 'Rose, don't let me have any more of what's in the flask. I mean it.'

'Oh, I think a little from time to time.'

'No. None,' I said firmly. Then my weakness swept over me. 'At least, not until—'

As the Maid of the Vale, she had been well educated in all its disciplines, medicine among them. 'You're given up to the drug, is that it?' she asked quietly.

I wiped my sleeve over my sweating face. 'Yes.'

'Ah.' She was silent a moment. 'Mother must send us water, then.'

She was right about that: I was already very thirsty from the fever. To avoid thinking about it, I asked, 'What's to do first?'

'Find the first painting chamber. It should be fairly close to the entrance.'

We began to walk, or more accurately, to shuffle, as she wasn't sure of the flooring, and I could barely feel my feet anyway. I could hear her free hand tracing along the stone walls. My bad ear was ringing again, and I could not block it shut with my hurt hand. The chiming became worse with every step until it was a physical sensation, as though my eardrum were being tickled by feathers. We made a turn in the tunnel, and the sound diminished abruptly. Greatly relieved, I licked my dry lips, and we walked on for some moments until my poppy-numbed brain did a slow turn. I pulled her to a stop. 'Rose, wait a minute. This painting chamber: would there be things of magic, of power as you would say, in it?'

'Quite possibly. I know what charms must be said, and I know a little of what to expect when I have pronounced them, but what else there is, I do not know. Why?'

'Back here. The first chamber is back here, we passed it. Can you retrace our route accurately?'

'Yes. I've been counting.'

'It's like that day in your cottage at the Vale, when you used the ring. Remember how my ear rang? It did that back here a little way. I'll know when we get closer.'

With no hesitation, she turned us about, and we began a faster walk back. She counted aloud in the darkness. '. . . forty-two, forty-three, forty-four—'

My ear was thundering. 'Here!' I gasped. 'Where's the opening?'

She kept hold of my hand and ordered me not to move my feet. When our fingertips barely brushed, she said triumphantly, 'Got it, by Mother's Milk! And we turn left to leave. All right, come this way, and mind your head – it's low here.'

Hunched over my wounded hand, I followed her under what appeared to be a squared lintel. On a hunch I tugged her to a stop, let go her hand a moment, and reached to run my hand along the stone above my head. My fingers traced a leaf. 'Yes,' I said. 'This is it. Now what?'

Her hand clasped mine again, leading me into the chamber a little. 'Close your eyes a moment. I'm going to make a light.'

It was as well she warned me. Even with my eyelids shut, the sudden glare made me throw up my wounded hand to shade my eyes. Rose let go of my other hand and inhaled. Cautiously I opened my eyes.

Color! That's what struck me first. The whole of the small chamber seemed alive with color, for painting covered the ceiling and walls. Only the floor, of bare sand, was untouched: a painting floor, ready and waiting for the colors I didn't have. I shook my head to clear it of the poppy, but the illusion of color remained. I looked up, weaving, and began to study this masterful tapestry

258

Next to me, Rose began to chant and her ring waxed brighter, so that the colors began to smoke and swirl, blurring a little and becoming somehow more real.

I had an instant of terror when I realized there was, indeed, a kind of mist growing, but then my breath caught in my throat and I was on the floor with Rose placing the pot in my left hand. But I couldn't open the seal one-handed, and I couldn't breathe for the cloud. The colors flickered and dimmed and I spun slowly away . . .

The sand was warm under my naked back, and the air moved softly, smelling of flowers and fruit ripening in the sun. The surf murmured near at hand, and I was exquisitely comfortable.

Sand trickled on to my chest. I pretended a groan. 'What are you doing?'

'Paint.' She giggled.

I opened my eyes. Black hair, black and wet as a seal's, eyes just as dark, mouth like a strawberry. I pulled that mouth down on mine, savoring. She bit my lip and pulled away.

'While Marner made big sleep, look-see what Tanu find.' She was pointing toward the water.

Lazily indulgent, I raised my head to look. The next instant I bounded up and raced into the surf to catch the waterlogged section of planking before the tide washed it out again.

She followed me. 'Piece Marner boat, aye?'

'Aye.' The deck prism, by the Five! The complacent sleepiness had vanished in an instant. I could get home! I was thinking how long it might take to fell enough of the island's tall trees, and whether they would season like our own, and how I could make pitch to caulk them . . . When I looked up, her eyes were troubled, the light in them that had delighted me snuffed out. She turned and walked up the beach.

I thought she might have hindered me, but instead she sent her brothers and male cousins to help, and daily the new ship grew under our hands, long, sleek, strong. I named her *Tanu*. In the language of the place it is to say, 'Beloved'. And every night I stretched out on the warm sand beside my hull and hoped she would come back to me, but the stars wheeled overhead and I fell asleep alone.

Finally we gave the *Tanu* a sea-trial, a quick navigation around the island. She handled beautifully, but I worried about the sail, made of material so unlike our own. There was no help for it, though. I sent the laughing boys to their homes and took a last walk along that sweet-smelling shore under the stars.

When I returned to the ship, she was waiting. A bundle was at her feet. 'I go Marner house,' she announced proudly.

I held her beautiful face between my palms. 'No, Tanu, you can't come. It isn't safe. I don't even think I'm going to make it home with that sail.'

'Tanu swim like fish.'

I smiled. 'Yes, much better than I do, but the water is very cold at my house. In fact, the air is very cold, too cold for you. You would be like a flower frosted.' I kissed her hair.

She had been prepared for me to say no, I saw that when she gestured to the sack. 'Food, water. Marner . . . um.' She waved a hand abruptly the length of my body.

'Clothes?'

'Aye, cloes. Tanu save.'

It was small wonder she couldn't remember the word. I touched her gently, and she began to cry. Somehow the sand was under us, and the moonlit shadow of the boat over us, and the island breeze came sweet and warm.

Later she lay in my arms, and we watched the stars wink and shine. 'Marner come back some life, Tanu say.'

It was a belief of theirs, this business of a person's having more than one voyage. 'Will I?' I just wanted to hear the sound of her voice, low, musical, like wings across the sky.

'Aye. Then no go away, by Five!'

I laughed, she was so fierce about it, and the oath sounded so strange from her lips.

She rolled to look down at me. 'Will. Marner say.' She jabbed an imperious finger into my chest.

By all the Powers there were, she would be worth coming

back for, lifetime after lifetime! 'I promise. I will come back to Tanu, who taught me what love is, not just some life, but every life.'

Above me she grinned suddenly and did something wonderful. 'Maybe Marner too tired go in morning, hey?' she suggested slyly.

'Maybe,' I agreed. 'Let's find out.'

Her eyes, green as the summer sea, danced, and sometime in the night they went golden brown, and I touched the Power.

I sailed with the morning tide.

came back to find Rose beside me on the floor, seemingly deep sleep, her ring a low glow holding back the darkness. My injured and was throbbing horribly, and I was sick to my stomach.

But there was a painting on the floor. A very embarrassing one, saw as I lurched around it. I made it to the corridor outside efore vomiting.

The light went out. 'Aengus?' she called.

'Stay there,' I managed to say. 'Don't – don't move. My color it is by you.' Another wave came, and I heaved.

When I crawled back into the painting chamber, I couldn't ll where the scene ended, so I may have dragged myself ght across it. Her hands found me. 'Mother! You're burn-g up!'

My teeth were chattering suddenly. Through them I asked, 'Are u all right?'

'Fine, though I had the oddest dream. It was the drug, I expect. d you paint?'

Yes. Don't make a light, though! I mean, I think you should ve your strength. You may wind up carrying me.' I wanted to ow what she had dreamt, but I didn't dare to ask. 'There's other door in this chamber, ahead of us and to the left.'

Yes, that fits. That would be the way out of this room. Can u walk?'

The shivering was making my muscles ache. 'I'll have to. Rose, it a minute. In my belt pouch, there's a needle. It has the drug it I gave Timbertoe. When the time gets near, if you think re's a chance to be gained, stick me with it, would you? I'd like to see the sun again, if I can.' Jackass, I thought. Just as though she wouldn't like to.

But she understood, I think. 'Come, Painter.' She took my uninjured arm, warming my cold hand in hers, and we shuffled forward, finding the exit and inching cautiously through it. 'Tell me when you hear the chiming.'

The cramping started soon after that, first in the forearm muscles above the damaged hand, and then spreading to my other arm and legs. Between trying to massage the knots out for me and keep me upright, Rose lost her count of steps and numbered openings. 'Aengus, I'm lost. Can you hear anything, anything at all?' she finally asked.

'S-sorry, my fault. Where's the wall? Let me lean a bit.' The stone felt cool against my cheek. I was unaccountably on the floor a moment later, one foot bent upon itself with muscle spasm. I groaned, gasped that it was my foot, and she tugged my boot off to rub it out for me. 'That's got it,' I finally said.

'All right. About the sound, Aengus?' She held the boot for me once more.

'Oh. Right.' I drew a breath, leaned my head against the wall and listened. 'Faint. I'm not sure, it could be just phantom noise from the fever.'

Her lips brushed my forehead, a gentle caress of comfort. 'I don't think so, my lord. I think you and Mother are well in accord. It's a terrible thing to say, I suppose, but I'm glad you're here with me.'

Basest flattery, or heartfelt sentiment, it worked. I hauled myself up. 'Bear leftish, if you find openings leading that way.'

She led off once more with me stumbling at her heels. I have no idea how long we walked. It seemed an eternity to me, and I think near the end I was nearly out on my feet, but she would shake my arm a little every once in a while and ask me what I heard. Eventually the din of the chiming itself roused me out of my stupor. 'It's right here,' I told her.

She circled me at the extent of her arm's reach. 'There's no opening,' she reported.

'There must be,' I mumbled, exhaustion pulling me down into sleep. My hand slipped from her grasp.

'—ngus, can you hear me?' Her fingers were on the pulse in
y wrist.

I tried to answer, but it was too much effort, so I merely
ghed.

'There's a door or hatch of some kind under you. Can you roll
little? Ah, good.' She was searching for a handle.

There was a reason she shouldn't pull the door open, but I
uldn't remember what it was, so I rolled back on to her hands
d thought about it while she struggled free. I tried to lick my
s, but my thick tongue just rasped over my cracked lips. 'Is the
or marked with a leaf?'

'A what? Oh, a leaf? Wait. Move, can't you?' she said a
tle impatiently. 'There's something carved here,' she agreed
moment later, 'but I shouldn't take it for a leaf. Give me your
nd. Feel it?'

My hand did not want to work very well, but I traced the lines,
ing to force my spinning head to make some sense of it. No, it
s not a leaf, nor was it a sugan. It was . . . two jagged lines. 'Not
is door,' I said. 'If you open it, we die right here. It's marked for
e Flame.'

'Mother! And I nearly pulled it open!'

'Another time, maybe, we'll go down,' I said woozily, 'but
t tonight. I don't want to, tonight.' My voice sounded hollow
d weak.

No, I don't care to go that way, myself. But you hear the
ging in your ear, don't you?'

n truth, I could hear little else. 'Try the ceiling.'

Clever pirate.' Her feet shuffled near my shoulder. 'You're
vonder, Painter,' she said proudly a moment later. I heard
od moving against wood, and then a smack as she pushed
door open.

Rose, I can't make it. I can't pull myself up into the painting
mber. Unless you give me some of the poppy.'

he dropped down lightly near me, and I hallucinated that I
rd the cork drawn and felt the bottle against my mouth. I
ped, but of course there was nothing to swallow. If I'd had
strength, I fear I would have hit her. Rose's hand smoothed
hair from my burning forehead. 'There's a ladder,' she said
n satisfaction.

Again the flare of light, more painful this time, striking through my head like a crystal lance. Her voice beside me, saying words could not understand. The painted walls beginning to blur . . .

We stood under the bower of flowers, laughing a little self-consciously while friends and kin of hers tossed barley and sang the songs, and at the end Dilin himself planted a kiss on his daughter's cheek and gave her hand to me. We were wed, though she was a king's daughter, and I but a stranger in that place.

Her eyes laughed sometimes, and they laughed later that day when I fumbled at the laces of her dress, hasty and impatient. We found we suited each other very well, though sometimes when I held her I thought of Tanu. She kept me home for nearly a year, but then the sea wind called, and the gull pointed a way I had not gone, so I pulled my boat to the water and sailed away, just for a little while, I told her.

When I put again into our little bay, she came running down the path from the house, kicking her skirts up like a girl, red-cheeked and wholly winsome. She smothered me with kisses for a moment, then drew back, breathless, to press a woolen bundle into my arms. 'Isn't he beautiful?'

My son, thin down of red hair, bright blue eyes, ten tiny fingers all clenched and trying to fit into his mouth at the same time. I was afraid I'd break the little mite, so I stood stock-still, but I never felt stronger. Her eyes laughed as I kissed her. 'Like his mother,' I whispered.

'I waited for you to name him.'

'Duncan, then.' It was my father's name and would please him when I took my wife and son home to meet him someday.

The name was an unfamiliar one to her, and she frowned a little, but then the folk of our holding were come to greet their lord's homecoming and the merrymaking lasted all that day. We had a seisun, and I painted them my voyage. They liked the t'ing, but they did not believe in it as a real beast.

It was a wonder to me how Duncan grew. At first King Dilin and I were much occupied with riding out to parley with the border lords, and it seemed the next time I was home, the boy was crawling. I dandled him on my knee, and he pulled my beard with a right good grip. He'd be a good swordsman.

When the second bairn was born, I was on a voyage for Dilin, trading for tin and slaves in the Wyvins. I came home out of an autumn storm to find Branwen by the hearth with the infant at her breast, and Duncan tugging at her skirts. An older woman, the housekeeper, made haste to swing the stew back over the fire. Bronwen put her face, pale, up to be kissed, smiled when I drew back the blanket to stroke his soft head, still a little misshapen from birth. 'All babies are like that,' she said at my look. 'Don't worry, he's fine. I've named him Derric. All right?'

'It's a good, strong name and suits him,' I approved. Then I swung Duncan toward the rafters, and he shrieked with glee.

'Hush, you two. Duncan, you may stay up to greet your father for a few minutes more, then it's off to bed. There will be plenty of time to see Dad in the morning.'

Of course he set up a clamor. I tried to shush him so he would not wake the baby, but he only wailed louder, purple and stamping with passion.

'Oh, too bad,' she said serenely. 'I guess you won't get to hear a story, after all.'

The torrent of tears slowed to a leak, and he stood with a finger in his mouth, watching her hand the baby over to the housekeeper. 'He needs a change, Maura, if you wouldn't mind.'

'Of course, me lady.' She made a half-curtsey to me and went out with the son I hadn't yet held.

Bronwen got up to dip me some stew and slice bread. When I was at the table, she sat down once more and drew Duncan on her lap. 'Somebody's tired,' she murmured in his ear. He snuggled contentedly, and she eyed me over his head. 'Is the stew hot enough?'

'Fine. I want to hear the story, too.'

She chuckled, rocked the boy a little, and told a shining little tale of a bad little boy who doesn't do what his mother tells him and winds up being chased by something wild in the forest. At last his mother comes, tells the beast to behave itself, and walks him home. (It turns out the beast was only wild because his mother had been killed by hunters. Eventually he and the boy became good friends.) And for ever after, the boy minded what his mother said.

Duncan was asleep by the time she was done, and she finished the story strictly for our own private amusement. I finished painting the chastened wolf pup, and she laughed low. 'It's good to have you home, my lord.'

We lay together in the huge carved bed, but she was still too sore. I drifted off to sleep, pleasantly stifled at being home.

After that, there was a hard birth. I was there for it, and I never forgot her screams all through the night. Maura told me tartly that the second one had been nearly as bad, but she expected the sound didn't carry well to the Wyvins. I struck her for that, though I regretted it later.

This boy was slow to take weight from his nourishment, but in time he came along as well as the others. His name was Donal. I was hung about with boys, and we fished, hunted rabbits, painted on the scant sand of the beach. Duncan was quite the lad now, and began to call me 'Father'. I never taught him to do that, and I missed his way of saying 'Dad'. Derric was a rascal, and I had to teach him some hard lessons sometimes, but he was funny, and I wound up laughing more often than not. The wife said I spoiled him, and she was probably right. Donal was quiet, shy around me, closer to his mother, but he had the best eye of any of the boys, and came in time to be the best archer. All three of my boys went to serve Dilin at court.

We had not expected Conor. His birth nearly killed Bronwen, and he remained tiny. It was Maura's daughter who became his nurse, her own baby having died in the night. I will confess I was not home much while he grew. I'd had a geis put on me, and fulfilling it took many voyages. At length, though, I was finished, and I thought to stay home for good. Finally, I thought, my wife and I would have our time together.

But one day Duncan came home and sought me out for a walk and a talk. He was ever the moving one, Duncan was. When he broached the idea, I rejected it immediately as too dangerous, and not worth the risk, but he persisted. Eventually he awakened in me a longing to see the river country again, and to make my son king of it, if that is what he wanted.

Bronwen was appalled. In all the years of our marriage, I remember it as the only time she was truly angry with me. Witless vanity, she called it, and she was right. But as I told her, the young men would go, with me, or without me, and I might be able to temper the heat of their headlong pride. She would not come to the dock to see us off, and that hurt. Little Conor was left alone to watch us into the sea haze.

The poison my brother gave us burned like fire, and I lost all three of my boys. Macguiggan saved me out of the wreckage of my life, and I cursed him for it. At the Vale, I came to know the Power I had been seeking all those years, all those voyages, and the bitter thing was that she had been at my own hearth for nigh thirty-five years, and I had not recognized her, because I was looking for eyes like a summer sea and a mouth like a strawberry.

I have been a very great fool, and I am still one.

y eyelids were gummed together, and my lips tasted of salt. 'rink?' I croaked, but there was no answer in the dim chamber. or some time I could not summon strength even to turn my head, at finally I managed. There was color on the sand floor, but from is angle I could not tell what I had painted. Rose was sitting ainst a wall, her knees drawn up, head down on her arms. I ed again. 'Drink?'

No good. I'd have to get it myself. I kicked myself over onto y side, let my head rest against the sand for a moment, then nched up on to an elbow. Damn the woman! What was she ing sleeping at a time like this? 'Rose!' I bellowed hoarsely.

'Damn the man, just when I finally drop off to sleep, too!' e muttered to her knees and raised her head tiredly. 'You're rsty, I expect. Aengus, I think you have to take the drug now. e nothing else for you to drink, and we've come so far.'

The flotjin would taste so good. I swallowed with difficulty. There was logic to what she said, but an instinct deeper than reason told me I could not let myself drink it. Wearily I shook my head. Rose put the bottle back into her girdle and came across the chamber. She wiped the salt from my mouth and cleaned my crusted eyes with a corner of her skirt. I lay with my head in her lap and looked up into her green eyes. 'I painted?'

'Mm-hmm.' She supported my head so I could look at it.

I let myself relax, breathing heavily at the small exertion of lifting my head. 'She's waiting for him to come home still,' said to explain the figure.

She nodded and smiled a little, though not with humor, merely with understanding. 'I wouldn't have.'

'You're the Maid of the Vale,' I sighed.

'Painter, we've got to move. I let you sleep, but if we're going to finish in time, we must move on.'

'I can't.'

'At least try to get down the ladder for me. After that, I'll try to carry you.'

Well, that pricked. It was all well and good for me to have carried Timbertoe, but he was a mate. Besides, she wasn't strong enough.

I couldn't stand, though, so I wound up crawling to the second ladder – like the first chamber, this one had an exit in a different place. But I couldn't stop crawling when I got to the opening and I just went sailing out into space.

The cold water closed over my head and felt delicious at first. A strong grip on my collar pulled my head above the surface. 'Swim, damn you! Help me!' she yelled in my face. My right arm, monstrously swollen, tried to drag me down. We were moving. There was a current here. I tasted the water, then drank and drank. I didn't much care whether I ever got out of it, truth to tell.

Finally I'd got my fill. 'I know where we're going,' I said smugly. 'First it was the Maid, and then the Mother. You know who's next.'

'Yes, the Crone. And that must be where the Realm is locked because both other paintings have been fine. Rouse yourself, Aengus, or all this struggle will have been in vain.'

'Vain, anyway,' I mumbled, then choked on a breath of water
s the cramp hit, doubling me like a dead wasp. I was dimly
ware that she was struggling to get my head above the surface,
nd I suppose my instinct for survival took over, because I gulped
nd found air before the current began to rage around us, or
aybe it was only the roaring of blood in my ears, and I went
own for good.

When I came to, I was lying doubled up with sand under
my cheek and cold water lapping my numbed feet and legs.
I raised my head a little, but everything was darkness.
'Rose?'

There was no answer, but for an echo which whispered
away and left it even more quiet.

'Grandson.'

I would have known his voice anywhere, even in the halls
of the dead. 'Bruchan! Where are you?'

'I don't know.'

I snorted a little and sat up painfully. 'That makes two of
us.'

'Thee's brought only the one color pot?'

I was panting, straining for breath. 'All I could save. I'm
sorry. I've not been a very worthy heir.'

He laughed, and it was like a breath of warmth in that icy
place. 'Thee's done well to save as much as that.'

My back straightened a little, and out of that sprig of
courage I was able to ask the thing important to me above
all else: 'Bruchan, do you blame me?'

'Nay! 'Twas not thy fault!' He sounded startled that I
asked. His voice hardened, though, when he said, 'At least,
the painting was not thy fault. The murders thee's done
since I do not like, for thee's been changed by them. Did
think to carry such a heavy burden of guilt to thy grave?'

I tried to draw my feet out of the cold water. 'I think that's
ust what I've done. Where's Rose, do you know?'

'I do not. I think she is not here.'

'All right, then, tell me what's to do.'

'Take up the pot. Thee remembers my countenance well
nough? Paint it, then.'

I let my hand tell the truth of him, a man not so old as he had seemed to me at fourteen, with long white hair caught back in a leather braid, a silver beard with some black still showing in it, those mysterious mismatched eyes, one brown, one blue. He watched me as I painted him a gray robe of good Inishbuffin wool.

'Ah, thank thee, lad. It is some comfort against the chill of this place.' The sword was slack in his hand for a moment, and he looked back over his shoulder. 'They're holding back,' he observed.

'Waiting to see whether I can open the Gate.'

'Yes, I fear so.'

'But that's Rose's task. Her ring—'

My grandfather's eyes returned to me. 'Paint her.'

At once, I saw what he meant. My hand moved swiftly, surely, and she stood beside us, ring hand raised to cast a flood of illumination in that dark, level place where nothing lived.

'Peace, Reverend Daughter,' my grandfather said.

She looked as though she'd like to have given him a peck on the cheek, but we knew living flesh could not touch spirit and survive. 'Peace, Master. Quickly, please; it is hard to keep the light in this place.'

'Paint the Gate, Aengus,' he directed.

I drew the bars of it between us, and to my surprise it was lichened wood. 'It's a garden gate,' I explained to myself.

'Of course,' Rose said lightly. 'What else would it be? Stand clear now, both of you. There's going to be a rush of walkers when I open this.'

I stood aside, color pot in hand. She touched the Mother's ring to the latch of the gate, and it burst open, sagging from its leather hinges as the cataract of poor shades fled from the sere and bitten Garden to Earth-Above. It was dangerous, for some of them would seek to warm themselves with living blood, but we had no choice if we were to help the Lady.

I surveyed the trackless, featureless plain. 'Aengus, thee knows how the Realm should look, having painted it before. Do thee paint it again.'

'Here?'

'Indeed. The Maid and thee cannot cross, otherwise.'

So I threw down a green wash, and it spread at the ends of my fingertips as far as the eye could see. Then I limned strong trunks, gray, black, and white to support the green canopy that was the ceiling of Earth-Below, dappled with a strange light that was not sunlight, but seemed to be. Then I bent to the flowers, and these I tried to make as Finian would have done, a luxurious tapestry of bloom, fruit, and leaf.

When I was done, my grandfather nodded appreciatively, a light of hope rekindled in his eyes. 'Yes, just so.'

Rose took my hand once more to lead me, but I gave her my arm instead, to cross this land where, tonight, I was king.

We went carefully, the sands puffing up at our footsteps, for the garden did not yet live. That was the Lady's gift to bestow, not mine.

When we drew near the small island in the midst of its lily pond, Bruchan lifted his sword to shield us from Tydranth, the Dark Fire who waited for us with the mantled figure of the Hag, his sister, behind him. Of the Lady there was no sign.

Tydranth smiled, and I felt it pierce me like the death of love. 'So, Painter, we meet again. You did this, you know,' he continued, waving a hand at the ice that underlay my sands. 'You gave me no Realm of my own, so I took what I wanted. I'll take all of them, in time.'

'Withdraw, Lord Fire,' my grandfather told him steadily over the sword.

'Ever the fool, Bruchan, still trying to honor all four of us equally. Well, it's time you learned the truth of power.' He threw his Fire, catching the Master in a burning net that enveloped his sword arm and ate toward his heart, the essence of him.

My ring lit of its own accord, and I brought it up to hurl my own Fire, a rainbowed light that met the dark for a moment before Tydranth smiled and turned it aside. I thought he would kill me then, but maybe I was already dead, for he extinguished his flame. Bruchan slumped to the floor and lay still.

I advanced on the Dark Fire, color pot in hand.

'Whatever you do will go awry,' he told me.

'Don't listen to him!' Rose called anxiously behind me.

'You'll never paint again,' he warned.

'That's not true!' Rose objected hotly. 'Mother—'

'Is not here, little wench,' he finished smoothly, 'and I don't like your interference.' He raised his hand.

I stopped walking at the verge of the frozen pond. 'Stop,' I told him. Simply that. I jerked my head. 'The Gate is open. Get out.'

'You're mine, Painter, you're marked with my sign.'

'And you're marked with mine, my lord. Leave now, or there will be no place left for you, I promise it, by the Five.'

His eyes stretched, like jaws of a snake, but he strode down from the little mount of the island, crossed the icy pond, and kicked his way through the Realm, swirling some of my sands in his passage.

Within her cowl of darkness the Hag watched me approach. 'I squeezed your heart once, Painter. I can do it again, thus.'

No, I was not dead, not yet, the pain told me that. I went nearly mindless with it, the burning that whipped through my injured hand, up my arm, and exploded in my chest. I could not walk, and though I thought Rose said something, I couldn't hear what it was. I kept my eyes fixed on that dark hood and crawled across the ice. When I made it to her stone seat, I reached as carefully as I could to fold back her cowl.

Gray as death, old as earth itself, bloodless as stone, but her eyes were alive and watching me.

I lay my head in her lap. 'Heal me, Mother.'

'If can do a thing for me first, Painter.' Her voice rustled like old leaves.

So I took the pot awkwardly once more and painted a teardrop on that withered cheek, giving her back the compassion her brother had robbed her of. Then I was too tired to care and for a time I simply rested.

When I woke, the dappled light shone green and living through the heavy boughs of a huge tree, and the perfume of its white flowers filled my spirit with peace. I drew a deep breath of it and sat up. 'Ah, just in time!' a merry voice I knew quite well greeted me. Ritnym stood under the laden cherry trees, beckoning with Rose at her side.

I tucked my color pot into my tunic and went to meet them, the ring on my finger dulling to a low shine. 'Good morning,' I bid them.

The women exchanged a smile. 'It is, indeed,' Rose answered. 'Come, now, dear. It's time we were gone. Mother's given me the seed.'

I sniffed of the winey air. 'I can't stay, can I?'

Ritnym smiled kindly. 'No, I'm afraid not. He is up in Earth-Above, son, and you must drive him from there.' I nodded. I had known it. Kneeling to kiss the hem of her robe, I felt her touch, light as feathers on my hair. 'Someday, Painter. I promise.'

'Thy will, Lady.'

I got up, took Rose's hand in my unhurt one, and we went back through the lichened gate, the scent of flowers fading as we walked on . . .

staggered to my feet on the riverbank, wet and cold. My whole body was an aching pulse emanating from my blackened hand, where my ring still glowed feebly. That gray light over the mountain's shoulder must mean dawn was approaching. I looked out, trying to retrace how I'd got to the slopes of Cnoch Aneil, but I could not. A huddled form lay only a few feet away on the sandspit in the river. Awkwardly, I lowered myself to my knees and touched her hair. 'Rose? Rose, wake up, it's all over.'

'Over?' she murmured, still held in the dream.

I jiggled her shoulder incessantly until she woke, frowning. Then as she saw my face a brilliant smile flooded over her features and, to confirm the memory, she opened her tightly clenched hand. About the size and shape of a pea, the seed lay in her cupped palm. 'We did it,' she breathed.

'Aye, lady, we did.'

She hugged me, and I gasped with pain at her touch. Rose jumped up at once, her face going still and sick when she saw my arm. 'I think it's time for the needle, Aengus.'

I grinned loosely. 'It's long past time, lady. It won't do any good now. Save it. We may need it yet. Where are we, do you know?'

She studied the terrain for several moments, then turned me to point toward the summit, where a fire shone against the graying stars. 'That's where Jamie will be.'

But I had caught sight of something else. 'I don't think so,' I said with utter despair. She whirled to see.

It wasn't fair. That's all I could think in that moment.

Jorem swung down from his horse, his battered guards darting glances everywhere in the lightening gloom. Their horses were lathered. It must have been a rough night. He had seen the seed. 'I'll take that.' He held out one gloved hand as though he expected her just to yield it up.

I stood up, legs planted. '*Stop*,' I told him. Simply that.

Our hands shot up at the same time, the rainbow light and the black fire meeting with a shock that reverberated down Cnoc Aneil like thunder. My hand was burning, seared with fire, and I stood it as long as I could to cleanse the wound. Then I ducked under his fire and pulled him from the saddle. His men had fled or, more likely, their sensible horses had run.

I knew he was raining blows on me, but I never felt them. Quite deliberately I twisted his sword from his hand and set to work. One foot for Timbertoe I took, and he screamed. Then I hewed the other leg, and he went limp, frothing. I had the tip of the sword poised over his hand to impale it when Rose screamed at me, a cry of horror and warning.

Something woke in me, and I shook myself as if coming out of a long dream. The archpriest still twitched, his eyes staring at me.

Sickened with myself, I splashed into the river and began to wash, though in truth the blood had already stained too deep for cleaning.

'Aengus!' she cried, and her slender body hurled me into the water. I had just time to see the bone dart as it took her in the breast.

I bludgeoned Jorem with a fist-sized stone from the river until I was sure. Then I crawled to her and pulled her all the way out of the water. The bone point broke as I drew it out, and I fumbled in my belt for the needle. I didn't know whether there was an

274

Iag's Embrace left on it, but it was the only thing I could do.
When I gently pricked her neck with it, she jerked and lay still.

I held her on my lap, cradled with my good arm, until the
pounding hoofbeats broke out of the early morning fog, bringing
with them the first glint of rising sun.

Beod flung himself off his horse, bellowing, 'Surgeon, to me!'
He knelt. 'Powers! Is she—'

'No, not that. It's a drug. Get us to Mistress Neilan at the Vale,
Beod, as you love her. Nothing else will do. Tell her there's a
bone point in Rose, and one in my hand as well. She'll know
what to do.'

'SURGEON, damnit!' His face was sick. 'Aengus, your hand . . .'
I fumbled to open Rose's clenched fist and held up the seed.
'For Jamie. Tell him it's Mother's Gift, and to guard it with his
life. It isn't given to every king to be called "Son".'

He thought I was wandering. He beckoned the field surgeon
roughly, and the fellow skidded in the gravel as he knelt. 'No
poppy, and save the ring,' I told the bloodstained apron. 'Don't
cut the ring. Take off my finger if you must to get it off, but don't
touch the ring.' He was looking at me oddly, so I leered and told
him the ring would curdle his privates if he touched it. I thought
that might make it safe from his paws.

Beod laughed a little, and the healer held his fingers against
the pulses in my neck and felt my forehead. 'Timbertoe?' I asked
past him.

My Ilyrian friend smiled. 'All's well. The old fellow is stumping
round Dun Aghadoe in a fine temper, wondering what's happened to you, I'm told.'

I nodded and started to ask about Ja-Solem, but the healer
did something very stupid with my hand, and I knew it was
time – before he took any more foolish notions. I pushed him
roughly away, and pulled the needle from my cuff where I had
threaded it while I'd waited for them. 'I'm going to sleep now,' I
announced.

And I did.

Sheila Gilluly

RITNYM'S DAUGHTER

THE TRIUMPHANT CONCLUSION TO
THE MAGICAL FANTASY EPIC

The Queen approached the painted mural. Quickly she scanned the picture. At this edge, just inside the vine-and-leaf border, the Crystal Keep stood with a sunrise sky behind it, exactly as she had found it upon her return from the Tower of the Winds. Reaching out from the centre of the mural was the Greenbriar itself, the Rose that was the symbol and foundation of her sovereignty, twining into the washed blue sky as it always had. Then she stared. The hare that had always crouched under the overarching shrubbery was gone. In its place was a shattered mess, the nauseating details of a hare savaged by a fox or marten. From the painting something bright red and liquid was trickling . . .

It should be a time of jubilation at the Greenbriar court. For the Lordling, Prince Gerrit, has come of age and the folk of many lands are gathering to celebrate.

But others, too, are gathering – Shadows, servants of the Dark Lord who feed upon the blood of innocent babes and bring the freezing death to humans, dwarves and Littlefolk alike.

It is at the court of Ariadne, the Greenbriar Queen, that the first devastating blow is struck, when her Crystal of Healing is stolen by the Dark. Her power of Healing lost with the final battle scarcely just begun, Ariadne, Gerrit, and their loyal allies must search desperately for some weapon to wield against Shadow and Dark. And their only hope rests in a riddle as ancient as time . . . a riddle no one has ever been able to solve.

ROGER TAYLOR

THE CALL OF THE SWORD

The Chronicles of Hawklan

Behind its Great Gate the castle of Anderras
Darion has stood abandoned and majestic for as
long as anyone can remember. Then from out of
the mountains comes the healer, Hawklan – a
man with no memory of anything that has gone
before – to take possession of the keep with his
sole companion, the raven Gavor.

Across the country, the great fortress of
Narsindalvak, commanding the inky wastes of
Lake Kedrieth, is a constant reminder of the
peace won by the hero Ethriss and the Guardians
in alliance with the three realms of Orthlund,
Riddin and Fyorlund against the Dark Lord,
Sumeral. But Rgoric, the ailing king of Fyorlund
and protector of the peace, has fallen under the
malign influence of the Lord Dan-Tor and from
the bleakness of Narsindal come ugly rumours.
It is whispered that Mandrocs are abroad again,
that the terrible mines of the northern mountains
have been re-opened, and that the Dark Lord
himself is stirring.

And in the remote fastness of Anderras Darion,
Hawklan feels deep within himself the echoes of
an ancient power and the unknown, yet strangely
familiar, call to arms . . .

FICTION/FANTASY   0 7472 3117 6

ROGER TAYLOR

THE FALL OF FYORLUND

The Chronicles of Hawklan

The darkness of ancient times is spreading over the land of Fyorlund and tainting even the Great Harmony of Orthlund. The ailing King Rgoric has imprisoned the much-loved and respected Lords Eldric, Arinndier, Darek and Hreldar; he has suspended the ancient ruling council of the Geadrol; he has formed his own High Guard, filling its ranks with violent unruly men; and Mandrocs have been seen even in Orthlund. At the centre of this corruption is the King's advisor, the evil Lord Dan-Tor, who is determined to destroy the peace won by Ethriss and the Guardians eons ago, and surrender the land to his Dark Lord, Sumeral.

The people look to Hawklan to make a stand against Dan-Tor. But he is a healer and not a soldier – though, deep within himself, Hawklan has felt an ancient power, and when threatened has been seen to fight like a warrior out of legend. Hawklan knows he must confront Dan-Tor before the land falls forever to the encroaching, eternal night . . .

FICTION/FANTASY   0 7472 3118 4

BRAD STRICKLAND
MOON DREAMS

A brilliant new fantasy in the bestselling
tradition of *Spellsinger*

On Earth, Jeremy Sebastian Moon is a master of
dreams – of the glib phrases, the fantasies, the easy
selling lines of the advertising industry. But his own
dreams are haunted by bizarre images of reality
turned upside down.

Then, on one terrible night, Jeremy finds himself
catapulted into another world. A world where magic
works, where fantasy is reality. A world where his
double is a dangerous wizard who has summoned
him to take his place – and face the wrath of the
Council of Mages.

Jeremy Moon wants to go home – before his alter
ego can wreak too much havoc. But first he must
help the Mages in their struggle against the evil that
has arisen on the world of Thaumia. And that means
a journey into danger with stranger companions
than he could ever have imagined: a green-eyed
enchantress, a beautiful, broken-nosed thief and Nul
the pika. They *might* prevail – if Jeremy's earthly
talents can be turned, NEW AND IMPROVED, into
magical powers.

MOON DREAMS

Discover a new world in the great tradition of
Spellsinger

FICTION/FANTASY   0 7472 3299 7

A selection of bestsellers from Headline

FICTION

WINDSONG	Unity Hall	£5.99 □
HIGH WATER	Peter Ling	£4.99 □
HALLMARK	Elizabeth Walker	£5.99 □
DARK MOUNTAIN	Richard Laymon	£4.99 □
THE RED SWASTIKA	Martin L Gross	£4.99 □
THE PALACE AFFAIR	Una-Mary Parker	£4.99 □
POLLY OF PENN'S PLACE	Dee Williams	£4.99 □
THE PIRATE QUEEN	Diana Norman	£5.99 □
GAMES OF THE HANGMAN	Victor O'Reilly	£5.99 □
GLEAM OF GOLD	Tessa Barclay	£5.99 □
A GARLAND OF VOWS	Harriet Smart	£5.99 □

NON-FICTION

THE QUEEN	John Parker	£6.99 □
TRAVELLING PLAYER	Michael York	£6.99 □
GINGER: MY STORY	Ginger Rogers	£6.99 □
LES ANGLAIS	Philippe Daudy	£7.99 □

SCIENCE FICTION AND FANTASY

GUARD AGAINST DISHONOUR	Simon R Green	£4.50 ■
THE ULTIMATE FRANKENSTEIN	Byron Preiss (Ed)	£4.99 ■

All Headline books are available at your local bookshop or newsagent, or can be ordered direct from the publisher. Just tick the titles you want and fill in the form below. Prices and availability subject to change without notice.

Headline Book Publishing PLC, Cash Sales Department, PO Box 1, Falmouth, Cornwall, TR10 9EN, England.

Please enclose a cheque or postal order to the value of the cover price and allow the following for postage and packing:
UK & BFPO: £1.00 for the first book, 50p for the second book and 30p for each additional book ordered up to a maximum charge of £3.00.
OVERSEAS & EIRE: £2.00 for the first book, £1.00 for the second book and 50p for each additional book.

Name ....

Address ....

....

....